The
Lincolnshire Tramp

Brian Pentangle

Copyright © Brian Pentangle 1998

No part of this book may be reproduced by any means, nor transmitted, nor translated into a machine language, without the written permission of the publisher.

Pentangle Publications
PO Box 535
Maidstone
ME15 8FP

A CIP catalogue record for this book is available from the British Library.

ISBN 0 9533123 0 5

Printed and bound in Great Britain

Chapter 1

It was late in the evening when the accident happened and, like most accidents, it was swift and spontaneous. In the first instance, a dishevelled tramp was shuffling along a railway track which passed over a viaduct, and in the second, he lay in a heap on the road below. His crumpled body rested awkwardly on the sharp edged grit of the macadam surface and, in the pale incandescent light of a street lamp, he began to groan and vomit. He was not aware of the blood oozing from his own human frame (severely damaged when he was forced through a brick wall to plunge a good twenty feet and land heavily like a sack of wheat), nor was he aware of any pain; such being the numbing effect of too much alcohol and the onset of shock.

All around, a profusion of dead leaves danced and scurried in a chill autumn wind, whilst a scattering of debris (masonry from the viaduct) remained passively where it had fallen. Apart from the intermittent howl of the wind and the incomprehensible utterances from the distraught tramp, no other sound could be heard. The whole place seemed desolate and quiet. Even the solitary figure of a man sitting astride a bicycle barely disturbed the eerie scene.

The man had been cycling towards the main arch of the viaduct when he caught sight of the falling body. He stopped abruptly and since then had adopted an attitude of mesmeric inertia. He was unwilling to move from his side of the road and he was certainly not prepared to render any assistance to the injured tramp, yet he had no intention of continuing his journey. All he could do was to prop himself up on the seat of his machine and stare. Indeed, he might have remained so for another hour had not a small saloon car pulled up beside him.

The driver of the car, a woman, peered through a partly opened window and asked, "What's happened here?"

"Accident," muttered the man, his eyes closing and opening involuntarily.

"What sort of accident?" Demanded the woman, alighting from her car and crossing over to where the tramp lay.

"A falling accident," replied the man.

"This old boy is in a bad way," reflected the woman as she surveyed the prostrate tramp, and then, in a louder voice, she enquired, "Has anyone sent for an ambulance?"

"I don't think they have, lady," returned the man. "You see, it's only just happened."

The woman cast a reproachful glance towards the man and retorted, "Then I suggest you go and call one – immediately."

"Just missed me – he did," explained the man, more intent on relating his version of the event rather than obey a command, "Came from up there." He pointed to the brick structure high above their heads.

The woman automatically looked up and was alarmed to see part of a railway carriage protruding precariously over the parapet wall of the viaduct. Silhouetted against the moving cloud of the night sky, it gave every impression of an imminent descent and would surely topple over should the slightest of movements upset its balance; in which case, it had nowhere else to go but to crash down on top of them.

Too terrified to move, for fear it might be she who would derange the whole equilibrium and induce the fateful consequence, the woman stood frozen with horror and paid little attention to the man who insisted on completing his account.

"Fell like a bundle of old rags," sniffed the man. "Cor! Didn't half hit the ground with a thump wonder he stayed in one piece."

Just then the railway carriage rocked slightly and caused more masonry to fall. The women let out a shriek and hastily stepped back, soon after, half a brick struck the tramp and he cried out in anguish. "For Christ's sake go and get that ambulance before he dies," screamed the woman and, as the man with the bicycle departed, she added, "Get the police and fire brigade as well." She watched the man disappear into the darkness and began to wonder if he had the sense to call out the services, or would she have to wait until someone else came along. In the meantime, she must do what she can for the poor wretch lying in the road.

Drawing on her limited knowledge of first aid, she knelt down beside the tramp and began to unfasten the top button of his outermost coat. Her intention was to loosen the tightly fitted clothing about his throat but her plan suffered a temporary setback when the stench from his body forced her to reel away. The unsavoury cocktail of excrement, urine, alcohol, and spew mixed with warm blood proved too powerful an odour for her to take and she felt herself reaching into the pit of her own stomach. Determined not to succumb to the inevitable, she resorted to taking great gulps of fresh air and then sniffing at a scented handkerchief (withdrawn from the left sleeve of her cardigan),

When composed, and with the scented handkerchief held firmly over her nose and mouth, she proceeded with her intended purpose and struggled to peel away each coat collar in turn. "Why does he wear so much clothing," she muttered as she exposed his grubby neck. Then, when she had convinced herself that he was breathing more easily, the tramp appeared to choke on something. "Oh God!" she cried, "Dentures! I must remove his dentures."

Without further thought, she started to probe inside his gaping mouth but when her fingers came into contact with warm, slimy, semi-digested food her own nausea returned. This time she could not quell the convulsions building within her own abdomen and, there and then, she was violently sick.

The spasms abated eventually but it left the her, feeling very hot, very sweaty, and very tearful. She sat back on her heels, wiped her mouth, and contemplated the possibility of finding a bucket of hot water and some disinfectant, But, before she had a chance to look up and down the road to see if there were any houses within the immediate vicinity, the tramp startled her. His groaning had given way to incoherent shouting – only the swearing was audible

Taking this to be a sign of consciousness, the woman leaned forward again and endeavoured to make the tramp's head comfortable; at which moment, he opened his eyes and swore at her.

"What the fuckin' hell are you doing?" he roared. "Get your fuckin' hands off me."

"There's no need to start swearing. I'm only trying to help you."

"I don't want your bloody help. You interfering cow."

"But you do. You've had a nasty accident and an ambulance will be here soon to take you to hospital,"

"I'm not going to the bloody hospital."

"You'll have to. You're badly hurt."

"Go away and leave me alone."

"Will you tell me your name so that I can tell them at the hospital?"

"I told you I'm not going to the bloody hospital so clear off before I break your fu..."

The word died on his lips since severe pain (brought on by his efforts to raise a hand with which to strike the woman) caused him to sink back into a coma.

She looked on helplessly as his eyes rolled and his head flopped over. Her first reaction was to shake him vigorously and demand that he wake up, but when that failed she was at a loss to know what to do. On reflection, however, she realised she should not have been so brutal – probably added to the poor man's injuries.

In future, before trying anything else, she would think it through beforehand. She relaxed a little and considered her options. The kiss of life sounded like a good idea, but then, she would have to face his filthy mouth again and there was no chance of that; besides, he was breathing well enough. Perhaps his heart had stopped, how could she tell? With so many old coats wrapped around his body it would be impossible to hear a heartbeat. Anyway, he might have some broken ribs and imagine how disastrous that would be if she were to start pumping at his chest. "Damn!" she grumbled, "In matters like this I'm so totally inadequate."

Further plans to administer first aid were abandoned, at least for the time being, instead, she would concentrate on finding out his name. "Do tramps carry means of identification?" she said tentatively, thrusting her hand into his nearest available pocket. The pocket was deep and wide and easily housed a plastic bag containing a wad of card and paper. This was extracted without undue difficulty and carried to the woman's car where she could examine it under better lighting. To her utter amazement she found a series of sketches depicting animals, birds, and landscapes. They were all neatly drawn and coloured on various pieces of discarded cereal packet and odd scraps of paper. Unfortunately, none of the sketches were signed, nor were there any personal papers bearing his name – which she clearly expected to find. If he had any written identity at all it would have been in the packet, she was sure of that.

To be certain she had not missed a single signature, the women sifted through the sketches several times and the more she saw of them the more she admired them. Very soon, she began to think about keeping them for herself and not return them to their rightful owner; after all, nobody knew she had them. But the desire had to be quickly suppressed, it was not in her nature to steal, and if she had, she would forever live in fear of the tramp. With some reluctance she put the sketches back into the plastic bag and returned it to the pocket from whence it came.

She stood and watched the tramp for a few seconds and allowed her mind to deliberate his lifestyle, and the outcome of his present predicament. Then came an uncanny moment when she felt a definite affinity with him, she thought she knew him and understood him and that they had been together at some time perhaps in another life.

Out of compassion she bent down to take hold of his hand and to check his pulse. Then, in that mournful light of the street lamp, she saw the telltale signs of flea bites on his pallid wrist – and then a flea. A wild shriek passed her lips as she stepped back in horror and frantically brushed at her skirt; for some time to come she would itch all over, believing herself to be infested with fleas. "My God!" she exclaimed, "How can a man get himself into such a despicable state?" The moment of togetherness had slipped by and they were separate items once again.

Wringing her hands in despair, she paced up and down the road and looked hard in every direction. "Where's that damned ambulance got to?" she moaned, "I bet that fool never called it. Now what am I going to do?" She paused to listen to the distant sounds of the night but heard nothing to appease her anxiety. "I can't understand it," she continued, "this is usually such a busy road. Surely someone else should have come along by now."

Her mind was all but made up to get into her car and drive away because, as her argument deduced, she was not obliged to stay there, no law said she had to, and there was nothing more she could do for the tramp anyway, So why not go home? If it had not been for the voices coming from the viaduct high above her head she may well have convinced herself to do exactly that. However, the voices offered fresh hope and she promptly called out to them, "Hello! Is there anybody up there? Hello!"

Desperately she scanned the huge, brick structure in a bid to catch sight of the railway men she assumed to be up there but when they did not appear she resorted to shouting even louder. As it happened, her exertions were not only unproductive but unnecessary, for out of the darkness there came an ambulance, heralded by a flashing blue light and a wailing siren. "At last!" she murmured as the vehicle drew up beside her. "Thank God it's arrived."

"What have we here, Luv?" asked the driver, climbing down from his cab.

"This tramp has fallen from the bridge up there," volunteered the woman, "And I think he's badly hurt."

"That's quite a drop," observed the driver without looking up. "I don't suppose you know his name?"

"Sorry, I couldn't find it out."

"No matter."

"Careful, he's got fleas!"

The warning was accepted with a derisory grunt as the driver dispensed with the woman and went to assist his colleague. Between the two of them they made a swift, yet thorough, examination of the tramp and prepared him for a journey to hospital. In a matter of minutes, they had him, made comfortable, strapped to a stretcher, loaded into the ambulance, and on his way. They departed with the same efficient urgency with which they had arrived, and the woman, stranded like a castaway, breathed a sigh of relief; at last the tramp was in safe hands and she could go home with a clear conscience.

As for the tramp, he had very little recollection of his journey to the hospital nor was he ever fully cognizant of his progress through the sanative departments, casualty, operating theatre, and surgical ward. He knew even less about the sedulity of the nursing staff who had the unpalatable task of cleaning him up – a deed he would have savagely resisted, especially when they shaved away his beard. Therefore, his waking moments would he realized through a haze of sedation, hallucination, and confused reality. This did not occur until the early hours of the following morning and then he gradually came to terms with the situation.

Merging existences turned a blissful mind into a troubled one; in the first place, his free spirit ran with wild, white horses as their flowing manes and dancing hooves revelled in unbridled liberty; and in the second, a dream fragmented by clumsy human indulgence as a person snored in a nearby bed.

The unfamiliar troubled the tramp most, clean sheets, pillows, a proper bed, a warm room, a roof over his head. All so strange and alien to his nature. Mentally he groped in the dark, searching for an explanation; or, at least, something to cling to, something to bring his mind to order. He needed to understand his dislike for bedsheets and warm rooms, and why he preferred not to be in the company of others. Formerly, his disembodied mind had floated in a state of levitation, completely oblivious of the body it should be controlling but now, with increasing awareness, the extent of its commitment became all too apparent. It had to accept the ponderous body that felt sore and unmanageable, the tired limbs that were restricted and remote, and the heavy head that ached unmercifully. Slowly, by degrees, the tramp regained consciousness.

He opened his eyes and tried to look around the darkened room. Vaguely he could see the other beds and the patients who occupied them, he could also see the double doors at the end of the ward. A way of escape, he thought, but the likelihood of such an event arising was prevented by the existence of a protective canopy at the foot of his bed – without the use of his legs he could not go far. Anyway, in his weakened condition he was not capable of resisting the medical attention being administered to him let alone making a dash for freedom. He would have to remain as a prisoner in the hospital and forget his carefree wanderings even though he hated the very thought of it.

Being a tramp had been his way of life for the past five years and any former existence had been banished from his mind but now, in the subdued atmosphere of the ward, it all came flooding back. His past was there to haunt him.

***

Joseph Albert Glasson (Joe to his friends) had led a moderate and peaceful life until his forty fifth year. He was content with his wife, Marjorie, and their comfortable home – a semi-detached house in a pleasant suburb of Spalding. If he had any regrets at all it would be over the fact that their union had not been blessed with children, otherwise, life moved along sweetly enough. Apart from her domestic duties, Marjorie had many hobbies and she belonged to more than one charitable organisation. Whereas Joe, on the other hand, enjoyed but few interests outside his work, perhaps listening to classical music, some light gardening, or an impromptu walk in a nearby park.

Through honest, hard work, Joe had attained the position of chief accountant to the joinery manufacturers, Harrison & Beck. He was the most senior of the salaried staff and had direct access to the partners of the firm; Herbert Beck (a master craftsman who started the business, but now in retirement), Alfred Harrison (a financier who forged the partnership and adopted the role of managing director), and Keith Harrison (the son impatient to step into his father's shoes). Alfred dearly wanted his daughter, Virginia, to become a partner but the young woman had plans of her own and opened up a clothes boutique elsewhere in the town.

Joe took pride in his work and never quibbled about the countless, unpaid hours he spent in the office, besides, he considered his salary as being adequate for his needs. He also maintained a close working relationship with Alfred Harrison, they were always in complete accord no matter what the complexities of any given situation. However, dealings with Keith were often less amicable and the younger partner would regularly be at loggerheads with his chief accountant, usually over money.

Generally, such confrontations never progressed beyond heated exchanges, but at one meeting in particular – about fourteen days before the Christmas holiday – an exchange of words erupted into a furious row. It all started when Keith burst into Joe's office and demanded, "Come on you bastard, what the hell have you done with my claim for expenses?"

The suddenness of the action caught Joe by surprise and it left him momentarily speechless. Seated at his desk, he had been immersed in the firm's accounts ledgers and was having trouble balancing the figures, therefore, any intrusion would have been unwelcome, least of all a sudden one. His face paled and his mouth dropped open as he stared back in astonishment. When he did speak he found anger motivating his comments. "In this establishment," he said coldly, "It is considered polite to knock on a door before entering an office and it is also considered polite to speak when it is convenient to do so."

Keith remained impervious to the remarks and continued to pursue his claim. "Don't give me all that crap Joe, where's my money?"

"I must finish this analysis – which you so rudely interrupted – before I can attend to anything else." Joe was being evasive.

"For Christ's sake, how long does it take to draw up a cheque," exploded Keith

"I can't pay out any more money until I've sorted out these accounts." Joe's outstretched finger stabbed at the ledgers to emphasis his point. "We do have a cash flow problem you know."

"Nonsense," rejoined Keith haughtily, "The company's awash with money. Business has never been better."

A sardonic smile crossed Joe's lips as he said, "Come off it Keith, you know damned well it's a competitive market out there and we're having to trim our prices to get a tiny part of it, and you also know we have a lot of debtors. People are not paying their bills."

"That's your fault," sneered Keith, "You're supposed to chase up the outstanding accounts."

"How can I?" countered Joe. "They are all your cronies and every time I put pressure on them to pay up they come running back to you to have their credit extended. We'll never get our money that way."

Being an habitual liar, the truth always embarrassed Keith, yet he believed he was skilful enough to play it down and do so with convincing aplomb. "They are all sound companies with rock solid backgrounds," he tried to assure Joe, 'And they'll all pay up in time, you'll see. It's as good as money in the bank."

"Don't talk rubbish," chided Joe, "Fly-by-nights every one of them. We'll be lucky to see another penny from that quarter, I can tell you."

"Huh!" grunted Keith sulkily, "Is that all the credit I get for slogging my guts out to bring the business in."

Joe was in no mood to show pity and pressed on with his attack. "If you were to bring in orders from reputable companies who paid on time, then you'd deserve credit, but all the time you sit around on your backside and do nothing you won't."

"Bloody impudence," roared Keith, "I've worked day and night to keep this factory together. And if it wasn't for me none of you would have jobs here today."

Greatly enraged, Joe leapt to his feet to deliver his next verbal assault. Probably the effusion had been on his lips for many years but now it was all to come out. "You bloody well wind me up Keith, d'you know that? You burst in here and demand money which I know you are not entitled to and then you try and tell me that my livelihood is down to you – my God! All this nonsense about you working your guts out has got to be some sort of a joke, you haven't done a full weeks' work in the ten years you've been here. Herbert Beck, your father Alfred, and I built up this business and made it successful, your only contribution lies in your ability to drain off the profits. Fair enough, I'm only working for the partnership but I have earned my place here which is more than can be said for a bloody parasite like you. And, in case you're interested I can tell you here and now that if I'd had any say in the matter you would never have been made a partner."

Keith had turned a deaf ear to much of what Joe had said but quickly picked up the last word. "Partner," he shouted, "That's right, I am a partner and you are an employee, so do as you are damned well told and give me my money!"

"Doesn't anything ever get through to you?" asked Joe despairingly. "I've just told you – there is no more money. If you want more money then you'd better start coming up with positive results."

"Father shall hear of your attitude," threatened Keith.

"It's your father's instructions," Joe returned.

Keith seemed to foam at the mouth as he paced to and fro. "Very well," he said, " if it's positive results that you want then it's positive results you will have. Townsend will be back by the weekend and he'll have a pocket full of contracts, hefty contracts. Believe me, we shall be rushed off our feet."

"Empty words , Keith, and you know it."

"It's the truth I tell you. I spoke to Townsend on the telephone last night and it was all good news. The cash will come pouring in, you'll see."

"What a liar you are."

"Take that back!"

"If you've spoken to Townsend within the past week I'll eat my hat."

A moment of panic seized Keith, for he did not know where the wayward Townsend was and he wondered if Joe did. This was dangerous ground and a change of tack was needed; better to forget the salesman and continue to bully the accountant. "Look here," he said assertively, "I've had enough of this argument. Either you pay me now or you're fired, Do you understand?"

"If I were you I would think very carefully before I tried anything like that," warned Joe, "after all, a lengthy court action is the last thing you need right now"

Again Keith was thrown and again he changed tack. "Damn it all, Joe," he pleaded, "I've paid that money out of my own pocket so I'm entitled to have it back."

"But you have had it back," said Joe, "Many times over. Be honest about it. I mean, I've seem the same luncheon chits time and time again as well as the same list of railway fares to London and the same dinner receipts. You can't possibly do so much entertaining, it's not practicable."

There was no denying Joe's accusations but Keith, desperate for money, refused to be deterred. "Be reasonable, Joe," he begged, "It is coming up for Christmas and you know what an expensive time that can be, I need the cash for the wife and kids. I can't disappoint them – can I? Not for a few measly pounds. Even you wouldn't spoil their Christmas for that."

Joe stood in silence and mockingly admired the performance, it was worthy of much applause even though he knew it was coming. Keith invariably introduced his wife and children into an argument in the misguided belief that compassion would win the day. But, as ever, the ploy was doomed to failure through lack of substance – everyone knew that doting grandparents provided well for the family.

"Well?" Demanded Keith.

"Well nothing," Joe responded firmly. "Everybody here has to pay for Christmas out of his, or her, annual income, and if they can do it so can you."

"Maybe, but they can do it out of their Christmas bonus."

"I wouldn't think so, they don't get that much."

A fresh approach presented itself to Keith and he readily took advantage of it. Cunningly he surmised, "So – by your own admission – the bonus doesn't do much for the workforce and, as you have made so abundantly clear, we've suffered a trading loss this year, therefore, they shouldn't get too upset if they don't receive so much this time. You see what I'm getting at – don't you Joe? We could knock a fiver off each one and they wouldn't be any the wiser. That five hundred pounds could do me a power of good and certainly get me out of a difficult situation."

"That's what this is all about, isn't it?" exclaimed Joe. "You want the money for other reasons. What is it this time, gambling debts or a whore?"

"That is a disgusting accusation," roared Keith, "and unless you withdraw it immediately I shall be forced to see my solicitor."

"See him by all means," urged Joe, "Then the truth will come out. You know as well as I do that it is common knowledge around the works about your mistress with expensive tastes and your gambling debts."

Caught off guard, Keith was speechless for a while and unable to gather his scattered wits. Presently he blurted out. "Remember this Joe, one day soon the old man will retire and then I shall be in the driving seat. You'd all better watch out for your jobs then, I can tell you."

"And how long will it be before the firm goes bust, I wonder." observed Joe dryly.

Yet again, Keith hoped to profit by twisting Joe's comments. In a loud voice he proclaimed, "The way you've been fiddling the books just lately I doubt if there'll be any firm left for me to inherit."

Joe's eyes narrowed as he stared hard at Keith and said, "What exactly does that mean?"

"We all know what you've been up to." accused Keith with sarcasm. "You thought nobody knew about your little secret but we found it out. For months now you've been milking the firm for every penny you can get – and we can prove it. Thousands of pounds have gone missing."

"That's a pack of lies and you know it."

"Ah! but mud sticks,"

"Don't push your luck, Keith."

"I don't have to. It's not my head that's on the block, it's yours. I have only to lift that phone and the fraud squad will come running,"

A mask of bemused disbelief spread across Joe's face, he did not know whether to laugh at Keith, or punch him on the nose. He chose the former and with a wry smile he said, "My books are accurate to a decimal point and there isn't an auditor in the country who can prove otherwise. Sorry, but the charge of embezzlement can never be laid at my feet."

"But you can be stitched up though."

"You haven't got the guts or the brains to do it."

Keith flew into a temper. "I warn you, Joe, if I don't get my money I'll... "

"You'll what...?"

"This..." he swung a clenched fist at Joe (only to have the blow parried by a left forearm) and shouted, "Pay up you bastard."

To protect himself from further attack, Joe picked up a heavy wooden ruler and shouted back, "You've tried every dirty trick in the book to get your own way, even violence, but you won't get another penny, understand! Not another penny."

Keith, fearing the wooden ruler in Joe's hand, looked around for a suitable retaliatory weapon and snatched a potted plant from the top of a nearby filing cabinet. Soon after, the clay pot and its contents hurtled through the air and crashed against the wall behind Joe's head.

In a moment of anger, Joe stepped forward and was about to grapple with his assailant when the office door burst open for the second time and Alfred (Keith's father) stormed into the room. "What the hell is going on in here?" he demanded, "The noise can be heard all over the building."

With a rapid change of mood - from assailant to injured party – Keith entreated his father. "It's all Joe's fault," he bemoaned, "he won't give me my money."

Alfred, dumbfounded, stared at his pathetic offspring. The contempt in his steel grey eyes demonstrated the animosity he held for his avaricious, self centred, ungrateful son. "You're not getting any money." he hissed, "So get out."

Keith, never able to look his father in the eye, glanced at the floor and burbled, "I ought to be entitled to my money."

In a flash, Alfred kicked out at his son, who had turned to leave the room, and caught him high on the thigh. "Money, money, money, that's all you think about," he roared. "Get out of my sight."

By now several members of the staff had gathered in the doorway. They were there under the pretext of being to hand if needed but, in reality, morbid curiosity was their main motive. Keith had to push his way past them and in doing so he barked, "Get back to work, all of you." They allowed him to pass but did not obey his order until it was confirmed by a nod from Alfred.

Alfred deliberately closed the office door from the inside before admonishing Joe. "I'm really quite ashamed of you Joe," he said in a calm voice, "I never expected it of you to behave so badly."

"I know," apologised Joe, "Keith somehow got under my skin and I lost my temper. I'm sorry."

"I suppose he was in here after that damned expenses claim again."

"He was, and he wouldn't take no for an answer."

"I really don't know what he does with his money, he always wants so much of it."

Joe declined to comment, more out of loyalty to Alfred than to Keith.

Meanwhile, Alfred crossed the room to examine the damage caused to the wall. "In future," he said, "I think it would be a good idea if you were no longer responsible for issuing sums of money to my son. Perhaps I should handle all his claims for expenses from now on." He knelt down to inspect the distraught plant – now separated from its earthy bed and shattered pot. "I shall make this perfectly clear to him in a short while and, further more, he shall be banned from this office until he mends his ways." He paused long enough to reach out for a sheet of paper on which to place the plant. "Do you know, I think I can save this begonia for you."

Joe had reservations about the begonia but welcomed the idea to keep Keith out of the way. A simple, "Thank you Alfred." covered both proposals.

"Let's keep a steady ship until Christmas," suggested Alfred, rising to his feet. "Then get off to a good start for the new year – what d'you say to that?"

"Suits me fine." Joe nodded in agreement.

"And talking of Christmas," Alfred continued, "How are the arrangements coming along for the staff party?"

"Don't worry," Joe assured him, "I have it all under control." He knew how much Alfred enjoyed the annual party and how he liked playing host and benefactor to the entire workforce. It was one of the highlights of the managing director's year.

"Good, good, good!" Alfred muttered happily and then, with his precious charge, he left the office.

Chapter 2

A large function room annexed to the town's premier hotel had been hired by Joe to stage the firm's Christmas party. A regular venue on an annual basis. Its walls were festooned with brightly coloured paper chains and sparkling tinsel, whilst the ceiling displayed a myriad of florid, paper spheres hanging impassively between the more permanent illuminating globes. Red berried holly, sprigs of mistletoe, and bobbing balloons were very much in evidence, as was a tall spruce dripping with fairy lights and glittering baubles.

Soon the party burst into life and the room throbbed with the sound of live music and the merrymaking of the revellers. It was, in a sense, a fancy dress affair since all participants were requested to present themselves dressed as tramps – a request enthusiastically responded to by all except one. The *tramps* consisted of joiners, wood machinists, bench hands, foremen, apprentices, drivers, draughtsmen, salesmen, typists, clerks, cleaners and a tea lady, all with their respective spouses (or lovers). The one exception was Keith, he wore evening dress with black tie and had deliberately neglected to bring his wife.

Joe and his wife, Marjorie, both suitably attired, stood to one side and contentedly watched the antics of the fun loving company. There issued spontaneous good humour and much laughter as the workforce cast off the shackles of year long toil and began to enjoy the festivities.

A smile spread across Joe's face when he saw Alfred making his way towards him, "Good old stick," he mused, "At least he's made an effort."

The managing director had donned a very old tweed suit, his gardening shoes, his fishing hat, and a threadbare cravat tucked into the neck of a neatly ironed shirt. He could have easily been mistaken for a head gardener, but never a tramp. In contrast, his accompanying daughter, Virginia, looked like a very beautiful tramp. Her immaculate make-up complemented the designer tramp suit which hugged her trim body.

"Congratulations Joseph," beamed Alfred as he grasped Joe by the hand. "You make an excellent tramp. Really do look the part."

"Yeah! And he even smells like one" interjected a cheeky apprentice who had overheard the conversation as he danced by.

Joe darted forward and deftly tipped the lad's battered bowler over his eyes. "Saucy young sod," he chuckled, "I'll dock your pay for that." He then returned to Alfred and Virginia and thought it prudent to admire their costumes. "Well done you two. Well done indeed." He stepped back to offer his full appraisal.

With that, Virginia twirled herself about in a manner which might suggest showing off and giggled, "I think this dressing up like tramps is a gas Joe, where did you get the idea?"

"It came to me when Marjorie tried to throw out some of my old clothes," Joe confessed.

"Smelly old things," interrupted Marjorie "They should have been thrown out years ago."

Alfred laughed politely and then said, "My late wife had the same opinion about my old clothes but as you can see, I managed to hang on to them."

"Daddy, they are absolutely *aw*ful," squealed Virginia, stressing the penultimate syllable.

"Men are all the same, dear," declared Marjorie "they hate changing their clothes."

"A jolly good turn out, don't you think, Joseph," observed Alfred as he focused his attention on the dance floor. "It looks as though everyone is here tonight but it's a bit difficult recognizing some of the faces. The disguises are so good."

"Yes, it can be a problem trying to see exactly who is behind the grease paint," said Joe, brushing aside one of the many paper streamers that had been aimed at them.

"But I don't see Townsend anywhere," continued Alfred with some concern. "Is he here?"

"As far as I know he is, although I haven't actually seen him,"

"Just wanted to know how he got on with the Benson contract, that's all."

"Tut! tut!," scolded Joe in good humour, "Shop talk at the staff party? That will never do."

"Quite right too ," acquiesced Alfred gleefully rubbing his hands together "And to show I'm in the party mood, the drinks are on me. Shall we..." He disengaged his hands in order to show the ladies the way to the bar. They graciously accepted and led the way.

Keith, already at the bar, sported a drink paid for by his secretary's husband and, whilst idly flicking cigarette ash from the lapels of his dinner jacket, bored the poor man with supercilious sales talk. He droned on with his one sided conversation until he caught sight of Alfred's party coming towards him, whereupon, he quickly downed the drink and (much to the husband's relief) turned to greet his father. "Dad – what are you having?" He offered generously, somewhat confident of the reply.

"Thank you my boy, but this round is on me," Alfred replied as he sought the attention of a barman.

"Okay! If, that's the way you want it." Keith may have allowed his voice to falter in feigned rejection but his actions proved otherwise; with a swift movement he thrust his empty glass towards the barman and said, "Mine's a double scotch."

Alfred looked scornfully at his son before nodding an approval to the barmen and then, with a fresh smile on his face, he addressed his guests, "Now, what's your pleasure. Marjorie?"

"White wine please, preferably sweet."

"Virginia?"

"Bitter lemon please Daddy."

"And Joe?"

"Half a lager will suit me, thank you."

When satisfied that all drinks had been correctly dispensed, including a gin and tonic for himself, Alfred toasted the season and prosperity. "Merry Christmas and a happy new year," rejoined the others.

After the toast, there came a lull in the conversation and Virginia took the opportunity to upbraid her brother. "Surely you could have found some old clothes to make up a tramp's outfit instead of wearing that damned suit. And why haven't you brought Shena with you?"

"Because – my dear sister – I have to go on to a business dinner with some very important clients after this shindig is over, and I won't get home until the early hours. You can't expect me to keep my wife out all night especially when our regular babysitter let us down."

"I don't believe you," fumed Virginia, "There isn't a word of truth in anything you say." She turned her back on her brother and despised him for the way he treated his wife.

Keith openly appealed to those standing around him and implored, "Now what have I said? What's all the fuss about? Just because I don't want to dress up like a tramp I get all this hassle. Whose daft idea was it in the first place?"

Before either Joe or Virginia could retaliate, Alfred intervened. "Would it have hurt your pride too much to join in with us on this one occasion," he barked at Keith. "Why does it always have to be you who spoils the evening'"

Virginia quickly took hold of her father's arm and said, "Come on Daddy he's not worth arguing with. Let's enjoy ourselves – let's dance."

Alfred was unwilling at first because he desired to stay where he was and give his son a thorough lambasting, but he could not refuse his pretty daughter's request and soon found himself cavorting amongst the happy throng on the dance floor. In fact, he was to stay there for quite a while as a succession of attractive ladies requested the pleasure or a dance with him. He was enthralled by it all and enjoyed every moment of it; and he never suspected that Joe had stage-managed the whole affair. Since the ugly scene with Keith had soured the evening for Alfred, Joe had been determined to redress the balance, therefore, he discreetly organised the flow of dancing partners.

In the meantime, Keith inched his way along the bar in search of more soft touches and when he was certain that he had swallowed his last free drink he slipped away from the hall and on to his next rendezvous.

As the evening progressed, the festivities became more intense; the music grew louder, the humour more boisterous, and the laughter more vociferous as the rising crescendo rang out from every corner. The party was in full swing.

Joe, having so carefully orchestrated the event, stood back to admire his handiwork. There was of course, the odd hiccup to be attended to, the minor adjustments needed to ensure the smooth running of the schedule, and an eye to be kept on the younger element of the group – drunken excesses in that department must be avoided. All things considered, he was extremely pleased with himself and his achievement.

Alfred, exhausted by the dancing, extricated himself from the crowd and declared in a breathless voice, "It's an absolutely wonderful party Joe. The best ever." He paused for a moment, partly to catch his breath and partly to wallow in the atmosphere. It gave him immeasurable pleasure to see his staff enjoying themselves because, in his vision of things, it was important for them all to work and play together as one big, happy family. Then, having become aware of Joe's lone being, he asked,

"Where are the ladies?"

"Marjorie has gone to help with the buffet," Joe replied, "and Virginia is over there by the double doors and seems to be amusing herself by playing a cat-and-mouse game with two lovesick lads from the drawing office."

"Ah yes!" said Alfred, catching a brief glimpse of his daughter, "I'm glad she's having some fun. She's been looking forward to this party and deserves to let her hair down. Been working terribly hard you know."

"At her dress shop?"

"Yes."

"How's she getting on with it?"

"I'm glad you asked, Joe, I've wanted to speak to you about it."

"Nothing wrong I hope?"

"Oh no! It's doing very well apparently. It's her book-keeping that worries me. She will insist an doing it herself,"

"Not a bad thing in my opinion."

"Perhaps not, but when you don't really know what you're doing it can have some serious repercussions." Alfred fell silent in order to consider his next move. He desperately needed Joe to look over Virginia's accounts, but how dare he ask him – especially when he worked so hard for the firm. It would be grossly unfair to take advantage of Joe's good nature.

Perceiving Alfred's dilemma and anticipating his request, Joe promptly offered, "I could go through the accounts with her, if it would be of any help."

"Would you, Joe?" said Alfred, showing genuine relief. "Be a load off my mind if her books were in order."

Joe gave the matter a little consideration before he said, "I could do it tomorrow morning if you like."

"Really?"

"Well - make a start anyway."

"That's marvellous. Virginia will be pleased. I'll go and tell her right away, but first..."

Eager to show his gratitude, Alfred snatched the empty glass from Joe's hand and headed towards the bar. "Let me get you another drink," he called back.

"Honestly, Alfred," protested Joe, "There's no need." The protest passed unheeded and before long Joe found himself sipping at a fresh drink whilst watching Alfred thread his way across the crowded dance floor.

A lorry driver carrying a tray of drinks passed by and asked, "What's the, Old Man up to? Seems to be nippin' about a bit tonight."

"At the moment he's looking for his daughter," confided Joe.

"Then he's going in the wrong direction." said the driver.

"So he is," Joe agreed, "and it looks as though he's going to buttonhole Townsend. This should be good for a laugh."

The Lincolnshire Tramp

The driver grinned and moved on leaving Joe to his own expectations.

As expected, Alfred made frantic efforts to attract the attention of the wily salesman but Townsend, anxious to avoid the confrontation, pretended not to notice and tried to blend in with the crowd. It was not to be his day; for well meaning revellers cleared a path which lead Alfred directly to his quarry

"Bravo!" chuckled Joe, greatly relishing the incident.

Time passes quickly when fun is to be had and only the lateness of the hour can terminate such merrymaking. Thus it was, for as midnight approached partygoers began to drift away, Alfred and Virginia amongst them. There had been speeches, presentations, toasts, raffles, prizes and an abundance of seasonal good wishes. Much food and drink had been consumed and many pranks performed. It had been an evening to remember.

The lights dimmed to announce the last dance and, as the couples swayed to the rhythm of the music, Townsend tapped lightly on Joe's shoulder. "Could I have a word, Joe" he said.

Joe turned to face the salesman and was alarmed to see the anguish in the man's eyes, "What's wrong, Vernon" he begged, "You look worried."

"I am worried." Townsend admitted. "That's why I've come to you. Things aren't looking so good."

"The Benson contract you mean – we didn't get it,"

" 'Fraid not."

"But an hour ago I saw the Old Man congratulate you. I thought it was in the bag."

Townsend shuffled his feet uneasily.

"I hadn't the heart to tell him the truth," he confessed, "I told him we were still in with a chance."

"And you're telling me we are not?"

"There will be no contract."

Joe was puzzled. "What went wrong?" he asked. "Surely nobody has under-cut us. We trimmed our prices to the core to get that contract."

"We'd have got the work all right," said Townsend, "and as far as I know there was no one else in the running. The truth of the matter is, Bensons have decided to cancel two of their biggest developments. They have abandoned plans to build six hundred spec. houses. They claim that the money market has dried up and mortgages are no longer available. They won't take the risk."

"And we lose six months' work." Joe pondered the prospect of redundancies on the shop floor.

Townsend continued. "It seems pretty general all round, the money just is not there. Rumour has it that the building industry is plunging into a deep recession."

"Prophet of doom aren't you, Vernon. Things can't be that bad."

"Believe me, Joe, they are and they're getting worse. Plenty of firms will be going bankrupt before this little lot's over, mark my words."

Joe thought for a moment and then said, "What about the builders merchants ? Do they predict a slump?"

"The firms that I've called on are already feeling the pinch," Townsend replied sincerely. "I very much doubt if many will stock joinery at the present time."

"Damn!" cursed Joe softly, "We were banking on that contract. At the most, we have a couple of weeks work for the new year and that's all."

A blank expression spread across Townsend's face as he stared at the floor. He searched in his mind for something constructive to say but he knew he was a spent force in a dying market. For him there could be no heroism; he could not ride off into the mists of despair and snatch up golden opportunities to return in triumph; his was not the lot of a saviour. Even he did not consider himself as a salesman of any particular merit – certainly not in the world of high pressure selling. His mind was completely devoid of constructive suggestions.

"Oh well!" sighed Joe sympathetically, "There's nothing we can do about it this side of Christmas. You might as well forget about it for a few days and enjoy the holiday."

"What about the Govenor?"

"Best keep it on ice for now and I'll tell him about it soon after Boxing Day. But be warned, the fireworks will start when he finds out and he'll want an eyeball to eyeball with you."

"Thanks Joe, you're a pal. Made me feel a lot better."

"A word of advice – if you haven't told anyone else about it then keep it that way. We don't want panic to set in before we've had a chance to sort things out."

"You can rely on me," assured Townsend, taking Joe firmly by the hand. "And thanks again, you've been a great help. Merry Christmas." He warmly shook the hand and then departed.

"Merry Christmas, Vernon."

The concluding moments of the party precluded any further contemplation regarding the lost contract because Joe was prevailed upon to finalise the evening's proceedings. He ushered out the last of the guests, payed off the band, awarded small gratuities to

The Lincolnshire Tramp

the hotel staff, and made sure that the function room was safe to leave. After a final check, he and Marjorie went home to retire for the night.

The following day (Christmas Eve) started early for Virginia. She hurried across town to open up her shop in readiness for a last minute rush which might, or might not, happen; it was always an uncertain time of the year to sell ladies fashions. Nonetheless, the shop would be open on time and any customer who chanced to enter would receive a cordial welcome. Lights came on, heating came on, background music came on, mail was scooped up from the mat and a feather duster was flicked at the display models – all part of the morning ritual before coffee.

A quick glance up and down the street assured Virginia that she would not be disturbed for several minutes. Time enough for her to tip the contents of a floppy, leather bag onto a wooden table in a small room at the rear of the shop. Items included were, invoices, statements, cheque stubs, paying-in books, tax demands, telephone bills, electricity bills, VAT returns, sundry scraps of paper of vague significance, and half a dozen – started but abandoned – slim ledgers.

Insouciantly she viewed the untidy pile of papers (the result of her two years of book-keeping) and giggled. "Well! " she announced to the musty, room. "There it is – all my own work. What a bloody mess." She giggled again and then, with a nonchalant shrug, she turned away and made her morning drink.

Within the space of fifteen minutes or so, half a dozen young women had entered the shop and were, by varying degrees, in the process of selecting and purchasing dresses when Joe arrived. "Good morning, ladies." he called out as he passed by them.

The half hearted response from the women was more then amply compensated by the gushing greeting from Virginia.

"Joe – hello! So good of you to come. Everything is ready for you in here." She opened the door leading into the small room and followed Joe as he entered.

Inside the room, Joe slipped off his coat and looked with suspicion at the confusion on the wooden table.

"I know, I know," confessed Virginia, "I've made a hash of it. But I'm sure you can sort it all out. You're clever at these things."

"I'll do what I can." said Joe, reaching out for a chair which he drew closer to the table, but before sitting down he set out his pens, pencils, note pad, and calculator.

"I shall always be grateful to you," promised Virginia, kissing him lightly on his forehead as he sat down. "I must go back to the shop now but I'll return as soon as I can – Okay?'"

Joe smiled. "There's no hurry, take your time."

A slight commotion in the shop hastened Virginia's departure, leaving Joe to scrutinize the first docket he picked up. The slip of paper was soon identified and placed carefully on the table and was to be the foundation for a pile of similar vouchers. Other piles were formed as the remaining documents were allocated to their respective places. Gradually the financial history of the small venture began to unfold.

The morning passed quite pleasantly. Virginia, staying for the most part with her customers in the shop, made brief visits to the back room to check on progress. Whilst Joe, finding his industry agreeable, patiently formulated the accounts.

The onset of the luncheon interval provided Joe with a chance to discuss his findings with Virginia and not be disturbed. She had secured the shop door against the public, found herself a chair, and settled down beside him.

"Well, how am I doing?" she asked.

"Very well indeed," Joe replied, "in fact you're making too much profit. We shall have to offset it with some kind of expenditure."

"Such as?"

"A car for instance. You do have one – don't you?"

"Doesn't everyone?"

"And you use it in connection with the business?"

"Of course – I'm always running around getting things."

"Therefore, you are entitled to claim for it." Joe scribbled notes between questions.

"How much did you pay for it?"

"I didn't pay anything for it. Daddy bought it for me. We could ask him."

"What about the road tax and the insurance?"

"I don't know that either. Daddy sees to it."

"What about petrol?"

"Oh yes! I buy my own petrol."

"Do you have the receipts?"

"I didn't think I needed them."

"You may be asked to produce them as evidence if you're going to claim an allowance."

"Really, Joe, is all this necessary?"

"If you want to reduce your income tax liability it is."

The Lincolnshire Tramp

It all seemed so tiresome to Virginia, but the desire to be regarded as a successful business woman demanded a certain awareness of taxation problems. Claims and allowances obviously had their place in the functional world of accountancy and, therefore, had to be recognized. She took from the left sleeve of her cardigan, a scented handkerchief which she held to her nose as if to stimulate concentration. "Is there anything else I should be claiming for?" she asked with renewed resolve.

"Business premises," said Joe "do you own any part of this building?"

"Not exactly - you see, Daddy owns it so I expect it will come to me in his will."

"Do you pay him any rent?"

"Don't be silly, why should I pay rent when the building belongs to us?"

Joe could understand her simple logic but he also knew that she must change her attitude if she intended to survive in commerce. Gently he insisted "You must get a rent book and pay the full amount agreed by an independent assessment. A local estate agent could arrange all that for you."

"How absurd," sniggered Virginia. "Pay rent to my own father – ?"

"I strongly recommend it," urged Joe, "That and buying your car off of him at a realistic price."

"I suppose that includes the money Daddy lent me to start the business?"

"It certainly does, and you should consider paying it back either by a lump sum or regular payments spread over a period of time. Whatever method you choose should be backed by a written agreement."

"Poor Daddy, I don't think he's going to like it if I have to give him money."

"No doubt he can find a way of giving it back to you without putting it into your business. The main thing is to show that you have made the payment and that they appear in your accounts. Joe stood up. "Now," he said, "I suggest we have a spot of lunch and then, this afternoon, I will file this little lot for you." He referred to the piles of dockets on the wooden table.

Virginia, deep in thought, rose slowly to her feet and said, "I'll have to think about your recommendations, Joe. I'll see what Daddy has to say."

"That's okay," he assured her, "These accounts need not be fully compiled until next March so we have plenty of time."

Chapter 3

The second morning of the new year loomed cold and dark. Outside, the roads and footpaths were encrusted with frozen snow, ribbons of gnarled grey icicles hung from every house gutter, and a raw, easterly wind chilled the bones of anyone who dared venture there. For the personnel of Harrison & Beck the Christmas holiday was over and a reluctant return to work gradually gathered momentum.

By the time Joe arrived at his office the workshops were buzzing with activity, blowers roared, machines hummed, extractors rattled, timber screamed, handsaws rasped, voices shouted, and steel hammers rang out in confused staccato. The loyal workforce was completely unaware of the imminent threat to its industry, nor did it know about an emergency meeting to be held in the managing director's office to discuss its future.

Townsend entered the works and hurried up the stairs to the first floor office complex where he caught sight of Joe standing in the corridor. "Have you spoken to the Old Man yet?" he asked; disregarding formal greetings.

Joe, slightly taken aback, answered, "Yes – I've told him."

"How did he take it?" Townsend was nervous.

"Quietly, very quietly indeed."

"That means I'm for the high jump."

"I don't think so. He didn't directly blame you,"

"Is there going to be a meeting?"

"Yes – so start getting your act together and be ready to come up with some good suggestions."

"How much time have I got?"

"You haven't. The meeting will start as soon as Keith arrives. Alfred is already in his office."

"Oh my God!" cried the hapless salesman, "What can I do?"

"Just take your hat and coat off and dump them in my office," said Joe resignedly, "then come on in. Maybe you'll think of something as the meeting progresses."

The corridor cleared as Townsend went to divest himself of his outdoor clothes and Joe entered Alfred's office. "Townsend has arrived." he said and waited for an acknowledgement.

Alfred stood in silence and stared at an overcast sky through a window moist with condensation. He was clearly worried about losing the business he had devoted so much of his life to. He had nurtured it from its early stages right through to its present maturity;

The Lincolnshire Tramp

always at his desk, always attending to details, and always on hand to make the critical decisions. He was the very nucleus to which the enterprise had clung and developed, But now, when the whole thing threatened to fall apart for reasons beyond his control, he felt completely powerless. Never before in his considerable career had he faced such depressing prospects. Undoubtedly, slumps had occurred in the past but then it was possible to look ahead and take precautions to counter them. Today the situation was different no longer a localised problem with a solution around the next corner, this time the whole nation was plunging into a recession. Alfred had read all the signs and he knew it would require nothing short of a miracle to achieve economic recovery. Worse still, it would take time. He allowed a few seconds more for his reflections and then turned to Joe and said, "Sit yourself down, old chap." A limp hand offered one of the vacant chairs deliberately placed in front of the spacious desk.

Joe, in need of a place to lay out his papers, selected a chair nearest the desk and sat down. "Don't look so gloomy, Alfred, " he said, "I'm sure we can ride out this storm."

A flicker of a smile crossed Alfred's lips as the well meaning words of encouragement briefly raised his spirit. He gravely doubted Joe's prediction but gladly warmed to his ardent optimism. "Have you got those figures for me?" he asked, dropping down in his own chair.

"They're all here," said Joe, "and I have an assessment."

"How much longer can we hold out?" Alfred was afraid of his own question and would have preferred not to know the answer.

"We have enough cash in the bank to pay wages and running costs for the next three weeks and – " Joe paused to make a small correction to his figures, "If we get prompt payment for our present contracts and chase up some outstanding debts we could stretch it for another two."

Before Alfred could comment further, the office door opened abruptly and Keith, sheepishly followed by Townsend, entered the room.

"Hurry up you two and sit down." snapped Alfred, irritated by their intrusion.

Townsend responded immediately and meekly sat down whereas Keith, in need of a whisky and soda, sullenly flopped into his chair when he found the drinks cabinet firmly locked.

"When you are quite ready" snarled Alfred, "I will explain the purpose of this meeting." He looked at each face in turn. "What we have to do today is to find ways and means to keep this firm alive during the economic crisis now gripping the country."

"Change of government, that's what we need," snorted Keith with a dogmatic air.

Alfred ignored the remark yet made a point of raising his voice above that of his son. "If we keep going as we are without the benefit of new contracts then we shall have to close the works within five weeks."

Keith, genuinely astonished by the severity of the statement, hysterically exclaimed, "What! Close down the works? You must be joking." His remarks, as before, were ignored.

"As you know," Alfred continued, "midwinter is, for obvious reasons, not the best time of the year to get new orders, we don't usually see them until March or April. Nonetheless, we've never been without work especially during the winter months. Unfortunately that is no longer the case and we are left facing a double edged problem; an the one side we have a shortfall in our workload because orders have slackened off in the run up to Christmas, and on the other, we are most definitely in the grip of a deep recession which could go on for many months to come."

"I can't believe any of this," laughed Keith, nervously, "five more weeks and we all pack up and go home, never to return. It doesn't make sense."

"That's if we can hang on for five weeks," warned Joe "it might be sooner."

"Still, a lot could happen in that time," offered Townsend. "I mean, something could turn up – couldn't it?"

"I think we are looking for something a bit more positive than that, Vernon." observed Alfred.

"I see it all now," ranted Keith as he rounded on Townsend, "this is all down to you, isn't it? If you were anything of a salesman you'd have a full order book now and we'd have no problems. What the hell do we pay you for anyway?"

Townsend's timorous disposition came from doubting his own abilities rather than fear of fellow man, therefore, he was quite capable of standing up to Keith and not being browbeaten by him.

"Before your big mouth gets you into more trouble," he said, "let me tell you a thing or two. About a couple of months ago I realized something was wrong but I didn't know what it was. Apart from spending a lot of time chasing the Benson contract I also trebled my usual number of calls and everywhere I went the answer was the same; nobody wanted joinery because the building industry was grinding to a halt. The general consensus of opinion suggested waiting until the new year and see how it goes."

True to character, Keith paid little heed to Townsend's explanation and continued to harangue him. "You can't fob us off with rubbish like that. A good salesman would sell snow to the Eskimos' and not fall for a lot of lame excuses. Obviously you're not doing your job properly and, in my opinion, your incompetence has cost us our firm. I think you've outlived your usefulness and you should be relieved of your position as of today. If nothing else it will save us five weeks wages."

"And cost the company thousands of pounds in severance pay." Joe intervened.

"Trust you to look after your own kind," Keith snapped at Joe "talk about bite the hand that feeds you."

"For Christ's sake, Keith, shut up," Alfred shouted angrily. "I'm sick and tired of your petty squabbling."

"Well I didn't get the firm into such a bloody mess, did I?"

If anything was designed to compel Alfred to change his ground it was Keith's attitude to business, thus, he switched from bemoaning the loss of his firm to staunchly defending it. "The firm isn't in a mess as yet," he said to Keith, "Nor will it be if you bucked your ideas up. We are a well organised outfit with a good track record and there is no reason why we shouldn't pull through."

"Then what's all the panic about?" retorted Keith.

"The survival of the fittest, that's what the panic is about." Alfred looked contemptuously at his son. "Thousands of firms like ours will be preparing to meet the challenge, some will come out on top but many others will go under. I don't intend to be among the losers. So, if you want to save the business and step into my shoes, you'd better come up with something constructive."

Keith leaned forward and wagged a finger at his father. "Right," he said, "I'll show you how to save the business. I shall tell you what we can do."

"Come on then," urged Alfred, "let's have it."

"Lay off half the workforce, it's as simple as that"

"What! And have a strike on our hands."

"Even better," said Keith gleefully, "all the time they're on strike we don't have to pay their wages. Like that we could hang on for months and pick up again when trade improves." Thinking this to be an extremely clever idea, he sat back in his chair and smiled smugly.

However, Alfred thought otherwise, "You really are a fool," he said, "a prolonged dispute with the workers will lessen our chances of survival, not increase it. A strike now will finish us for good because what little trading there is in the market will go to the firms who are in a state of readiness and who are hungry."

"That's my point exactly," Keith interposed, "if we reduce the entire workforce by 50 per cent, then those who are left will have to work harder or lose their jobs, therefore, we must become leaner and more competitive."

"And what do you think the unions will say to that?" Alfred asked.

"Damn the unions," said Keith, "they're nothing but a millstone around our necks. This might be the ideal time to get rid of them once and for all."

"There will be no redundancies." Alfred roared, "My men have been loyal to me for all these years and I intend to stand by them. Loyalty cuts both ways you know, we are responsible for each other."

"Really, Dad, with a negative attitude like yours I don't wonder we are going bankrupt."

The remark infuriated Alfred but he could not find words to counter it; the predominant thought in his mind called for kicking Keith's backside out of the office. But in the end he did no more than reiterate his former statement, "There will be no redundancies."

"All right then," whined Keith sulkily, "keep your bloody workforce. I suppose we can always borrow money from the bank to pay for it." He half turned away as if indicating his reluctance to take further part in the debate.

Joe, who had been patiently waiting to comment, cleared his throat and said, "Money is very expensive to borrow at the moment and we'd do well to avoid that course of action. I think we should look at another option before committing ourselves to heavy borrowing."

Mildly surprised, Alfred enquired, "Does this mean you have something up your sleeve, Joe?"

"Nothing concrete you understand," cautioned Joe, "but I have prepared a draft proposal which I would like you to consider." He handed a typewritten sheet of paper to Alfred. "It consists of three dependent parts."

The group sat in silence whilst Alfred read through the proposal. After a while he made a noncommittal grunt and began to question Joe.

"Can you explain what you mean by – stock items?"

"Yes I can. If we manufacture a selection of stock items to run concurrently with our commissioned work then we can stay fairly operational for five to six weeks. I'm thinking of things like, window frames, door frames, doors, and staircases. All of which must be made to standard sizes and able to fit into any new house. I've checked with the yard and timber stocks are good, but care will be needed to use it wisely ."

Alfred started to shake his head. " I have grave reservations about a stock pile of spec. joinery." he confessed.

"I'm afraid it is a crucial part of my plan," Joe insisted, "I need it to buy time. The main thing is to keep up the morale of the workforce and still have a saleable commodity at the end of it. It's one of the risks we have to take."

To Alfred, taking a risk suddenly implied a chilling consequence, it sounded too much like losing money. "I'll have to think about that," he said, "but in the meantime let's look at part two of your plan – the four day week"

Joe chose his words carefully as he explained, "Without the extra work the figures become irrelevant. You can reduce the working week how you like, four days, three days, or two days, depending on how long you want to drag out the existing orders. Mind you, I think anything less than a four day week will not be acceptable to the men and a strike could be on the cards. On the other hand, if the stock items are included you can assure them of a regular four day week for a prescribed period and probably keep the unions off your back."

Whilst Alfred declined to comment and Keith continued to sulk it seemed incumbent on Townsend to break the silence. "Of course I have no real say in the matter," he said, "but I do think Joe has the right idea and it's well worth trying."

"Think so, do you?" challenged Alfred, peering into Townsend's eyes. "And do you know what the third part of this plan involves?"

"No – I don't"

"The hard sell, that's what. It's no good making a lot of joinery if it's just going to sit in the yard. It has to be sold and I mean really sold, high pressure stuff. Do you know what I'm saying?"

Townsend, apparently bewildered, said, "Yes – you want me to go out and sell the new stuff, but it doesn't make sense to me. Did we not conclude, only a few minutes ago, that the market was dead?"

"I think you are missing the point here, Vernon," stated Joe, "I'm sure we are all in agreement about the local market but we must go beyond that, our targets must be set further afield. From now on our customers should be drawn from the greater part of England and Wales."

"What!" exclaimed Townsend. "Are you seriously suggesting I should traipse all over the country to get orders. It's not on Joe, it's too much for one rep."

"Not one rep," said Joe, "but three."

A sombre frown hung on Alfred's brow as he demanded of Joe, "How can you talk about employing more salesmen when we are so close to laying men off?"

"I do not propose to engage more salesmen," Joe declared, "not when existing resources can be utilized. As you can see from this drawing," he presented Alfred with a sheet of paper bearing the outline of the British Isles, "I have divided the chosen area into three parts, a division each for three of us in this office."

Alfred gave the plan some earnest consideration, then he faced Townsend and said, "If this scheme goes ahead do you think you can handle the eight or so counties in the south east?"

"That sounds more like it," beamed Townsend, "I could easily work that area – no problem."

"And you, Joe," Alfred continued, "I see you have yourself down for the south west and Wales I must confess don't see you as a salesman."

"If I manage to sell this plan of mine to you will that change your view." Joe's response was light-hearted.

The smile which might have appeared on Alfred's face was quickly discouraged since Keith had to be informed of his part in the scheme, a directive which would not be well received. "Keith, you are to cover the Midlands." Alfred's comment was brief and precise.

Keith, breaking his long silence announced emphatically, "I'm not in favour of any part of this stupid scheme and I've no wish to be connected with it, so count me out."

Again, because of his son's uncharitable attitude, Alfred was persuaded to change his ground and he accepted Joe's proposals without further reservation. Hitherto, he had been dubious about the scheme and had inwardly fought against his chief accountant's more businesslike approach, but now, with Keith set firmly against him, he decided to back it.

"I'll have another look at this, Joe," he said and picked up the proposal to examine it more thoroughly. "I can see you've given it a lot of thought."

"Spent most of the holiday working it all out." Joe modestly admitted. He knew, at that moment, Alfred was hooked and it would be only a matter of time before the proposals became a reality.

Joe passed more sheets of paper across the desk . "Here are lists of standard joinery sizes and designs," he said, "also our manufacturing costs. All profit will come from the best deals we can make in the market place, in other words, we should not sell below those prices. Of course, if the economy picks up we can return to our usual profit margins."

Apart from the odd perfunctory grunt, Alfred made no other comment until he had completed his survey of the figures and then, addressing Townsend, he said, "Do you understand what Joe means about pricing the new range of spec. joinery?"

"Yes. It means I can be flexible with the prices if I think I can get a sale."

"Precisely," Alfred nodded, "but remember, while stocks must be cleared it should not be at a total disregard for profit. Survival depends on profit."

He handed all of Joe's papers to Townsend and instructed, "Get yourself photocopies of this lot and be on your way to the south east."

Townsend stood up to receive the papers and dared to ask, "It's been an expensive holiday and I'm a little short of funds, so I wondered..."

"Yes, I know," sighed Alfred, "I'm sure Joe will fix you up with something before you leave."

It was a happier salesman who quietly dismissed himself from the office for Townsend had spent a miserable Christmas worrying about his future, but now, instead of losing his job, he had been given a fresh incentive with greater responsibilities. He was now a man with a mission, a man with new scope and power and a man with a chance to make a name for himself. He resolved to do well in the south east and so justify the faith entrusted in him.

As soon as the office door was closed behind Townsend, Keith seized the opportunity to lodge an incisive protest. "Take it from me," he said, "selling is not my scene, so I hope you don't expect me to go on a wild-goose chase like that."

"Not at all," Alfred observed dryly, "you are going on a sales campaign. As from today – and for the next five weeks – you will be hawking our wares around the counties of the midlands and you will not be expected back in your office unless you bring with you orders amounting to many thousands of pounds. Do I make myself clear?"

"You can't do this to me, I'm senior management not a bloody sales rep."

"You'll be senior nothing if the firm packs up. Either you go out and sell joinery or you leave the firm. The choice is yours."

"You can't make me do anything I don't want to."

"I can and I will. Just remember what I said to you the other night,"

Memories of a past confrontation flooded back into Keith's mind and he recounted the harsh conditions set by his father at the time. "You bastard!" he shouted as he got up, kicked over his chair, and stormed out of the room. The violently slammed door sent tremors pulsating through the walls, causing the smaller and less permanent objects to waver and slip. Joe sprang from his seat and tried to steady as many as possible whilst Alfred sat tenaciously at his desk.

"If Keith concentrated his energies on selling joinery instead of smashing the place up we might be in with a chance." Joe remarked as he put the room back into order.

"Come and sit down, Joe," Alfred urged, "I'd like a private word with you."

The behest had an air of confidentiality about it which, seemingly, demanded Joe's immediate attention, therefore, he had to resist the temptation to make a final adjustment to a hanging portrait and return to his chair.

Alfred continued. "I'm sorry I gave you a bad time just now," he said apologetically. "I know you were doing your best to save the firm and I was being bloody minded. The trouble is – and I tell you this in the strictest confidence – I am having some personal financial problems at the moment and I can't put any more money into the business – something I was afraid you would ask me to do."

He hesitated; should he confide in Joe or should he not; after all, family squabbles are private matters and not for general concern. On the other hand he needed somebody to talk to, somebody he could trust, and especially somebody who could offer good counsel, "Damn it all, Joe!" he blurted out, "I may as well tell you the whole story. A few nights ago, Keith came to me and asked for eighty thousand pounds to clear his gambling debts. He said he had been threatened and his life was in danger. We had one hell of a row but in the end I agreed to pay it. For my sins, I am his father and I would never forgive myself if anything violent happened to him. However, it took every penny I had plus a mortgage against my own house."

Joe was sympathetic, "I had no idea," he said "it must have come as a shock to you."

"It did," Alfred gravely admitted. "Apparently it's been going on for some time – the gambling I mean - but it's all going to stop now. Keith has pledged never to get involved again. He burnt his fingers and learned his lesson. Further more, he has promised to makes real commitment to the firm."

The doubt in Joe's mind became all too obvious by the expression on his face. "I hope, for your sake, Keith doesn't default again," he offered.

Alfred smiled and said, "Don't worry, I have a plan which will keep him in check. I shall appoint a board of directors to run the business, providing we can save the firm. Apart from Keith and myself there will be you and two others – probably Townsend, if he does well on the sales campaign, and somebody reliable from shop floor. I shall remain as a managing director and hold the chairmanship but we'll all have equal voting power on major decisions. I've given it a lot of thought, Joe, so I hope you'll back me up."

The unexpected proposal caught Joe off guard and all he could manage to say was, "Risky! I mean – we could vote Keith off the board altogether."

"Exactly," agreed Alfred, "but I hope it will never never come to that – all the same, Keith will have to watch his step if he's to keep his place."

"It's an ingenious plan, Alfred, I'll grant you that – and I'm more that grateful to you for offering me a directorship."

"Good – it's settled then. I shall make all the necessary arrangements whilst you're away," he stood up to shake hands with Joe, "and when you get back the new company will start running the firm."

"It's a generous gesture, thank you." said Joe also rising. Then he added, "Is Vernon to be told of his pending appointment?"

"Not in so many words," advised Alfred, "just tell him to do well with his sales campaign with a view to a future promotion – that's all."

A loud knocking on the office door brought the conversation to an abrupt end. Before either of the two men could respond, the door opened and the stocky figure of Bert Seedon swaggered in. "Excuse me, Mr Harrison," he growled, "But Keith has been talking about redundancies on the shop floor and, as trade union representative, I'm here to see if there's any truth in the rumour."

"Glad to see you, Bert," Alfred said warmly, "I was just about to send down for you."

His sincerity belied his true feelings for, above all things, he hated dealing with the unions. His obvious course of action was to dump the problem in Joe's lap and distance himself from the confrontation; something Joe was well aware of. "We do need you co-operation in a little matter," confided Alfred, guiding the union man to a vacant chair, " But I'll let Joe explain it to you – he's so much better at it than I am."

"Should I talk to Bert in my office?" Joe suggested.

"No, no," Alfred asserted as he edged towards the door, "you can stay in here for as long as you like, meanwhile I'll pop along and have a word with the draughtsmen."

It was an unburdened man who stepped lightly into the corridor and headed for the drawing office.

Bert, left alone with Joe, thought himself the victim of a conspiracy and demanded, "What's all this about then?"

"It's all about trade slackening off and lack of orders," Joe explained. "To be honest with you, Bert, we've barely enough work to keep the men going."

"Ah! So there is going to be redundancies?"

"Not at all. We are committed to saving all your jobs even if it means a four day week."

"Forget it, Joe. We are definitely not going down that path to cutbacks."

"Would you prefer redundancies then?"

"I must make myself clear on this point, no redundancies and no four day week."

"It's either a four day week or a no day week, so make your mind up."

"Don't threaten me, Joe, you know my position. If any of my members loses so much as one hour's pay through management cutbacks then we'll be out on strike before you know it."

Joe, tired of standing, relaxed and sat casually on the corner of the desk. "I envy you, Bert," he said with a smile, "Everything in your world is clear cut – it's either black or white. As for me, I have to move into the grey areas where nothing is straightforward. This morning, for instance, I've had a hell of a time of it trying to convince Mr. Harrison to manufacture a quantity of stock items just to keep the jobs open, and then you come along to jeopardize the whole scheme with threats of strike action."

Bert refused to give way, "I have to consider the interests of my members." he insisted.

A note of firmness crept into Joe's voice as he warned, "For what it's worth, I can tell you this – a strike would close the works for good. We would all lose our jobs from the youngest apprentice to the Harrisons themselves and no matter how long you picketed the front gate it wouldn't make the slightest scrap of difference. So if you went to put principles before jobs that's down to you,"

The union man, skilful negotiator that he was, could not argue against the facts presented by Joe, nor could he be seen to lose face. Warily he said, "Tell me more about the stock items you mentioned."

"It will guarantee five more working weeks for the men instead of two and it will give some of us from the office time to go out and sell the new joinery."

"All four day weeks?"

"Yes."

"Why can't we have four five day weeks?"

"Because you are asking for normal working and that would not be sustainable for four weeks. We need to stretch the workload out and save running costs where we can. The advantage of the four day week is that it can be extended beyond the five week period as demand for joinery increases. With any luck we can be back in full production by the spring."

Despite a nagging fear of being hoodwinked, Bert condescended to accept the plan. "I suppose I shall have to go along with it," he said begrudgingly, "but I don't like it – not one bit of it."

"You won't have any regrets," Joe assured him.

"I'd better not," growled Bert as he stood up and prepared to leave. "All the same, I'd better have it in writing and signed by Mr Harrison."

"You shall have it," promised Joe. "In the meantime, Bert, try and keep the men together. Be a good chap and try not to rock the boat whilst I'm away."

"Why – where are you off to?"

"I'm going down to the south west on an intensive sales campaign. I'll probably be away for a couple of weeks or so."

"I hope you know what you are doing, Joe."

"I think I do," said Joe with confidence, "I have faith in this firm even if no one else does."

"Well — I wish you luck,"

"Thank you."

The two men, each believing they had won a moral victory, harmoniously vacated Alfred's office and set off to implement their respective charges. Bert returned to the shop floor where he confirmed union backing for the four day week and Joe spent the rest of the day in his office planning the sales campaign.

By four in the afternoon the firm had switched to the new arrangement. Townsend had departed to the south east to explore his new territory, Keith had solemnly declared to do likewise in the midlands, Alfred re-acquainted himself with office management and the first batch of speculative joinery began to appear on the work benches. Harrison & Beck had committed itself to the biggest gamble in its, hitherto, judicious history.

Chapter 4

The third morning of the new year was no different from the second, it was still cold, damp, and very dark. Not that it bothered Keith too much, because he took advantage of his authorised absence from the office to stay in bed for all but the last hour before midday. He demanded a cooked breakfast when he finally made an effort to get up and then, having washed and dressed, he cast a cursory eye over a road map before sitting down to the meal. Kettering looked nice and handy, he thought, less than thirty miles away and he could be there and back within the remaining hours of daylight, it would also allow time to visit his sister, Virginia; something he had been meaning to do for days.

The morning papers were late arriving but Keith did not find this altogether unacceptable especially when he found out that he had backed three winners from the only race meeting of the previous day. He calculated his winnings to be in excess of five hundred pounds, with so much money to play with and his luck riding high Kettering suddenly seemed insignificant, anyway, there was always tomorrow. A belated lunch with his bookmaker and a careful study of form became the priorities of the day.

The evening had already closed in by the time Keith eventually entered Virginia's dress shop. He had been celebrating his good fortune and his breath smelt of strong drink. Virginia was not pleased to see him and made him wait until she had dealt with the last of her customers – a decision which could not be in her best interests for it gave Keith a chance to assess the value of the small enterprise.

"And what ill wind brings you here?" demanded Virginia as soon as they were alone,

"I've had a marvellous day," beamed Keith, somewhat stupefied, "so I thought I'd just pop in and see my little sister. Good will visit you might say."

"But you're supposed to be away on a sales campaign, aren't you? For your firm?"

"Just got back from Kettering." Keith lied, "Thought I'd do all the local towns whilst the weather is still bad."

Virginia was suspicious of him. "Did you sell anything?" she asked.

"Too soon to say, old girl," he bragged, "but I did get some useful leads."

"I do hope you aren't going to let Daddy down this time," Virginia pleaded, "It would break his heart if he lost the firm."

His sister's remark brought Keith nicely to the point of his visit and it also permitted him to stake his claim without alarming her. "He won't lose his firm if we all stick together as one family," he said.

"What do you mean by that?"

"Dad tells me you are planning to break away from us and run your business as a separate concern. Bad move old girl, don't you know there's safety in numbers. If we can keep the businesses linked up then we shall have the financial clout to ride out this recession. Surely you can see that."

He was well aware of Virginia's success and he needed to be in the right position to muscle in on her venture should the joinery firm fail and he be without a source of income. If she divorced herself from the family now then he would certainly be left out in the cold.

"It would be rather dodgy to go it alone as things are," he pressed "I mean – suppose you got into difficulties – we wouldn't be able to help you out – not unless you were part of the group."

"But Joe thought it would be better to run this as a separate concern," argued Virginia without conviction; Keith's comments had caused her a change of heart.

"Joe!" sneered Keith, "what does he know? Dad wouldn't be in trouble now if Joe was any good at accountancy."

"Oh come on! That's not fair."

"Okay – so Joe can draw up the men's wages every week but he knows nothing about business. The best thing you can do is to forget his advice."

Virginia could not completely ignore Joe's advice, nor could she that of her brother, or her father. So much conflicting advice was confusing, therefore the matter had better be left unresolved for the time being. "I know Joe is away at the moment," she said, "so I won't take any action until I've had another talk with him on his return. How will that do?"

"Not a bad idea." admitted Keith who saw yet another opportunity. "Better still, why not wait and see if Joe can get Dad's firm out of trouble first. That way you will be sure – see what I mean?"

Virginia nodded. "Yes – I like that," she said and believed it to be the best way to appease everyone concerned.

As for Keith, he was highly delighted, his day was going really well, all it needed now was a successful evening at a gambling club just to put the icing on the cake. He bid his sister farewell and hurried home to get ready for an evening of self gratification.

Whilst a carefree and confident Keith prepared to leave the comfort of his warm home to spend a night on the town, a cold and disconsolate Joe searched for hotel accommodation. Unlike Keith, Joe had not had a good day. The numerous calls he made during the journey from Spalding to Gloucester were not beneficial to himself or his firm. Selling a product was more strenuous than it would appear, it was a soul destroying task which could dampen the spirits of the most good humoured of men. Townsend's assessment of the market proved all too accurate, it was dead and trade reps. were about as welcome as a winter cold.

Tired and hungry, Joe entered a small hotel where he had booked a room – or thought he had.

"Sorry sir," said the girl at the reception desk, "But there seems to be a most dreadful mistake, you see, somebody has made a double booking on that room and it has already been taken. Sorry. "

"And you've nothing else I suppose," retorted Joe testily.

"No sir, 'fraid not. You could try the commercial down the road, about a quarter of a mile on your left. They might be able to help you." The girl said as much with her hands as she did with her voice. Joe reluctantly picked up his suitcase and trudged wearily back out into the night. He drove the short distance to the recommended hotel and was dismayed to find a large, drab building seemingly in need of repairs. It was not well advertised and not in the least way inviting, Surprisingly, its car park was almost full which, in an odd way, belied the impression given by the outward appearance of the establishment. Joe had misgivings about the place and doubted if it was worth his while to ask for a room. For a full five minutes he sat in his car to consider the situation; should he put on a brave face and go in to order a room, or should he abandon the entire mission and go back to Spalding? It had been a long day and a tiresome journey – the way back could be interminable. A room in the hotel was his only option.

To his amazement, the hotel seemed even larger on the inside and it was warm, bright, and vibrant with a distinctly masculine feel about it. Countless men (attired in business suits) moved freely throughout the lounges to enjoy the facilities on offer and did so with such familiarity that Joe began to realize what the girl in the previous hotel had meant by commercial. These men were nearly all commercial travellers and this was one of the hotels they frequented. For the first time in many hours a smile spread across

The Lincolnshire Tramp

his face; what better place to pick up the latest information and, perhaps, a few tricks of the trade.

The prospect of good company alone was enough to lift his flagging spirits so, having booked a room, freshened up, and had a meal in the dining hall, he entered the lounges to mingle with the real salesmen.

With a glass of beer in his hand, he moved from one group to another to eavesdrop on their conversations. To a man they were salesmen and, of course they were talking shop but with such a diverse range of products on sale no two conversations followed the same line. The main topic was the recession and the means to counter it but as soon as a particular product was mentioned Joe was able to discard the speaker until the whole group had been eliminated, then he moved on.

An hour – and many conversations later – Joe lined up at the bar to have his empty glass replenished and whilst he waited he found himself listening to a man who had an unusually loud voice. "They'll need cement of course," said the voice, "and lots of it." Joe casually turned to catch sight of the speaker and saw a robust man addressing a small group of colleagues as they sat in a corner of the room. The speaker continued, "And let me tell you, we've got a particularly attractive offer on at the moment. They'll never get cement cheaper anywhere else, believe you me."

"I do hope you're not going in for the bricks as well, old man," piped up an elderly rep. with a jocular air,

"Not at all, Barney," replied the loud voice, "You can quote for all the bricks you like, we're not interested. Not enough profit in bricks."

Joe almost chuckled with delight, he could hardly believe his luck, a group of building trade reps. at last. His hand trembled slightly as he paid for his beer; he then walked nonchalantly towards the group and asked, "Is that seat taken?" He referred to an empty chair close by. A member of the group indicated that it was not so Joe quietly sat down to listen.

He was to remain there for the rest of the evening and glean what information he could from the banter that passed between the reps. Some facts that he could be sure of did emerge. Principally, a large building site would soon open up somewhere in the south west and it was to be government sponsored, secondly, the London based contractors had taken a suite in a Bristol hotel to conduct a series of meetings to discuss sub-contract tenders, and finally, the meetings start Thursday (the next day).

It was an opportunity Joe could not afford to miss, somehow he had to find out the name of the London contractor and the name of the hotel in Bristol. Obviously only a limited number of people were privileged to such information and he would be told nothing if he dared ask without grounds for doing so. In what little time he had left at his disposal he devised a simple plan; he would memorize all the faces in the group so that he might recognize any one of them at any time during the following day, he would also get up early in the morning to record the details of each man's car as it departed for Bristol. He was certain that one of them would lead him to his objective.

Half an hour later the man with the loud voice declared that it was time for bed and the group, without breaking off the conversation, vacated the corner and headed off towards the bedrooms. Joe had intended to follow soon after but was waylaid by a member of the bar staff (clearing tables of empty glasses) who confronted him with a bulky briefcase.

"I think this belongs to a member of your party, sir" said the man as he forced the briefcase into Joe's hands, "Perhaps you would kindly do the honours."

Joe, taken aback by the man's actions, stammered something that sounded like, "Thank you – I will," and hurried out of the lounge in pursuit of the reps. He hoped to catch up with them somewhere on the landings or in the corridors but, by strange coincidence, the whole place appeared to be deserted, the landings and corridors were devoid of all human forms. As he could hear sounds and voices coming from behind closed doors he assumed that all hotel guests were in their rooms and it would not be worth his while to knock on every door just to find the owner of the briefcase. It would be easier to return to his own room, open the briefcase to find the owner's name, and then phone down to the reception for a room number.

Prying into another person's business was strictly against Joe's principles, therefore, opening the briefcase to find a name was an affront to his dignity especially when he had to remove a large section of its contents to find that name. By then it was too late – he saw too much. Before him lay not only the rep.'s name but the joinery manufacturer he worked for, also, full details about the London contractor and the hotel where the meetings were to be held. A feeling of guilt came ever him as, in his view, he stole the vital names and addresses; he had to do it for the sake of the men and women who depended upon him. Anyway, as he was to remind himself, all is fair in love and war. He knew there would be more

The Lincolnshire Tramp

for the taking if he had the nerve – a search through the documents would reveal the quality and the quantity of the joinery required, also his rival's costings.

With his hand poised above the papers, Joe paused to deliberate the integrity of his behaviour; should he or should he not cheat to gain advantage. After due consideration he deemed there to be too much at stake to let slip this once in a lifetime opportunity which had providentially come his way, he had to know what he was up against. Surreptitiously he delved into the other man's documents and found all the information that was needed. However, before he could settle down to a long night of plagiarism, he called reception for a room number. He learned, without divulging his reasons, that the owner of the briefcase occupied a room on the same landing as his own.

Seven a.m., Joe decided, was the best time to leave the carefully re-packed briefcase outside the door of room no.43; it could easily be assumed to have been put there by a porter when he cleaned the shoes and brought up the morning papers. It meant that Joe had barely five hours sleep but that was a small sacrifice to pay if he succeeded in winning a contract for his firm.

By mid-morning of that Thursday, Joe entered the city of Bristol. He lost no time in locating the hotel suite hired by the London contractors, and boldly approached a representative of the firm. He fully expected to be thrown out for not having a proper appointment but instead, he was treated to a cordial welcome, given a complete set of plans and specifications, and invited to submit his estimates on the following afternoon.

All pangs of conscience deserted him as he found himself yet another hotel room and set up a makeshift office. He devoted the rest of the day to a thorough examination of the plans and specifications followed by detailed costings of every scrap of joinery contained therein. Many times he tried to make telephone contact with the Spalding office but the lines were always engaged, this did not deter him, however, because he carried with him enough bill headings and the like to draw up a presentable quotation. All he wanted for was somebody with the correct machine to put his submission into a type written form; this could be done at some time on the morning before his appointment. The knowledge of one rival's estimates gave him an edge on the others but he would have to take pot luck where they were concerned and hope to pitch his prices at just the right level.

Heavy cloud rolled in from the Atlantic as Joe sought the services of a typist in the heart of Bristol on the Friday morning, and the same cloud formation heeded towards Spalding where Alfred sat in his office and listened to Bert Seedon's accusations. The union man had discreetly organized a surveillance team to monitor Keith's progress and, when he thought nothing was being done to support the firm, decided to report to Alfred.

"Joe and Mr. Townsend have gone down south to sell our doors and windows," observed Bert Seedon, "And I thought Mr. Keith was going to do the same out Manchester way."

"That's right," agreed Alfred, "So what's the problem?"

"The problem is, Mr. Keith ain't left Spalding, that's what. And I don't think it's fair on my members to be cut back to a four day week when the management won't pull its weight."

Alfred became angry. "How do you know?" he demanded.

"I have my spies." retorted Bert Seedon, matching Alfred's anger.

"You've no right to spy on my son, " Alfred shouted. "His affairs are none of your business."

"Look here," Bert Seedon shouted back, "I was led to believe we were all going to work together to save the firm and that included Mr. Keith, otherwise I would never have agreed to the four day week." He wagged his finger. "And if the men down there find out they're on short time so that Mr. Keith can go gambling then I won't be able to stop a mass walkout." Alfred leapt to his feet and roared, "Get out of this office, d'you hear, get out!"

"Right!" snapped Bert Seedon coldly, "On your head be it." He walked towards the door.

Suddenly Alfred had a change of heart, "Wait!" he called. "Come back here, Bert, and let's talk"

Slowly the union man turned and retraced his steps. "You'll deal with Mr. Keith then?" he said. The request was by way more of a condition.

"Yes," sighed Alfred as he flopped back down into his chair. "I'll speak to him later this morning on my way back from the bank."

"If I'm right," Bert Seedon suggested, "Then you'll find him at home."

"I'm sure I will," conceded Alfred and then he urged, "I'd be obliged if you'd keep this conversation to yourself, Bert. I don't want it spread about the shop floor, I don't want a strike on my hands."

A nod from the union man was enough to satisfy Alfred.

It was bad form to spy on a man and equally bad form for that man not to be doing his job in a time of crisis. If Bert Seedon was right, and Alfred had no cause to doubt him, then Keith was guilty of the accusations made against him and deserved to be severely reprimanded; besides, he was bringing the family name into disrepute and that was unforgivable. These thoughts and others like them passed through Alfred's mind as he drove from the bank (where he had collected cash for the firm's wage bill) to his son's house. He desperately prayed not to see Keith's car parked on the drive or, at least, not to find him at home. Pensively he rang the doorbell and waited for the door to be opened.

Keith, unshaven, dishevelled, and in his night attire, was startled to see his father standing on the doorstep. "Oh – it's you Dad!" he stammered, "You'd better come in."

Alfred pushed past his son and snapped, "I didn't expect to find you at home today –"

"Just a touch of 'flu, that's all," Keith followed his father into the lounge. "I'm expecting the doctor to call at any moment."

"Don't lie to me, boy, " barked Alfred, "You weren't so ill that you couldn't go out gambling last night."

Keith laughed nervously. "I don't know what you are talking about," he said, "I was here at home – in bed."

"You were seen entering the Tawny Owl night club."

"Sounds like someone has been telling tales," snorted Keith, "I bet it was that creep Seedon, I thought I saw him hanging around outside."

"So – you were there." Alfred glowered at Keith.

"For no more than five minutes – and that's all. The place is due for a refit soon and we are quoting for the joinery so, I popped along to make an appointment for a measure up,"

"Lies, lies, lies!" stormed Alfred. "You were there for the best part of five hours and that means you must have been gambling."

"You can't prove that," Keith insisted.

"I don't have to," raged Alfred, "The look on your face says it all."

"Oh, for God's sake, Dad! I'm old enough to do as I please and you have no right to order me about."

"And you have no right to fritter the family fortune away, night after night." So furious was Alfred that the anger in his heart quickly turned to pain and that pain, rapidly increasing with intensity, spread through his chest to seize his arms. Feeling nausea and dizziness, he groped for something to cling to and, at the same time, tried to cry out in anguish; instead he fell heavily to the floor, unable to catch hold of anything supportive or to utter a single word.

Keith was dumbstruck. For several minutes he could do no more than stare at his unconscious father but after a while his senses returned and he characteristically set about dealing with the matter. He would gladly have dumped the problem onto his wife had she been at home, but as she was out on a shopping expedition with their children he had to make his own arrangements. Calling for an ambulance was easily the most obvious thing to do and, with that done, he had to consider his own position.

With his father incapacitated, be it temporarily or otherwise, Keith would surely be expected to take over the running of the business and the sooner he took command the better it would be for everyone. Impulsively he knelt down to search his father's pockets for keys to house, office, and car; yet he would not have made the same gesture to administer aid or comfort to the unfortunate man.

The keys were soon found and Keith realized that a bag containing money for wages was in his father's car. That bag had to be transferred to his own car and concealed before anyone else saw it, and it had to be done before either his wife or the ambulance turned up at the house. Not a second was lost as he dashed out into the drive to switch the bag, he then returned to the house to quickly wash and dress prior to greeting the ambulancemen on their prompt arrival.

Whilst Alfred received expert medical attention, Keith loitered in the lobby by the front door and anxiously looked for the return of his wife. And then, when her car entered the drive, he hurried out to speak to her,

"Don't look so worried," he said, "It's only Father – he's been taken ill."

"Oh dear!" exclaimed his sad-eyed wife, "I saw the ambulance when I came round the corner and I wondered what was wrong, I do hope he's all right."

"Listen," interrupted Keith, "there's trouble at the works and I have to get over there immediately so I can't stay with Father. I want you to take over. Make sure he's put safely into the ambulance, dump the kids with your mother, and then go on to the hospital. I'll call you later – okay?" He barked his orders in his usual tone which served for both dog and wife alike and he departed in the same brusque manner, even to the point of driving his car across the frost hardened lawn to avoid the traffic littering his driveway.

It took him no more than ten minutes to drive to the joinery works and less than a minute to be inside his father's office. After a pause for breath he settled down in the big chair and became master of all he surveyed. Presently he called for his father's secretary and demanded to know where the firm's cheque book was kept.

"I'm not sure if I should tell you that, Mr. Keith," said the secretary, "Mr. Alfred gave strict instructions."

Obviously an explanation was needed and Keith had to think fast, "Ah!" he exclaimed, "I see you haven't heard yet – I did ask the police to phone."

The secretary looked glum. "We've had no phone call from the police," she said.

"Oh yes!" Keith continued, "Father is with them now. He was waylaid and robbed on his way back from the bank, you know. Very nasty business."

"All that money stolen!" The secretary was horrified. "And poor Mr Alfred – was he attacked and hurt badly?"

"They just snatched the bag of money and ran," said Keith, "Father wasn't hurt at all but he won't be in for the rest of the day. Luckily I had a local appointment this morning so I'm able to take his place and the first thing I must do is make provision for the men's wages. So – if you can get me the cheque book and tell me how much cash we need to draw out I'll get something organized."

"The cheque book is in Mr. Alfred's safe but I'm afraid I haven't got a key."

"No problem – Father let me have his keys." Keith fished the bunch from his pocket and selected the likeliest of the keys. "This should do the trick." He sprang from the chair to confront a large, old fashioned, square safe which resided unobtrusively in the corner of the office. The precision engineering of its lock responded mechanically to the key and a heavy, steel door swung open. Keith reached inside to pick up the coveted cheque book and almost gloated over the prized possession; the very feel of it seemed to give him power.

Controlling his emotions, he returned to the desk and signed the first available blank cheque which he then plucked from the book and handed to the secretary. "Fill this in with the relevant details," he instructed, "Then hurry along to the bank to cash it and take somebody hefty from the shop floor to ride shotgun. We don't want a second lot of money to go missing." The dumbstruck secretary automatically accepted the cheque and in doing so committed herself to carrying out the command even though she thought it to be in breech of her contract. Her one consoling thought as she left the office came from knowing that she alone would be responsible for making sure that everyone concerned received their hard earned pay: However, she did make a point of protest by slamming the door as she went out.

Keith ignored the woman and set about unlocking the drinks cabinet whereupon he poured himself a large whisky and soda. He carried the drink back to the desk and, sitting down in the big chair once again, he began to systematically turn out the drawers. There was nothing of any great value or of any real importance apart from one folder in particular. Such a folder in itself presented no offence but its contents were enough to send a shiver down Keith's spine for there he found a draft proposal to appoint a board of directors to run the business. Apart from himself and his father, three other directors were to be appointed; Joe was definitely listed whilst Townsend and a long serving foreman from the shop floor were pencilled in.

After some moments of thought, Keith realized the deeper implications of the proposal and he knew that if it (in its existing state) became perceptive his position would be very precarious indeed. Based on the assumption that his father would be too ill to function further as the head of the finer, he, Keith, would take control by right of succession, therefore, he had no intention of allowing the likes of Joe and Townsend to get in the way.

"The old bastard!" muttered Keith, "He's not going to get away with a dirty trick like that." In a fit of temper he tore the proposal to shreds and burnt it piece by piece in a convenient ashtray. "I am the head of this firm now – let nobody make any mistake about it." The announcement was made to an absent audience although he did intend to make his position clear to the workforce at a later date.

Complacently he sat back in the chair and contemplated how best to use the money concealed in the boot of his car. It was a tidy sum and it would serve him for several evenings at the club. His run of bad luck had to turn any day now and, as he calculated, his investment could increase by tenfold. That would shake them, that would show them he had real business potential, especially if he ploughed most of the money back into the firm. He sipped at his drink and relished his new found freedom.

However, his immediate euphoria was not to last; at two-o-clock in the afternoon he was summoned to the hospital to be at his father's bedside and an hour later he was to mourn the loss of his parent. Alfred had died without regaining consciousness.

Chapter 5

By unfortunate coincidence, the moment of Alfred's demise occurred shortly before Joe's interview at the Bristol hotel. Joe, of course, was not to know that as he entered the hotel foyer, although he may have had a premonition a second or two earlier when he noticed how dark the sky had become, and the fall of the first snow flake as it landed and dissolved on his sleeve. He paid but little attention to it at the time because he had other things on his mind and, if anything, he was glad to be inside and out of the snow storm that raged soon after.

The meeting with the contracts manager of the London company went extremely well. The manager was impressed by Joe's assiduous application to the task in hand and the thoroughness of his estimates. An instant rapport developed between the two men and the time passed swiftly as they discussed almost all aspects of an impending contract. Therefore, because the interview overran its allotted span before a conclusion could be reached, Joe was invited to attend a business lunch on the following day (Saturday) if he was available.

Joe readily accepted the invitation although he had planned to be back home in Spalding long before then but with such a good connection having been established he would be foolish not to alter his plans. He thanked his host warmly and excused himself from the hotel to return to his own rented room.

Because he had no desire to become entangled in the Bristol traffic he had previously walked the distance between the two hotels but now, in the height of the blizzard, he sought the services of a taxi.

"It looks as though you're in for a difficult night," he said to the taxi driver as the drifting snow hindered their progress.

"It do lay heavy on the outskirts of the city," observed the driver, "and it be getting worse by the minute. 'Tis forecast to snow right through the night 'til morning."

"In that case I don't envy you."

"I shan't stay out in it long, don't you worry."

The journey by taxi was of short duration and Joe was soon to pay off the driver, plus a handsome tip and some advice about returning to the comfort of home. It was six p.m. and too late for Joe to telephone his office but he could ring Alfred's private line and tell the senior partner to expect some good news. The telephone kiosk in the hotel lobby was vacant and Joe, somewhat ebulliently, dialled the Spalding number but instead of hearing Alfred's voice he heard an operator saying, "Sorry, the lines are busy at the moment. Please try again later...sorry, the lines are..." Joe replaced the handset and cut the voice off; there was plenty of time to try again later.

As it happened, the winter storm was not confined to the Bristol area alone but had engulfed virtually all of the British Isles. It came with such ferocity that it almost brought the nation to a standstill. Snow choked the major highways whilst minor roads completely disappeared under a blanket of white, penetrating ice crippled the railways as electric motors burnt out and points froze up, and strong winds played havoc with power lines. By midnight, all communications and essential services suffered regular breakdowns and there seemed to be no hope of restoring the telephone link between Bristol and Spalding.

With the dawn came the problems. The storm had abated but chaos was strewn in its wake. All over the country, men and women toiled to free themselves from the shackles of the restricting snow and ice. Strenuous efforts were made merely to move from one point to another and progress towards releasing the nation's infrastructure from the grip of a freezing environment proceeded at a painfully slow pace; and often to suffer setbacks.

Joe spent most of the morning watching weather reports on a television set. His main concern was with the condition of the roads and his chances of driving home later that day. There was much talk of certain roads being passable by late afternoon – which suited his arrangements nicely providing the weather did not deteriorate in the meantime. About three p.m., according to his assessment, he would be able to leave; the business lunch would have been concluded by then and perhaps the roads might be clear.

Contrary to Joe's assessment, the business lunch ran on for a full hour and a half longer than he would have liked and he came out of it with mixed blessings. It may have made him late for his journey home but, for his trouble, he had been awarded a contract for his firm to make the joinery for the first stage of the new development It did necessitate him being back in Bristol by the coming Monday for final confirmation and the signing of agreements, but at least he would have Sunday at home.

Joe's spirits were high as he drove east from Bristol to pick up the A46 road to Gloucester. It had been a hard week but a successful one and he counted himself lucky to have landed such a useful contract. All he needed now was a clear way back to Spalding with as few delays as possible. Care was obviously needed to travel the partially cleared roads but it could be done, and done at a reasonable speed.

In the darkening night, Joe found himself sometimes passing desolate, polar landscapes, and sometimes rugged walls of heaped up snow looking like dirty icebergs. Another twenty minutes into the journey and the horizons became less clear until they were eventually obscured by drifting snow. Joe reduced his speed to compensate for the ever diminishing distance of visibility and braced himself in case he lost control of the car.

Windscreen wipers thrashed from side to side whilst the car's raised headlights merely served to illuminate the white flakes of the swirling vortex instead of burning a great hole in it. With the wind picking up and a fall of fresh snow adding to the confusion, the road ahead began to recede under a carpet of opalescent ice crystals; and before long, the carriageways, verges, and hedgerows began to merge into a solid mass of frozen snow.

A few vehicles kept moving but many had been abandoned and Joe knew that one slip would render him vulnerable to the same fate. His car was going well and it seemed perfectly capable of contending with the wintery conditions. But, unwittingly, he had turned off from the A46 and was following a minor road.

The occasional high hedge and the unbroken lines of telegraph poles were the only indications Joe had of knowing where the road lay but there was nothing to warn him against hidden hazards. Then, for a brief moment, he lost all sense of direction and plunged his car into a deep snowdrift where it became firmly stuck. For several minutes he toiled with the gears and clutch in a determined effort to shunt the car out, but the more he struggled the more it resisted.

Resignedly he got out of the car to assess the situation and his worst suspicions were soon confirmed, the car had its front wheels down in a ditch and it would need a hefty vehicle to pull it out. Joe cursed his luck and started to look around to find his bearings; only to curse again when he discovered he was on the wrong road. Everywhere he looked, no matter the direction, he saw nothing but falling snow and when he listened, he heard nothing but the soft howl of the wind. He was a being alone in a hostile wilderness, completely lost and out of touch with his fellow man. There was not a house or any other building in sight, there was no other car on the road, no telephone box, no friendly light, no encouraging sounds, no smell of a comforting fire, and no means of calling for rescue.

He shivered and got back into his car, at least with the engine running he could use the heater to keep himself warm, he could also listen to the radio and pick up local information. Furthermore, he had to consider his plight and decide what best to do. Police advice desired that he stay with the car and wait to be rescued. That was all very well on a busy trunk road where police made regular patrols but on a remote country lane the chance of seeing a policeman was almost nonexistent.

After ten more minutes, he decided that he could not spend the rest of the night in the car. It would be better, he thought, to follow the road for any length of time until he found a house willing to give him shelter, or maybe find an inn.

Although already wearing winter clothing, he decided to supplement his outfit by donning an extra sweater (taken from his suitcase) plus a pair of wellingtons and an old coat (always kept in the back of the car for such emergencies). The suitcase, being too heavy to carry over a distance, had to be hidden and locked in the car whereas the briefcase, being smaller, could be packed with the more valuable of his possessions and taken with him.

A final check round assured him that the car was being left in as safe a condition as could be, before he resolutely set off in search of refuge. He tried to follow the crown of the road to avoid further pitfalls but it was not easy to walk in the snow; the very act of having to lift his feet high with every pace was in itself, exhausting.

After half an hour, Joe began to despair. The road, as it narrowed, twisted, and turned, seemed to be leading nowhere, and the ghostly light emitting from the snow covered terrain was never enough for him to see very far at a time. He paused to peer into the darkness and listen out for a friendly sound – but there was nothing there to encourage him, nothing to dispel the tiredness in his limbs or the cold that gnawed at his toes, hands, and ears. The freezing conditions, so easily draining the energy from his body, caused him to think about people perishing in the snow and he understood how simple it was to succumb to death's beckoning finger – survival was much harder.

Determined not to be a candidate for the undertaker he trudged wearily on. Then upon rounding the next bend, he saw something which gave him renewed hope, wheel tracks made by a heavy farm vehicle, undoubtedly they were of recent occurrence but they did present something of a poser to him. As they appeared to have come up the road towards him before turning at a right angle into a field, which way should he go? Was there a farmhouse down the

The Lincolnshire Tramp

road, or across the field? He was too tired to walk in the wrong direction only to find he would have to walk back again.

Whilst he stood and deliberated, a distant engine burst into life and before long the lights of a farm tractor came into view as it trundled back towards the road from across the field. Joe remained stationary and waited until he was picked up in the tractor's lights whereupon he made a frantic gesture to attract the driver's attention. The hot, noisy, oily, machine with its little trailer crunched to a halt and the driver (a farmer) leaned over the steering wheel to see what was amiss.

"Not a good idea to be out in this weather." The farmer shouted above the roar of the engine, "Be something wrong."

Joe moved closer. "I wonder if you can help me," he called, "You see, my car is stuck in a drift about a mile back and I can't get it out, so I need somewhere to stay for the night. Is there a pub or a boarding house anywhere near here?"

"Well – I dunno about that–" said the farmer thoughtfully, then he said, "We do let rooms in the summer like, for the visitors – but we never does it in the winter. I suppose I could ask the missus."

"I don't want to put you to any trouble." Joe called out again.

The farmer chose to ignore the comment and called back, "You best jump up on the back and come up to the farmhouse with I. Leastways, you can have a warm up 'til us sorts this thing out."

"Thank you," said Joe as he heaved himself onto the little trailer. He then had to find a way to squat down on the wisps of hay and straw which cluttered the snow covered floor. The tractor moved off with a jerk and the little trailer followed somewhat hesitantly. Joe thought his bones would never stop rattling as the combined vehicles bumped along the uneven surface of the road.

The journey took several minutes and Joe, though shaken up, was glad that he did not have to walk it. Inside the farmhouse, all was warm and friendly. The farmer's wife – because Joe was a business gentleman far from home – willingly prepared a room for him, then she cooked him supper. After the meal they sat and chatted until bedtime, Joe recounted his adventures which eventually led him to their part of the country, and the farmer explained how he happened to be in the right place at the right time to save Joe from further exhaustion; he had been tending his sheep. It was an extremely grateful Joe who went to bed and slept that night.

He had all the more reason to be grateful that weekend because, being completely cut off from Spalding, he was obliged to stay at the farm until Monday morning. And when (on Sunday) he was told that Bristol was less than twenty miles away he recalled his appointment for the following afternoon. Upon hearing this, the farmer and his wife did their utmost to make sure that Joe kept the appointment. The farmer insisted on taking his tractor (and Joe) to the abandoned car where he succeeded in pulling the vehicle from the snow drift and towing it back to the farm; and his wife – catching sight of Joe's suitcase – would not rest until she had washed and ironed two of his shirts and some underwear. "Must have you looking smart for the interview," she had said whilst Joe suffered mixed feelings of gratitude and embarrassment.

Even then the good deeds did not come to an end, for on the Monday morning, when it was realised that the roads were still impassable, the farmer started up his tractor once again and towed Joe back to the A46. He carried on towards Bristol for a mile or so until he was sure that Joe could continue the journey unaided. The two men parted with a handshake and a promise to meet up again in the summer, the farmer then returned home and Joe went on to Bristol.

Later that day, with thoughts of the farmer and his wife far from his mind, Joe entered a police station. In his briefcase was a freshly signed contract just burning to be displayed to the Harrison's and their loyal workforce. All Joe had to do now was to get it back to them but firstly he needed to know if the way was free from obstruction. The police were most helpful and told him that; whereas some roads had been cleared many remained blocked and his best chance of getting through would be tomorrow morning when a slight thaw was expected. Joe reluctantly heeded the advice and found himself yet another rented room in which to spend the night – he dare not risk being trapped in the snow again.

At seven thirty on Tuesday morning, he left Bristol for the last time. Before leaving, he made a final effort to telephone Spalding but the lines were still down, however, it was of no consequence because he anticipated being back there within a matter of hours.

The thaw had set in and the roads were better, especially the motorways, and Joe, as he drove, began to contemplate the reception he would get when he arrived at the works; particularly if his arrival was unannounced. He imagined the flurry of excitement that the new contract would enthuse as the news spread from the office to the shop floor. And he imagined himself accepting – modestly of course – the acclaims and accolades showered upon him by his appreciative colleagues. It would be a rapturous homecoming.

His journey home proceeded without undue interruption and by midday he entered the suburbs of Spalding. Feeling triumphant,

The Lincolnshire Tramp

he headed towards the main gates of the works but, alas, his jubilation was to be shattered for there at the entrance stood Bert Seedon and some of his cronies. Bearing makeshift placards and adopting an air of self-important superiority they stood around a blazing brazier which greedily consumed offcuts of kiln-dried timber.

"I hope you don't intend to cross that picket line, Joe." Bawled Bert Seedon.

Joe was stunned by the remark – he could not believe his ears. Anyone would have thought he had just popped out for a sandwich instead of being away for almost a week. There was no: "Welcome back Joe, how did things go?"; or, "Hello Joe, nice to see you again." In fact there was no sign of a greeting whatsoever. Had downright bad manners superseded common courtesy, he wondered as he pulled up beside the picket.

"What the hell is going on, Seedon?" He demanded

Bert Seedon stepped forward. "You've got a nerve, coming back here," he said. "And to think I trusted you."

"For Christ's sake, will you tell me why there's a strike on?"

"Don't come the innocent with me, Joe, you know bloody well why! When Mr. Keith phoned you yesterday to tell you Mr. Alfred had passed away, you told him to start the cutbacks and lay off fifty men. Now I already warned you about that, didn't I. Cutbacks are not acceptable to my union so I've no choice but to call a strike."

Joe was both mystified and angry, He could not. easily accept the news about Alfred's death and let it slip to the back of his mind as anger became the predominant emotion.

"I've had no phone call from Keith," he snapped, "Haven't spoken to him since last Tuesday."

"I'm not interested in management squabbles," retorted Bert Seedon, "All I want to know is, are the sacked men to be reinstated or do we stay out?"

"My advice to you is to stop behaving like spoilt children and get back to work immediately – it's for your own good."

"Not until terms have been negotiated."

"Then you are a fool, Bert. A fool to yourself and to the men you represent."

"A fool to believe you – maybe, but I'm not selling my men down the river to save your bacon. You've made a hash of things, Joe, so you might as well admit it. The only way to resolve the situation now is for Mr Keith to come out here and give us all our jobs back"

Bert Seedon's declaration was supported by a chorus of affirmative yells from the men standing around the brazier. Their intention to remain defiant was abundantly clear.

Joe grew impatient with the futile argument and resolved not to waste another word on it. "Where's Keith now?" he asked and prepared to move off.

"In the office," Bert Seedon replied tartly, "and remember – there's a picket line."

"Balls to your picket line," roared Joe as he drove off to shouts of "Scab." Seconds later he pulled up outside the apparently deserted office complex and in an agitated state he hurried into the building. Having a shrewd idea where he might find Keith, he headed straight for Alfred's office. Without knocking he entered the room and saw Keith sitting at the desk.

"I expect you've heard the news," Keith said coldly, "About Father I mean."

"Only that he had passed away."

"Had a heart attack last Friday," continued Keith, "and no wonder – the way you treated him."

Joe was astonished by the remark and stammered, "I, I treated him? What do you mean by that?"

"You put him under too much pressure, that's what, All your fancy ideas about restructuring the firm. It was too much for him."

"I'm sorry to hear about your father's death but I'm sure it had nothing to do with me."

"Ah! But it did have something to do with you," Keith said slyly. "You see — he found out about the money you embezzled. I told you he'd find out didn't I."

Joe laughed sardonically. "Now I've heard everything," he said. "I get back here after an extremely exhausting week away and what do I find – the place is a shambles. Men are on strike because of some fictitious order from me, Alfred has died because I'm supposed to have put him under stress, and finally I'm accused of stealing money I know nothing about. What's it all about, Keith? More of your dirty little tricks?"

"Let the facts speak for themselves, Joe. A great deal of money has disappeared and you cannot account for it, the firm is in ruins because of your policies, and you choose to crawl into work on a Tuesday – at lunch time I may add – because you're not averse to taking the odd day off now and again. Seems to me you are nothing but a liability to this firm and the best thing you can do is resign."

"So that's your plan, you evil bastard, a scheme to get rid of me. Well you needn't have bothered because I'd never work for a worthless idiot like you." At that moment a strange feeling came over Joe, it was as if nothing about Harrison & Beck mattered any more. Gone was the thriving industry he had enjoyed and cared for throughout the past years and gone were the many friends that he knew. The once active works had become an industrial mausoleum, cold, dusty, and dead, and, its present custodian seemed content to keep it that way. The new contract might have put life back into the works but Joe doubted it, besides it would probably be in his best interests to sell it elsewhere.

"Did you pick up any new orders on the way?" demanded Keith, butting in on Joe's thoughts. "Because if you did, they are the property of this firm and you should hand them over."

Joe sidestepped the question to exclaim, "Congratulations, Keith, you've managed to kill the firm off once and for all – and it only took you a couple of days. It will be something of a miracle if this place ever produces joinery again."

"That's what Townsend said when I sacked him," retorted Keith. "But I'll prove you all wrong. In a month or two this place will be running at full capacity with masses of overtime and all the men working here will be rolling in money."

"Pie in the sky," snapped Joe, "You haven't got a cat in hell's chance. Not that I'm bothered one way or the other. Quite frankly, I don't give a toss what you do or what happens to the firm. It will never be the same now that Alfred has gone."

"Then why are you hanging around," snorted Keith, " You might as well clear off now."

There was nothing more that could be said to change the course of events and Joe knew it; an era had come to an end in which he would play no further part. With a twinge of regret he made his way out of the office complex end returned to his car.

The picket at the gate continued to behave like adolescent rabble as Joe drove out of the works. They jeered, cheered, and generally called out obscenities as he sped by. "The fools," he muttered, "If they only realized how stupid they were."

To get home, Joe had to drive through the town which meant he would be passing Virginia's shop so, thinking it appropriate, he stopped to call in on her and offer his condolences for the loss of her father. Unfortunately he was not greeted with the same benevolence, Virginia did not welcome him at all and was positively hostile.

"Murderer –!" She screamed, "I don't want you anywhere near me, so get out of my shop." She tried to push Joe back out of the door.

"I don't know what you are talking about," said Joe; the inflexion in his voice insisted on an explanation.

"You killed my father because of your ambitions," hissed Virginia. "You knew he had a weak heart so you deliberately tricked him."

"Come on, Virginia, you know that isn't true." Joe pleaded with her.

"It is true," she insisted. "You told Father that Keith had stolen some money and you wouldn't tell the police if you were given a full partnership in the firm. Poor Daddy was so frightened that he agreed, but my brother would lose everything he'd worked for and that upset Daddy. Too bad for you he died before signing the document otherwise you would have ended up with it all. Luckily Keith found the document and burnt it so you're the loser in the end. "

Joe could do no more than be generous with his own introspection. He was fond of Virginia and did not wish to enter into a pointless argument with her. The shock of her father's death coupled with a web of lies spun by Keith had confused her, therefore, she had every reason to be distraught and emotionally unpredictable. He wanted to take her into his arms and comfort her but she was too distant for that, Instead he had to be content with his intended statement. "I called in to say how sorry I am at the death of your father, and to offer you consolation in your hour of grief. If there is anything I can do to help..."

"Please go away and leave me alone." Once again Virginia tried to usher Joe out of the shop.

"Perhaps I could come back at a later date to sort out some of these misunderstandings," offered Joe as he backed out into the street.

"Get it into your thick head, Joe," screeched Virginia, "I never want to see you again — ever." She slammed the shop door in his face.

He waited outside for a moment but when he heard a key turn firmly in a lock he knew the brief interview was over. Reluctantly he got back into his car and vowed, "One of these days I'm going to get hold of Keith and bang his head against a wall for the trouble he's caused."

His thoughts, during the short journey home, toyed with the idea of selling his services – and his contract – to a rival joinery firm. He might even consider buying into a partnership if the price was right. After all, in view of the recession, it could be said that he was holding three very good cards.

With a sigh of relief, he pulled up at his own front door. It was good to be back after being away for so long and he looked forward to being with his wife again, he also relished the prospect of peace and quiet in the comfort of his own home.

Thinking to surprise her, he silently let himself into the house and carefully put his suitcase down on the hall floor. There was no immediate sign of Marjorie but music was coming from an upstairs room. "She must be doing some sewing" he mused as he ascended the staircase.

The music came from the main bedroom so Joe opened the door to look inside. What confronted him was enough to shock him rigid, for there on the bed he saw the bare back and buttocks of a naked young man arched between Marjorie's fleshy, pink thighs. To Joe, the whole scene had a nightmarish unreality about it and he was reluctant to grasp the severity of the drama unfolding before his eyes. Perhaps it was a figment of his imagination and after a while it would go away and leave things as they should be.

However, matters did not improve, for Marjorie (catching sight of Joe) let out a wild scream which alarmed the young man, and he, unable to avoid the audible squelch of a hastily extracted penis, rolled over and tried to cover himself with some bedclothes. Joe, trembling violently and at a loss for words, entered the room and stared hard at Marjorie and her lover.

After an interminably awkward silence, Marjorie thought it prudent to introduce the young man to Joe, "This is our window cleaner," she said and immediately realized it was a stupid thing to say; under the circumstances the two men were hardly likely to be the best of friends.

"How long has this been going on?" Joe's voice faltered as mixed emotions of anger and grief affected his speech.

"You shouldn't have come home at this time," scolded Marjorie as she reached for a dressing gown. "You've never come home in the middle of the day – not once in ten years," She got up from the bed and wrapped the gown around her naked body.

"D'you mean to tell me you've been carrying on behind my back for ten years?"

The idea was so ludicrous that he would never have believed it if she had said yes.

"You could have phoned me," bemoaned Marjorie "and let me know you were coming." She hunted for (and found) her bedroom slippers.

The Lincolnshire Tramp

"How could I?" snapped Joe, "The phones are out of order."

"All the same – you could have waited until this evening."

"Don't be daft woman – I live here. Anyway, how was I to know anything was going on?" Much to his own disgust, Joe found himself excusing his wife for her infidelity when he should be castigating her. He somehow lacked the incentive to adopt a firm line and deal with the matter aggressively, and for the second time that day he had the feeling that nothing mattered any more.

"I expect you want something to eat." said Marjorie as if she and Joe were the only two people in the room. "Go and take your coat off and I'll be down directly to cook you a little snack."

Joe could not believe his ears, only a few minutes ago this woman was passionately coupled with her young lover, now she was calmly offering to prepare a meal for her husband as though nothing was amiss. How could she be so fatuous as to pretend that adultery had not occurred when she had been caught in the act and the man involved still cowered in her bed. Such irrational behaviour was too much for Joe

He never knew exactly why he had to leave the house but leave it he must; maybe it had become oppressive and crowded in on him at a time when he needed to be alone and free to think, or maybe it had been tainted by a sordid little affair which now rendered it shabby and undesirable.

Slowly, sadly, and solemnly, he turned and walked out of the bedroom for what was to be the last time. He did not look back as he descended the staircase to cross the hall and slip out through the front door. With the music from the bedroom radio still haunting him, he climbed into his car and drove off.

Chapter 6

If asked to account for his movements from the time he left his home in Spalding until the time he was stopped from driving the wrong way in a oneway street in Cambridge, he could not. His memory for that period of time (some three to four hours) was particularly patchy. He would not have easily remembered the roads that he had travelled, or the towns he had visited, or, indeed, the landmarks that he had passed. Such was the state of his mind that he drove from place to place without really knowing where he was going.

Throughout the journey his mind was persistently troubled by the callous conduct of Keith, Virginia, and Marjorie. In Keith case such behaviour might have been predictable, but far less so in Virginia's and not at all in Marjorie's. How could they all have turned so ruthlessly against him at time when they needed him most? If they did but know it, their destiny rested with him but they were too blind to see it.

Joe's miserable meandering were abruptly brought to halt when a police constable stepped out and flagged him down.

"Do we usually drive against the established flow of traffic, sir?" Said the constable in response to Joe's apprehensive appeal.

"I don't know," flustered Joe as, stricken with panic, he frantically looked around to find his bearings and when nothing became familiar to him he confessed, "Sorry constable, I seem to have lost my way."

"Come far have we, sir?"

"Only from Spalding."

"Not a great distance for you to get lost in is it? Have you got your driving licence with you?" Then, whilst Joe searched for his licence, the constable made an external check on the car and when satisfied that all was well he returned to examine the pink document offered to him through the car window. Without another word, he removed his gloves and tugged a note book and pen from his breast pocket. A little white form was selected and meticulously filled in with the requisite reference to the licence. Presently the form and the licence were handed to Joe together with a verbal caution. The constable had one last duty to perform, that being, to ensure that Joe turned safely round in the street and drive off in the proper direction.

"I think you'd better pull over and take stock of the situation," Joe said, catching sight of his reflection in the driving mirror, "'seems to me you're losing your grip." Seconds later, he brought the car to a halt in a quiet cul-de-sac and set about contemplating his immediate future. A return to Spalding was definitely out of the question; any feelings he had for Marjorie had irretrievably soured, therefore, it was beyond the realms of possibility to face her again, besides, he still harboured the notion that his bed (and, indeed, his home) had been dishonourably violated. He could not go back there.

Another strange bed in another strange room seemed to be the inevitable option, unless he desired to sleep in the car. A shiver ran down his spine as he considered the prospect, after all, it was mid January and freezing cold outside. It would have to be a rented room and an inexpensive one at that because he was running short of money and it would have to be somewhere in Cambridge to avoid driving to another town; after so many hours behind the steering wheel, he was totally exhausted.

Following some explicit instructions given by a passer by, Joe easily found a bed and breakfast establishment in the southern outskirts of the city. He was greeted by a plain little woman who looked every bit as austere as the building she owned and the rooms she had to offer, nonetheless, the cost of the accommodation was well within his means and he was happy to accept it. Unfortunately, no evening meal could be provided but there were many restaurants in the vicinity and it should not be much of a problem to find hot food.

The absence of any real luggage caused Joe some minor anxiety but he made great play with his briefcase and purported to get another case (something he did not have) from his car which was parked in the next street. The plain, little woman showed no interest in his explication, instead, she thrust a pen into his hand and urged him to sign her register before taking him to his room, then she disappeared into the darker recesses of the house and left Joe to his own devices.

The room was suitably furnished and clean but it offered no other amenity beyond that of its intended purpose – somewhere to sleep. It was definitely not the kind of room for a troubled mind to be in, its sombre ambience threatened to lay heavily on the slightest of human miseries; Joe needed to drown his sorrows, not add to them. With deliberate deftness he placed his briefcase beside the bed and retreated from the room to seek solace in the streets outside.

The Lincolnshire Tramp

Sometime later, after a supper of fish and chips from the paper, he entered a public house and ordered a pint of beer. The beer, when it arrived, tasted flat and insipid but seemed in keeping with Joe's melancholic mood and the general feel of the place. For within that dreary public bar with its smoke stained ceiling and chipped paintwork there existed a need for kindred spirits to come together. Faded wallpaper and outdated advertising in league with unpolished furniture and well worn linoleum, cried out to share their anguish with a fellow sufferer. Years of neglect was the cause of their bane whereas Joe, on the other hand, became all too swiftly aware of his.

The soul has been knocked out of this room as it has me, he thought as he watched a fire struggle for survival in a crumbling grate. Then, as a pale lick of flame made a vain attempt to devour a large piece of damp coal, he remembered the fires he used to make at home and how Marjorie enjoyed sitting by them on a cold winter night. It was his job to lay and light the household fires as it was the job of any good husband and, if nothing else, he had been a good husband to Marjorie, always hard working, honest, and faithful. He considered himself to have been a most attentive partner and had no reason to doubt his ability to satisfy his wife's sexual desire – so why had it all gone wrong? Why did she need to take a lover?

He peered into his pint pot as if expecting to find the answers in the remaining dregs of beer, but when none emerged, he drained the pot, and ordered a fresh pint. The lethargic barman stubbed out the butt of a cheap cigar in a chipped, glass ashtray before attending to the order. "Never known it as quiet as this," he said, carefully gauging the frothy head on the pint of beer. "Business is dead tonight and no mistake. Don't suppose I've served more than six drinks all evening." He passed the beer to Joe. "There's a couple in the saloon and only you in here, hardly worth opening up is it?"

"The recession I expect" suggested Joe.

"I know it's usually slow at this time of the year," continued the barman, "but this is ridiculous!"

Joe, being emotionally unwilling to continue the conversation, reverted to his former meditation whilst the barman shook his head in disbelief and picked up an evening newspaper.

The aged, but accurate, clock behind the bar continued to tick away the seconds until, eventually, its monotonous click was subdued by the sudden intrusion of a swarthy young man bursting into the room. "Give us a whisky, Dave, and make it a double," he called, tendentiously closing the door.

"Celebrating are we, Digby?" asked the barman, dispensing the drink with his customary indifference.

Digby gulped down half of the measure of whisky before stating, "Do you know what that cow's done now?"

"The wife you mean?" substantiated the barman.

Digby nodded and took another swig of whisky. "Only been tommin' it with that git from the baker's, ain't she." he declared.

"Really! I didn't know,"

"Oh yeah! They've been 'aving it off for a couple of weeks now. Found out about it didn't I? Bloody caught 'em at it, didn't I?" He finished his drink and thrust the glass forward for another one. "Sorted it out now though, gave 'em both a bloody good 'iding and sent 'im packing. He won't come sniffing around again, you can be sure of that, and she knows where she stands —you'll see."

"Will that stop her?" said Joe, unintentionally allowing his thoughts to slip out.

"What was that, mate?" demanded Digby – not fully hearing Joe's comment yet taking immediate exception to it.

Disconcerted by his own outburst and fearsome of Digby's wrath, Joe decided that discretion was the better part of valour and tried to gloss over his error. "I know how you feel," he said, "I've just suffered a similar experience myself."

"What?" asked Digby coarsely.

"Adultery," Joe replied.

"You don't look the sort," returned Digby, mildly astonished. "I mean – without being rude like – you're too old for that sort of thing."

"Age has got nothing to do with it," snapped Joe, "It can happen to anyone at any time just as it happened to me today."

"Your missis – right?" enquired Digby.

"Yes" said Joe, "This afternoon when I got home from work I found her in bed with another man. A bloody window cleaner of all things." Until that moment Joe had not associated occupation with lover but now that he had he found it to be all the more distasteful.

Digby, showing genuine concern, moved closer to Joe and said, "Did you belt 'im one, mate?"

"No – I didn't."

"Why not?"

"It never entered my mind."

"What did you do then?"

"Nothing really – I just walked out."

"You should 'ave belted 'im."

"Perhaps "

"So – you ain't been back then?"

"No."

"Well now" Digby surmised, "They could still be at it." Then he offered, "Want me to come back with you now and sort 'em both out?"

"Thank you for your offer," said Joe politely, "but I don't feel like going back there any more. I'd rather stay here and get drunk." And to establish his intention he drank emphatically from his glass.

"You do just that, mate." comforted the barman, "Women ain't worth it and I should know, I've had two broken marriages."

"I know!" exclaimed Digby, "Let's all get drunk," he snatched the glass from Joe's hand, "the round's on me so fill 'em up again Dave – and one for yerself."

The barman was known never to refuse a drink nor remain sober, therefore, it merely became a matter of time before the three men were stupefied with alcohol. At the end of the evening, when normally permanent objects no longer stayed in place and the whole world started spinning in the wrong direction, they drank to a final condemnation of women and then set about getting each other safely to their respective beds. Quite how this was to be (or indeed) achieved remains a mystery.

When Joe awoke the following morning he was confronted with the inevitable hangover but despite his discomfort he went down to breakfast and endured the meal under the scornful eye of the plain, little woman. No doubt she looked down upon him because she saw him (in his inebriate state) return to her house at some time during the night – something he certainly had no recollection of. However, he consoled himself with the notion that she must be thinking of him as being too drunk to have shaved properly when, in fact, he had no razor; he had left it in his suitcase in the hall of his home.

There was no need for Joe to linger in the guest house after breakfast so he settled his account, picked up his coat and briefcase, and made an unceremonious departure. Had he known what the future had in store for him he might have paused for a few moments and paid homage to that humble abode. Instead he hurried away with a new set of plans buzzing around inside his aching head.

He was convinced that the precious contract in his brief-case was his passport to a new job and he had to find that job as soon as possible but first, he had to do something about his appearance.

The Lincolnshire Tramp

Leaving his suitcase at home was a silly mistake to make, it contained so many of the things he needed. Now he would have to slip back into Spalding (preferably without meeting Marjorie) to retrieve it, also get some extra cash,

Before he could put his plan into operation he had to find his car but, to his utter bewilderment, it was missing from the place where he had parked it. He walked up and down the rows of parked cars but it was nowhere to be seen yet he distinctly remembered parking it in that particular street.

To satisfy his curiosity, he searched (without success) the adjacent streets until, after much walking, he braced himself to accept one of two possibilities, either it had been towed away by the authorities, or it had been stolen. A visit to the local police station would, no doubt, provide the answer.

The police station proved easier to find than the car and after a short discussion with the desk sergeant, Joe agreed to assume the car had been stolen. He was then shown into a C.I.D. room where a detective meticulously logged the details of the missing vehicle and warned not to expect too much as a recent spate of car thefts in the area remained unsolved.

With the advice to return home, contact his insurers, and await developments still reverberating in his ears, Joe once again found himself out in the Cambridge streets. A fresh wave of depression came over him as he counted his losses, firstly his job, then his wife, and now his car. What next? – he wondered. Why should he be made to suffer when others have committed the wrongs?

In a fit of desperation he shouted, "What's the meaning of it all that's what I want to know." His outburst served no real purpose other than startle the more immediate pedestrians. He ignored their bemused glances and ambled off to conduct his own search for his lost car; he half expected it to be abandoned somewhere in the vicinity.

By midday he gave up the search and decided to return to Spalding no matter what the consequences. Unpropitiously, the money in his pocket would not buy him a good lunch let alone pay the train (or bus) fare back to his home; if he was to get there at all it would be by hitching a lift.

Being on the south side of the city, he was not in the most favourable position to hail a passing motorist, it would be better if he made his way to the opposite side and pick up one of the roads leading to the north. As he stood at the kerb edge to consider his best route to the desired roads he became aware of a car drawing alongside of him. "Hey Joe!" called a voice, "How you doin', mate?"

The Lincolnshire Tramp

Joe glanced suspiciously at the car but relaxed when he recognized the driver.

"Hello Digby!" he called back, "How are you feeling?"

"Woke up with a bit of a hangover," Digby explained, "but I'm all right now." Then he offered, "Hop in and I'll give you a lift somewhere."

A heaven sent opportunity, thought Joe as he settled into the passenger seat, perhaps things will start taking a turn for the better.

"Cor! We didn't 'arf get through some wallop last night," laughed Digby. He selected a gear and the car moved off.

"It was a bloody good night from what I remember of it," Joe agreed. "But I don't know how you got me back to my digs."

"Strange," exclaimed Digby, a puzzled expression on his face, "I thought you come over to my place first."

"I don't think so," said Joe thoughtfully "We were going to, but I'm sure we decided not to in case your wife was there."

"Nah!" chaffed Digby, "She couldn't 'ave – leastways, when I got up this mornin' she'd already packed 'er bags and gone."

"Left you for good, you mean?"

"Yeah! Done me a favour really, now I can go back to the Smoke with my old mates."

"Is that where you come from? London?"

"Battersea – until I joined the army. Then I was posted up 'ere and got married up 'ere. Been 'ere ever since —can't say I like the place, there's no night life."

"There's plenty to do in London, is there? Jobs I mean?"

"You'll always find work – I promise you. 'Ere, why don't you come down with me and try your luck, after all, what have you got goin' for you up 'ere?"

"True," acknowledged Joe, pensively considering the proposition. If he could not sell his contract in a city with the economic clout of London, where else could he sell it? For him, this could be the chance of a lifetime, the break he deserved. "Okay," he said, "If I can find some digs and somebody to lend me same money until I get on my feet again, then I'm all in favour of it. "

"No worries," encouraged Digby, "We can sort something out for yer – promise. Now, if you look in my bag be'ind you there's a couple of cans of lager, we'll 'ave one each to celebrate."

Sure enough, Joe found the lager in a canvas holdall and he handed one can to Digby who had no difficulty opening it and drinking from it as he drove.

Joe was dubious about drinking the lager because his hangover forbade him further alcohol but the thirst burning in his throat demanded to be quenched and must receive instant attention. The cold, bitter liquid belied its initial intention and did not offend the palate as expected for it had an unusually soothing quality which brought welcomed relief.

Joe and Digby continued with their journey, they sipped lager and chatted aimlessly on whatever topic came to mind. Each expounded his plans for the future and each advised the other on how best to achieve them. The journey was pleasant and seemed surprisingly short considering the ninety minutes it took to reach the northern suburbs of London. However, things were to change dramatically when Digby saw something ahead which did not please him. Swiftly he brought the car to a halt and stalled the engine whilst doing so.

"This is the end of the line for us, Joe," he said, reaching into the back of the car for his holdall, "From now on it's every man for 'imself." He opened the car door and, in his haste, almost fell out of the driving seat but he recovered sufficiently to shake Joe by the hand and warn, "Don't 'ang around 'ere, old mate – get movin', Good luck." He left the door to close by itself as he darted across the road ,mingled for a moment with pedestrians, then disappeared down a narrow side street. It was as if he had never existed.

The speed at which Digby had departed left Joe baffled, he could not understand what all the fuss was about. Not until he saw the police checking vehicles less than fifty metres away and that there was no key in the ignition system did he realize the truth. "Christ!" he exclaimed "This car is stolen!" In a moment's confusion, he thought it was his car and that Digby had stolen it from him even though he knew perfectly well it was not.

The half dozen cars already waiting to pass through the checkpoint started to move slowly forward and Joe, unable to keep up with the convoy, prepared for a surreptitious getaway. Picking up his brief-case, he stepped out of the car and strolled purposefully past the inquisitorial policemen as if he had business to do in a nearby office block. So casual was his manner that nobody noticed him leaving the scene of the offence, least of all the drivers held up behind the abandoned car; he was able to walk away unchallenged.

"That Digby's a cool customer," he said, chuckling to himself as he skirted the office block. "A bit of a crook but likeable enough. The trouble is – he's dropped me right in it. What do I do now?"

Barely two hours of the working day remained if he was to profit from it; it would mean finding somewhere to lodge his precious contract and finding suitable accommodation. Although his money was almost spent he still had some personal possessions which could be pawned or sold to raise funds "All is not yet lost, old Joe," he muttered confidently to himself, "There's a future here for you." Renewed optimism lifted his spirits and added impetus to his gait.

Taking his bearings from the postal districts marked on the street names, he progressed steadily towards the centre of London, passing through Edmonton, Tottenham, Stoke Newington, and Shoreditch. With every step he hoped to meet the desired situation, perhaps it would be around the next corner or at the next junction. Surely, in a city of such a size there must be an opening for a man of ability, there must be something for Joe.

Disappointment came all too often for whenever he came across an establishment proffering to manufacture joinery he found it to be boarded up and deserted.

By the time he reached Liverpool Street railway station, his feet were sore and his legs ached, he was also hungry and cold. Seeking warmth and a hot drink, he entered the main concourse of the station. He would have liked something to eat but feared his money might not run to it – even a cup of tea can seem expensive when cash is in short supply.

It was late afternoon and time for the mass of diurnal commuters to make its nightly exodus from the city. People of all walks of life poured into the station and divided themselves into either queues at barriers or lines on platforms. In other cases they simply disappeared from view as they were sucked into waiting trains.

The bustle and excitement of the homegoing disturbed Joe, he felt the urge to join in and return to his own home. But then, as he contemplated boarding a train to Spalding, his line of reasoning was countered by another – he had no desire to see Marjorie again nor did he desire to return home as a failure.

Watching other people depart may not have been good for his morale but he had resolved to stay and stay he would. All he had to do was to somehow get through the night, make himself presentable in the morning, and try again for a job. He could wash and shave in one of the station's toilets provided he could get hold of a cheap razor – the disposable type would do. And he would have to keep his shirt as clean as possible.

Now that his arrangements were clear in his mind, Joe settled down to face the long night. He would, until asked to leave, stay in the comfort of the station buffet where he could mull over the contract and its appended estimates. The sight of the documents gave him fresh encouragement and, for a while, he forgot his problems as his busy calculator checked the figures.

Later, when the buffet had closed down for the night, Joe wandered around the near deserted station. Wearily, he looked for somewhere to sleep but he had to be careful – railway police were winkling out the vagrants from the bona fide passengers. He found some wooden packing cases in a remote part of the station less frequently visited by the police. Unfortunately, they were sealed with their contents safely entombed; it meant he would have to sleep on top of one of them rather than crawl inside, also, they might be moved at any moment. On the other hand, they could stay there for days. Whatever the outcome, it was worth trying to snatch some sleep.

Joe climbed onto a packing case where he could be least seen sleeping and tried to repose. It was harder than he had anticipated and not at all comfortable. However, a fitful sleep soon overcame discomfort as moments of waking during longer periods of sleep became the pattern for the night and with the dawn came the deepest sleep.

The fitful slumber continued for several hours until, at length, he was abruptly awakened by the general hubbub of the station. The bright morning light and the volume of pedestrian traffic suggested the lateness of the hour. Heavy eyed and stiff limbed, he sat up to check the time but, to his astonishment, he found his wristwatch was missing. Thinking it to have fallen between the packing cases, he leapt down and made a thorough search of the area.

The wristwatch had vanished and (as he soon discovered) so had his wallet and his brief-case; they had been taken from him whilst he slept. The wallet was of no consequence because it contained nothing of value whereas the contents of the brief-case and the wristwatch were potential fund raisers.

It took a second or two before Joe tumbled to what had happened and when the penny did drop he flew into a furious rage. "The bastard!" he shouted, "What dirty, low down, little, sneak thief did this to me? Christ almighty!" He kicked out angrily at the packing cases.

"I don't understand any of this," he continued to rant, "Why is it happening to me? Why is everybody picking on me? What have I done to deserve it? I mean – I haven't embezzled any money, I haven't stolen anything, I haven't injured anyone, I haven't committed adultery, I haven't raped women, and I haven't abused children; so why am I being punished?"

He proceeded to pace to and fro like a demented moth who has lost its sense of direction. His fists were clenched and his brow was heavy with anger. "If I get my hands on the scum who stole my property" he vowed, "They'll wish they had never been born. And if I ever get back to Spalding that bloody window cleaner had better make himself scarce because I'm going to break his neck. It's all his fault, if he hadn't been in bed with that cow of a wife of mine I wouldn't be in this state now. Mind you, if that bitch had been a good and faithful wife then I would have been at home this morning and not stranded here. It's no good going back now; she doesn't want me any more; she's made that clear enough. After all these years of marriage how can she do it to me? Laying there with a stranger between her legs and making me out to look a complete fool, and she didn't show the slightest sign of any regret. Did I mean so little to her? I suppose I should go back and claim what is rightfully mine but what's the bloody point of it – there's no future for me now."

He aimed another kick at the packing cases.

"God almighty, what a start to the new year! It's barely three weeks old and I've lost everything; reduced to certain obscurity and for no apparent reason. To think that I've been working my guts out for those greedy, selfish bastards up there just to be treated like this,"

His pacing became more agitated.

"What's the world coming to – that's what I want to know? From now on is it to be all lying, cheating, and stealing with no respect for decency and honesty? Do we have to live in fear of each other and crawl around in this ball of crap suspicious of everything that moves? Is it to be a sewer life where hatred and malice become commonplace and the meaning of trust taken as dirtier than the sewer itself. Because if this is to be the case then I am just about ready for it. As from now I'm going to be really bloody nasty and I'm not going to give a damn for anyone; I shall walk all over people just as I have been walked over. I've got a genuine grudge against society, make no mistake about it."

He broke off his oration when he noticed a small crowd had gathered. Their expressionless faces were turned towards him as they stared blankly at his unscheduled performance. They were not to know what triggered his rampage although many opinions were formed; some leaning to insanity.

"What are you staring at – you stupid looking imbeciles?" Joe raged, turning on the crowd. "Make the most of what you see and remember it because you'll end up like me one of these days."

Alarmed by his appearance (unshaven face, wild eyes, uncombed hair, crumpled clothes, and angry speech), the crowd, pretending not to have been concerned and therefore not required to participate further, quickly melted away. Joe screamed after them, "That's it – bury your heads in the sand; don't face up to reality; it'll always happen to somebody else but never to you! "

A party of schoolgirls, seemingly reluctant to leave, made light of Joe's remarks as they exchanged witticisms between themselves amid peals of laughter. But when they became aware of their isolation and the evil in Joe's eyes as he set off to approach them, they turned and fled.

"You'll laugh on the other side of your faces if I ever catch up with you again," he roared, pursuing the schoolgirls out of the station. "You won't find it so funny then."

The briskness of his gait was not intended to chase schoolgirls (they were simply in his way) but to get him to any small cafe in the streets behind the station. He was extremely hungry and had decided to spend the last of his money on a cheap, yet sustaining, meal. He stormed from street to street until he found a dingy, little cafe with soiled curtains at it window and a smell of stale food to greet its customers. Its grubby interior was even less inviting and did nothing to encourage the slightest of appetites. It did, however, have two things in its favour; it was warm and the food was cheap.

Joe demanded, rather than requested, two rounds of bacon sandwich and a mug of hot tea; he also omitted to say please and thank you. Such courtesies no longer had a place in his vocabulary

Although it had cost him the last of his money (barring a few coppers) he sat down to devour his breakfast with a self satisfied relish; it seemed so long since he had last eaten. The grease from the bacon lodged in the stubble on his chin and glistened in the harsh glare of a solitary electric light bulb which hung above the counter, and the thick, sweet tea (pleasant to drink as it was) coated his teeth with a dirty yellow stain.

Whether he was aware of it or not, Joe was undergoing a process of transformation from respectable business man to slovenly vagrant. His whole personality was changing by the hour and soon he would enter a lifestyle incongruous with anything he had previously known.

Chapter 7

A bitter disagreement between Joe and the cafe proprietor resulted in immediate banishment and Joe found himself yet again, out on the streets. It was his own fault because he had been the main antagonist and had stubbornly argued a point with aggressive rudeness . Normally, such a minor irritation would have passed without comment but now – with his world turned upside down he flew off the handle at the slightest provocation.

Issuing curses against the cafe and its proprietor, Joe ambled off (with no particular purpose in mind) to follow each street as it came. He picked his way through Moorgate, Princes Street, and Queen Victoria Street until he came to Blackfriars Bridge. The buildings that he passed were plain, grey, and dreary, not at all what he expected and certainly not as romantic as their street names suggested.

The bridge (spanning the Thames) he knew well from national news bulletins as a place where many of London's homeless slept at night. Its wide underpass provided a rudimentary shelter and there was often a chance of hot soup brought round by the local charities. Joe spent a few minutes checking out the underpass before moving on but he knew he would return to it later.

From Blackfriars Bridge, he walked along Victoria Embankment, keeping his eyes on the river for most of the way. The more he saw of the murky Thames the more he thought about committing suicide. All he had to do was to slip unnoticed into that ice cold water and let death take its inevitable course. No doubt it would be painless; freezing conditions would shock a body into numbness and drowning would follow as a welcomed release.

He moved nearer to the embankment to look for a suitable place where he might immerse himself discreetly into the river. There were many; and, what is more, so few people about to prevent his intention. It all seemed too easy, so easy in fact that he had cause to reconsider his objective. What would he achieve by ending his life now? Certainly not the revenge he lusted for. How convenient it would be for Marjorie, she could continue her lascivious life free from the shackles of a fruitless marriage. Virginia would be mistakenly vindicated and Keith would laugh himself silly, deriving much pleasure from Joe's demise.

No – his death must not be contemplated, not even if it could be contended that his spirit would rise from the grave to haunt his persecutors. For Joe, who had little or no faith in the supernatural, doubted if an apparition was capable of exacting the same fear in anyone as he could in his human form, therefore, in order to avenge his grievances he had to stay alive.

Turning away from the river and dismissing all thought of suicide, he set about the more practical side of survival. There was much to be discovered about living rough and self protection.

In the weeks that followed he roamed all over London, seeking food and shelter. His food came by way of, handouts, foraging in dustbins, and stealing whenever an opportunity presented itself. Often he would visit street markets to pick up discarded fruit and vegetables, and, on other occasions, help himself to a pint of milk from an unattended milk float.

His sleeping arrangements were just as diverse, sometimes sleeping in shop doorways, or under bridges, or in derelict buildings, and, as a last resort , in churchyards. Keeping out the cold was his main preoccupation during the long winter nights and he rarely slept for more than three or four hours at a time. Nevermore did he attend to personal hygiene; he did not wash, he did not shave, he did not clean his teeth, and he did not comb his hair. His clothes were dirty and soiled, and never changed. Eventually came the grime and with the grime the obnoxious stench of body odours.

For a while he openly begged for money in the streets but his bad temper and offensive attitude earned him little reward; he picked up more money from the roadside gutters than he ever did from a begging bowl. It was preferable to ignore him rather than offer sustenance.

Needless to say, he did not associate with anyone, particularly the rest of London's homeless. He despised the teenagers who had run away from their homes in the midlands and the north (misguidedly believing they were heading for a better life) and he had no time for the mentally retarded whom he considered (contemptuously) to be displaced persons. Of other vagrants, he was even less considerate; always pushing them out of his way and never a kind word to exchange. He soon gained a reputation for being disagreeable and was intensely disliked by all factions of the homeless fraternity. Above all, he was a loner and he intended keeping it that way.

Towards the end of March, Joe decided to leave London and head north. The bitterness in his heart was sufficiently tempered for an intended confrontation with Keith and Marjorie; he would

The Lincolnshire Tramp

deal with them first before he settled his other debts with society. His aim was to put fear into them and deprive them of lasting peace, to disturb their minds and to cause trouble in their lives.

With vengeance on his mind, he set off to walk through the northern suburbs of London and enter into Hertfordshire. By evening he was content to rest up on the outskirts of Cheshunt, the rural town within the grasping tentacles of the Greater London conurbation.

His shoes (worn since his arrival in the city) were very much the worse for wear, therefore, during the early hours of the following day, he broke into a garden shed on an allotment patch and stole a pair of sturdy boots. Triumphantly, he threw his old shoes away and pulled on the freshly acquired boots and when he found how well they fitted he was extremely pleased. "One up to Joe." he shouted, gleefully.

Audaciously, he walked through the streets of Cheshunt before taking to the main road which would lead him to the next town – Hoddesdon , and as he walked he hoped the gardener (to whom the boots belonged) would suffer the same sense of loss as he had done when his effects were stolen.

The road to Hoddesdon took him out into the less overdeveloped countryside as grey buildings gave way to a greener landscape. The last vestige of winter had gone and the new season shone from every corner. Bright green leaves, freshly coloured petals, healthy new shoots, and buds bursting, announced the arrival of spring.

In happier times, Joe would have appreciated nature's wondrous endeavour but now he could not give a damn for the wild primroses he trampled underfoot or the daffodils he kicked out of his path. All living things were an affront to his current purpose.

He continued his journey, passing through Hoddesdon, Ware, and the Hadhams. Just beyond Little Hadham, on the road to Bishop's Stortford, he stopped off to enter a little spinney which was situated opposite the village school. It was late afternoon and the children had gone home for the rest of the day thus the school, and the spinney, were left to a period of absolute quietude. It seemed a good place to spend a night.

Joe shuffled through a thick carpet of dead leaves as he weaved his way between the slender trunks of the silver birch trees. He was looking for a suitable place to lay his bed and was not aware of watchful eyes, following his every move.

The onlooker was Bumble Drage, a seasoned tramp known throughout Hertfordshire. He was fifteen years older than Joe and had been on the road twenty years longer. He had come from a wealthy family and had been well educated. Unfortunately he was an habitual homosexual. Hence his vagrancy, cast out by an intolerant family. His real name was John Sebastian Drage but his nickname seemed more appropriate and stuck. Despite his shortcomings, he was a gentle man with a very persuasive manner.

Desiring to make contact with Joe and not startle him, Bumble came out of hiding and casually picked up sticks as if to kindle a fire, then, with a look of surprise on his face, he made a direct approach. "Hello there!" he said with his refined voice.

"Haven't seen you in these parts before have I?" Joe did not answer directly, instead he stood in silence and made careful observations. Usually, when such meetings occurred, it was his practise to curse the other fellow and send him on his way but, somehow, Bumble's magnetic personality precluded this. After a while Joe could no longer resist the inquiry and admitted, "I've never been here before – this is my first visit."

"Then let me welcome you to Bumble's spinney" enthused Bumble Drage. "By the way – have you had dinner yet?"

"I haven't eaten since this morning."

"You shall dine with me tonight." confided Bumble, "The fare is modest but substantial." He laid down his collection of sear sticks and whipped a dead rabbit from the poachers' pocket of his greatcoat. "There's fresh meat on the menu and a selection of vegetables." A swede and some potatoes emerged from the same pocket. "And," he continued, "a fine table wine to wash it all down." Out came a grubby wine bottle containing a cloudy, reddish liquid.

There was little, or nothing, Joe could do, the hypnotic Bumble had temporarily taken over his life. Within minutes of their meeting he felt that he had been reduced to a minor role and, as he accompanied Bumble to a clearing where they were to light a fire and cook the meal, he likened himself to a probationer following his master. Indeed, Bumble was to become Joe's mentor until they parted company.

"In case you're wondering about this dear little bunny," explained Bumble as he skinned and gutted the rabbit, "I found him caught in a snare. Somebody else set the snare of course but I took the rabbit. You have to do that you know – let somebody else do the hard work whilst you cream off the profit." He poked a green stick through the carcass to form a roasting spit over the open fire and, whilst the meat roasted, he prepared the vegetables. His method was to chop the vegetables into great chunks (skins included) and drop them into stream water simmering in a sooty billy.

"If you want to survive in the country," said Bumble, "you take whatever comes your way. Take a moonlit night last week for instance – there was I standing in the shadows when a fox came racing across the field towards me and in its mouth was a nice plump chicken. 'Hello', I thought, that looks like a tasty meal, so I did no more than leap out and scare the fox off. The silly arse dropped the chicken and ran for his life. I soon had a fire going I can tell you, and that bird tasted delicious. No doubt the fox got himself another meal, after all, he's more adapted for it than I am."

If this man outwitted a fox, thought Joe, then he must be well skilled in country ways. With animal cunning like that you could easily live off the land and not rely on the contents of dustbins. The problem is, how do you acquire the skills ? Being in the right piece at the right time obviously had something to do with it.

Bumble, raising his grubby bottle aloft, interrupted Joe's thoughts and declared "If you have a mug about you we could have a little aperitif before dinner."

Joe, showing no hesitancy, pulled a blue enamelled mug from under his coat and presented it for a measure of the cloudy, reddish liquid. Bravado rather than desire, caused him the drink greedily from the mug but the draught was stronger than he had anticipated and he almost choked an it. When he did get his breath back , he was compelled to ask, "For Christ's sake —what sort of drink is this?"

"Don't you know, dear boy," gurgled Bumble, drinking from his own mug, "it's a very compatible blend of red wine and methylated spirits."

"But– that's bloody poisonous."

"Not in moderation, dear boy, not in moderation."

Tentatively, Joe took another sip from his mug but this time he tasted it before swallowing. Clearly (for him) it was a drink to be sipped and not gulped down.

"Drink up," urged Bumble, forcing more of the noxious mixture into Joe's mug, "this stuff is quite harmless really, mainly a fruity elderberry wine with just a dash of meths. It will soon make you feel good." His own mug was then topped up and he drank insatiably from it.

The rabbit and vegetables, when they were ready, were more to Joe's taste, in fact, he thoroughly enjoyed the meal and vowed to have many more like it; if and when the circumstances permitted. In a philosophical way, he thought of the meal as an initiation, a sort of coming of age or passing out parade whereby he had graduated from greenhorn vagrant to fully fledged tramp (if such a distinction ever existed).

Darkness had descended on the little spinney by the time the meal reached its conclusion but it was far too early for sleep and (as friendships have a habit of developing) much had yet to be discussed. The fire was rekindled and, as glowing sparks and acrid smoke spiralled up through the trees, the conversation ran on.

By midnight, when Bumble thought he had the advantage over Joe and the venomous concoction of the wine bottle had all but been consumed, the conversation was switched to Bumble's favourite subject – homosexuality.

"How often did you have sex with your wife?" Bumble asked with sincerity.

"Not enough it appears," retorted Joe, bitterly.

"Was it always straight sex? You know – man an top of woman? Or did you deviate?" Bumble's eyes lit up and he began to foam at the mouth as the thought of other people copulating aroused his own sexual desires,

"Most of the time it was straightforward sex," admitted Joe, "In the early days we sometimes tried it doggie fashion, but she never liked it."

"Did you ever bugger her?"

The question may have excited Bumble but it annoyed Joe. "Why should I need to shove it up her arse when her cunt was available." he snapped, tetchily.

"Women do have their bad weeks, old boy," countered Bumble, "And when the vagina is out of commission the anus is always available." He licked his lips. "Dammit all, a chap must have his daily ejaculation."

"There are other ways," insisted Joe.

"Of course there are," smiled Bumble, "The countryside is full of animals – take pigs and sheep for instance – have you tried any of them yet?"

"Certainly not, " Joe was horrified by the suggestion, "I don't care that much for sex anyway."

The disapproving remark momentarily threw Bumble but he quickly cast it aside and pressed on with his quest. "So you've only known one woman then, I mean, did you fondle other girls?"

"I've had intercourse with just the one woman," said Joe, "Unlike others I could mention."

"What about when you were a boy – in the Scout's perhaps – did you play with each others' cocks. Did you suck the next boy's cock

The Lincolnshire Tramp

and wank him off?" Yet again, Bumble hyped himself up with sexual fantasy.

"I was never in the Scouts and I never played that sort of game with other boys. If I needed to masturbate I did so in the privacy of my own room."

"Masturbation is such a solitary pursuit " declared Bumble, "So much better to share your pleasure with others."

"Why don't you go and find yourself a woman," said Joe, growing tired of the conversation,

"I tried a woman once," confessed Bumble, "But it was a hopeless disaster. Give me the well rounded buttocks of a young boy any day."

"Whatever turns you on," mumbled Joe as he set about preparing his bed and making ready to sleep, This involved tightening his greatcoat around his body and covering himself with a layer of dead leaves.

"It all started long ago," said Bumble, reminiscing, "In the dorm at boarding school, you know. After lights out we had a whale of a time and in the morning the sheets were covered in blood, semen, and excrement. God knows what Matron must have thought. I particularly remember the last day of school and I had a medical check up. The doctor declared that I was absolutely shagged out, what he didn't know, of course, was that I'd had five of the younger boys the night before. My God – I could come my cocoa in those days."

Joe cast a glance of suspicion towards his companion and, in the fading light of the dying fire, he could see Bumble's erect penis. "Don't you come near me with that," he hissed.

"I thought you might oblige me, old boy," grinned Bumble, "After all, we are men of the world."

"If your prick comes within a yard of me I'll cut it off with my knife," Joe warned.

"Couldn't you give it a few strokes then," persisted Bumble, desperate for sexual relief.

"Yeah! I know what your game is," snarled Joe, "a few strokes will lead it straight up my arse, I told you – keep away from me." He pulled out his knife and threatened Bumble with it.

"There's no need to get violent," said Bumble, sourly, "I just thought you might care for a little pleasure before you went to sleep, that's all."

"Pleasure is the last thing I need right now," said Joe, firmly. The idea of two filthy old men engaging in a carnal relationship was abhorrent enough – let alone participating in the grotesque act. In his conception of sexual matters, intercourse was something practised only between male and female, and in the appropriate circumstances; fresh young bodies in a scented boudoir would be his criterion. Anyway, he was far too bitter to contemplate the delights of sex, to the contrary, it would be his preference if such an activity caused great displeasure to others, including Bumble.

As for Bumble, he laid back against a mossy bank and continued to stroke his penis but the moment had gone and his erection collapsed before achieving the desired orgasm. Feeling cheated and disappointed, he gave up and consoled himself with a pipe full of tobacco. For a while, as he smoked his pipe, he refurbished his mind with memories of past lovers until he eventually fell asleep.

Squirrels, darting to and fro, disturbed the leaves about Joe's head and awakened him. He sat up and rubbed the sleep from his eyes. "Bloody animals" he cursed, "Do they ever respect man." A particularly obdurate squirrel sat before him and chewed monotonously on a seemingly endless acorn. Its very presence infuriated Joe and he lunged out at it. "Clear off you little bastard," he shouted. The squirrel, in a series of rapid, jerky movements, departed from its breakfast place, skirted the pile of cold ashes, and shot up the mossy bank where Bumble had been sleeping.

There was no sign of Bumble or his impedenta he had gone as if erased from the scene; even his part of the spinney appeared tidy and undisturbed. The remains of the fire alone bore witness to the events of the previous evening and of Bumble's existence.

Joe stood up and stretched, he was not altogether bothered to be on his own once again although he would have welcomed more of Bumble's knowledge. The spring morning was warm and bright and encouraged a great deal of unseen business in the little spinney. High aloft, a lark winged its way up into the blue sky and sang of its joy to be alive. As Joe listened to the lark another sound emerged to disadvantage its rapturous song, that of childrens' voices coming from the nearby playground. A thought suddenly occurred to him and he headed for the road which ran between the spinney and the school.

"I thought so," he said, catching sight of Bumble, "Guessed you'd be here."

"Good morning, dear boy," said Bumble half turning to greet Joe, "Come and have a look at this." He drew Joe's attention to the playground where fifty or so young children played happily, their games observing two basic rules; no standing still, and no staying

The Lincolnshire Tramp

silent. "A fair number of good looking boys in that lot, don't you know," observed Bumble, drooling at the mouth.

"They're making too much noise," said Joe, curtly, "especially when the girls start screaming."

Then, as if Joe had pressed the button himself, a bell started to ring and the children formed themselves into disciplined lines. Soon after, a plumpish woman, emerging from the gaggle of tiny arms and legs and ushered the children into the school building.

Bumble stood transfixed until the last little bottom disappeared through the school door. "Well," he sighed, "That's that." He stepped out of the spinney and on to the road. "I'm going up to Bury Green now – to see if I can find a breakfast. Are you coming along?"

Joe accepted the invitation with a solitary grunt and the two men set off to follow the narrow lanes which led to the tiny hamlet of Bury Green. Along the way, Bumble (who did most of the talking) pointed out the advantages of living in the countryside, and the pitfalls. He had many anecdotes with meaningful messages which were to stick in Joe's mind, and serve him well, in the years to come.

Bumble's rhetoric did not stop at obtaining food but went on to cover other aspects of survival; how to blend into the background or move quickly without being seen, how to find bearings without the aid of a compass, how and where to shelter during inclement weather, and how to minimise the discomfort of being homeless. Living the life of a tramp was an art form to Bumble, it gave him untold freedom and a certain sense of power.

Thirty minutes later, they came to a small clearing beside the lane; a parcel of land unclaimed by local farmers yet not under the jurisdiction of the district council. In fact, a piece of common land used in the main by gypsies.

The place gave rise to some excitement in Bumble as he hurried onto it to examine the ground. He carefully surveyed, tyre tracks, the remains of a fire, odd shreds of material, and other discarded objects. To his obvious delight, the evidence added up to a significant conclusion. "They're back in the county,'" he exclaimed, a twinkle in his eye.

"Who?" asked Joe.

"A gypsy family I know of" replied Bumble, "They were here yesterday and moved off this morning – probably be on Hatfield Forest by tomorrow."

Undeniably, Joe was impressed by Bumble's powers of deduction but why the euphoria over a gypsy family? What was so special

The Lincolnshire Tramp

about gypsies? He shrugged his shoulders and waited for Bumble to make the next move.

"I'm glad I came this way," said Bumble, nodding with self satisfaction "I thought they'd be back." Smiling contentedly to himself, he beckoned Joe to follow him back to the lane and on towards the hamlet; a ten minute walk.

"When we get there," Bumble explained, "We shan't walk across the green — that will be too obvious. However, there is an orchard to the left which runs behind the houses, it affords plenty of cover and it goes all the way to the chicken farm. With any luck we shall have eggs for breakfast."

The lane wound its way past isolated cottages and small meadows until it was obliged to traverse an open area of grassland. The grassland, or green, had little cottages dotted around its circumference and had two separate farm entrances at its furthermost point. It also had a timeless tranquillity about it which defied the march of progress.

Before Joe could fully appreciate the scene, Bumble slipped away into a hawthorn thicket and was soon gone from view. Joe followed, though not with the same dexterity, and found Bumble waiting for him on the other side.

"This is the orchard," said Bumble in a hushed voice, "But we'll go around the edge and come up on the chicken houses from the far side."

The thought of stealing eggs in broad daylight and under the nose of the chicken farmer appealed to Joe's newly formed sense of justice; of course, a handful of eggs (and a pair of garden boots) was but little compensation for a stolen car nonetheless, time was on his side and he would use it in his efforts to redress the balance.

Basic knowledge and exceptional expertise soon had a clutch of eggs in Bumble's hands as he and Joe crouched in the shadow of the outermost chicken house. But, just as they ware about to sneak away with their spoils, a noise from behind startled them. For a few frozen moments they hardly dared to move then Bumble looked cautiously over his shoulder and began to grin. "Here – take these," he whispered, thrusting the eggs into Joe's hands. "I've just seen our supper."

The casual interloper who had startled the tramps happened to be a runaway hen. Its freedom, however, was short lived for the wily Bumble soon had it cornered and tucked away in his special pocket. "Can't hang around here," he urged, "We'll have to kill it later." And with that said, he moved stealthily towards the northern boundary of the orchard.

The Lincolnshire Tramp

Joe dogged his footsteps until they cane to a rustic stile which offered a way through the thick and thorny hedgerow. The stile opened onto a large, arable field laid fallow for the winter season and beyond the field lay an extensive area of woodland, an ideal place to cook breakfast.

In no time at all, the tramps had climbed over the stile, crossed the field and set up a fire well within the periphery of the woodland. After a meal of fried eggs, which Bumble somehow contrived to cook in his faithful billy can, Joe was shown how to ring a chicken's neck. It looked so easy in Bumble's experienced hands.

There followed a period of rest after which the two men set off to cut across county to the market town of Bishop's Stortford. En route, Bumble visited various farm building; in an attempt to provision himself with fresh vegetables He was out of luck where the vegetables were concerned but he did chance upon a bottle of cider which became his property the moment he set eyes on it.

He and Joe took it in turn to drink from the bottle as they walked through the near deserted streets of the market town. It was half day closing and most of the shops had barred their doors, those that stayed open did so out of necessity – to combat the crippling recession.

Joe was reminded of this when he saw a newsagent's placard denouncing the latest figures, it brought back unpleasant memories and was one of the reasons for his present situation. He tried to broach the topic with Bumble but received a negative response.

Bumble was completely out of touch with present day politics and knew nothing about recessions, he was more interested in finding the sports field annexed to the town's school for boys. He did find the field but was disappointed not to see the boys playing. "Pity – I do like to see those skimpy football shorts," he mused.

Rain began to fall as the sky clouded over, it was steady at first but threatened to increase during the remaining hours of daylight. Bumble decided to make for Great Hollingbury on the outskirts of the town where he knew of a disused pigsty which offered a dry shelter. They could rest up for the night and cook their chicken.

The night might have passed without incident had not Bumble been up to his usual tricks, first he spiked what remained of the cider with methylated spirits, then he grabbed a passing dog and proceeded to stimulate its genital organ with his grubby fingers. The bemused dog, sperm dripping from its penis, had no option in the matter and tolerated the treatment with resolution.

"You dirty old bugger," accused Joe, "Don't you ever think of anything else?"

"It's all there is, dear boy," giggled Bumble.

Joe was too disgusted to say any more and, turning his back on Bumble, he sought out the driest spot in the pigsty and settled down to sleep. In fairness to Bumble, Joe had no reason to complain – had he not enjoyed three hot meals in twenty four hours? In fact he could not recall when he last had a hot meal.

There was more to come, for when he awoke next morning he found the industrious Bumble cooking porridge. "Where on earth did you get that?" asked an astonished Joe.

Bumble looked up and smiled. "I just happened to have the oatmeal about me, dear boy," he explained. "All I needed was something to put with it so I went out last night and milked an obliging cow – quite simple really."

"My word –What clever fingers you have." An unpalatable connection between dog and cow gave rise to Joe's acerbity.

The remark had no effect on Bumble as he happily stirred the simmering brose. "Got a busy day today – so must have a good start," he said.

Why should one day be any busier than the next when you are a tramp, thought Joe. After all, one of the pleasures of vagrancy was not having to schedule time. He sat down beside the fire and waited for his share of the porridge.

It soon became apparent what Bumble had in mind when, later in the morning, he and Joe entered that part of Hertfordshire known as Hatfield Forest. It was more like a large park than a forest, it was crisscrossed by tracks from all directions, and encompassed a small lake.

"That caravan has got to be around here somewhere," asserted Bumble as he hurried from one part of the forest to another.

"Not the damned gypsies again," muttered Joe, tagging along behind. He would have liked to explore the forest at a more leisurely pace.

It was well after midday when the caravan was eventually sighted. Bumble recognised it instantly as it nestled discreetly on a grass verge wedged between the forest and a lane that meandered into Hatfield Broad Oak.

The gypsy family, parents in their thirties, a boy of twelve, a girl of six, and a baby, were engaged in various activities around a blazing fire. An older man, presumably a father to one of the parents, tinkered with the engine of their battered truck.

Joe had expected Bumble to go over and greet the family in the manner of a close friend but it was not to be so. The prurient Bumble held back and was content to watch the family from behind a screen of established saplings. Plainly, he wanted to see them without them seeing him (at least, most of them).

For what reason Bumble should have for staring at the gypsy family, Joe could not discern, all he could be sure of was that Bumble's attitude suggested a long stay and he wanted no part of it. "Look here," he declared, "You can stay here for as long as you want but I'm off to see what I can find."

"You do that, dear boy," acquiesced Bumble, "See if you can rustle up something for our supper."

There were a few houses actually situated within the confines of the forest and many farms that bordered its circuitous boundary; plenty of scope for Joe to go scavenging. Of course, such dwellings were spaced well apart and it would take time and patience to reconnoitre each one, therefore, by the time he returned with a few scraps of food it was almost dusk.

Bumble no longer stood within seeing distance of the caravan, he had moved off to a more secluded part of the forest. Never the less, Joe knew where he could be found and the new location was reached within a couple of minutes. The rendezvous did not meet with Joe's expectations, he thought Bumble would be attending to his customary fire or smoking his pipe, instead, he found the old tramp compromising the gypsy boy.

The boy, his grubby trousers around his ankles, leaned forward and clung to the lowest bough of a stunted oak. His eyes were closed and his mouth gaped open as he emitted a low, unmelodic moan; a rasping mix of ecstasy and anguish. Behind him, with his loins pressed against the boy's bare buttocks and his weather beaten hands gripping the boy's pale hips, panted a resolute Bumble .

Oblivious to all around him, Bumble urgently thrust his penis into the young body in an endeavour to reach an orgasm to beat all orgasms. With glazed over eyes and lolling tongue he continued his rhythmic jerking and was not distracted by the skirt of his greatcoat as it flapped against the boy's legs. In fact nothing would distract him now – not even the arrival of Joe, Bumble was doing the thing that he loved doing most and no power on earth would dissuade him; it was the only thing he lived for, Joe was disgusted by the whole scene and promptly turned his back on it. He was particularly annoyed with Bumble for not having confided in him, all that time spent chasing after a caravan just for a few minutes of sexual gratification. No doubt the gypsy boy would be offered to Joe as soon as Bumble tired or him but, as Joe was to remind himself, such pleasures were not for him, therefore, he would probably kick the boy's backside out of the forest.

There and then, Joe decided to part company with Bumble. It had been an interesting relationship and Joe had definitely gained from it, but Bumble's way of life detracted conversely from Joe's original intentions; Bumble sought to give (and receive) pleasure whereas Joe intended to deride it.

Without a backward glance, he walked deliberately away from the place and found a track to lead him out of the forest and into the darkening night. He was not sure if Bumble had seen him or not and resolved not to care a damn if he had – at least there would be no methylated spirits in Joe's drink that night.

Chapter 8

A distant clock chimed midnight and Joe cursed – he did not want to know the time. He cursed again a few moments later when he came upon a sign welcoming him to Great Dunmow; he thought he was heading north – not due east.

Since leaving Hatfield Forest, he had walked steadily through the night and without consideration for sleep – his mind was far too active for that. The brief encounter with Bumble Drage hung about him like an incorporeal mantle and the events of the past two days had an air of unreality about them. Yet it all had been real enough, Bumble did exist and Joe could not deny it. "The dirty old bastard," he was to declaim with a chuckle, time and time again.

Hitherto, Joe had had no cause to be wary of the traffic passing along the primary route from Bishop's Stortford to Great Dunmow. It had been busy at the start of his journey but had gradually decreased as the night progressed, therefore, he did not expect to be run down by a car.

He first became aware of it when he heard it coming at great speed and when he turned to face it he was dazzled by its powerful lights. Then using his hand to shield his eyes, he saw it deliberately swerve towards him with every intention of knocking him down. Desperately he tried to jump clear but was caught a glancing blow by the rear nearside of the car as it slewed into the grass verge. There resounded a dull thud as Joe was sent tumbling into a soggy ditch much to the applause of the car's occupants (half a dozen young men) who cheered loudly at the sport

Brakes were firmly applied and the car screeched to a halt some sixty feet further on, then it shot back in reverse gear to the spot where it had sent Joe reeling from the road. Side windows were wound down and six heads looked out at the darkened hedgerow.

Joe partly raised himself from the bed of the soaking ditch and roared, "You bloody roadhog," at the car's driver.

"You bloody hedgehog," returned the driver to the obvious delight of his companions.

In the awkward moments that followed, Joe expected to be set upon by the young men but they, presumably, had more urgent business elsewhere for the car moved forward and sped off to its next destination.

"You won't get away with it," shouted Joe as, with knife in hand, he scrambled out of the ditch. "I know who you are and there'll be hell to pay when I catch up with you." His voice fell away as further threat became pointless – the car had gone from view and he was alone once again.

A body check carried out in the darkness revealed no more damage than mere cuts and bruises, all the same such abrasions were not sustained without pain and Joe was to suffer the discomfort as he continued on his way into Great Dunmow.

Having explored the town for what remained of the night and finding nothing to his advantage, Joe ventured out into its eastern flank and settled down on a grassy bank to watch the sunrise. With heavy eyes he sat back against a garden fence and watched the sky turn from grey to pink and when the sun came up over the Essex marshes it warmed his body and induced a pleasant sleep.

When he awoke, some three hours later, he did so to the sounds of daily, rural activities; animals brayed, bleated, or barked, birds chirped and chattered, farm machinery rumbled and rattled, voices greeted voices, and the town's traffic roared to a crescendo at the height of the morning rush hour.

The sounds were warm and friendly but Joe disliked them intensely, it was no longer his desire to live in a pleasant world. Grudgingly he got up from his gramineous bed and was immediately reminded of the incident with the car. The soreness in his limbs soured his mood still further as he set off down the grassy bank toward the river Chelmer.

Following a river suddenly seemed more inviting than following a road, at least, he would be safe from cars for a while. Unfortunately, there are very few signposts along a river to direct a traveller and Joe, not yet skilful in the art of navigation despite Bumble's teachings, made another miscalculation and found himself heading south once again, this time towards Chelmsford.

The wildlife of the river remained generally unperturbed as Joe ambled by despite his vociferous condemnations of the young men who had caused him such pain. "Those bastards needn't think they're getting away with it," he vowed. "One of these days I'll catch up with them and they'll regret ever trying to knock me off the road. I'll know that car if ever I see it again – a big American job with a left hand drive. Pink it was, I distinctly remember that – saw it by the light on the number plate. I'll get even with them – you see if I don't".

The Lincolnshire Tramp

Empty words considering he had made no attempt to find the car or the young men, and following a river to the back of beyond was hardly conducive to tracking down adversaries. But, by curious coincidence, that is exactly what did happen – the river led Joe to the car.

There was barely two hours of daylight left when he reached the village of Little Waltham. Leaving the river bank, he skirted the village in search of food but, when sounding out an old barn, he found the car instead. Cautiously he entered the barn and made a thorough examination of the vehicle – it was the same car all right, he was sure of that. Then, suppressing a desire to leap into the air and shout out with glee he applied his mind to finding the best way to exact his revenge. That car was going to be destroyed no matter what.

A dog barking in the near distance brought Joe quickly to the barn-door and when he looked out he saw two young men emerging from a row of farm cottages situated not more than a hundred yards away. The young men had some stern words to say to the dog and ordered it back into one of the cottages before they turned and swaggered towards the barn.

There was not time for Joe to make an escape so he had to hide somewhere in the barn – he dare not risk being caught by the young men. With one half of the barn piled high with bales of straw, it was not difficult to find a hiding place.

Joe was well hidden by the time the young men entered the barn yet he was able to hear them planning their evening as they climbed into the car and started its engine. A second or two was allowed for the engine to warm up before the car jerked forward and bounced along an uneven track to pass the row of cottages and on into the village lane.

The swift departure of the car caused Joe a moment of despair for he thought he had lost his opportunity, however, reason soon returned and he realised the car would eventually come back. "Joe can wait," he said, "Joe's got plenty of time." He knew that many hours would have to pass before the car returned in the meantime his safest bet was to stay in the barn. There would be much to occupy his mind, rummaging around to see what could be of use to him, keeping an eye on the cottages in case any of the other tenants had an interest in the barn, and making sure he did not attract the attention of the dog.

One by one the lights went out in the cottages until all was in pitch darkness. The night was very still with hardly a breath of wind and Joe, once again hiding in the bales of straw, waited apprehensively for the young men to return. There had been some false alarms when one or two vehicles passed through the lane but nothing had entered the barn or the farm yard.

Joe was about to give up on the idea and move off to another part of the village when the dusty beams and the rough-hewn rafters of the barn suddenly became illuminated by a bright light, and the whole place reverberated to the droning throb of an engine. Soon after, the engine was killed and the lights extinguished; the car stood motionless and the young men retired to their cottage.

An hour was to pass before Joe made his move, he wanted to be sure that everyone was asleep. From broken bales he took the straw to place under and around the car then he soaked it all with paraffin oil (found earlier at the back of the barn). More bales of straw were dragged over to the car and stacked against it, they were also doused with paraffin oil. Then, with the will of an executioner, he struck a match to set the fire going. A wry smile lurked beneath his matted beard as he watched the fire take hold and when he could no longer tolerate the heat and the smoke he made a hasty exit from the building.

The oak-framed barn with its timber-clad walls and thatched roof did not take long to become engulfed by fire, especially when a southerly wind picked up to fan the flames. Although the fabric of the building and most of its contents were highly combustible it would take time to burn thoroughly through and Joe (concealing himself in a nearby field) had reservations about it. Would the car be destroyed before the fire brigade arrived?

With strident crackle and fearsome roar, the raging inferno drowned all other sound as it swept on to even greater intensity. Clearly, such a noise could not continue without attracting some attention and, before long, people began to appear to investigate the disturbing interlude. Silhouetted against the incandescent flames, they scurried from place to place but were incapable of dealing with the situation.

Not until heavier parts of the structure caved in, sending great showers of sparks cascading into the air, did the first of the fire appliances arrive. Barely had it time to disgorge its crew when a second appliance pulled up, then a third. From initial confusion came order as the well drilled firemen set about damping down the fire and the surrounding buildings, a task that would take many hours. When the fire was finally brought under control it was clear that the barn had been irretrievably lost, also its contents.

Joe did not hang around to see the ultimate result of the fire because the coming of the dawn necessitated an urgent retreat. Inevitably, there would be an investigation and any stranger found within the vicinity would be questioned, he did not want that. In any case, he was well satisfied with his effort to permanently immobilize the car – that particular vehicle would never run him into the ditch again.

Leaving the smouldering barn behind him, Joe returned to the river and continued to follow it into Chelmsford but not before he had taken a short sleep. His feelings at that time were surprisingly impassive, he was not over elated by his new found powers of destruction nor did he suffer the slightest remorse for the damage he had caused. To him, it was simply another score settled.

Chemlsford did not present Joe with any extraordinary incident even though he was on the lookout for one during the six days he spent wandering around the sprawling town. For most of the time he was in a belligerent mood and spoiling for a fight with anybody less advantaged than himself, be it man or beast. In their infinite wisdom, timorous creatures of either genus gave him a wide birth and avoided the violence in his temper whilst those of greater confidence ignored his extravagant rantings.

After the sixth day he came to a decision; the proposed visit to Spalding would have to be postponed in favour of a lengthy stay in Essex. The accessible county encouraged him to spend the spring and summer months exploring its other towns as well as its coastal resorts and its open countryside. However, he did have his reservations; he did not want to be to Essex what Bumble Drage had become to Hertfordshire – its resident tramp. With this in mind he set off for the next town but vowed to be in Suffolk by midsummer.

On the walk from Chelmsford to Billericay he sensed there would be fresh opportunities to continue his campaign of deliberate vandalism and to indulge himself with food and drink at the expense of others. The first opportunity came sooner than he expected for on a wet evening in a quiet suburb of Billericay he chanced upon a near deserted off-licence – and old lady manning the till appeared to be the only person in sight.

Joe could hardly believe his luck, the street lighting was poor, the shop was devoid of customers, the falling rain kept people indoors, and the road was clear of moving vehicles. The shop itself could be entered and left without attracting too much attention and it lacked a workable security system. Providing nobody was working in the back of the shop, Joe had no problem – all he had to do was, enter, subdue the old lady, and take what he wanted.

It was all over in less than a minute; the old lady, suddenly confronted by a vile tramp with menace in his eyes, let out a stifled scream and became paralysed with fear. Whilst she trembled, Joe gathered up several tins of food, four packets of biscuits, two bottles of whisky, and some cigarettes. With his pockets bulging, he made a final threat to the old lady and then slipped out of the shop to disappear into the night.

An hour later, having consumed almost half of one bottle of the whisky, he staggered and rolled along the road to Basildon. Passing cars blasted him with their horns as he swayed unsteadily into their path. He responded with his usual curses, albeit belated and with slurred speech.

The whisky tasted wonderful (especially after Bumble's wild concoctions with methylated spirits) and Joe fully appreciated its intoxicating power. So much so that he felt exhilarated about the way he had obtained it. "A piece of piss!" He exclaimed, referring to his success. "I just walked in and helped myself." He took another swig from the bottle "I could have taken the whole bloody store, there was no bugger there to stop me. That old bag couldn't stop me , she just sat there and shat her knickers the minute I walked in. She couldn't stop me. Nobody can stop me."

At that moment he swayed a little too far and fell clumsily onto the road. Swearing profusely, he picked himself up but his balance was not good and he pitched over yet again, this time away from the road. His second attempt at attaining the perpendicular and staying there almost succeeded, for a few seconds he stood perfectly still with his legs wide apart and his arms outstretched. Then, in an effort to walk forward, he stepped back three paces and fell over for the last time. He landed against a paling fence and was sound asleep before his head touched the ground. It had stopped raining but the grass verge still held a quantity of moisture.

After seven hours sleep, he awoke to the inevitable hangover and dry mouth yet his clothes were wringing wet. It took him a few moments to establish who and what he was and, thus done, he reached for the whisky bottle to seek a remedy for his ailments. The alcohol gave some relief but not enough for real comfort, what he needed was a good fire to dry out his wet clothing and to warm his chilled bones. Later, when he was restored to some sort of normality, he made his way into Basildon. The whisky bottles, for the time being were stashed safely away and would not be brought out again until his head had cleared. In the meantime, he would see what mischief could be made in the town. But, for there to be a disturbance of any kind certain elements must come into being, there has to be something readily available to be abused together with the means and the will to do it.

The means came by way of the whisky bottle on his second afternoon in the Basildon suburbia; his sudden craving for alcohol demanded to be appeased with equal expedition. On this occasion the whisky did not have the desired effect, instead of being pleasantly relaxing it made Joe depressingly morose. Increasingly, memories of home life haunted him as he sat in a park and watched gardeners attend to flower beds. He recalled the walks with Marjorie in their local parks and gardens, and he remembered his own garden with its carefully preserved flower beds. He had spent so many happy hours amongst his roses, tubers, and seedlings.

With their day's toil done, the gardeners loaded their tools onto a wheelbarrow and set off towards a distant greenhouse, they had worked hard and were justly proud of their exertions.

Bitterness and resentment gave Joe the will to perpetrate his next act of vandalism, and the park gardens provided the object to be abused. In fact, it was not only the park gardens that were attacked that night for many a private garden suffered a similar fate and by early dawn a trail of damaged property followed Joe on an easterly route out of the town. He had ripped up plants and flowers, churned up lawns, wrecked greenhouses, and broken garden furniture without disturbing a soul, not even a dog barked as he went about his furtive business.

In the weeks to come, stealing alcohol and destroying property became a regular part of his life. In Southend-on-Sea he was responsible for starting a dozen major fires whilst in Maldon he smashed shop windows. With great cunning he practised his destructive skills and made it a policy not to commit the same offence in the towns he visited; too much of a common factor (he reasoned) would be easily detected. Therefore, private cars were his target in Witham, industrial units in Braintree, and churches in Colchester.

However, by the end of June he had grown weary of his unrelenting pursuit of wasting other peoples' property and, on the road from Colchester to Sudbury he decided to postpone his activities until such time as he might be provoked into renewing them. Not that he had extracted a full measure of retribution from society, far from it, he had yet to fully satisfy his grievances. He needed to rest because the effort required to plan and execute deliberate destruction was exhausting and he had done little else for the past two months.

For this reason alone, he avoided entering Sudbury and at Cornard Tye he walked away from the main road and headed north into the Suffolk countryside. In the days to come he was to confine himself to the fields and hedgerows and only approached a domestic dwelling when he wanted food.

The summer days were long and hot but Joe was unwilling to shed any part of his clothing. Whenever he became overheated he merely stood still until he cooled down, otherwise he was quite content to sweat profusely under his heavy greatcoat. Before long, stale sweat became the most dominant of the foul odours emanating from his body.

On a particularly hot afternoon in July, he paused to mop his brow and scan the distant horizon. He had all but completed a lengthy trek across open grassland (an ambulation hindered by too many barbed wire fences and low hedges) and was on the lookout for somewhere to rest for a while. Ahead, with copious foliage breaking the skyline, a clump of shimmering trees offered indispensable shade against an unrelenting sun; just the place for a weary tramp to rest up or, even, spend the night.

Joe pressed on towards the trees but was halted in his tracks a few minutes later – from behind the sturdy trunks, something glittered and he was momentarily dazzled. Unsure of what he might find, he proceeded with caution until he eventually crossed over into the shade and there, less than twenty paces away, stood a baby's pram. It was brand-new and its chromium plated frame and wheels mischievously reflected the sunlight.

A pram with a baby in it, thought Joe, must have parents or other adults nearby. He stood quite still and listened, and then moving only his head, he contrived to look in every direction possible. All seemed quiet, he neither heard nor saw another person.

Stealthily he moved closer to the pram and looked in at the quiescent baby. He knew nothing about babies but be felt confident that there was nothing amiss with this one apart from the absence of a mother. In fact, the child's mother was not so very far away as Joe was soon to discover, she was sound asleep on a rug which she had spread out a few feet from the pram and almost out of sight.

Joe caught his breath and stared at the young body stretched out before him. She lay on her back with her legs slightly apart and her head turned to one side, her cotton skirt was pulled up to her waist to expose white thighs and her unbuttoned blouse hung loosely about her arms. The nursing bra she wore looked far too cumbersome for such a hot day, nevertheless, it served its purpose and supported her heavy, milk laden breasts.

In her naivety, the young mother believed she could relax in complete isolation and not be disturbed. She desired no more than the freedom to feel the warm, summer air soothing her traumatised body whilst her legs were being treated to a healthy sun tan. Never in her wildest dreams did she expect to be the object of a dirty tramp's lecherous desires. This was her place, her very special place, a place where she and her lover spent many blissful hours, and a place where their child was conceived As far as she was concerned, no other person was allowed there.

Hardly able to believe his unexpected fortuity, Joe wasted several long seconds contemplating the young mother's body. He knew he would have to rape her, the arousal in his loin told him that for a start; then there were Marjorie's indiscretions to be taken into consideration – he would have to rape a lot of women to balance out that particular wrong; finally, and of paramount importance, it was his first opportunity to degrade a woman by abusing her body. He – in his filthy, unwashed condition – would take his pleasure and not give a damn for her feelings.

By now the adrenaline was flowing and his heart was pounding in his ears as he moved closer to the young mother and knelt down beside her. To wake her too soon, he realised, would severely curtail his intentions and prevent him from satisfying his obsession. Therefore, with his sharp bladed knife, he deftly cut through the narrowest part of her bra and as the padded cups fell away so her breasts tumbled out.

Quickly, Joe put the knife back into his greatcoat pocket in order to leave his hands free to fondle the young mother's breasts and after a while he lowered his head to take one of the inflated nipples into his malodorous mouth. As he lasciviously sucked the warm milk from the excited teat he let his coarse, right hand run over her body until it came to rest between her thighs. Feverishly, his grubby fingers slipped under her white, lace-trimmed briefs to toy with the pubic hair above her vagina. Any moment from then on, he would force an entrance and so the rape could commence – so he thought.

In the event, rape was not an option. The young mother's reaction was far from what Joe had expected and he was totally unprepared for it. Hitherto, he assumed she would put up some sort of struggle and as a counter measure he planned to hold his knife to her throat, and keep it there until he reached his climax. By then, of course, it would be too late for her she would have been defiled and made to feel shame whilst he would have reaped the pleasure of ultimate satisfaction.

In a state of confusion, the young mother woke abruptly from her sleep and after a short period of adjustment (a mere split second) she assessed the situation and began to fight Joe off. Although he had steeled himself against her opposition he succumbed to a moment of panic when she started to scream. Instead of reaching for his knife he clamped his hand over her mouth in a bid to silence her; but as the mother's cries were muffled so the baby (startled from its slumber) gave out with its own unremitting screeching.

Joe glanced towards the pram but he refused to be discouraged from his business, in fact, the baby's crying made it all the more urgent. With his free hand he undid the fly of his trousers and rolled over an top of the young mother.

She, with her breathing restricted and unable to throw off the great weight now forcing down upon her, reached deep into her mind for renewed strength to repel him. But then a new sensation came over her, a sensation she was all too familiar with, a sensation she feared – the onset of an epileptic seizure. She recognized it for what it was and knew that she could control it under normal circumstances but now that she was about to be raped it all became too much for her, it required too much energy to deal with both problems at once. She slipped into unconsciousness and as she entered the earlier stages of the fit she grabbed held of Joe's straggly beard.

Joe became alarmed when he saw her eyes rolling wildly around in their sockets, and even more so when her body tensed up and the grip on his beard tightened. He did not know what was wrong with her, nor did he want to know; all he wanted to do was to get away from her. Taking his dampened hand away from her mouth he noticed the frothy saliva coating her lips and (much to his disgust) he was being drawn closer to the saliva. He tried to release his beard from her grip but, short of breaking her fingers, he could not get free. Besides, he doubted if it was possible to break her fingers – she seemed to have so much strength in them, but he had to do something because his hair was being pulled out by the roots and it was becoming extremely painful. His only means of escape came by way of his knife – he had to hack off that part of his beard caught in her grasp.

Seething with rage, he scrambled to his feet and then kicked out at the young mother, the blow caught her on a lower thigh and might have caused her more damage had not her twitching limb cushioned it. "You dirty little cow!" he bellowed, "You ought to be bloody well ashamed of yourself." frustration as well as anger motivated his comments.

The baby, its tear stained face getting even redder, redoubled its efforts to attract attention by crying all the louder. "If you don't shut up," shouted Joe, kicking out once again and this time sending the pram slightly askew, "I'll bloody shut you up for good."

The suddenness of the attack stunned the baby into a brief silence which lasted just long enough for Joe to hear a Landrover sounding its horn as it made its way across the open grassland towards the clump of trees. "Christ Almighty!" exclaimed Joe, his anger turning to panic, "I'd better get out of this place."

Correctly supposing the driver of the vehicle to be the baby's father and not wishing to be seen near the distressed infant nor its half naked mother, Joe hastily departed from the scene. Clutching his paltry belongings and fearing for his life, he ran like a startled rabbit as he set off to put the greatest possible distance between himself and the Landrover.

From his early youth he had never been very good at running and now, when he was at his least fittest, he found it to be an extremely uncomfortable experience. Nonetheless, he dare not slow down or take a breather because he knew it would only be a matter of time before the driver discovered the truth and followed in pursuit.

Five minutes into the run and Joe began to suffer; his lungs felt as though they were about to burst whilst his heart crashed against his ribs, a sharp pain stabbed at his upper abdomen and his legs began to buckle. A few paces further on, he fell to the ground and gasped for precious air, By this time his whole body was racked with pain and only clean, fresh air could soothe it but (adding to his discomfort) the heat of the day made breathing more difficult.

Believing that Landrovers were coming at him from all directions, he was compelled to search for cover, therefore, he scrambled to his feet and half crawling, half lurching, he progressed forward until he was clear of open fields. But then, the country lane into which he had staggered offered little in the way of protection; it would have been impossible to hide a thimble in its sparse hedgerows.

Panting heavily, Joe paused again and tried to regulate his breathing, he also looked despairingly at the exposed terrain surrounding him. Just as he was about to give us hope of finding a hiding place he realized he was being deceived by the lane, for although it ran straight and flat it did, in fact, pass over a stream. A bridge some hundred yards further on may not here been apparent at first glance, but it did exist and it did offer a suitable place to hide.

Joe was instantly elated by the prospect yet he had to check himself before charging towards the place of safety; a 'Bumble Drage' lecture on the art of concealment came flooding back into his mind. "Never cut a swathe through a bed of stinging nettles which would lead a predator to your lair." Bumble warned. With this warning to guide him, Joe made a wide detour to approach the bridge without leaving the slightest hint of a trail, and without being seen by anyone. Once there, he tucked himself up tightly under one of its haunches and merged into the darkened recess. He planned to stay there for many hours because summer days are long and it would be late in the evening before he could venture out under the cover of darkness, besides, it would give him time to recover from his exertions.

The rest of the afternoon did not pass without incident. Within minutes, a police car sped by on its way to the young mother and when it returned (half an hour later) it stopped on the bridge to let out a police constable who promptly searched the area. Although Joe was not spotted it did confirm his suspicions – he was a hunted man. Other cars too came and went but Joe remained motionless and out of sight.

In time, the western horizon swallowed the fiery, red sun and the last glimmers of daylight surrendered to the nocturnal hours. It was time for Joe to come out of hiding and stretch his stiffened limbs, it was time for him to move on through the night.

Chapter 9

After the incident with the young mother, Joe kept his head down for a few days but before long his former arrogance returned. Damn it all! He was Joe and nobody had the right to persecute him – he could roam wherever he liked and do whatever he pleased, and do so without being harassed by any man. No longer would he hide from the police or keep out of sight of Landrovers.

With renewed confidence he stalked the streets of Stowmarket; although the intent to rape was still on his mind another opportunity did not present itself, instead , he was forced to concentrate on the more mundane problems of keeping cool and feeding himself.

Suffolk was particularly sleepy in the height of summer and the relaxed way of life did not suit Joe's belligerent mood, he could not find the means, or the motive, to express his pent-up emotions. However, he stayed in the county until the early days of August when his wanderings took him from Ruckinghall Inferior to Blo Norton and subsequently into Norfolk. He then followed the road into Diss where he spent a couple of days before heading for Norwich.

He was not a complete stranger to Norfolk for he had, in the past, spent many of his summer holidays on The Broads or in the coastal resorts of Lowestoft and Great Yarmouth. Therefore, because of his holiday memories, be decided not to travel any further east of Norwich; he was not quite so familiar with the countryside west of the city and could afford to be curious about what it might have in store for him.

As there was no great urgency to get to Norwich, Joe did not take a direct route from Diss – he thought rich pickings could be had from the many villages between the urban sprawls. But, after a period of twenty one days he was not satisfied with his achievements and thought he should have gained more from the venture. Admittedly, he had stolen food and alcohol and had frightened the daylights out of a small boy he found innocently playing in a wheat field, but he had not seriously disrupted anybody's life. He desperately wanted someone else to abuse, someone who would suffer as he had suffered.

Giving up on the villages, he moved on to enter Norwich via Caister St Edmund and spent the following week probing the outer limits of the city. He knew his presence would irritate the local inhabitants, they would watch him carefully as he passed by and at night they would make sure their doors were securely locked. He was encouraged by such attitudes and he became all the more obnoxious.

The summer holiday came to an end for the city's school children and they dutifully returned to their respective schools. Normally such a mass movement of children twice a day would not have concerned Joe and he would not have made a serious effort to stray into their regular routes to school, but (because he felt cheated out of sexual satisfaction with the young mother) he found himself inexorably drawn towards adolescent girls. Unintentionally he harboured a penchant for the clumsy blazers that cocooned the nubile young bodies; beneath such coverings he visualised budding breasts and voluptuous vaginas.

A place much favoured was a local park where he could conceal himself amongst the shrubbery and watch the girls as they came and went, and late afternoon was the best time because they were in no hurry to get home. His stratagem was to grab any girl walking alone, drag her into the bushes, silence her by threatening her with his knife, and then rape her – it would be all too easy.

Very rarely do girls in their early teens walk alone, they always seem to be in little gaggles and have so much to talk about. This presented Joe with a problem and he was becoming extremely frustrated by it, so much so that he dared to venture out from his place of concealment on a September afternoon and approach a group of three girls. He calculated that two of the girls would run away and leave the third to her fate. As he drew nearer he could see they were trying to ignore him so he put out his hand to attract them. "Hello girls!" he said, "And how many of you have had sex lately?"

The girls, their conversation petering out, stood in silence as each left it to one of the others to volunteer a comment.

"What's wrong," continued Joe, studying; each girl in turn, "Don't you like sex?" he watched their downcast eyes and waited for some significant response but when none came he decided to stir things up by putting his hand inside the blazer of the girl nearest to him and squeezing her breast.

"Leave my tits alone you filthy old bastard," shrieked the infuriated girl as she pulled herself away and swung her heavy school bag at him.

Instantly grabbing hold of the bag, Joe, tried to pull it and the girl into the bushes but his efforts were thwarted by the other girls who also shrieked and swung their own heavy bags into action. Joe might have been able to cope with the girls but certainly not with the boys who came to their assistance. At least six or seven fourth formers, whooping like Red Indians, raced across the park and were clearly intent on rescuing the girls.

Obviously outnumbered Joe let go of the bag and retreated into the shrubbery where he waited until the boys drew level with the girls. He thought the two groups would exchange information and then decide to continue on to their homes; it was hardly likely they would go to the police since nobody had been seriously hurt; and, besides, how often do the police take any notice of fourth formers.

Joe was almost right on both counts, the girls did go on to their own homes and nobody bothered to make a complaint to the police, however, the boys had other plans which had not come into his reckoning. They sensed that much fun could be had from tramp baiting and accordingly spread themselves out in a straight line before entering the shrubbery.

"There he is!" exclaimed a sharp eyed boy catching sight of Joe.

"Let's get him!" shouted others as they gathered up stones from the loose earth footing the laurel bushes and hurled them through the air.

At first, Joe was prepared to stand his ground and deal with each youngster as he came – proposing to pick them off one by one and give each a sound thrashing – but being pelted from so many sides and with such ferocity he was at a disadvantage. Although he made a determined effort to return the missiles he could not compete with the boys (whose numbers were increasing anyway) and was forced to retreat even further into the shrubbery.

No matter where he went, for the following hour and a half, Joe could not escape his persecutors. They forced him out of the shrubbery and into open parkland where he fled from tree to tree and from bush to bush in a bid to outwit them. But no matter where he went they streamed after him and always with a plentiful supply of rounded pebbles, and always able to keep him within the confines of the park. The gang of boys, high spirited and jubilant at their sport, were keen to keep up the chase whereas Joe, cut, bruised and revengeful, was desperate to put an end to it. Again and again he turned on then to harangue them with the foulest of oaths and, as always, he met with the same response – jeers and more accurate stone throwing.

As the evening shadows lengthened so the gang began to diminish, in ones and twos the boys drifted away to attend to other matters and it gave Joe the chance to escape from the park. Not that it ended there, for the battle was to continue as he darted from one street to another but at least he was confident of gaining the upper hand.

The cluttered streets soon restricted the activities of the stone throwers and presented Joe with a few more options – he could either retaliate or evade the boys altogether. With their number now down to five, he thought he stood a good chance of seeing them off once and for all and from an adjacent doorstep he scooped up empty milk bottles which he lobbed at them. The first bottle smashed on the pavement in front of the boys and sent a shower of glass splinters flying in all directions, and the second bottle bounced off a parked car and went flying over their heads.

Now that private property (the car) had become entangled in the conflict, the boys deemed it wise to call off their action; they knew all too well who would be blamed if such property was damaged, anyway, they had achieved their aim and the tramp had been punished for touching a teenager's breast. In a final gesture of defiance they kicked away fragments of glass before turning their backs on Joe and walking off.

Still clutching the third, and last, of the empty bottles, Joe stomped off in the opposite direction and swearing profusely he vowed to get even with the fourth formers. Of course, he had no idea who they really were or how he should exact his revenge.

Throughout the rest of the night he was to be constantly reminded of the experience. For the second time within a month he had to run for his life and as a result of it his limbs ached unmercifully. He believed his whole body was covered with bumps and bruises whilst his face was stained with congealed blood from innumerable cuts. To make matters worse he was without sufficient alcohol to use as an anodyne.

Sleep eventually numbed the pain and for a few hours his body benefited from the rest, unfortunately, his temper did not. Burning with anger, he set off in the early morning to search for a school; any school would do as long as it catered for fourteen to fifteen year old boys. As a matter of urgency he had to find a school before the children emerged out onto the streets in case any of them should recognize him, and when he found a school he planned to stay out of sight until his chosen moment.

In due course he found a school and , unbeknown to him, it was an establishment attended by many of the boys who had chased him through the park. Across the road from the school, an unmanned building site provided him with cover until it was time for him to make his protest.

He waited patiently for the boys to arrive and when a sufficient number poured through the main gate he made his move. Crossing the road, he walked boldly amongst them until he reached the first in a series of buildings where he stopped and turned to face the, now curious boys. Deliberately he whipped the empty milk bottle from his pocket and (holding it by the neck) pointed it at one of the boys. "This is for you," he snarled and then in a frenzied movement he spun round and smashed a pane of glass in the nearest window within reach. With the bottle still in his grip he singled out another boy, "And this is for you –" a second pane was shattered. A third, a fourth, and a fifth followed in quick succession – each one dedicated to a particular boy.

A burly teacher of metalwork (on playground duty) heard the commotion and went to investigate. His huge frame the boys knew well as he separated them to form a path to Joe, "And what in hell is going on here?" he demanded, clamping a huge hand on the tramp's shoulder.

"It's a madman, sir," piped up a shrill voice,

"And he's breaking windows, sir," proclaimed another.

"I can see that," said the teacher, "But why is he breaking windows?"

"Don't know, sir."

"Said it was for us, sir."

The teacher, seeing that no sensible answer would come from the boys, put the question to Joe, "Why are you breaking these windows?"

"Because those little bastards were throwing stones at me last night and I'm paying them back," Joe replied.

"I don't quite see how breaking glass settles a grievance," observed the teacher sternly.

"Making a point," said Joe. The school authorities will want to know why, and when I explain, they'll find the boys responsible and punish them."

"The boys who threw the stones at you," queried the teacher, "do you see any of them ?"

"All of then, I would have thought," snapped Joe.

After a moment's thought, the teacher took the empty milk bottle out of Joe's hand and said, "I think you had better come with me to the headmaster's study, see if he can get to the bottom of this." He gripped Joe's arm in readiness to lead him away but before doing so he barked at the boys, "Get along to assembly – all of you, and you, Henson, find the caretaker and ask him if he can do anything about this mess."

Talking excitedly amongst themselves, the boys moved off in small groups and headed for the school's main hall, meanwhile Joe was marched unceremoniously to the headmaster's study.

The stoney faced headmaster listened in silence to the metalwork teacher's report before delegating the deputy head to take the morning assembly and the school secretary to phone for the police. He had taken an instant dislike to Joe and, considering him too dirty to sit in any of the chairs, made him stand in the middle of the room. Furthermore, the headmaster (unlike the metalwork teacher who had some sympathy for the tramp) would not listen to Joe's explanation.

"Look here," said Joe, wagging his finger at the headmaster, "Boys from this school caused me a great deal of pain and discomfort last night and I want to know what you are going to do about it?"

The headmaster looked disapprovingly at Joe and then asked with a hint of sarcasm, "Were you on the school premises at the time?"

"No," said Joe, "I was in the park."

"Then what do you expect me to do about it? I mean, when they go out of the school gates in the afternoon they're no longer in my charge."

"They should be brought in here and flogged, that's what!"

"And of course, you should be excused of causing damage to public property –."

"They had no right to attack me."

"And you had no right to break my windows." The headmaster became very angry and thumped his desk with his fist to emphasise his point. "A man of your age should know better."

"I can see I'm wasting my time here," snarled Joe as he made ready to leave, "Obviously there's no discipline in this place."

"You stay exactly where you are," ordered the headmaster, partly rising up out of his seat, "The only place you're going is to the police station."

"That's what you think," Joe retorted, but when he turned to go he saw that his way was barred by the bulk of the teacher of metalwork who, adequately, blocked out the office door.

Not even Joe's knife could help him out of this situation and he would not risk using it unless he was absolutely certain of escape. Brute force was not the way to get out of the study, it required something more subtle.

The Lincolnshire Tramp

For the next five minutes, Joe was totally ignored by the headmaster who busied himself by making notes and exchanging comments with the teacher. Nonetheless, Joe remained unperturbed by his isolation and applied his mind to achieving freedom. During his contemplation he felt the need to answer a call of nature but just as he was about to ask permission to go to the toilet (where he would make his bid to escape) another idea struck him – an idea he liked so much better. With a smile on his face he allowed his penis to hang down inside one trouser leg and urinate on the carpet, it was not the most comfortable of things to do but it did have the desired effect.

"Christ Almighty!" roared the headmaster, "He's pissed all over the floor. "Get the dirty sod out of here" He leapt from behind his desk to take Joe by the arm and spin him round, and the teacher (prior to taking Joe's other arm) opened the study door. Between them they marched him out into the corridor which ran past the school offices.

"We've got to get him out of the school before he stinks the whole place out," complained the headmaster. "And where have the police got to?"

"Over there," affirmed the teacher nodding towards two uniformed officers who had just entered the corridor.

"Thank God for that," sighed the headmaster as he dragged Joe over to meet the constables.

After some earnest discussion between the headmaster and the policemen Joe was given a once-over and the damp patch on the study floor examined before they all moved off to inspect the damage caused to the windows.

The caretaker had swept up the last of the broken glass when they arrived and he stood to one side whilst the headmaster and the policemen examined the destruction. Meanwhile, with his role in the matter now done, the teacher of metalwork retired from the scene to take a class. He was followed some three minutes later by the headmaster who had the caretaker in tow – no doubt a bucket of hot water laced with strong disinfectant would be called for.

As soon as the headmaster was out of sight the policemen escorted Joe to their car and ordered him to sit in the back, thus done, they moved off a few paces for a quiet consultation.

"I don't think we want to take that dirty old bugger back to our nick do we?" said one of them softly.

"Sarge won't like it – I know that," observed his colleague, "Got my balls chewed off the last time I ran a vagrant in."

"Exactly," agreed the first officer, "And look what happened — went before the beak and got bound over to keep the peace. Wasn't worth the paperwork."

The second officer gave a moments thought to the problem and said "Let's give the old boy a chance to decide his fate." He walked back to where Joe was sitting and, opening the car door to pop his head in, he explained, "I want you to wait here whilst we go and check out a few details – so no running off now, right?"

Joe nodded and sat back in the car seat to reassure the officers of his good intention but he knew he would get away given the right opportunity. Meanwhile, the officers returned to the building with the broken windows and, knowing it to be empty, went inside. Ostensibly, they were going to examine the damage from the inside but in reality they lit up cigarettes.

After their smoke the first officer stubbed out his cigarette and surmised "I expect the old bugger has gone by now so we'd better go back to the station and tell them how the cunning sod managed to give us the slip."

Joe, thinking himself, indeed, cunning, scurried through the quieter streets of Norwich; having escaped from the police car he was now bound to leave the city. He followed the lesser used roads and passed through Spixworth, Frettenham, and Stratton Strawless on his way to Aylsham, where he spent a few days in and around the town before continuing his leisurely perambulations of the northerly parts of Norfolk. He went on from Aylsham to North Walsham (where he stole two bottles of gin) and then to Bacton on the Norfolk coast (where he threw the empty bottles away).

The ten miles of coastal road from Bacton to Cromer took Joe longer to walk than usual for whenever the road strayed near the coast he paused to look out over the North Sea. Something about the sea mesmerised him and for long periods of time his mind wandered away from his body. On the other hand, when he was in control of his faculties, he ventured down onto the beach in the hope of finding a lone woman either walking or bathing, but he was never to encounter such a person.

October days in and around Cromer forewarned of the coming winter; the sun no longer felt warm and the nights had a definite chill about them. It was time for Joe to turn to the west and head inland, and also time for him to find some warmer clothing. This did not necessarily mean a change of clothing, just extra garments added to, and worn over his existing apparel, that is apart from his greatcoat – that was always worn over everything else.

The Lincolnshire Tramp

A week later, at Little Snoring near Fakenham, he found what he wanted. A neglectful wife had left her washing out on the line overnight and it provided Joe with, a thick sweater, a pair of jeans, and a pair of woollen socks. They were, of course, ringing wet but within a matter of hours a blazing fire soon dried them out and it did not matter if they reeked of wood smoke.

Feeling comfortable in his newly acquired clothes, Joe spent the next six weeks zig-zagging approximately ten miles north to ten miles south of a line running from Fakenham to King's Lynn. His purpose lay not in a desire to visitevery small town and village in the area but to expend the weeks leading up to Christmas. He planned to be in Spalding for that event.

However, before then he was to disgrace himself still further and sink to greater depths of depravity.

It happened early one morning on the road from Wormegay to Blackborough End when he chanced upon a solitary house which stood alone and without any immediate neighbour. He would have passed it by had not hunger forced him to stop and consider the prospect of obtaining food, even if it meant stealing it.

In the darkness of the morning, and at some distance away, he carefully surveyed the house and tried to determine how many people might live there. The impression it gave was one of dilapidation and abandonment, and certainly not inhabited, yet a cock crowed (somewhere at the back) and downstairs lights came on. Soon after wisps of smoke climbed lazily away from the chimney stack and a roundsman called at the front door to deliver milk and newspapers.

In all probability, thought Joe, a postman would call at the house but as soon as he had gone there would be no more scheduled visitors for the rest of the morning – time enough to get a breakfast. In fact, the familiar red van did not stop and sped by without the slightest hesitation.

Joe gave himself a few more minutes to consider; whether to knock on the door and ask for food or simply to break in and steal it, but before his deliberations were complete a door at the side of the house opened and an old lady stepped out. She wore, headscarf, old mackintosh, and Wellington boots, she also walked with a stoop and used a stick to support herself. In her free hand she carried food for her chickens.

Joe (convinced that the old lady lived on her own) saw his opportunity to slip into the house and take what he wanted, and as she waddled off down her garden path, and out of sight, he dashed up to the side door and let himself in. He passed through a dimly lit scullery to enter a spacious, yet archaic, kitchen which was cluttered with years of constant living; even the central table barely had room to lay out a meal. A larder, with its fly-screened window and stone cold-shelf, was situated just two paces inside the kitchen and it was to this that Joe turned his immediate attention. No sooner had he stuffed half a loaf of bread into one of his greatcoat pockets and some cheese and cake into the other than a voice startled him.

"That's not you – is it Mother?" croaked an old man, "So who is it then? Rentman?"

To see from whence the questions came, Joe looked over his shoulder and saw the old man sitting in an armchair close to the kitchen range. He sat very still and listened intently to every sound which brought Joe quickly to the conclusion that the man was blind.

"Have you come to collect the rent?" demanded the old man.

"Keep your mouth shut!" snarled Joe, "Or I'll slit your throat."

Upon hearing Joe's voice the old man became very agitated and, in his panic, divulged certain information which he had intended to withhold. "Don't you touch Mother's handbag," he blurted out, "She knows exactly how much she's got in it."

"So – " muttered Joe as his eyes scanned the kitchen, "She does – does she?"

"If you touch her bag I'll get the police on to you," threatened the old man.

The bag was amongst the clutter on the kitchen table and Joe soon spotted it. In an instant, he had it torn open and its contents tipped out.

"Please don't take our rent money," pleaded the old man, changing his ploy. "If we don't pay our rent, we'll be thrown out of here."

"Too bad," quipped Joe but, as yet, he had not found the rent money. A closer examination of the bag revealed an inner pocket with a bulky, brown envelope lodged in it; being full of treasury notes it had become wedged and could not fall as freely as the other contests. "Found it!" exclaimed Joe and trembling with anticipation he peered inside the envelopes and saw the money. There must be a couple of hundred here, he thought, although he did not have time to count it there and then.

By this time, the old run had picked up a poker and was waving it frantically from side to side, with his other hand he gripped the arm of his chair as he raised himself up and forward in a bid to strike Joe. "Leave that money where it is, you thief , and get out of here" he croaked.

The Lincolnshire Tramp

"Sit down, you blind old idiot," sneered Joe, "You don't know if I've found the money or not."

"Get out! Get out! Get out!"

"Don't worry I'm going – but keep your voice down." Joe tucked the envelope inside his greatcoat where a convenient pocket awaited and then, as a last defiant gesture, he seized hold of a packet of sausages and a tin of beans before walking out of the house.

Leaving, as he had entered, by the side door he encountered the old lady who had returned from her garden chores. She was about to wipe the mud off her Wellington boots when Joe came out and when she saw him, and the food he carried, she instantly guessed what had happened. Showing no emotion whatsoever, she leaned heavily on her stick and swung her arm, and the wooden trug in her hand, through the air to catch him a stinging blow on his ear.

"You – cow!" he shouted, and in a fit of temper he kicked her stick from under her, and as she fell screaming to the ground he stomped on the wooden trug and broke it. "I'll teach you to keep your hands to yourself," he hissed.

The old lady tried desperately to get back on to her feet but every time she managed to raise herself a few inches above the ground Joe knocked her down again. She was very frail and no match for the callous tramp but it was not her spirit that failed her in the end, just a lack of energy. Completely drained and without the will to continue the struggle, she lay prostrate after the last knock down.

Satisfied with himself and believing he had taught the old lady a lesson, Joe stepped out into the road and headed back to Wormegay. He strolled off haughtily and whistled loudly just to make sure that the old lady remembered the direction he had taken. He knew, that in due course, his exploits would be reported to the police and he would be a fugitive once again – possibly arrested. He could not allow this to happen, especially now that he had money, therefore he would have to lay a false trail. This he achieved by walking a short distance along the road to Wormegay then doubling back across the fields (making sure he was not seen from the house) and picking up the road to Blackborough End.

Meanwhile, at the house, the old man had heard his wife's cries for help and had unsteadily probed his way from the kitchen to the side door where he endeavoured to pick her up. It took many long minutes for the old couple to help each other back into the warmth and security of the house but it was to be many hours before anybody heard of their ordeal. Much later in the day, the police mounted a full scale manhunt in and around Wormegay but when the callous tramp could not be found the inspector in charge commented, "The trail has gone cold because we were not called in soon enough." It did not occur to him that he was on a fool's errand and the vagrant he wanted was five miles to the north entering King's Lynn via Brow-of-the-Hill.

Joe was a little more cautious than usual during his brief stay in King's Lynn and he managed to keep a low profile whilst adding to his food stock. A decision to leave the ancient port coincided with the first day of December although Joe was not aware of it as he crossed the Great Ouse on his way to Lincolnshire. He guessed he had a week or two in hand before his intended visit to Spalding and he could easily check the date nearer the time. Until then he meandered from one small town to another and planned his campaign of terror.

At Terrington St Clement, he decided to target all three – Virginia as well as her brother, Keith, and his own wife, Marjorie. Hitherto, Virginia's name had not been uppermost on his hit list because he had held a certain affection for her but now she was just another name to come to terms with, after all, did she not turn against him when she needed support.

Christmas Eve, thought Joe with a vivid recollection of the previous year, that's the best time to catch her. She would surely be in her shop and open for the last minute rush, he could then present himself and spoil her Christmas for her. She would never look forward to Christmas ever again.

With his plan to upset Virginia perfected, Joe moved on from Terrington to Long Sutton and as the winter days grew colder he warmed himself by contemplating some unpleasantries for Keith. Most likely, Keith would spend Christmas at home with his wife and children but only after he had done the rounds and sponged off as many people as he could. In one way or another, Joe would catch up with him and embarrass him in front of his family, or his friends. Keith would be shown up for the louse that he was and everyone would hear how he had driven Joe to destitution. Instead of Santa Claus, it would be a dirty, old tramp calling at the house this year and whatever Christmas cheer there was would be turned sour. Keith would forever rue the day he ran foul of Joe.

The bitterness mounted in Joe's heart as he journeyed on from Long Sutton to Holbeach, he was getting nearer to home ground now and nearer to Marjorie. He hoped to find her at their old house and then, by his very appearance, to shock her system as she had shocked his. In fact, nothing short of heart failure would settle the grudge he nursed in his own breast.

It had been almost a year now since he had discovered her in bed with her lover and at that time he was too taken aback to do anything about it, but if her lover was still there then he had better be wary of Joe's knife. For should that knife be used then twelve months of pent-up hatred would be behind every thrust. Joe reckoned he had nothing left to lose so he could be as reckless as he liked without fear of the consequences and without concern for his future.

On the morning of December the 24th he entered Spalding having followed the road from Holbeach, but as soon as he reached the centre of the town he found himself on the horns of a dilemma. His mind was split in two directions, one part felt as though it was good to be back home amongst the familiar surroundings and urged him to stay, whereas, the other part took an immediate dislike to the place and wanted to get as far away from it as possible.

However, he could not let his emotions interfere with his plans so he set off to find Virginia's shop but when he got there it did not meet with his expectations. Instead of being brightly lit and selling the latest fashions it was in darkness and boarded up. The tattered posters on the dusty windows and the street litter heaped against the step suggested a lengthy vacancy.

Momentarily thrown by the revelation, Joe could do no more than stand and stare at the building, eventually he came to terms with it and proceeded to examine the posters in case Virginia had left a forwarding address – there was none. A feeling of sadness came over him but it soon passed when he remembered Keith and forgot Virginia.

Soon after midday, Joe walked along the street where he knew Keith to have his house, and as he walked he prepared himself mentally for the coming confrontation. He need not have bothered because on reaching the house he realized Keith would not be at home for it, like the shop, was completely empty – an estate agent's board confirmed this.

"Damn it!" cursed Joe, "The bloody Harrison's have obviously upped sticks and gone." Anger replaced the sadness he felt earlier.

Half expecting his own house to be up for sale, Joe approached it somewhat gingerly ninety minutes later...To his relief there was no sign of an agent's board and the curtains were still up at the windows, unfortunately the garden had been neglected and was wildly overgrown. Unexpectedly, a strange sensation came over him when he fully realised he was back at the place where he had spent the greater part of his past life, and then a sudden apprehension at the prospect of meeting Marjorie once again.

His acute anxiety kept him at the gate for quite some time and as he stood and stared at the house it dawned on him that something was wrong – surely on such a dull and overcast day there would be some lights on. It was curiosity that compelled him to open the gate and walk along the drive towards the front door, but it was the cobwebs that confirmed this suspicions when he saw them sealing the door in its frame. Clearly, Marjorie was not living at the house and had not done so for many months, also, her imminent return seemed most unlikely.

Joe could not account for his wife's strange behaviour, nor could he (in all honesty) be really bothered about it. He was annoyed, however, because he could not show her just what she had done to him: and what he had become thanks to her selfish indifference. His intention to punish her may never be fulfilled since their paths were hardly likely to cross, therefore, he might as well turn her out of his mind and deny all knowledge of her; besides he could punish someone else if he had a mind to.

Before leaving his Spalding home for the second, and last, time, he gave some thought to spending Christmas Eve in his garden shed but with so many happy memories of the festive season – especially the firm's dances – to haunt him, he dismissed the idea. it would be better, he concluded, if he left Spalding immediately. It was not the place for him to be at Christmas.

Chapter 10

Joe spent the night of Christmas Eve at Cuckoo Bridge just a mile or so south west of Spalding and on Christmas Day he walked the road to Market Deeping. Believing the winter to be warmer in London than anywhere else in the country, he decided to return to the city and, providing he was not delayed in any way, expected to be on the Embankment by the first week in January. However, finding his way without the aid of a road map was bound to be erratic although his journey need not be one of great urgency since the winter, so far, was considered to be mild. He could have chosen a straightforward and direct route had he gone to Stamford and picked up the A1 arterial road to the south but, because he preferred the solitude of the countryside to the roar of traffic, he opted for the minor roads instead.

On Boxing Day he set off to cut across the north western corner of Cambridgeshire and passed through the villages of, Maxey, Southorpe, and Stibbingtan before resting up at Fotheringhay (Northants). He spent the night in a tumble-down cow shed where he cooked himself a meal with his rudimentary untensils and as soon as he had eaten he sat back to mull over his futile visit to Spalding.

The next morning, he allowed himself a rare privilege and slept in longer than usual, and when he did stir it was not to the conventional frosts of the previous days but to a warm southerly breeze. It created the kind of weather that fooled, the plants, the birds, and the small animals into early preparation for the spring even though it was ten weeks too soon. Joe welcomed the change in temperature and thought he would chance his luck in the fields to see if he could catch a rabbit.

There were rabbits a plenty but they were too agile for Joe and he could not catch them. After an hour he gave up the chase and paused to take his bearings. A church, with its ambient cemetery and all important weather vane, stood no more than a field away; just the thing to direct him south. But as he approached the churchyard he noticed a deep ditch which ran between it and the field he was in. Although it did not stop him from seeing the weather vane it did prevent him from entering the churchyard.

Whilst Joe looked down into the ditch and tried to gauge the depth of the muddy water contained therein, a girl, suffering from Down's syndrome, entered the churchyard from the opposite side.

The Lincolnshire Tramp

She had her hands thrust deep into the pockets of her unbuttoned coat which flapped rhythmically against the thighs of her baggy jeans as she marched jauntily past the church and on towards Joe not until the church was behind her did she actually catch sight of him and when she did a broad smile shattered he mongoloid features. "Hello!" she called cheerily.

Joe looked up and was about to admonish the girl in his usual abusive manner but when it occurred to him that it might be in his own best interests if he did not frighten her away, he smiled back and said, "Hello!"

Being in her eighteenth year, yet with the body of a fourteen year old and the mentality of a ten year old, the girl happily retained a childish innocence and knew no fear of any man, least of all a dishevelled tramp.

"I've come to help the Vicar," she called out again, "Have you seen him?"

"No," Joe shouted back and then he suggested, "why don't you come over here so we can talk while you wait for him?"

"Okay," agreed the girl and picked her way amongst the tombstones until she was within ten feet of him. "Are you going to help the Vicar too?" she asked politely.

"I'm going to help you," smirked Joe, "What's your name?"

"Tracee –" drawled the girl and then she giggled.

"Tracy – that's a pretty name," he stepped back half a pace to look her up and down, "And you are a very pretty girl."

Taking the compliments to be sincere, Tracy blushed slightly and admitted, "My Mum gave me that name. I was a very beautiful baby you know."

Joe quickly latched on to her last comment and used it to further his own intention. "Would you like to have a baby?" he asked.

"Don't be silly," Tracy chided, "I haven't got a husband yet."

"You don't need a husband," assured Joe, "I could do it for you."

Joe's lewd remarks left Tracy in a state of confusion simply because he did not know what he was talking about; in her world, babies were given to mummies and daddies when they went into hospital and definitely not found in churchyards. In a bid to cover up her confusion she sought to alter the course of the conversation and asked brightly, "Do you want to know what I had for Christmas?"

"Tell me – what did you have?"

"I'll show you." Removing her hands from her pockets, she took off her coat and laid it carefully over a convenient headstone than, tugging at the hem of her new sweater, she declared, "This – Isn't it just lovely?"

"Very nice – " agreed Joe. His approval lay not in a genuine appreciation for the sweater but for the young torso it entombed. "Give us a twirl," he demanded, "I want to see more."

In an ungainly manner, Tracy twirled herself about and, thinking herself elegant was proud to do so.

Joe looked on with interest, but it was not her performance that attracted him – it was the curves of her hips. Uncannily, he sensed other delights might be revealed to him if he continued to coerce the girl. "It is a lovely sweater," he agreed, "And what other presents did you get?"

Tracy completed a final turn and stopped. With one eye closed and the other looking skyward, she began to count on her podgy fingers. "I had –" she drawled, "some cassettes – a pair of slippers – some make-up – a new nightdress – some underwear – and another pair of jeans."

"I bet the underwear looked nice," commented Joe. "What was it – long knickers?"

"No –" Tracy giggled, "I had a bra and panties – only little girls wear knickers. I'm a big girl now." To emphasise her point she posed provocatively then she said, "I'm wearing my new bra now – can you see it?" She thrust out her chest.

Joe shook his head. "I can't see it at all," he confessed, "because you have your sweater on."

For the briefest of moments, Tracy looked perplexed and when the smile returned to her face she admitted, "Silly me – of course you can't see it."

Without further hesitation, she bent forward and peeled off her sweater which was then placed, with care, on top of her coat. Thus done, she stood up and with outstretched arms, gave Joe the fullest possible view of her new bra.

"I like it," he said, and with a cunning smile he added, "But don't you think you might here it on inside out?"

Slightly embarrassed, Tracy peered down at her undergarment and said – with some hesitancy – "I don't think so..."

"Better make sure." encouraged Joe. "Take it off and start again."

"All right," she agreed willingly and with accomplished dexterity she unclasped her bra from behind and let it slip from her shoulders. Totally unconcerned about her near nakedness, she examined the garment to ascertain whether, or not, she had been wearing it correctly.

"There's no need to put it back on just yet," insisted Joe, "You've got a beautiful body and you should show it off more." He stared hard at her plump, fleshy, body and although it did not fully justify

The Lincolnshire Tramp

his extravagant appraisal, it did offer some erotic enticements – especially her breasts. They were firm and well rounded, and (despite the weather being mild there was still enough chill in the air to excite them) the nipples stood erect.

Greatly flattered by Joe's remarks, Tracy readily flaunted her body, in fact, there was nothing she enjoyed more than divesting herself of her clothing. Hitherto, she had always been discouraged from going around naked and was told never to strip off in front of anyone but, much to her own surprise, she had no qualms about doing exactly that in front of Joe – indeed, she found it most exhilarating. For a while, she ran her hands over her own body and ended up by cupping her breasts, lifting them up and out together she announced, "These are, my puppies. See – they have little pink noses."

Wow – this is going better than expected, thought Joe as he ogled the girl, and I bet she's still a virgin – if she is, the silly cow doesn't know what she's in for. He smiled benignly at her, although the dirty yellow teeth glistening through the straggly hair of his moustache gave a different interpretation of his intentions. "In a minute I will kiss your puppies," he promised, "But first you must show me your new panties."

Tracy's eyes brightened up yet again, "Oh yes – I haven't shown you, have I?" She unzipped her jeans and pushed then down to her ankles, "They're the same colour as my bra but Mum thinks they're a bit skimpy..."

Succumbing to his own erotic emotions and no longer able to control his racing pulse, Joe, once again, ogled the girl and could not take his eyes away from her loins. Her panties, obviously of an amatorial design, were indeed skimpy and (contrarily) seemed to reveal what they were supposed to cover. "I dare you to take them down," he inveigled, steadfastly maintaining his gaze.

Tracy accepted the dare, after all, what had she got to lose, she was almost naked anyway. With a giggle, she lowered her panties and left them slightly above the jeans at her ankles. Then posing, as she had seen in magazines, with one hand on her hip and the other raised aloft, she asked, "Do you like to look at me without my clothes on?"

Disregarding the short stubby fingers perched on her hip and the layers of puppy fat on her thighs, Joe sighed deeply as he stared unremittingly at the fine pubic heirs curled around her protuberant vulva. He could not claim to having carnal knowledge of many women and, therefore, could not consider himself a good judge of female anatomy but he was sure he was looking at the most perfectly

The Lincolnshire Tramp

formed genital ever seen on a woman. Tormenting himself, he was torn between the two choices, either he remained passive to admire the more pleasing aspects of this awkward, young girl, or he got on with it and raped her.

"Well," insisted Tracy, "Do you like looking at at me or not?"

"You look gorgeous," admitted Joe, his choice had been made, "And I've got something for you."

"What –" Tracy became curious.

"You'll see," he said as he proceeded to unfasten his greatcoat and trousers. "This is what I've got for you." He pulled out his erect penis.

"Oooh!" giggled Tracy, "That's naughty!"

"Naughty but nice," corrected Joe, "And if you come over here I'll show you how nice it is,"

In that brief moment when Joe looked down into the ditch to find a way across and Tracy stood and wondered what it was about a tramp's penis that could be nice, all hell seemed to break loose. It came from the direction of the church and manifested itself in the form of flailing black cassock and stout boots churning up the gravel as it sped towards them. Furthermore, and shattering the relevant quiet of the morning, the wrath of God echoed through the graveyard as an angry priest voiced his objections.

"What in God's name is going on here?" He screamed as he picked his way between the graves to bear down on Tracy. "Cover yourself up child. Remember where you are."

Tracy became rooted to the spot, looking in terror towards the holy man who had come to protect her. Fear rendered her too helpless to dress herself.

"For goodness sake hurry up girl," roared the impatient priest but when Tracy remained stubborn and refused to budge he forcefully pulled her panties and jeans up to her waist. "I don't know what your mother's going to say about this nonsense," he threatened as he tugged the sweater over the girl's head and body; he deliberately avoided the bra which she continued to hold in her hand.

"That's it, you dirty old sod," shouted Joe, sarcastically, "Fondle her tits before you take her into the vestry and screw her." He was extremely angry and spoiling for a fight with the priest.

Picking up Tracy's coat, the priest turned and tried to pin Joe down with an icy stare "I would prefer it if you kept your opinions to yourself and took your filthy body away from here," he snorted,

Fire burned in Joe's eyes. "Don't you come that holier-than-thou crap with me, you pious bastard. You don't have any power over me. you can't tell me what to do." He had thought to embarrass the priest still further by urinating in the ditch, but since he had no urgent desire to pass water, he could do no more than tuck his deflated penis back into his trousers.

For the time being, the priest ignored Joe and, with trembling fingers, attended to Tracy. He draped her coat across her shoulders and turned her to face the church. "You run along inside, child," he ordered, "and I'll join you in a moment. Together we'll pray and ask the Lord for his forgiveness."

The bewildered girl burst into tears and ran off towards the church.

"Well done, Vicar," chided Joe, "You've certainly ballsed things up for that girl. From now on she'll never know if she's coming or going."

"Look here," snapped the priest, "I've just about had enough of your insolence. When you insult me you insult the Lord – just bear that in mind."

"Don't tell me you really believe in all that bloody rubbish," sneered Joe. "When it comes down to it you're no different from any other man. You grab what you can the same as the rest of us."

"I do not rape young girls which is exactly what you were trying to do before I put a stop to it. If I had my way you'd be stoned to death."

Joe, almost exploding with anger, whipped his knife from the pocket of his greatcoat and pointed it menacingly at the priest. "And if I get my way!" he roared, "I'll cut your bollocks off." Then, to add meaning to his threat, he began to descend the steep bank on his side of the ditch.

"We'll soon see about that," countered the priest. His response carried but little weight and served only as a face saver for he had not the stomach to face a knife wielding madmen. Within on instant, he turned, lifted the skirt of his cassock, and set off at full gallop to find sanctuary in the church.

By the time Joe had traversed the ditch and come up onto the churchyard, the priest was too far away to be harmed, however, it did not deter Joe from picking up an empty jam jar (used for flowers) and hurling it after the disappearing cleric. It fell short of its target and broke into several pieces.

Bitter, resentful and angry, Joe looked about for sear twigs and branches or other suitable kindling material. In his temper he had resolved to burn down the church with the priest in it and would have attempted to carry out his resolve had not a party of parishioners arrived. For whatever purpose they were there was of

The Lincolnshire Tramp

no concern to anyone except themselves, but it did put paid to Joe's evil intentions, moreover, it would only be a matter of minutes before they, went into the church, heard the priest's account, and came back out to see for themselves. Joe was not willing to be the subject of their curiosity, nor was he prepared to hang around to be caught and incarcerated, he valued his freedom too much for that. After a quick glance at the weather vane, he set off at a brisk pace to leave the church behind him.

He headed south and after half an hour of brisk walking he slowed to his usual dawdle. The briskness of his former gait reflected his state of mind for he continued to nurse a grievance against the priest and relentlessly plotted his downfall. The man should be made to suffer terrible injuries for having thwarted his attempt to rape. Such reasoning lacked logic for with every step Joe took so increased the distance between himself and the priest and they were hardly likely to encounter each other again; but then, logic no longer had any place in Joe's mind.

It was late in the afternoon when he entered the little, Northants, town of Oundle and by then his temper had subsided. The town itself was of no great size which soon became apparent to Joe when he passed through it in less than twenty minutes. Nonetheless, he thought the place had some potential and decided to hang around until morning. He could explore the streets under the cover of darkness and rummage through the dustbins without attracting too much attention. Until then, however, he deemed it prudent to lay low amongst some yew and holly in a quiet cul-de-sac.

As he waited (concealed by the evergreens) he could see into the nearby houses, especially where the rooms were well lit, and in all cases the rooms displayed the trappings of Christmas – the festive season was by no means over.

One house in particular caught his eye because of a sudden rush of activity. A car arrived and parked outside the front door, its engine and lights were switched off and a man got out. He opened up the boot of the car before he went into the house and when he came back out again he was carrying a large, cardboard, box. The box, loaded with presents and good things to eat and drink, was placed in the boot of the car together with some bulging carrier bags and other bits and pieces brought out by the woman of the house. The man went back in to usher out two adolescent children and whilst he helped them into the car, the woman went back into the house. Presently, all the lights went out except one and that stayed on even though the woman came back out and locked the door. As she got into the car, the man set off to make a final check on the estate and when he was sure that all was well he returned to the car, strapped himself in, started the engine, switched on the lights, and moved out of the drive.

Joe watched the car disappear out of the cul-de-sac. "Looks like they're off to a party," he muttered, "might give their dustbin the once over later tonight."

It was nine-o-clock in tbs evening and the night was very dark. Joe had completed his scavenging in the northern part of the town and was on his way to the south when he came upon a group of five teenage boys standing outside a public house. They were obviously not old enough to drink alcohol on the premises but it seemed that nothing prevented them from drinking it outside.

Each boy had a can of lager in his hand and two older boys also carried four packs. They were boys trying to be men as they drank the beer with immature panache between bouts of noisy chatter.

When Joe saw the full cans of lager in the four packs he developed a craving for one of them and it was the need for alcohol which compelled him to ask for it. He approached the boys directly and with a gruff voice he asked, "Do you think I could have one of them cans?" He knew he would be greeted by verbal abuse but he hoped the Christmas spirit night prevail and the boys would be charitable.

"Piss off, you old cunt," jeered one of the older boys

"Go and buy your own fuckin' beer," snapped the other.

"Surely you can spare one can," persisted Joe.

"Bugger off," piped up the youngest of the boys, "you make the place look untidy. "

"Yeah! And you stink," added another

They all started to laugh.

Anger flared and died in Joe's eyes as he contemplated and dismissed open confrontation with the boys; a battle over a measly can of lager was not worth the effort. "Keep your rotten beer, you greedy wankers," he growled as he turned away. "I hope you choke on it."

With an eye on Joe's receding back, the eldest of the boys drained the last dregs from his can and called out, "Hey! Mister – you wanted one of these cans didn't you," he hurled the empty can at Joe, "Then have this one. Ha!ha! ha!"

The can struck Joe on the shoulder and fell with a clatter to the road. He realized it was empty as soon as it hit him yet his immediate reaction was to bend down and pick it up but, just as his hand was within an inch of it, he checked himself. No, he thought, don't touch it now. It might come in useful later on. He stood up and marvelled at the latest idea to come into his head. "I've got them now, he chuckled as he hurried off into the darkness.

The teenagers kept up a barrage of abuse until Joe was out of sight then they forgot about him and resumed their usual pattern of drinking and chattering. They were to remain there for another fifteen minutes until, after some argument, agreeing to go off and look for girls. At that time they did not know that Joe had stealthily doubled back and had been watching them at a discreet distance. One after another, the boys tossed their empty cans into the street and, as a group, walked off to find another location.

When they were gone, Joe came out of hiding. He carried a little stick in one hand and a plastic bag in the other as he stepped lightly to the place where the can had struck him on the shoulder. Deftly, he poked the little stick through the aperture in the can and lifted it off the road and dropped it into the plastic bag. He went on to pick up the other discarded cans in the same manner, all the time taking care not to get his own finger prints on them.

With his haul of empty cans, he set off to find the vacated house in the cul-de-sac. "If the family is at a party," he surmised, "Then they probably won't be returning until about midnight. I should have enough time to do it if I can find the damn place." His concern was for the timing of the deed rather than finding the actual house, he could find that at any time during the night but he would never be able to set the clock back. It was essential to his scheme to commit a crime whilst the teenagers were on the streets.

As it happened, he found the house with comparative ease and managed to get into its grounds without being seen. Passing between the main building and the garage, he turned a corner and came to face the kitchen window and the back door. The door was solid and well locked and could easily resist any attempt to force it. Undaunted, he placed his plastic bag beside the door and then searched in the darkness for a heavy object with which to smash the kitchen window. A part of a broken paving slab taken from the patio served the purpose and was flung with great force through the first available pane.

Joe dived for cover as shards of glass crashed noisily into the kitchen. He concealed himself behind an oil tank which abutted the rear wall of the garage and remained motionless until all had settled down. He wanted to be sure that, no burglar alarm would be set off, no dog would start barking and no inquisitive neighbour would come to investigate. Barely breathing, be allowed ten minutes to pass before making his next move.

The Lincolnshire Tramp

Taking care not to leave fingerprints, he came out of hiding and climbed on a garden chair to examine the broken window. He could see that it was possible to put his hand through the shattered pane and open a larger casement, one big enough for him to clamber through. It was soon done and once inside the kitchen he went to the back door and unlocked it. He opened it just far enough to reach out and retrieve his plastic bag.

Aware that a light was left burning in the hall, it was not necessary for him to switch on any other light, especially when, in that well lit hall, he spotted what was needed – a pair of gloves and a torch. The gloves were laying on a hall table and were clearly not the owners best pair, nonethless, they would serve Joe well and he quickly slipped them on. The torch stood on the floor beside the table and despite its battered appearance it functioned quite well.

A sum of money, left on the table top to pay off a tradesman, caught Joe's interest and as he pocketed it. He fancied more could be had if he searched the house. With the torch to guide him, be ascended the staircase and made his way into the first of three bedrooms. It was a room typical of a girl entering her teens; it was untidy rather than dirty.

Joe flicked on the torch for a second to get his bearings but was horrified to notice the tight, pale pile of the carpet and his own footprints coming in through the door. This was totally unacceptable. His master plan would be doomed from the start if a set of his footprints were found. He hoped the girl possessed some thick, woollen stockings and began a search to find them. He was lucky, they were in a basket of soiled linen and although they were not as big as he would have liked be did manage to pull them on over his boots.

Cash gifts as well as the usual run of presents had been given to the children and, like the presents, the money had been left laying around – a temptation not ignored by avaricious fingers. Joe not only took the money from the girl's room but the boy's room as well. And in the main bedroom he discovered more cash, it was hidden in a wardrobe together with a jewellery box. He did not particularly want the jewellery, mainly gold necklaces, bracelets, brooches and earrings, because he had no means of disposing of it; at least, not to his advantage. But he could not afford to leave it behind; he was setting up a crime and burglary was part of it.

With the jewellery and cash safely stashed in a sound pocket, he backed his way down the staircase and brushed away any footprint he may have left. On returning to the hall, he gathered up his plastic bag and sought out the sitting room. Again, he used the torch to light his way. The room could not have suited him better, the furniture was just as he wanted it and there was a well stocked cocktail cabinet. He was delighted to see the cans of lager on the floor beside the cabinet; they still contained their contents and, more to the point, they were the same brand as the empty cans he had in his plastic bag.

A sense of satisfaction came over him as he placed the empty, yet much finger printed, lager cans beside five of the most comfortable seats in the room. When done, he revisited the cocktail cabinet and stowed the full cans into the plastic bag. He then helped himself to three bottles of spirits, two of fortified wine and as many bottles of beer as he could stuff in the plastic bag and his pockets. Before leaving the room, he messed it up to make it appear to have been visited by the five teenage boys who had offended him earlier, he kicked over a magazine rack, upended an ashtray, switched on the television set and smashed a glass in the fireplace. "That'll make it look as though the little buggers were here," he said to a nonplussed budgerigar who perched motionless in a festively decorated cage.

Thinking to avail himself of some food, Joe left the sitting room and passed through the hall on his way to the kitchen, but before he had taken too many steps he paused and turned to look at the telephone. "I could phone for the police," he mused, "and really stir things up." He retraced his steps and was about to pick up the receiver when caution urged restraint. He realized the call could be traced and that would lead the police straight to the scene of the crime; much too obvious, they would soon smell a rat. Better if he called them from a public phone box and then give them only part of the information, just enough to keep them interested. Then, when the householder returned and reported the break in, they would be primed.

Yet again, when in the kitchen, Joe had to restrain himself. It was in his mind to steal a whole lot of food (enough to keep him going for a week or two) but he had to forget the notion. An astute mind would quickly deduce that so much and so varied an amount of food could only have been taken by a vagrant. He had to console himself with some cold turkey, a piece of Christmas cake and a couple of apples. It grieved him to turn his back on such a well provisioned larder but vengeance was the greater priority He desperately wanted to see the teenage boys punished for the crime he had just perpetrated.

It was with malice and hatred in his heart that Joe carried his ill-gotten gains from the house and ventured out into the darkness once more. In fact it was so dark that nobody could have seen him come and go. Maybe that was just as well because if he had encountered another person at that time he may have been tempted to use a smashed beer bottle to cause injury. He was in a bitter mood for he recalled the events of the day and it did not please him. He should have had that mongoloid girl and abused her in every way possible, then again, he should have got hold of that priest and knocked every ounce of hypocrisy out of him.

At least he was doing something about the teenaged boys. They may have merely been rude to him but that was enough to merit the full force of his wrath. Now, as he headed towards a telephone box, he was going to cause them some degree of suffering. Using the emergency number to contact the police, he began to explain how he he'd seen the youths breaking into a house in Oundle. He did not know the address of the house but he was able to give good descriptions of the boys concerned. However, the telephone call did have its awkward moments when the police wanted to know more about the caller than the crime being reported. Joe adopted the air of an indignant resident and demanded to know what sort of service he was getting for the money taken from the burdensome taxes he was paying.

Thinking he had been wronged, Joe stormed out of the telephone box and headed for the country park spread out to the south of the town. "Damn fool police," he ranted, "Hope they recorded everything I told them." He hurried on into the park, pausing only to snatch the woollen stockings from his boots. He did not start drinking the beer until he was well into the reserve and had found a place to rest up for the night. After the first bottle he was curious to know how much money he had accumulated since robbing the blind man and his wife. The loose change was of no real importance and quickly slipped back into a convenient pocket. The real power came in the wad of banknotes which, when Joe counted it out by the light of the torch he still retained, totalled four hundred and sixty pounds. Although unwilling to show delight, he could not discount the air of satisfaction that swept over him. It was good to feel so much money again because it gave him a certain authority. A down and out with four hundred and sixty pounds in his pocket was, assuredly far superior to one who had less.

On balance, perhaps he had not done on badly out of the day after all. With his hoard of beer, wine and spirits, plus extra cash and a pair of gloves to keep his hands warm, he could count himself considerably wealthier than when it had dawned. What little wealth there was in the beer soon abated, he drank most of it before going to sleep.

In the morning, when he awoke, he found himself covered with a hoarfrost. A long pull on the brandy bottle (one of those taken from the house) was needed to take the chill out of his bones; a second was needed in place of a breakfast. After a yawn, he stood up, stretched and then relieved himself. It was daybreak but not an early hour; such being the way with winter in the northern hemisphere. Not that it bothered Joe that much, he was going to amble out of the park and follow the first road he came to.

As it happened, he stepped on to a road leading to the hamlet of Stoke Doyle and soon after he cursed everyone and everything as he narrowly avoided being run down by a police car. He cursed himself mainly for his lack of vigilance; he saw it as putting himself into the hands of the police. Keeping a wary eye on the disappearing car, lest it should stop and reverse back to accost him, he merged into the hedgerow and proceeded with more caution. As the minutes ticked by he grew more confident and began to think he had seen the last of the police car. Then, when he assumed it was safe to pass through Stoke Doyle, he saw it parked up beside a cluster of houses. Instantly alarmed, he took refuge again, this time behind a large tree.

Upon hearing raised voices he peered out from behind the tree and saw two policemen at the door of one of the houses, they were questioning a youth and his parents. "That's one of the little sods who gave me a hard time last night," muttered Joe as he recognized the youth. "The gang leader, no less." For a moment it looked as though the police were not going to arrest the youth and Joe would have to go over and convince them to do otherwise; a most foolhardy notion he was to realize on reflection.

The policemen had no intention of returning to their station without the youth and despite protests from him and his parents he was escorted to the car and driven off at a lively speed. Joe believed his cunning plan had worked and five boys would suffer days of questioning. A celebration was in order and the brandy bottle came into play. He raised a toast to himself and his exploits over and over again.

Chapter 11

In an inebriated state, Joe made his way from Stoke Doyle to Thrapston; much of it via the waterways and lakes in that district. The brandy had had a pleasing effect on the landscape as rough edges became blurred and shapes blended harmoniously into one another. Also, alcoholic torpor committed nothing to memory, therefore, he could not (if he so desired) recount the strangers he had been rude to even though he had told them how good the brandy was and how disgustingly offensive they were.

Unfortunately, alcohol has a nasty habit of kicking back as he knew all too well and by nightfall, when he discarded the empty bottle, he tried to sleep it off. He had collapsed beside a five barred gate which he had intended to climb to gain access to a field but, no matter how he positioned his body, he could not sleep. If he lay on his back then the heavens started to spin wildly and if he lay on his side, the ground did the same. Propping himself up on his elbows made no difference nor was there any respite when he sat himself bolt upright – it seemed nothing would stop the spinning in his head.

After a while, he got to his feet again and leaned against the gate but since he was incapable of standing up all night his only solution was to drape his arms over the structure and hang himself on it. With his head lolling over the gate, he fell asleep and remained there for many hours.

A throbbing head, a dry throat and stiff limbs greeted his waking moments and, without opening his eyes, he reached into his pocket for the second bottle of spirit. It was not necessary to read the label for he would drink anything that came to hand, besides, the first mouthful or so would have no taste whatever it was. In fact, the bottle contained gin but it was no less a lethal a potion than the brandy and, to Joe's relief, had an instantly numbing effect.

For the next three days, he – in an alcoholic stupor – drifted from place to place, unable to control his drinking habit. He spent one might at Hargrave and another at Knotting Green – that saw off the bottle of gin and a bottle of whisky. It was left to a bottle of sherry to accompany him on the third day and that saw him into the outskirts of Bedford.

As a result of his four day bender, he was completely exhausted when he staggered into a derelict factory building situated on the periphery of an industrial estate. And as he flopped to the ground he did not care if the building had been used by vagrants on a regular basis for the past six years. Further more, he had no desire to be reminded that it was New Year's Eve when all he wanted to do was sleep.

The new year dawned bleak and cold – much as it had done on the previous year but without the frost and snow. Not that it would concern Joe for some hours to come because he was in a deep slumber and dead to the world. So much so, in fact, that he did not stir when Bumble Drage entered the building and gave him a hefty prod.

Bumble had come to the place expecting to meet his friends, the Obday brothers, and was surprised to see Joe there instead. At first, he did not recognise him and thought (in the grey light of the morning) that he was one of the Obdays. Only when the sleeping bundle refused to respond to his prodding did Bumble realize his mistake. "Good God! It's old Joe." he said in his dignified voice.

Ever curious, Bumble tried to see what Joe had in his pockets but fell short of actually putting his hand inside them – he knew Joe would be at his throat with a knife if he awoke suddenly and found himself being molested. On the other hand, Joe's plastic bag could be searched without disturbing anyone. At some time Joe must have bought some provisions, for the bag contained half a dozen rashers of bacon in a sealed pack and a tin of beans. These, Bumble asserted, together with his own half loaf of bread would make a fine breakfast for himself and Joe, when the latter became conscious. In the meantime, he could get a fire going and warm the place up.

The sound of sizzling bacon and the warmth of a fire brought Joe blissfully from his sleep but the bliss was short lived when a thunderous headache threatened to burst his brain. Not really knowing where he was yet aware of someone else's presence, he sat up quickly and peered into the smoke. "Who's there?" he demanded

"Dear boy! – you recognise old Bumble – surely?"

"What are you doing here?"

"At the moment I'm cooking your breakfast, dear boy. I found the stuff in your bag."

"I don't want any bloody breakfast – anyway, who told you to touch my stuff?"

"Come, come, Joe – let's not be uncharitable."

"Balls!" Joe turned away so that he could fish the last of the bottles from the pocket of his greatcoat. The bottle, with some measures already gone, contained a vintage port and deserved to be treated as such and not gulped down like a cheap cough mixture.

"I wouldn't mind some of that," said Bumble

Joe glared at Bumble and tightened his grip on the bottle – why should he share his drink with the old queer? Nobody had asked him to come and cook breakfast so why should he be encouraged to stay. He was, as far as Joe was concerned, unwelcome company.

Bumble's round, feminine eyes pleaded with Joe and did so in such a manner as to transmit their desire without the need for spoken word. This disturbed Joe and forced him to change his mind because he could not bear to be looked at in that way; fair enough, on this occasion it was a desire for a mouthful of port but it could easily have been a desire for his body. Begrudgingly, he passed the bottle to Bumble.

"Thank you, dear boy," said Bumble and put the bottle to his lips. After he had swallowed his share, he wiped his mouth with the back of his hand and gave the bottle back. "God! That's whetted the appetite." he declared without specifying whether it was for drink or for breakfast.

Joe's hangover forbade him to eat a meal and promised much discomfort if he did but, after the first bite, discomfort came there none and he thoroughly enjoyed the food.

"Do you know, " said Bumble, smacking his lips, "you upset me when you went off without saying goodbye?"

"Too bad," retorted Joe, "But I'm not into polite conversation any more. Besides, I didn't like what you were doing."

Bumble chuckled and settled back against a wall to savour the memory. The fire that he had made was only a few feet away and burned merrily on the brick floor of the building. Draughty walls ensured combustion as well as assisting most of the smoke to rise and disperse through the numerous holes in the roof. Therefore, it was not difficult for Bumble to lean forward and pick up a burning twig to light his pipe. "Have you met the Obday brothers yet?" he asked, drawing smoke through the stem of the pipe.

Joe finished the drink he was taking from the bottle before he replied. "Never heard of them," he said. he passed the bottle to Bumble.

"Local lads," explained Bumble, "Down and outs like ourselves but not hoboes in the strictest sense of the word." he took a swig from the bottle. "They do have a home here in Bedford but they spend much of their time sleeping rough on the streets," he took another swig from the bottle. "I think what happens is – every time they go home someone finds them a job so they run away again." He took another swig.

"How many of them are there?" asked Joe reaching out to snatch his bottle away and secretly vowing never to let Bumble have it back.

"Three," Bumble replied, "Jack is the eldest and then comes Dick - they have the same father. The youngest is Robinson and he and Dick have the same mother. If you see what I mean."

"Clear as mud," mumbled Joe, "But it doesn't really matter because I don't want to meet them."

"Funny you should say that," observed Bumble, "This place is one of their favourite haunts."

"In that case" said Joe getting to his feet, "It's time I was an my way." He drained the last drop of port from the bottle and tossed it into an opposite corner. "I'm feeling much better now."

"Didn't know you were poorly" observed Bumble with concern. "And if you take my advice, you'd stay here for another night until you were absolutely fit again,"

"I'm fit enough," Joe said scornfully, "And I plan to be in London in a couple of days." Having made sure he had left none of his possessions behind he walked towards the door, but before he could make his farewells to Bumble, he was confronted by the tall, gaunt figure of Jack Obday.

Jack, on his way into the building, blocked the door and spoke to Joe. "I wouldn't go out there if I was you, brother," he said, "It's started to snow and will be ten foot thick by nightfall." He stepped aside to allow Joe a chance to look out.

The snow was falling steadily and had already started to settle on the ground, beyond the tumbling flakes a leaden sky menacingly closed in and forewarned of snow yet to come.

As Joe watched it fall, some uncertainty crept into his thoughts. He wanted to leave and be on his way but, being mindful of a previous experience when he got caught up in a blizzard, he held back. On the other hand, when he heard Bumble greet Jack (to explain Joe's presence), he did not want to stay; he was far from feeling sociable.

Whilst Joe pondered over his present predicament, two more figures came out of the snow. They were trying to drag an overloaded perambulator towards the building and were having problems keeping the load in place. Dick and Robinson had found some old furniture dumped in a skip and when they told Jack about it he ordered them to deliver it to the old building; not, himself, volunteering to lend a hand.

The Lincolnshire Tramp

When the perambulator finally came to a rest outside the door, Robinson came up to Joe and complained, "Jack ought to be helping with this, you know." Although they had never met before, the Obday brothers (to a man) approached Joe as if he was an acquaintance of long standing and spoke to him with familiarity.

"Come on, Robinson," shouted Dick, "Give us a hand."

In that moment of brief conversation, Joe knew who each brother was and, not that it was forthcoming, any formal introduction became unnecessary. This did not alter his views about companionship and it remained his desire to be on his own. However, he could not leave the building because his way was barred by the furniture coming in and an apprehension of snow clogging the highways.

With a sigh of resignation, he returned to the corner he had occupied earlier and sat down. From then on he was content to sit and observe the antics of Bumble and the Obday brothers as they acted out some frantic charade.

Jack adopted a dominant role and took command of the situation in spite of the fact that his judgements were basically unsound and his instructions wars often ignored by the others. He strutted about the building and made great play with his arms to emphasise a point or an idea. "Fires should always be ten foot from any wall, brother," he said to Bumble more often than not.

Bringing in the furniture and arranging it around the fire was left solely to Dick and Robinson. It consisted of two armchairs, a settee, and a standard lamp. The armchairs and the settee were well worn but still had a useful purpose whereas the standard lamp was of no use at all and was only brought along because Dick had taken a liking to it.

As they worked, the two brothers displayed contrasting temperaments. Robinson was the youngest and had inherited his mother's habit of continually complaining. He rarely smiled and he lacked a sense of humour. He did have one thing in common with his brothers – all three were mentally retarded to some degree.

Dick was less volatile than Jack and more light hearted then Robinson. He was plump and had a nervous laugh yet he found something amusing in almost everything that went on around him. He had formed a close relationship with his grandmother and was prone to quoting many of her venerable sayings.

Arranging three pieces of furniture presented the brothers with, seemingly, endless problems. At first it was too close to the fire and then, when it was moved, it was too far away. One piece had to be moved because it was in a draught and another because it was in

The Lincolnshire Tramp

the smoke. Dick was unhappy because his standard lamp had been placed between the armchairs when he wanted it between an armchair and the settee. Robinson obligingly moved it but not without complaint.

When all appeared to be settled and Jack was designated an armchair he observed, "You shouldn't have a chair that backs on to a north wall, it's bad for the lumbago." Of course, he had no idea which of the walls actually faced the north.

Dick did not know either as he bent forward to move the chair and so set the whole process of rotating seats in motion once again. "Went all the way to Braughing to do a day's thrashin'. Got nothin' – that's somethin'," he chanted as he humped the furniture around.

From his corner of the building, Joe watched the proceedings with mild amusement and likened it to a small boy's train set, on a larger scale, as the pieces were shunted around and around the fire. Quite often, Bumble added to the confusion in his efforts to stoke the ingle in their midst until eventually he was forced to ask, "How much longer are you going to be with these damned armchairs ?' There was more than a hint of irritation in his voice. "You've been at it all afternoon ."

"Nearly done now, brother," assured Jack as he supervised the final arrangement.

"I don't know what you're moaning for," bleated Robinson "I'm the one doing all the really hard work 'round here." He paused from his labours to wipe, nonexistent sweat from his brow and whilst he was thus engaged, Jack sat himself down in one armchair and Dick sat in the other. "Hey! That's not fair. I should have one of them armchairs as well as Jack. Come on, Dick, get out of it."

"Are you talking to me or chewing a brick?" Dick was defiant and settled deeper into his chair.

"What about the rest of the stuff?" asked Jack, "What about it?" Robinson snapped back.

"You haven't brought it in, brother – that's what."

Sulkily, Robinson went towards the door. "Why does it have to me?" he moaned,

"Because you're the driver," Dick reminded him.

When the Obdays first came across the old perambulator they were delighted with it and quickly adopted it as their transport, and as every vehicle needs a driver, Robinson was appointed to the task.

Because it had been left out for so long, a layer of snow had settled on the perambulator, putting its remaining contents at risk. Robinson grumbled incessantly as he dragged the whole lot into the building. He was about to brush away the snow when Bumble interrupted him. "Hang on a minute." he called, "Did you bring any water with you?" He was banking on the Obdays to bring some food with them and if they had, water may well be needed in the cooking of it.

"No" said Robinson, "We ain't got no water."

"Have you brought your big billy can?"

"Yes," He reached into the pram and pulled the battered billy from the snow, he offered it to Bumble.

"Good – now fill it with snow."

"But that's to cook our dinner in," protested Robinson.

The manipulative Bumble sensed his supper was in the offing and began to scoop handfulls of snow from the pram into the billy can. "And what are you going to have for your dinner?" he asked.

"Stew. " said Robinson. "We've got some bones, and some carrots, and some chips."

"In that case, we'll certainly want some water," said Bumble as he set the billy down beside the fire. "We'll melt this lot first."

"Have you got something to put in our stew – Bumble?" asked Robinson anxiously.

"Oh! I don't need to put anything in," observed Bumble dryly. "I'm doing the cooking – that's my share."

"What about 'im over there?" Robinson nodded towards Joe, "Is he going to put anything in?"

"You mean Joe – " said Bumble, "We had his food this morning so I don't think he's got any left." He cast an inquisitive glance at Joe.

"I have no food at all," confessed Joe, "but I do have a little money if you want to buy some."

Jack, becoming bored with the petty conversation, leapt to his feet and rushed over to the perambulator. "Joe can have some of our stew if he likes and he doesn't have to put anything in." With frantic, arm movements he tugged three carrier bags out of the pram and tossed them onto the settee. "Here you are, brother, make us a stew out of this lot."

Bumble examined the bags and was not surprised to discover that they contained nothing more than waste scraps of food given to the Obdays by various tradesmen in the town. The bag from a butcher revealed mainly bones for a dog to chew on but there were a few odds and ends of meat amongst them. "All for the pot," announced Bumble as he tipped the entire contents of the bag into the billy.

The Lincolnshire Tramp

The greengrocer had been a little more generous with his contribution for he had included some apples with the seedy potatoes, wrinkle-skinned carrots, mouldy Brussels sprouts, and scar encrusted swede. These were to be added to the stew as, and when, Bumble deemed it necessary.

The third bag was something of a curiosity because it contained a quantity of cold chips. As it transpired, they were given to Dick when he begged outside a fish and chip shop at closing time. Subsequently, he thought they would make a tasty addition to the stew. Bumble agreed.

Late in the day, they all sat around the fire and watched the stew simmering. Joe had been given the use of one of the armchairs whilst Bumble, Jack, and Dick sat on the settee. The other armchair was occupied by Robinson who had been offered it as a bribe for taking Joe's loose change into town to buy some extra ingredients for the stew.

Joe could have surrendered more of his ill-gotten money and bought sufficient alcohol for all, but his new found meanness would never countenance such a generous gesture. He kept his wad of notes well out of sight.

The main topic of conversation between Bumble and the Obdays centred on a plan to steal a keg of beer from a brewers warehouse. Much talk flowed back and forth across the fire but little, if any, substance was added to the basic plan.

"I can tell you this, brother," declared Jack, "It will have to be done with military precision."

"I know what you mean," said Dick, "Like this – the Beds. and Herts. are a dirty lot. Lost their colours at Aldershot. Then they won them back again. In a battle on Salisbury Plain."

"What's the use of that?" said Robinson, rounding an Dick, but before his half-brother could respond a commotion outside the door attracted his, and everyone else's, attention.

Presently the door burst open and Lizzie Tish entered, she brought with her a variety of canvas bags. She was a short, stout woman of no discernable age (years of vagrancy and alcohol abuse had etched senility into her features) and she spoke with a cockney accent. "'Allo luvs" she called, "Guessed you'd be 'ere."

"It's Lizzie Tish," chorused Robinson and Dick.

"Hello Lizzie," said Bumble in his matter-of-fact way.

Lizzie set down her bags inside the building then she closed the door and brushed the snow from the outer of her many layers of old clothing. "Bleedin' snow," she wheezed, "Gets on yer bleedin' wick."

"Come and have a warm by the fire," invited Bumble.

Rubbing her hands in a bid to drive out the cold, Lizzie crossed over to the fire and stood by it. "Something smells good," she said sniffing the air. "What yer cookin'?"

"A nice stew." announced Dick proudly.

"You can have some if you want," offered Jack. "be ready soon."

"It's ready now," said Bumble stirring the stew with a stick, "So if you've got your begging bowls I'll dish it up." He used his mug to ladle the steaming brew into various receptacles.

Lizzie went back to her canvas bags to get a dish and a bottle of cider "We'll have this with our supper, lads." she said, holding the bottle aloft.

As the supper progressed, Lizzie swapped yarns with Bumble and the Obdays; Robinson gave up his seat to her and sat on the arm of the settee to be in the circle as the cider bottle passed from hand to hand. Indeed, he came in useful when more cider was called for, it was he who went to her canvas bag to fetch more bottles.

Joe did not move out of his armchair nor did he express a word of gratitude for the hospitality he had been shown. He greedily consumed the stew and drank the cider but made no great effort to join in the run of conversation. For the most part, he was content to sit and look about the building which might well have been designed to suit the needs of a vagrant. It was outside yet inside, in a manner of speaking, for the barn of a place offered limited protection against the elements. Fortunately the windows had been constructed high in the walls, therefore, the wind and snow blowing through their shattered pains went above the heads of the visitors and either dissipated in the roof space or out through other openings.

When there came a lull in the conversation, Lizzie stood up and stripped off some of her clothing. "Well – who's going to shaft me?" she asked boldly.

Bumble alone broke the stunned silence that followed and said, "Surely you don't expect me to offer, Dearie. Frankly, you're not my type."

"I'm not proud, Luvvie," said Lizzie,"But I am bleedin' randy, so one of you bastards had better come an' poke me." To add emphasis to her desires, and encouragement to a potential lover, she lifted her skirts and displayed her wares. The thick, woollen stockings, tied with binder twine above the knee, and the absence of underwear, knickers or otherwise, did nothing for aesthetic values but the sight of a vagina matted with hair might well instill animal lust in some other loin. "Come on then – who wants this?" she said, placing her hands on her thighs in order to force her vagina forward.

Joe looked at her disdainfully. Sex thrust at him on a plate, as it were, was not at all acceptable. It did not present him with enough incentive to be malicious, and intercourse, on her terms, was intended to be a pleasurable experience for both parties. From his point of view, any pleasure from the union was to be his alone whilst she must suffer everlasting humiliation as was his intention when he tried to rape the young mother and the mongoloid girl. Although he craved for sexual satisfaction on those occasions, the same passion could not be roused in him now, unless he could be brutal and abusive to Lizzie. No doubt a woman of her background was no stranger to abuse and if he tried any form of brutality, he would most certainly be at the mercy of Bumble and the Obdays.

"Well?" said Lizzie, glaring at Joe, "Are you going to fuck me – or not?"

"Definitely not," replied Joe as he looked away.

"Isn't there a bloody man in this place?" Lizzie called out furiously. "A real one I mean."

"I'm a real man." declared Robinson. He stood up in front of Lizzie and stuck out his chest,.

"It's your willy you want to stick out, son, not your chest," said Lizzie.

Apart from encouraging him the remark offended him, and he reacted accordingly. "You don't half stink," he said, And you're ugly."

"You don't look at the mantelpiece when you're stoking the fire," Dick chipped in.

"What d'you know about it," chided Lizzie, "you've never had a hard in your life." Her anger for Robinson was vented on Dick.

"Steady on old girl," said Bumble jumping to Dick's defence. "You won't get a lay that way."

"Don't worry, brother," drawled Jack getting to his feet, "I know what to do." He took Lizzie gently by the arm and steered her away from the group. "This way, gal," he said.

They had gone no more than four paces when Lizzie broke away saying, "'Ang on a minute, Luv, If I'm going to lay on the bloody floor I might as well do it in comfort." She returned once more to her luggage and after a moment or two she found what she wanted – her sleeping bag. "Right," she said, "Let's go and make whoopee!"

As she and Jack disappeared into the smokey gloom to find a suitably clear area at the far end of the building, Bumble put his hand on Dick's knee. "Don't be too upset," he said sympathetically, "Having sex with a woman isn't all it's cracked up to be." He assumed that Dick had been put out by Lizzie's unkind words.

Nothing was further from the truth for Dick had taken it as a compliment and was feeling pleased about it. So much so that he thought a riddle was in order. "If a chap takes a bath with a soul full of hope, what does he come out with?" he asked, but before anyone else could answer, he blurted out, "A hole full of soap — ha, ha, ha!"

Bumble thought the riddle was amusing and put his arm around Dick to give him a cuddle. "You're talking about my favourite part of the anatomy, dear boy," he purred.

Dick may have been blissfully ignorant of Bumble's intentions but Joe knew better. Any minute now, he thought, that stupid sod will get more than just a cuddle from Bumble. It's enough to make you want to puke.

Robinson sat down in the armchair vacated by Lizzie and – crashing in on Joe's thoughts – asked loudly, "Is there any cider left?" he pointed to the bottles on the floor beside Joe.

"Is that a request or an order?" Joe said curtly as he looked for the bottle that still had some cider in it. And when he found the right bottle he did not pass it directly to Robinson but drank from it instead.

"That's not fair," moaned Robinson, "I asked for it first."

"Don't worry, dear boy," said Bumble, "I'm sure Joe will hand it to you shortly."

Only when I'm good and ready, thought Joe as he allowed the fermented apple juice to trickle down his throat. It was a particularly strong brew and could not be taken in excessive measures, therefore, he was soon obliged to stop drinking and pass the bottle over.

"About bloody time," said Robinson snatching the bottle and putting it to his lips, but before upending it to take a swig he added, "There isn't much in here. 'That greedy sod must have drunk it all,"He threw his head back to drink from the upturned bottle.

Whether it was the effect of the cider making him morose or whether it was because Jack and Lizzie were fornicating and their love making disturbed him, or perhaps it was the thought of Bumble making ready to bugger Dick, or simply the whinging and whining of Robinson, Joe did not know – but something caused him to snap. In a fit of temper, he picked up the nearest bottle and hurled it violently at Robinson. "That'll stop your bloody moaning!" he shouted.

The bottle, flying through the air, caught Robinson high on the head before it rebounded and knocked the other bottle from his mouth. The sudden action had caught him off guard and, inherent of shock, he found his speech to be drastically impaired. A strangled scream was as much as he could manage.

Blood poured from the many wounds to his head, face and mouth, and when he could see it running down his clothing he went dizzy and passed out. He could not stand the sight of blood.

Stricken with panic, Dick leapt to his feet and shouted, "Joe's killed Robinson. Killed him dead."

Joe also leapt to his feet and grabbed another bottle, this time by its neck. He was not sure of Dick's intentions, or, indeed, that of the others, so he thought it advisable to arm himself in case he was set upon. Fearing reprisal, he stood his ground and braced himself for battle, his eyes were round and wild, and his face was red with anger. Above all, he was furious with the lot of them for the way they had created such a congenial atmosphere. He was annoyed with himself, for he had almost succumbed to their easy going life style. This was living the easy way, it was all about getting the best out of life; even for down and outs.

Bumble, completely ignoring Joe, went to see what he could do for the unconscious Robinson. He was soon joined by Lizzie who, upon hearing the commotion, had interrupted her love making to see what all the fuss was about. Between them they made every effort to staunch the flow of blood coming from the various wounds.

Jack, fastening his trousers, came into the firelight to see what was happening. After some consideration he said, "If Robinson is dead then someone is going to swing for it."

"Yeah!'" added Dick, "And I know who that someone is. Joe' going to be 'ad up for murder."

"He should have come round by now," said Bumble as he loosened the clothing around Robinson's neck. "Must be more serious then I thought."

"We got to get 'im to bleedin' hospital" insisted Lizzie. She cast a glance towards the pram. "Does anyone know where the hospital is?" Her appeal was directed at Jack

Lizzie's good counsel struck a chord with Jack and he instantly assumed responsibilty for it. "Get the ambulance ready!" he ordered with an emphatic wave of his arm.

Dick giggled light-heartedly as he went to the perambulator and tipped out what was left of its former content, the prospect of pushing the makeshift ambulance to the local hospital appealed to his sense of fun and, more importantly, it dispelled the fears and anxieties he held for his younger half brother.

When all was ready, Robinson was lifted carefully into the perambulator and made as comfortable as possible. Dick, appointing himself to be the official ambulance driver, wheeled the pram out of the building. He was followed by Jack and Lizzie (she having first instructed Bumble to take care of her belongings whilst she was away).

When they were gone and the place quietened down again, Bumble turned to Joe and said, "Why did you have to do that?"

Joe, still standing, put down the bottle he held and replied, "Because he was getting on my nerves, in fact, you all were. You were turning the place into a bloody brothel."

"You've spoilt the evening with that nasty temper of yours. I'm disgusted with you," Bumble looked about for more wood to burn. "I just hope that boy is going to be all right, that's all."

"The trouble with you and the rest of them," Joe snapped, "Is, you're all so bloody selfish. You only think of your own pleasures."

Bumble came face to face with Joe and said, "If ever we meet again I hope it will be under different circumstances and you've adopted a more amenable disposition." He turned his back on Joe and bent down to tend the fire.

His remarks and subsequent action left Joe in no doubt as to what was intended, therefore, he had no other alternative but to leave the building. He tightened his greatcoat around his body and headed for the door. Once again there were no farewells.

Chapter 12

The snow had stopped falling when Joe stepped out into the wintry night. The clouds had rolled away and left in their wake an inky sky littered with millions of tiny, bright stars. It seemed less dark outside the building than it did inside for the expanse of white snow reflected every glimmer of light and gave an uncanny luminosity to the area. In the distance, a warmer glow softened the skyline as the lights of Bedford tried vainly to brighten the subfusc heavens,

The wheel marks and footprints left in the snow by Lizzie and the Obday brothers caused Joe some concern. He cursed them for being there but, nevertheless, he was obliged to follow them until he was clear of the industrial estate. Then, at a road junction, the tracks veered to the left and were clearly heading for the commercial part of the town. Joe, wanting nothing more to do with the tracks, or – more to the point – the particular vagrants they embodied, perversely turned to the right and – effectively, his back on Bedford.

The road that he followed had been traversed by more than one vehicle therefore it was possible to walk on compacted snow without too much difficulty; so different from the previous winter when he struggled through heavy drifting and suffered from exhaustion. Besides, he was more physically (and mentally) aware of survival now than he was then and he had the confidence to face the elements no matter what. However, part of that awareness was knowing how long he could last in the freezing conditions without the prospect of food and shelter. Like the birds and small mammals he knew such essentials to life would be hard to come by in midwinter – especially in the countryside.

The fall of snow and the sudden drop in temperature had changed his attitude concerning the proposed journey to London, it became imperative to get there with all possible haste and not drag his heels as he had done at the start of the winter. The thought of hot soup (hand-outs by charitable organisations) spurred him on as he sought to find a major road southbound.

He walked the quiet roads for about fifteen minutes before he became aware of traffic moving freely along the A421 some way ahead and as he neared the flow of speeding vehicles he could see how clear the highways were; much credit to the local authority who had worked diligently even though it was throughout the remaining hours of a bank holiday. This was the road for Joe and he was sure he could make good progress as soon as he got on to it.

The hours seemed to slip away as he marched along the A421. The crisp air cleared his head and released him from the stuffy remnants of his last hangover whilst the meals he had eaten (albeit prepared by Bumble) fortified him against the cold. And as he marched, it puzzled him as to why he should want to walk all through the night and do so without a pause for a rest. Was it really because Bumble's activities had disturbed his yet again?

Resolutely, he followed the main road until he became lost in the deserted streets of Bletchley (Buckinghamshire). It was three-o-clock in the morning and he was confused because he could not place the town within the limits of his geographic knowledge. It was not one of the towns north of London, he was sure of that, nor could it be one in the east. It could mean only one thing – he had been making his way to the west instead of the south.

He had, in fact, passed two major routes (the M1 and the A5) which would have put him on course for London had he paid heed to the numerous road signs on sentry-go at the appropriate junctions with the A421.

Disgruntled and extremely annoyed with himself, he decided to go no further. A tiredness, no doubt brought on by the disappointment of finding himself in the wrong place, came over him and he sought somewhere to sleep. But, no matter where he looked or in whatever part of the town he searched, he could not find a place to lay himself down, not even for the briefest of naps. There was not a door, or yard gate, or deserted building open to him, nor was there any, alley, alcove, park bench, or overhanging structure free from the cold, damp snow. It seemed that the whole town was locked and bolted against him and that nothing was left available to afford him the slightest succour. Did the town know of his pending arrival he was to wonder as he searched in vain for a resting place.

With the arrival of the dawn, Joe was beginning to regret walking out on Bumble and the Obdays, at least he would have had shelter and a nights' sleep if he had stayed; such was the price he paid for spoiling their evening although it was little comfort to him now.

Fresh snow started to fall as the people of Bletchley stirred from their slumbers and brought the town back to life; not that is was any consolation to Joe – food and shelter for a vagrant was the last thing on the minds of the scurrying figures. Nevertheless, he hung around the town for a few hours in the hope of finding something

The Lincolnshire Tramp

to eat but when he found there was nothing to be had (he was detemined not to pay for food) he moved on.

Wandering through the outskirts of the town, he passed a steep bank where some children were playing in the snow. They were building snowmen, having snowball fights, sliding on slides and tobogganing. Their excited shouts echoed around the housing estate that nestled beyond the bank and their exuberance for the snow was insurmountable. They were having fun.

Joe, passing the bank at its lowest level, tried to ignore the children although he was irritated by the noise they made and, in all probability, he would have continued to ignore them had he not have been bowled over by a small boy on a runaway toboggan. Joe did not see the little sledge as it hurtled down the slippery bank and crashed into his ankles, he only became aware of it when he lost his footing and tumbled over in the snow. In a furious rage, he sat up and glared at the small boy who, having parted company with his snow vehicle, lay spread-eagled on the ground and stared back at him.

"You little bastard!" shouted Joe, "Can't you look where you're going?"

"Sorry mister," spluttered the small boy, "I couldn't help it."

"I'll give you sorry," sneered Joe as he scrambled to his feet. "I'll give you bloody sorry..." Using both hands, he picked up the little, wooden sledge and carried it aloft to a nearby fence post (an isolated stock no longer performing its original function). Then, with all the force he could muster, he brought the sledge down to smash it on the top of the post. The child's toy sprang apart and pieces flew in all directions. It would no longer operate as a toboggan – Joe made sure of that.

The small boy, now on his feet, burst into tears. He was both frightened by Joe's wild temper and upset over the loss of the cherished toboggan.

"It serves you right," snapped Joe, "Perhaps you'll be more careful next time."

Screaming for his mother, the boy turned and began to scramble back up the bank. He ran straight into the arms of the other children who had come down to remonstrate with Joe. They had witnessed the entire incident and were not happy to have their simple pleasures marred by the actions of a selfish tramp. "Why did you have to break his sledge, mister?" asked one girl. "'is dad will murder you when he come home from work," warned another.

"I'll murder the lot of you if you don't clear off," said Joe as he picked up the biggest piece of the broken toy and threatened to use it as a club. "I'll warn you now, I'll break the skull of the first one I catch." He lunged forward and growled.

The children fell silent and backed away, they were wary of the cudgel in a madman's hands. Then, since none of them wanted to be the first to get a broken head, they peeled away and clambered back up the bank.

Joe made a token gesture to pursue them but he knew he did not have the legs to make the climb, the long walk had rendered them too tired. Instead, he repeated his threat and did so with a voice that was sure to instil everlasting fear into the children. Not that they needed the second reminder – they were already frightened enough.

When the last of them disappeared over the ridge and went out of sight, Joe felt satisfied. He could now continue his wanderings without being bothered by immediate reprisal; of course he must expect some angry parents to come after him but he would deal with them as and when the need arose. In the meantime he could return to his former preoccupation – seeking something to eat and a place to rest.

Without waiting to consider his next destination he set off to follow the road ahead of him and, as he trudgd through the snow, he concerned himself with what might be around the next corner – surely something to his advantage. It was this hope alone that kept his tired body going and not the prospect of another involvement in another town.

Ninety more minutes into the day and the weather changed – a steady thaw set in. Very soon, the snow on the roads turned to slush and tiny rivulets started to flow along the roadside verges. Joe welcomed the change and stepped livelier as he made his way to Winslow.

It was about noon when he arrived in the centre of the rural town. The smell of cooked food from the coffee bars and small restaurants heightened his hunger but of course he would not be allowed to enter them to sate his appetite. Already he had been frowned upon by the people he had passed in the streets; they would rather see him run out of town than be seen eating in any of their refreshment rooms. Nevertheless, he was sure that he would get some hot food in due course, he had a feeling about it,

Whilst probing a side street in order to find a service area behind a cafe (where he would risk begging for food or searching dustbins) his attention was drawn to a young man who stood alone on the steps of a little-used chapel. Joe looked hard at the young man and soon likened him to Adonis for he was strikingly handsome with blue eyes, blond hair, and athletic body. But this Adonis was not a happy one, the look on his face portrayed a person most wretched; perhaps an Aphrodite somewhere had spurned his love.

Joe was puzzled by the young man's attitude and his attire. His attitude suggested that he was a down and out without visible means of support yet his clothing was quite clean and unsoiled considering the nights he must have spent sleeping rough. Furthermore, his clothing was hardly adequate for the ravages of winter, the long, grey overcoat that he wore over his shirt and jeans was made out of a lightweight material not designed to keep out extremes of cold. Worst still, he wore nothing on his feet and he stood barefoot in the melting snow. Almost suicidal, Joe thought.

In his hand, the young man held a green tomato. It had obviously fallen to the ground at some time because it had a lot of grit embedded in its flesh. With his free hand he carefully picked out each small spec of grit and cast it aside. His slender fingers worked slowly and monotonously as he made a great show of cleaning the tomato in readiness to eat.

So engrossed was he, in his pathetic little task, that he pretended not to notice Joe (who stood across the way and stared at him) or the two women who hurried along the street towards him. It was as if he wanted to turn his back on the world but he did not want the world to turn its back on him.

The young man may not have shown interest in the women but Joe did, he was particularly interested in the items they held out in front of them. Each one carried a plastic beaker which was capped and contained hot, liquid refreshment, they also brought ham sandwiches wrapped in cellophane and some fruit cakes in a paper bag. Joe quickly deduced that the women had seen the young man earlier and had taken pity on him. Most likely he was picking at the same tomato when they saw him so they decided to fetch him some food.

They stopped in front of the young man and offered him their gifts but he refused to take them. "Come on," urged the woman nearest to him, "take the food, It'll do you good."

The young man turned away from the woman and made it clear that he wanted nothing to do with them.

"Drink it while it's hot," encouraged the second woman as she tried to thrust her plastic beaker into his hands, an action which prompted him to complete his turn and face the other way.

"I don't think he'll take it if we stay here," observed the first woman.

"Better leave it somewhere for him."

You could be right," said the second woman. "Should we leave it on the steps?"

"Yes – a good place."

Without further delay, the women placed the food and drink on the stone steps beside the young man and hurried away. They were pleased with themselves for their good deed and if the young man took the food – they were certain that he would – then their money would have been well spent.

As soon as the women could no longer be seen in the street, Joe called out to the young man. "Hey – Adonis! Are you you going to eat that food or not?" He waited for a reply but when none came he repeated his question, "I said, are you going to eat that food? Be a pity to waste it."

The response from the young man was nothing more than a reproachful glance over his shoulder at Joe. He had not spoken to anyone for many hours and he had no intention of doing so for many more. Joe meant nothing to him so why should he bother to strike up a conversation by answering a question.

"You must have one hell of a chip on your shoulder," said Joe as he crossed the street to where the young man was standing. "But whatever it is, it's not worth starving for." He bent down to pick up one of the plastic beakers and deftly flicked the lid off. "It looks like tomato soup," he announced, "I can't allow this to be wasted." He greedily drank the soup and did not pause until he had consumed the lot. "That went down well," he said, "But it's not that hot, You'd be best advised to drink the other one before it gets any colder."

The advice was wasted on the young man because he felt he could only function properly if left to his own solitude. He might well have taken the food had not Joe been there, but he was, therefore, it was not possible to even contemplate accepting the meal. In the meantime, the miserable, green tomato would have to suffice.

"You got to be an idiot to turn this down," remarked Joe as he picked up the sandwiches and unwrapped them. "Never look a gift horse in the mouth no matter how sorry you are feeling for yourself." He took a bite out of the first sandwich.

Much to Joe's astonishment, the young man burst into tears and began to sob uncontrollably. Then, just as suddenly, he threw away his green tomato and started to run off along the street, his bare feet squelching in the melting snow.

"Go on then – you namby-pamby," roared Joe, "Run away from it if you can." He watched the distraught young man until he had gone from view. "Bloody touchy, that one. Must have given his mother a hard time when he was small. Don't know what's wrong with the youngsters these days, turn on the waterworks at the slightest provocation." He was mindful of the small boy he had upset earlier as well as the young man; the boy's anguish he could understand but the sobbing of the young man was unfathomable, not that it really mattered because he had not the slightest sympathy for either of them.

Joe stayed in the street just long enough to eat the sandwiches and drink the coffee (the content of the other plastic beaker) before he set off for Bicester. He was grateful for the food, although not to anyone in particular for providing it, and he saved the fruit cakes for a later feast.

He gave some thought to staying in Winslow for a few days but, percievably, the town was not big enough to support a hungry and troublesome tramp. Bicester, he presumed, would be more to his liking. Desperate for sleep, yet not willing to succumb to it, he started his next trek.

Had Joe been familiar with the area he would have known that the only direct route fron Winslow to Bicester was by rail and not by road. The roads that existed enlaced the open countryside as they bent out of their way to engulf the villages from the Claydons to Twyford, Poundon, and Launton; not a direct route by any stretch of the imagination.

Half an hour into the trek and persistent rain started to fall, it may well have washed the last of the snow from the roads but it did make walking extremely uncomfortable. Joe cursed his luck and then he saw an enclosed bus-shelter in the near distance. He hurried forward to it and was pleased to step inside and out of the rain. Better still, it had a wide, wooden bench so he was able to sit down and (for the first time in many long hours) rest his weary legs. It felt good to be in the dry and relaxing, so much so that it was not long before he stretched himself out along the bench and fell fast asleep.

His sleep was disturbed about an hour later when a small child ran into the shelter and stopped dead in its tracks. The tiny being, clad in hooded raincoat and red wellingtons, stood and stared unremittingly at Joe and remained so until its mother popped her head inside the shelter entrance. Within an instant she summed up the situation and decided it would be unwise to stay inside the scant building with a foul smelling tramp. She scooped her infant up in her arms and hurried to a spot a few yards away where she waited, in the pouring rain, for a bus.

Joe was partially awake by now and aware of the woman's presence. In former days, he would have gladly given up the shelter to the woman and her child but not anymore – his comfort came first. He had been on his feet far too long and been awake for too many hours to be robbed of his resting place now. The damned woman would have to stay out in the rain or else go back home unless, the thought occurred to him, she came back in and gave him a reason to rape her. It could only be a thought because he lacked the energy to back -it up.

He was about to doze off again when he heard the voice of another women, she had also expected to stand out of the rain whilst waiting for bus. "Why are you standing out here, Anne?" she asked the mother, "Is there something wrong with the bus shelter?"

"There's a filthy man in it, Mrs. Dale," Anne replied, "I didn't like to disturb him."

"We'll soon see about that," snapped Mrs. Dale. "Nobody has the right to make a small child like yours stay out in weather like this!" She stormed into the shelter and prodded Joe with her hastily furled umbrella. "Look here," she commanded, "this is not the place for you. This shelter was built for the benefit of passengers waiting for a bus and not as a dosshouse for tramps."

Joe slowly turned on his side and glared at the woman, "Piss off you old bag," he hissed, "Before I slit your throat."

Somewhat flabbergasted, Mrs. Dale drew back. She had expected the tramp to be a frail old man who was down on his luck and somebody she could easily bully, instead, she found a mean and unapproachable monster whose violence she knew she could not counter. However, she was determined not to lose face and, unfurling her umbrella once more, she warned, "Rest assured, I shall send somebody for the police. 'You haven't heard the last of this," She retraced her steps to offer Anne some space under the umbrella.

"He really is a nasty man," observed Anne calculating her remark to suit the comprehension of her child as well as Mrs. Dale.

"People like that shouldn't be allowed to roam freely," snorted Mrs. Dale "They should be behind bars."

"Hark at the silly cows," murmured a somnolent Joe, "Police indeed. Huh!" He drifted off to the sound of the rain beating down on the shelter roof and was no longer concerned about the women getting soaked through outside. He could count on them staying

The Lincolnshire Tramp

there until the bus arrived, they would be too frightened to disturb him again.

A third woman joined the group but she was too old to be of any assistance should it come to a concerted effort to dislodge Joe, anyway, the bus could be heard rumbling along in the distance and there seemed no point to stirring up a hornets nest. In a last ditch effort though, Mrs. Dale did complain to the bus driver and urged him to intervene but the driver tartly informed her that his contract allowed him only to drive the bus and collect the fares, he was not paid to perform any other duty beyond that. The bus moved off and it was the end of the affair for Joe, he slept on peacefully for several hours.

When he awoke it was dark again but the rain had stopped falling. He stood up and stretched his arms and legs before stepping outside and resuming his journey to Bicester. As he walked, he ate the fruit cakes and mulled over the events of the day; had he really upset so many people in so short a space of time?

The Oxon town of Bicester suited Joe well enough for almost a week and he was soon into pilfering for his simple needs. But, the lure of Oxford (as soon as he realized it was less than a day's walk away) dimmed his interest in the smaller town, besides, it was about time he moved on.

By coincidence, he sauntered into Oxford on the day of his first anniversary as a vagrant. He was not aware of the fact at the time nor would he have wanted to be – it was nothing worth celebrating. It was also the start of a less turbulent period in his life for although he remained abrasive and antisocial he was not to encounter further altercation with the general public for some months to come; not that he went out of his way to avoid trouble – it simply did not happen.

After five weeks in the Oxford area, Joe adjudged the worst of the winter's weather to have passed and it was worth the risk to set off on a lengthy ramble of the west country. He could always head for the larger town of Swindon if the weather deteriorated again, meanwhile, there were large tracts of Gloucestershire and Wiltshire to be explored.

On the occasion of the vernal equinox, Joe found himself entering the Wilts. town of Chippenham, well west of Swindon. He learned that Bristol was some twenty miles further on, as the crow flies, but he held back any plan to visit the city lest it should trigger off a whole series of memories he would prefer not to recall. Anyway, there was more than enough to occupy his mind amongst the many towns along the Somerset/Wiltshire border especially now that the sun was warming up again.

March soon became April and the wildlife in the countryside took full advantage of an early spring. Birds and small mammals mated frantically and generally busied themselves with preparations for parental responsibilities. All around, a bright, fresh greenness replaced winter's gloom and spring flowers defied the morning chill to display their vivid colours. But, as with the previous spring, it all meant nothing to Joe, he could not care less about the season so long as he could extract alcohol (no matter in what form) from the towns of Chippenhem, Corsham, Melksham, and Trowbribge.

Not until the beginning of May did he really understand the kind of world he was living in. By night, although he could not accept it, he belonged to the natural world and slept with the wild creatures yet by day he belonged to the material world and relied an domesticated man for his sole existence. Realistically, he could not divorce himself completely from the material world but he certainly changed his attitude to the natural one soon after an incident on the county border between Trowbridge and Frome.

He had taken it into his head to wander across the fields and ignore the public roads, it was late in the afternoon and he was alone. All went well until he came to a waterway which was too wide to leap over and, presumably,too deep to wade through, it could only be crossed by bridge. A short walk, following the course of the waterway, brought him within sight of a suitable span. It was a wooden structure but not used on a regular basis because it was poorly maintained, though it was passable. As for it attracting so little traffic, this may have accounted for a family of swans having a nest close by.

The pen sat serenely in the water with her young – yet mischievous brood around her whilst her mate, the cob, stood on the bank above and preened himself. He was, without a shadow of doubt, a magnificent bird, big and powerful, proud and elegant and in the prime of life. He had black legs and black markings above his organge bill otherwise he was completely white, his immaculate plumage shone with vitality. Above all else, he was the imperious protector of his family and, as such, he kept a watchful eye on any stranger trespassing too close to the family nest.

Oblivious of the cob's concern, Joe approached the wooden bridge. He had never encountered a swan in the wild before (especially at breeding time) and was totally unprepared for the confrontation and rancorous struggle about to absorb him. As a

The Lincolnshire Tramp

matter of fact, he had all but ignored the swans and thought only of crossing the waterway.

The cob had other ideas as he gauged the tramp's every step and the moment Joe put his foot over the prescribed, yet invisible, boundary (some ten feet from the bridge) the swan sprang into action. With outstretched neck, he lowered his head and began to hiss harshly, he also spread his wings and made himself look as big and as ferocious as any fighting bird could be. He then lunged forward at alarming speed and tried to gain the maximum height possible in the short distance; height enough to overpower his intended victim.

The suddenness of the attack took Joe by surprise and he found himself staggering backwards to avoid the vicious onslaught, furthermore – because he missed a breath – he did not have sufficient air in his lungs to ejaculate a single curse. The only noticeable sensations he was aware of were, his blood running cold, a shiver sweeping his spine, and the hair at the back of his neck standing on end. Not until he recovered from the initial shock was he able to utter a string of profanities.

Just as soon as Joe had retreated, so the cob backed off. He settled down on the ground and, with his head held high, he folded his wings before returning to his former post. He had done his duty and warned off the intruder. In reality, he meant Joe no harm and would not have harmed him no matter how often the stubborn tramp tried to cross the bridge, he merely wanted to frighten Joe away and so create a safe zone between him and the cygnets.

Joe did not see it that way, he misunderstood the cob and believed the bird to be a killer. Legends about swans having powerful wings – powerful enough to break a man's arm – flooded into his mind and he was convinced that he would suffer a similar fate if he let this one get the better of him. Guided by this thought, he looked around for a suitable stick to beat the cob with and when he found one he made a second, and more determined, move towards the bridge.

The cob responded immediately and, in full battle cry, he sallied forward to meet Joe's advance. Using the same tactics as before, he rose into the air and, once again, tried to force Joe into retreat.

This time, Joe was ready for the attack and, with both hands on the stick, he thrashed out at the cob in an endeavour to knock it to the ground. By chance, the stick Joe had picked up was too sear and with its moisture content lost, it no longer retained sufficient flexible strength to resist force thus, when it did eventually fall heavily on the cob, it broke into several pieces. Only the stump of the stick remained in Joe's hand but it was nowhere near heavy enough to use as a weapon when he tried to bludgeon the cob. In a moment of panic, he clenched his fists and tried to punch his way out of the confrontation but the cob was in control and, once again, Joe was forced to give ground. Thinking he was about to have his eyes pecked out, he stumbled backwards and fell over his own feet.

The graceless fall angered him so he lost his temper, "You bastard swan," he roared, "This time you're for it!" Fear lost out to rage and by the time he was back on his feet again his blood was boiling. Without losing sight of the cob (who had, by now, settled again on the ground and was strutting to and fro whilst maintaining constant eye contact with Joe) he vowed, "Attack me once more and you're as good as dead – Understand?" The cob stood his ground and defiantly hissed back – a gesture which prompted Joe to arm himself with a knife. "Back off, you bastard, or I'11 have your guts out," he warned.

If Joe had known better, he could have pushed his way past the cob and crossed the bridge without further harassment, and if the cob had not fretted about his family and allowed Joe a free passage, then a clash between them night never have happened. But, because each believed the other to bear malicious intentions, they entered into a violent struggle.

Joe made the first move to provoke the cob into assailing him and was almost caught off guard by the speed of the big bird when it retaliated. Its wings seemed bigger and more powerful than ever and Joe thought he might easily be smothered by them. In sheer desperation, he reached out and was fortunate enough to grab the cob by the throat. Hanging on for dear life, he held the bird in his left hand whilst he tried to stab it with the knife in his right.

Blood and feathers flew in all directions as the cob struggled to free himself from Joe's grip, and had he had tallons instead of webbed feet he would have caused his aggressor as much harm as he was suffering at the blade of the knife. Instead, he could only fight with what nature had equipped him with plus his great courage and a will for survival. Though badly wounded, he made a determined effort to fly a little higher and a little further forward. He clearly intended to overbalance Joe (which he succeeded in doing) and send him crashing to the ground.

It was not without pain and some discomfort that Joe found himself, yet again, on the hard path of the river bank. He had twisted his ankle in the fall and hurt his back but he hung on resolutely to the cob who fluttered and flapped above him whilst trying to release its head. So violent was its effort that Joe panicked and flew into a frenzy, he lashed out with his knife and slashed at anything within reach.

The ferocious battle continued for an indeterminate length of time until, in that most awful of moments, the cob fell limp and Joe was left holding the dead bird's head and upper neck; he had hacked at the swan in such a blind rage that he did not realize he was severing its neck from its body. He watched in horror as the life ebbed from the twitching body and he knew he had committed a terrible injustice against such a graceful creature.

Before getting to his feet again, Joe reverently placed the cob's heed beside its body, he then stood up and took a last look at the carnage he had caused – he was sickened by the sight of it. The blood on his hands began to haunt him so he hurried to the water's edge and carried out the uncustomary task of washing them. For him to worry about the mess on his hands and clothes at a time when he cared so little about personal hygeine was a mark of the guilt he felt for killing the swan. The birds and the animals were not to be held responsible for his present situation, so why should he use violence against them? His own kind were his enemies and it is amongst them that he should look for revenge; from now on, animals would be treated as equals and given every consideration. Other people were to blame for the hatred Joe carried in his heart, not the dumb creatures of the woodlands and waterways.

Fatigued and burdened with sorrow, he dragged his exhausted body accross the wooden bridge, pausing only for a moment to cast a concerned glance towards the pen and cygnets. She, being a wiser swan, had taken her family downstream and out of harms way. Joe turned away, there was nothing he could do for her she was on her own now and had to bring up her young without the assistance of her mate. He could do no more than wish her well as he hobbled off to face the setting sun.

Chapter 13

The death of the cob played heavily on Joe's mind as he limped through Midsomer Norton on the following day. For the first time since his fateful journey from Bristol to Spalding – all those months ago – he wished he could have set the clock back. If that particular day had not been marred by the maleficent behaviour of Keith, Virginia, and Marjorie, he would not be in Somerset now and he would not have killed the cob. Alternatively, why did he have to cross the waterway at that particular point? He could have gone on further and found another bridge, or he could have retraced his steps and gone back to the road. But no, he was not going to alter his course for the sake of a stupid swan.

With these thoughts buzzing around in his head, he dodged the traiffic on the busy A37 to cross at Ston Easton where he located a little lane leading to Chewton Mendip. It was along this lane that he became aware of a figure following him, it had been following him for almost half a mile, but whenever he looked back to see who it was it always slipped out of sight yet it continued to follow him when he resumed his journey.

Unnerved by the stranger, Joe left the lane and entered a coppice that bordered it. Ostensibly, he went in to relieve himself but this was merely an excuse to lay in wait for the stranger to pass by. And when that moment came, he was astonished to see a female vagrant of West Indian origin; this he easily determined by her brown skin, her strong features, and the bright colours in her clothing (unusually bright considering she was a tramp living under the same conditions as he). The lemon- yellow headscarf covering her tight, curly locks was tied at the back and its tails hung down over the shoulders of a sky-blue cardigan, beneath that she wore a pink blouse, a skirt decorated with red and green stripes, and white trainers. She also carried a brown, leather shoulder bag and towed and overloaded shopping trolley.

"HI! man," she called, cheerily, "How you doin'?" She came to a halt opposite Joe and smiled at him.

"Why are you following me?" he demanded.

"Ah'm not following you, man. I happen to be going the same way as you – that's all."

"Who are you and what are you? I've never seen a coloured tramp before, let alone a female one."

"Folks round here call me Mad Molly but I ain't really mad. What do they call you?"

"They don't call me anything," Joe said sarcastically, "Because I don't want to talk to them."

"But I can see you want to talk to Molly because you are curious about me. So what are you called?"

"Joe!"

Molly smiled again and dragged her shopping trolley into the coppice. "Well now, Joe," she beamed, "Have you got anything to eat?"

"It's no good coming in here to scrounge off me," warned Joe, "I haven't got any food." He was alarmed by Molly's brash approach and almost intimidated by it.

"I'm not scrounging," Molly said sharply, "Ah just asked in case you was hungry. Ah've got a whole new loaf in here," she tapped the side of her shopping trolley, "And ah could share it with you if you was a bit more friendly."

If anything was designed to break down barriers between strangers, thought Joe, it must be the sharing of food. It must be a practise inherent amongst the peoples of the world since time immemorial yet its philosophy was simple enough to understand – if you were hungry and uncertain of your next meal then it made sense to offer friendship to another who had food. This may not have been the case when he had supper with Bumble and the Obdays, he felt more hostile then and the evening had soured but now (affected by his killing of the cob) he was less antagonistic. Somehow he forced a smile and said, "It's ages since I had any fresh bread and I'd be most grateful for some now."

"This bread is fresh," boasted Molly, "Ah stole it off a baker's van this morning, but we can't eat it here," she pushed her way past Joe, "It just ain't good manners. We've got to find somewhere to sit down."

Beyond the coppice, and away from the lane, lay a grass meadow. It was fenced off with barbed wire to limit the freedom of a dozen reticent bullocks who were, at that time, in the distance. It was also bathed in sunshine and seemed the ideal place for a picnic.

Molly adeptly eased herself and her shopping trolley between the strands of barbed vire, then she ventured out into the field to find a suitable spot to sit down. She selected a place which did not lay in the shadows, was free of cow-pats, and not too close to a patch of stinging nettles. With the excitement of a child and the authority of a mother, she sat down and, by patting the ground deliberately with her hand, invited Joe to do the same.

Joe, thinking her behaviour extraordinary, did not put up any resistance and duly complied with her wishes. He sat in silence and watched her as she set about unpacking her shopping trolley, but long before she fished out the promised loaf did the smell of freshly baked bread reach his nostrils. Molly laughed raucously and held her prize aloft for all to see. But when no acclain came she lowered it again and, with her strong brown hands, broke it into two. It was as much as Joe could do to stop himself from snatching the largest half when Molly offered it to him, and he certainly did not thank her.

"Hey man! Haven't we forgotten something?" At the very least, Molly expected some sign of gratitude for her generosity.

A nod and a grunt was the most that Joe could offer, and this he did grudgingly as he pretended to have too much bread in his mouth to speak properly.

"Ah wanted some jam and some butter to go with this bread," explained Molly as she chewed on a crust, "But the baker was fresh out of them and ah couldn't hang around to see if he was gettin' any in." She laughed loudly again, that same raucous, yet nervous, laugh which, in time, would irritate Joe.

"Is this how you get all you food" asked Joe between mouthfuls, "Steal it – I mean?"

"Ah steals everything," Molly boasted. "If ah wants it, ah steals it."

"And your brightly coloured clothing – did you steal that as well?"

"Ah likes bright colours," declared Molly, "Which reminds me!" She put down her half of the loaf and had another poke around inside her shopping trolley, this time she pulled out a packet of coloured pencils; twenty in all and of various shades of red, blue, yellov, green,and brown. The packet was as yet, unopened therefore the colours shone vividly through the polythene wrapping. "Now here's colours," she sighed, "Lots of nice colours. Take a look." She offered the packet to Joe.

Showing only a mild interest, Joe handled the packet for a moment and then handed it back. "I suppose they look pretty enough," he said, "But what's the use of stealing pencils? What can you do with them?" And as he posed the questions he began to understand why the locals thought she was mad.

Molly, somewhat perturbed by Joe's lack of enthusiasm, stated, "Ah stole them because ah wanted them and because, man, ah does just what ah likes. Ah'm a free woman and other folks don't tell me what to do no more."

Joe could not argue with that observation, at least he and Molly had one thing in common – they were both relatively free from the trammels of legality and it was quite in order for them to live outside the law providing they were not caught. All the same, he could not see the value in stealing pencils. The jewellery, however, now that was something worth stealing and, what was more he was in a position to show Molly the difference. "Look here," he said, tugging a small bundle from an inner pocket of his grubby greatcoat, "I'll show you what's worth stealing." He put his chunk of bread to one side and then, with an air of self-satisfaction, he undid the bundle and spread it and its contents out an the grass. "There – what do you think of that?"

Molly's eyes grew large and round as she ogled the jewellery stolen from the house in Oundle. "Man, that sure is somethin'," she sighed as she ran her fingers through the golden trinkets. "Ain't nothin' a woman yearns for more than to have gold dripping from her ears, her neck, her wrists, and her fingers." She slid an eighteen-carat, gold bracelet over her wrist and held it out for appraisal.

"Here – that's enough of that," shouted Joe, snatching the bracelet back "I'm only showing you what is worth stealing. I didn't say you could have any of it."

"Ah was just admirin' it – that's all," claimed Molly in dismay and then in a more belligerent tone, she said, "Why d'you want to keep them when they is for women to wear?"

"It's none of your business," snapped Joe as he quickly bundled up the jewellery put it back in his inner pocket; there and then, he decided that Molly should not have any of it. He was in fear of softening up and betraying his avowed intentions, to get too friendly with this woman would undermine his entire strategy, and then where would he be? Perhaps he could ignore her and eat his bread in peace.

"My, my, my, you is touchy today," laughed Molly – that same raucous laugh. "But Molly has something in here to bring a smile to that gloomy old face of yours." Yet again she delved into the depths of her shopping trolley to seek out a bottle of gin. Normally she would never share her favourite tipple with anyone but now that she had seen the jewellery and nursed a desire to have it, sacrifices had to be made, Instinct told her that Joe would succumb to alcohol and she would get her own way, even if it did take the whole bottle. "Ah bet you wouldn't say no to a nip of this," she said, thrusting the bottle under Joe's nose. "It's the best."

Joe stared hard at the colourless liquid and licked his lips.

Molly read the signs but ignored his outstretched hand, she was too shrewd to let him help himself from the bottle, instead, she poured a measure of gin into a small, aluminium cup (an artefact which once capped a very old thermos flask) and passed it over.

A forced grunt of gratitude slipped through Joe's lips as he accepted the drink and downed it in one go. "It is good," he agreed but his opinion was not that of a connoisseur; a greedy man wanting more would be nearer the truth.

Without delay, Molly poured him a second drink. "We could trade," she said, topping up the little cup.

Sipping and not gulping the gin, Joe was bound to ask, "Trade what?"

"Mah coloured pencils for them jewels," announced Molly. "Is it a trade?"

Horrified by the suggestion, Joe lowered the cup and stared at Molly. "No – it is not a trade," he said firmly. "Hou can it be? The stuff in my pocket is worth a lot of money whereas your pencils are only worth a few pence."

"Ah doesn't see it that way," retorted Molly. "You stole them jewels so they didn't cost you nothin'. Same as my pencils – they cost me nothin'."

"So what?"

"Well – if they cost us nothin', they is worth nothin'. So their value is equal. Let's trade."

"With logic like that," countered Joe, "It's no wonder people call you mad." He looked away from her and continued to drink his gin.

"Ah could give you the rest of the gin as well as the pencils," offered Molly, hopefully.

Joe made no immediate reply preferring, instead, to watch the grazing bullocks as they chewed up the grass carpet which lay between him and them. His mind was troubled again because he felt the conversatian with Molly was going on far too long and she was beginning to get him down – especially that laugh of hers. With the alcohol taking effect, his former meanness returned and he looked for a way to disadvantage her. The solution was obvious – she would have to be raped.

In one continuous movement he, drained the gin from the cup and tossed the empty vessel at Molly, spread his legs apart and opened the fly of his trousers, and, whilst still seated, fished out his limp penis. "What you're going to get is a good fucking not a trade," he roared as he began to massage a stiffness into his drooping phallus.

Although alarmed by Joe's outrageous behaviour, Molly was determined not to show it. "You white boys is all the same," she observed as she casually repacked her shopping trolley, "see a bit of brown skin an' you come on strong," this time her customary

The Lincolnshire Tramp

laugh was all the more raucous as if to rule out any sign of nervousness.

Her, seemingly, casual attitude angered Joe and his knife was in his hand before he realized it, "See this," he snarled, "I'm not afraid to use it, if I have to." He got onto his hands and knees, and lunged towards her.

Instantly, Molly stood up and backed away. The knife in his hand terrified her but she continued to show composure. "Well, Mr. Joe," she said, "It seems ah'm going to have to tell you a few facts of life. Ah'm here for the taking because that knife of yours guarantees it but what you don't know is that old Molly has got somethin' inside her that you won't want to catch. You tries it if you want to but don't blame me if you gets something nasty."

Stunned by Molly's confession, Joe slowly got to his feet and considered the consequences of her remarks. Christ Almighty, he thought, the bloody cow's riddled with pox, or Aids, or something like that. Almost immediately his imagination conjured up a vision of a vagina lined with pustules of virulent diseases, any one of which could burst and sent it's vile puss into the blood stream of an unsuspecting intruder. No, definitely no, Joe was having none, of it. He did not want to risk catching anything like that, even though she night be bluffing. In a fit of anger, he roared, "Fuck off you old cow and never come anywhere near me again."

Relieved, but also deeply hurt, Molly meekly turned to walk away. She had barely taken a step when Joe threatened her yet again. Holding his knife inches from her face, he demanded, "Leave me the bottle of gin. That is something I will have off you."

He did not notice it but a sly little smile passed across Molly's lips as she handed over the bottle, it could have been that she was pleased for him to take it. However, as soon as the bottle was in his possession she hurried towards the barbed wire fence and dragged her trolley with her. Losing her favourite tipple was but a small price to pay to be free from Joe's distastefull company. Scrambling through the fence and feeling safer on the other side, she threw a final comment at Joe. "You is the nastiest person ah ever did meet – nothin' but white trash. You is rude and ungrateful, greedy and bad tempered – and ah hopes you rots in hell." With that said, she stormed off into the coppice and out of sight.

Molly's outburst amused Joe and he started to laugh loudly, but his laughter came as an embarrassment to him for he had not heard the sound of his own voice in that mode for many, many months. He was far too self-conscious of it to allow it to continue and had to suppress it with a large draught of the gin. Then he sat down before he fell down.

The Lincolnshire Tramp

He remained in the field for the rest of the day and gradually drained the bottle of its intoxicating liquor. The alcohol had a soothing effect on his aching body so he entered a state of inebriation. By dusk, he was flat on his back and snoring sonorously, the night was warm and the beasts in the field were tolerant company.

As dawn broke, Joe came out of his sleep, sat up, and licked his dry lips. In a daze, he tried to focus on his surroundings and put the events of the previous day into perspective. The bottle lay close by but when he lifted it, in a bid to quench his thirst with the last dregs of gin, he found it to be empty; not even the slightest of drips to run down his dehydrated tongue. However, the bottle jarred his memory and the interlude with Molly flooded back into his mind, and with it an alarming premonition he instinctively dropped the bottle and reached into the inner pocket of his greatcoat to feel for the bundle of jewellery. Instead, he found a packet of coloured pencils.

It was not difficult to discern what had occurred, Molly had not gone away after all but had hidden in the coppice until Joe had been rendered insensible, then she crept up on him and exchanged the pencils for the jewellery. He should have guessed what was in her mind when she so willingly gave him the gin but, there again, he did not think she would have the nerve to approach him let alone steal from him; surely she would have been too frightened of him to do that. Above all else, he was furious to know that he could still be robbed.

"The rotten cow," he roared as he threw the packet of pencils away, "How dare she do this to me?" He struggled to his feet and took several faltering steps to where the packet lay. "Whatever possessed the silly bitch to believe that I wanted her bloody pencils. I can't eat them, I can't drink them, and I certainly can't sell them." Driven by temper, he tried to stamp the pencils into the ground and crush them to pulp but his legs were unsteady and his aim was poor. No matter how hard he tried, he could not accurately lay a foot on the packet. The nearest he came to it was when he finally fell over and ended up with it only inches from the tip of his nose. The fall did nothing for his temper and he cursed the pencils. "Bloody useless things – not worth a bottle of piss!"

For a while he lay where he was and stared at the packet. "She hasn't heard the last of this," he groaned, "Because if ever I catch up with her again I'll shove a coloured pencil into every hole in her body. We'll soon see how she feels about a burnt umber poked up her nose and an ultra marine sticking out of her arse."

The Lincolnshire Tramp

It may have been an idle threat conceived in a moment of anger but in no time at all the idea had lodged in Joe's mind – he would track Molly down and carry out his threat. "She can't be too far away," he muttered, "And if I go now there's a chance of catching her." Once again he stood up and this time he picked up the packet of pencils. "She'll rue the day she ever set eyes on these," he vowed as he tucked the packet inside his greatcoat.

Firmly committed to finding Molly, he left the field, passed through the coppice and set off to follow the lane to Chewton Mendip. It was early in the morning when he entered the village, far too early for the villagers to be greeting the new day. The quiet cottages stood poised for the eventual activities of rural life but in the meantime Joe could wander amongst them as he searched for clues and (possibly) some food.

He was not fortunate enough to find a breakfast but his hopes were raised when he saw the wheel marks of a shopping trolley in a patch of soft earth beside a footpath, there was also a footprint which clearly indicated the direction taken by the trolley and its owner. It was enough to convince him that Molly had passed that way and she was heading for Wells or Glastonbury along the A39.

A second wheel mark south of the village added confirmation to Joe's assumption and he quickened his pace as he anticipated settling his account with Molly. He was convinced that she was on the A39 somewhere and that it would only be a matter of hours before he caught up with her, also, he believed he had the advantage because he would see her long before she saw him.

By noon, he was in Wells and by the evening he was in Glastonbury, but there was no sign of Molly. Throughout the long walk he had looked everywhere for her, all to no avail; yet he still nursed the feeling that she was no more than a few steps ahead of him. This could not be further from the truth because Molly was some twenty odd miles to the north widening the gap. She knew Joe would be after her as soon as he realized the jewellery was missing and she calculated that when he did, "He would surely follow his nose." She could almost count on him going forward and not backtracking. That is why she went into Chewton Mendip at midnight and laid a false trail. On her return, she carried her shopping trolley past the field in which Joe slept and for half a mile further on. To be honest, she was absolutely petrified when she crept past the field but when she heard Joe snoring her fears began to fade. By sunrise she was her contented self once again; her simple philosophy told her that it was easier to lose someone rather than to find them.

Chapter 14

The more Joe thought about Molly the more he convinced himself he should have raped her. If she was prepared to steal from him then she deserved to suffer the ultimate degradation. Who knows – he might yet rape her and do so just as soon as he caught up with her; providing he took precautions of course. Instantly he could have kicked himself for such a stupid thought. Who was he, a dirty old tramp, to contemplate the purchase of condoms - how ridiculous. What a fool he would look if he went into a chemist's shop to ask for a packet of three.

Paradoxically, he did have a place in society (albeit a lowly one) and, therefore, he was obliged to exist within the parameters of such a fixed order. Hitherto, he believed his new found freedom was limitless and that he could do whatever he pleased and go wherever he liked, but now he had to accept that certain activities were no longer available to him. The purchase of condoms was one of them.

Shamed by his own foolishness, he toured the dustbins of Glastonbury for scraps of food. Yet, whilst thus engaged, his mind would not completely rule out the desire to rape. Was his need simply to humiliate women, he wondered, or was it more deeply rooted than that? Was it really to spite Marjorie or to satisfy his own sexual craving? Whatever the reason, his mind would not let go of the impulse and it became all the more imperative to have the deed over and done with.

In the past his attempts had come to nothing because they had been ill-timed and clumsy, but from now on more detailed planning would be required if a future attempt was to succeed. Whether the victim was to be Molly or anyone else was not the issue, the important thing was to work out the details beforehand and leave nothing to chance.

Joe retired to the outskirts of the town and settled down for the night. He kept a wary eye open for Molly but, of course, he fell asleep without seeing her. The night passed without incident and early the next morning he was on his way south to the slightly larger town or Street. It was there that he finally gave up his search for her. Intuition told him that she had given him the slip and he was unlikely to see her again. He cursed himself for not seeing the truth sooner, he should have known what sort of woman she was. From now on he would be on his guard and be ready for the next scheming female who tried to take advantage of him, he would not be duped so easily again.

In a mood – best described as foul – he stomped out of the town and, turning his back on the mid-morning sun, he ventured into the Polden Hills. His irascibility was to hang over him for the rest of the day as he roamed the rolling hills. Indeed, he preferred to sulk rather than shake off the melancholy. As dusk closed in he was drawn to the sound of a woman's voice somewhere in the near distance, she was calling out for her wayward pet.

"Tyke, Tyke, Tyke," called the woman, her clamorous voice shattering the stillness of the evening. "Tyke, Tyke, Tyke," she continued.

Joe instinctively moved towards the voice and located the woman at the garden gate of her isolated cottage. He had come upon her by way of some high grassland and, whilst concealing himself, he was able to look down at her and her cottage. A narrow lane ran between him and the building; it was to this lane that the woman sought a sighting of her adopted cat.

In the time it took for the lethargic animal to manifest itself and entwine its furry body around its mistress's legs, Joe came to several conclusions. The woman was a widow and lived alone, he was sure about that, and she was no more than ten years older than himself. He was sure of something else – he had found his victim.

The widow scooped up the cat and hurried into the cottage, gently scolding the beast as she went. The cottage door closed behind her and Joe distinctly heard the bolts being slammed home. He was not unduly perturbed by this because he had no immediate intention to assault the women there and then. He could wait until he picked the right moment and he would not be rushed into it. Breaking into the cottage late at night was not an option – there might be someone else in there apart from the widow, and that would ruin his plans.

During the earlier part of the night Joe was confident enough to approach the cottage through its established, yet weary, garden. He was careful not to step onto the gravelled drive, knowing full well the noise that particular aggregate makes when crushed by a heavy tread. His mission was simple – spy out the area and establish the identity of the cat; it was essential to be able to recognize the animal at a later stage because it would provide the key to the cottage door.

It could not have been easier, a gap in the curtains (for they had not been properly closed) enabled Joe to see into the well lit living room. The widow sat back in a comfortable armchair and watched the restless images on a television set. On her lap dozed a carefree Tyke, a tabby with unusually large head and paws. Joe watched the widow for a minute or two then he tried to see as much of the room as possible to give himself some idea of the pattern of her daily life.

After a while he was satisfied with what he saw and, confident that his evil plan would work, left the garden to find somewhere to sleep, somewhere not too far away. Come the morning he would perpetrate the deed and so exact a little more retribution for the harm that had been done to him, this time he intended to be more calculating and more cold blooded about it.

As was his custom, he awoke early to greet the new day but, on this particular morning, he was in no hurry to leave his place of rest. Guessing, correctly as it happened, that the widow was not an early riser, it would not be in his best interest if he approached the cottage too soon; not many people would open a door to a stranger before an acceptable hour. It would be better, he reasoned, to be invited into the cottage rather than forcing an entry, that way he could take the widow by surprise and gain valuable time.

His chosen place of rest served him well as a vantage point for he could watch the cottage with ease yet remain inconspicuous, moreover, be was out of sight of anyone passing along the lane. As expected, the usual tradesmen came by but they did no more than deliver their wares before moving on, then at about nine-o-clock and when the sun was beginning to warm the earth, the front door of the cottage opened and the widow stepped out.

Still wearing her night attire (supplemented by a jaded, pink dressing gown and sturdy slippers) she basked in the sunlight for a few moments. Tyke, the tabby cat she held in her arms, became restless and wanted to be on the ground where he could roam the garden unhindered. The cat landed heavily on all fours as the widow stooped to drop him and pick up a bottle of milk, he went off with his tail in the air whilst she slipped back into the cottage closing the door behind her.

It was time for Joe to make his move but firstly he had to attract the attention or the cat and do so without being seen by the widow. He eventually cornered the inquisitive animal in a secluded part of the lane and then, having befriended the beast, he rendered it unconscious with a swift blow to the head. He was pleased with the result for now he had the means to gain access to the cottage.

Showing considerable care, he carried the limp body of Tyke to the front door and rang the bell. "Is this your cat, missus?" He put

The Lincolnshire Tramp

the question to the widow as soon as she came to the door. "I found him in the lane. I think he's been knocked down by a car. He is yours, isn't he?"

A look of horror spread across the widow's face as she reached out in a bid to take the cat. "Yes, yes he is mine," she said. "Oh! dear, he is in a bad way. Must be serious!"

Joe was not prepared to let go of the animal, at least not yet. "If you can show me the way to the kitchen sink," he offered, "I'm sure I can do something for him."

The unsuspecting widow, concerned only with the welfare of her cat, eagerly led the way into the cottage. "This really is kind of you," she said over her shoulder, "He's never been run over before, he's usually such a careful cat."

"It happens all the time," Joe replied nonchalantly, "See a lot of it on my travels." He followed the widow into the kitchen where she stood aside to allow him access to the sink. "Now, my little friend," he said, holding the cat's head under the cold water tap, "Let's see if this will help." He had only the one recourse to restore the cat to normality and that was based on a cold water treatment,but, as he was to tell himself when he turned on the tap, he could not have cared less if the animal responded or not, he had got what he wanted – admission to the cottage.

Nobody was more surprised than Joe when the cat came round. Its body tightened up and then it shook itself, soon after, it began to purr as if nothing had happened. But before Joe could utter a word, the widow rushed forward and scooped the cat up in her arms. She kissed it and cuddled it as if it had come back from the dead.

"I can't thank you enough," she beamed at Joe, "And, really I must give you something for your trouble. Some money," she hesitated briefly when she suddenly realized she was addressing a tramp, "Or some food perhaps?" She was annoyed with herself for not seeing the vagrant behind the Good Samaritan, she also became alarmed by his presence.

"I don't want your food or money," said Joe, coldly. "I want something else." He stared at the jaded, pink, dressing gown and lusted after the warm body beneath it. "You know what I want."

The widow was in no doubt about his intentions – the look in his eyes made that quite obvious, however, she was not willing to acquiesce to his desires without protest. She attempted to talk her way out of the situation. "I really am grateful to you for saving my cat," she said trying to check the faltering in her voice, "But I can assure you there is nothing else here for you to have apart from the food and money I've already offered. Why not take it and go before somebody comes along and sees you, I'm expecting a visitor at any moment."

"I don't believe you," snapped Joe, "What's more, we're wasting time so get your clothes off."

"He'll be here soon," screeched the widow. "My son is visiting me today and if he catches you doing something nasty to me I don't know what he'll do, he's a very violent man. He was a soldier and he's killed people before now."

"Enough of this nonsense," shouted Joe, banging his clenched fist on the kitchen table. "Strip off – now!" Such was the suddenness and violence of his action that it startled the cat, the widow, and the crockery on the table. The cat leapt out of the widow's arms and fled from the kitchen, the widow trembled with fear, and some pieces of crockery tumbled from the table to smash on the kitchen floor. "Don't give me any more shit about visitors," continued Joe, "I've been watching you for a long time and I know you live alone."

The mere thought of being watched over a period of time struck fresh horror into the widow's heart and she began to feel faint. This is no act of lust, she thought, it is more evil than that; she must stay in control of her emotions if she is to defeat this man. "My pills," she begged, "I must have my pills. I can feel my blood pressure rlsing.",She edged towards the kitchen door. "I must go and get them, they are out here somewhere."

Before Joe could grab hold of her she slipped out of the kitchen and tried to escape from the cottage. Indeed, she might here made it had her legs (enfeebled with fear) not buckled. The recalcitrant limbs failed to support her and she stumbled towards the front door where she ended up on her hands and knees. In a moment of panic, she deemed the front door (which was firmly closed) to be too difficult to unlatch whereas the door to the living room stood wide open and offered immediate sanctury. Without hesitating, she half crawled and half lifted herself into the room and made a desperate bid to close the door behind her. But her efforts were to no avail because Joe had caught up with her and with his foot against the doorjamb the door could not be closed.

"Go away and leave me alone," screamed the widow. "Go and pick on somebody else."

"See this," shouted Joe brandishing a knife he had brought from the kitchen, "I'll cut your bloody tongue out with it if you don't stop screaming." He stood in the doorway and,to the widow, he was a menacing sight. His eyes were ablaze with fury and his hands trembled with emotion. Beyond all doubt, his deranged mind had set him on his concupiscent course and he was going to rape the widow no matter what the outcome. The more she fought him off the more frenzied his attack would be, it would be up to her as to how much pain she need suffer.

Drawing on her last ounce of energy, the widow dragged herself to her feet and made a final effort to fend off her attacker. Grabbing hold of an upright chair and gripping it by its seat and back, so that its legs were aimed at Joe, she wailed, "Keep away from me you filthy beast. Keep away, d'you hear."

Joe, having the superior strength, easily disarmed the widow as he snatched the chair out of her hands. He then flung it across the room where it collided with a coffee table and sent a bowl of fruit and some framed photographs clattering to the floor.

Fearing further damage to her home and furniture, the widow gave in. He was going to have his way despite her efforts to stop him. She would have to submit to his carnal desire and get it over with. Resigned to her fate, she fumbled with the knot in the belt of her dressing gown and prayed for a speedy conclusion to the pending ordeal. If ever there was a moment to fast forward the clock this was it.

Joe, almost out of control, snatched the dressing gown from her shoulders and demanded, "Now get your knickers off." But when she lifted her nightdress to remove the designated garment he was astonished to see a second pair of briefs under the first. "Why?" he asked, "Why two pairs of knickers?"

"To protect me from being raped," replied the widow sheepishly.

"Much good it'll do you," muttered Joe as he allowed his greatcoat to slip to the floor, "Now lie down," he added and gave the widow a shove. He undid his trousers and flopped down on top of her, forcing her legs apart as he did so.

The penetration was not as comfortable as it could have been and both parties suffered some pain. The widow more so because her vagina was nowhere near moist enough to admit his stiffened member and because she was, in effect, trying to reject him. And as the intercourse developed she realized further discomfort, mainly from the hard floor on which she was forced to lay and the soreness to her thighs caused by the chaffing of his soil encrusted trousers. She was also subjected to the foul odours transpiring from his body and, as he began to puff and pant from his exertion, the vile smell of his breath. The encounter was proving to be far worse than she anticipated as every renewed thrust became more repulsive than its predecessor. Please God, she begged in silent prayer, let it be over soon and make him leave me alone.

The Lincolnshire Tramp

There was nothing to hinder Joe now as he hammered into the near naked body of the widow and, as he did so, he had not the slightest concern for her feelings. He had waited a long time for this moment and would not be deterred from achieving his objective, not even by the pitiful pleading from the woman he was abusing. Her part in the exercise was a negative one, no more than a means to an end, a mere instrument on which to practise his violent intercourse until he had exacted a fair measure of retribution as well as gratification.

To maximise his effort, he held the widow by her buttocks (such unusually small buttocks for a woman, he thought) but the arrangement served only to remind him of BumbleDrage and the incident with the gypsy boy; he hated Bumble for that. The reminder may have forced Joe to release the widow's buttocks but the anger it induced urged him to thrust harder into her loin.

Such anger, a second or so later, turned to a deep loathing for when he happened to glance down at the widow's thighs he saw Marjorie's thighs and the lewd window cleaner between them. How he wished he could thrash the pair of then to within an inch of their lives for the misery they had caused him.

The furious jerking of Joe's coition brought a breast tumbling out al the widow's nightdress and with it came a vision of the young mother and her own milk-laden breasts. He should have had the young mother and released his pent-up emotions on her.

Then he thought about the Down's syndrome girl and the temptation of her young body. He would have screwed her, make no mistake about it, if that damned vicar had not been there.

Then there were the schoolgirls; he should hare violated all three of them, one after the other.

And then, Molly. He should have fucked her.

And fucked her again, and again.

Suddenly it was all over, a final heave brought both pleasure and despair as seminal fluid passed from male to female. The pleasure came in the briefest of moments when Joe ejaculated in orgasm but after that both he and the widow suffered varying degrees of despair and disgust.

Gasping for breath, Joe lifted himself up to deliver his final insult he spat on the widow. "You dirty cow," he wheezed rolling his body away from hers and propping it against a settee. He wanted to add further insults but the strenuous assault had drained him of all energy, he was too exhausted to utter another word.

The widow did not move, at least not immediately. Her mind had drifted into another world, a world without meaning, a world of hopelessness. She saw herself carrying her own dead soul through a labyrinth of underground tunnels whilst stabbing fingers came at her from out of the half light and discordant voices chanted, "Unclean... Unclean..."

Slowly, she drifted back into the real world and made a half hearted attempt to come to terms with it. This obliged her to, raise herself from the hard floor, pick up her dressing gown, and walk dispassionately from the room. She was even indifferent to a thin stream of rejected semen that had oozed from her vagina and had trickled irritatingly down her leg.

She had but one thought on her mind as she ascended the staircase to her bathroom and that was to cleanse herself of the whole sordid affair. She had been defiled by the dirtiest of tramps and must now rid herself of the lingering contamination. Her only course of action, it seemed, was to wash and scrub her entire being until the last traces of the evil contact had gone. A bath full of soapy, hot water must disburden her of the pain, the smells, the touching, the memory, and the abuse.

Completely unmoved by the widow's plight, Joe sat back and contemplated breakfast. He listened carefully to the bath being filled and correctly deduced the widow's intentions. "She'll be in there for hours," he told himself, "Should give me time for a fry up".

The prospect of fried eggs and bacon together with freshly made tea stirred him into action. He quickly adjusted his clothing and went from the living roon into the kitchen. Everything he needed was to hand – as he expected it to be – and he soon set about preparing the biggest breakfast he had ever eaten. In the past, breakfast had been a modest meal even before he became a vagrant but now, because he was in a dominant mood, he thought he should have a meal to match his ego. Besides, being on the road he had not enjoyed many fried breakfasts so all the more reason to make the most of the opportunity when it arose.

The meal was not to be hurried for he did not feel under pressure to wolf down the food and make a hasty getaway, He ate at leisure and drank many cups of tea. However, a commotion in the bathroom did cause slight concern during the meal but not enough to spoil it. The widow had obviously decided, after she had drained her bath, that she was nowhere near clean enough and a second bath was needed. The entire cleaning process would have to start all over again. Joe sniggered and poured himself another cup of tea.

About a quarter of an hour later, whilst selecting food to take with him, he heard a car in the lane and then the unmistakable crunch of pneumatic tyres on the gravelled drive. "Christ almighty," he blurted out, "So she has got someone coming." In a moment of panic he, gathered up the food, let himself out of the back door and sought refuge in the garden. He was annoyed by his own stupidity, he should never have lingered over the meal, now he risked being caught.

In the shadow of a garden shed he paused to check out his bearings and also establish the identity of the visitor. In fact, the car brought four visitors, a man (the widow's son) his wife and their teenage daughters. They all appeared to be getting out of the car at the same time and were excited at the prospect seeing the elder relative.

"Run along in girls," ordered the man, "Go and find Granny. We'll bring the rest of the stuff."

"Okay Dad."

"Granny - we're here."

"I hope the old dear is up and about," said the man, addressing his wife. Joe froze to the spot and his heart leapt into his mouth when he thought he recognized the man's voice. Surely it couldn't be, his mind slipped into turmoil, it must be someone else. He tried to get a closer look at the man's face which was, more often than not, impeded by the bulk of the car but he saw enough to come to the conclusion (although he could not accept it) he was watching a former colleague.

"Townsend!" he gasped. "Is it really Vernon Townsend?" He blinked sereral times to make sure his eyes were not deceiving him. It would be too much of a coincidence for the erstwhile salesman to impinge on his life at that particular moment, he did not want to see friends from the past.

As Joe stood and stared in disbelief; the youngest of the teenaged girls came out of the cottage and called to her father. "Quick, Dad, come quick, something has happened." The urgency in the girl's voice summoned immediate response from her father and he rushed into the cottage to see what was amiss. His wife followed at a slower pace.

Any minute now, thought Joe, they'll find out the truth and come looking for me. No doubt, they'll kick up such a stink the whole nation will join in. Good luck to them.

He could not really be surprised to find himself fleeing furtively from the scene as he ducked and weaved his way through the open countryside trying to blend in with local surroundings and be as inconspicuous as possible. He needed to travel a great distance under the cover of darkness but, exasperatingly, the night was a long time coming.

The Lincolnshire Tramp

It was essential to keep his wits about him to avoid being caught, a lapse in concentration and things could go disasterously wrong. Yet it was not so easy to stay alert whilst his mind suffered the constant bombardment of disagreeable thoughts; thoughts centred on Townsend.

Why did it have to be Townsend visiting his mother? Why couldn't it have been any one of millions of other men in the country? Why did it have to be today? Then the worst thought of all struck Joe, it slowly dawned on him that he had raped Townsend 's mother.

"Oh! my God," he roared, "How on earth could it be possible? Of all the women to rape it had to be the mother of somebody I know. What sort of bloody world am I living in to have my life screwed up like this? Why can't I, for once, get my own back without it backfiring on me? It's so bloody unfair."

He continued to blame everyone and everything for his own misery until well into the night and he dearly wished for a bottle of spirit with which to drown his sorrows. But he was to endure his problems with a sober mind and very little chance of respite.

Chapter 15

Since fleeing from the widow's cottage, Joe had squandered many hours ducking and diving, weaving and waiting. The state of his mind had urged greater caution, every step forward had to be taken with extreme care. Often he stood quite still to listen for the sound of an impending pursuer or scan the horizon in all directions to be certain of crossing an open space without being seen. In this manner he progressed throughout the day and well into the night before finding a suitable place of refuge; this time it was a wooded area some five miles south of Taunton.

Moving stealthily through the trees he knew that they and the night would afford him sanctuary. For a few hours, at least, he could rest without the fear of being discovered. although, if he was to be honest with himself, he had to admit that he had not seen a single person looking for him – be it police or otherwise. Yet he must not be too complacent, the crime he had committed would not go unnoticed and must, eventually, be reported to the proper authority. Come daybreak, somebody, somewhere, would be on his trail. With this in mind, he settled down on an earthy bank and tried to sleep.

As it turned out, he was to be denied the benefit of deep slumber and in its stead become a victim of night terrors. He so desperately wanted to sleep but he could not settle comfortably and, above all, he was plagued by a series of bad dreams. Very soon a regular pattern emerged, every time his body suffered some discomfort it would awaken him in a dream and he would have to adjust his sleeping position. Barely conscious of the disturbance, yet annoyed by it, he would doze off until the next delirium; each dream being more perturbing than the previous one.

The ultimate nightmare came at a time when he resolved not to sleep any more. Extremely disgruntled, he vowed to stay awake and put his mind into some sort of order but he could not resist the temptation of suspended consciousness and drifted back into the uncertain twilight.

How much time was devoted to sleep and how much to nightmare, Joe could not tell. All he could recall was his presence in a crowded courtroom and an eagle-eyed judge bearing down on him.

"How do you plead?" shouted the judge, "Guilty or not guilty?"

"To what?" asked Joe believing himself to be innocent of all crime.

The Lincolnshire Tramp

"To the charge that you did sire a child out of wedlock," challenged a female voice from somewhere in the shadows.

"Impossible," retorted Joe.

"Not so," continued the voice as a barrister came into view, "And I will prove as much to this court."

Joe was taken aback when he saw the face of Tracy coming at him from out of the wig and gown, he could not believe the achievement of the Down's syndrome girl.

"Well - ?" demanded the barrister, "Do you deny that you are the father of this child?"

"I'm not the father of any child," snapped Joe, "I've never been able to father a child."

"You'll have to convince the jury of that."

"I tell you I can't. Marjorie and I tried for years but we just could not have a baby."

"My very point," smirked the barrister. "Marjorie was at fault because she could not conceive. That does not prove you infertile."

"But I haven't had sex with anyone else so I can't have fathered a child."

"Come now – you don't expect us to believe that." The barrister gave a knowing wink before gathering up her papers and then, taking Joe by the arm she said, "I want to take you to my chambers, I have something to show you."

He was taken from the courtroom and guided into a sumptuous bedroom where the barrister brushed aside her wig and allowed her blonde, curly hair to flow freely. Thereafter, she tossed her papers into a corner, adeptly unfastened her collar with one hand whilst slipping her shoes off with the other and, as a final gesture, loosened her gown so that it could drop to the floor. She stood completely naked before Joe and begged, "I want you to make love to me and sire me your baby." Her voice was low and seductive.

Joe could see the beautiful young woman before him but he was not aware of any arousal in his own body. He was no more than a floating head devoid of all feeling. "I can't do it," he confessed. "I just can't."

"Oh yes you can!" coaxed the beautiful young woman (no longer appearing as a barrister), "You can give me a baby right now." She laid down an the bed and spread her legs apart.

"It's no good," Joe tried to explain, "I can't do it in a bedroom. I live outdoors now and have no need for beds." His argument seemed pointless but it was the only one he had.

"Even better," purred the beautiful young woman as she got up from the bed and commenced to lead Joe (via the french window) into the garden. "To conceive outdoors – how wonderful. And I know the very place."

Joe felt himself being whisked along behind the beautiful young woman as she ran out of the garden and into a field. He was compelled to stay with her for he lacked the ability to escape. She ran on towards a river and to a spot where breeding swans had had a nest. "This is where I shall conceive," she declared. Effortlessly she flung Joe to the ground and sat astride him as he lay on his back amidst down and feathers.

He looked up into her bright,blue eyes and was horrified to see them changing shape and colour. The heavenly blue turned to coal-tar black as they went from oval to round and become expressionless. Even the voice changed, it went from soft and sensuous to cold and clamorous. "You killed my husband and left my children without a father," it scolded, "Now I'm going to kill you."

Fearing for his life, Joe tried to struggle free but he did not have the strength and energy to do so. He was trapped by a ubiquitous mass which weighed him down, a mass getting heavier by the second. "I don't know what you are talking about," he gasped, "I haven't killed anyone..." His voice fell away when the metamorphosis before him finally emerged as, a swan – a very large swan.

Suddenly it all became clear, this was the mate of the swan he had fought and killed and she was obviously out for revenge. Towering above him she struck fear into his heart as he came to terms with the brutal truth,he was destined to certain doom. The frantic beating of her huge wings droned in his ears as he wriggled and writhed beneath her. And then he saw that she had venomous talons instead of webbed feet and the talons were biting into his flesh. Although he could feel no pain he knew his life was ebbing away and it was doing so to the sound of those beating wings intermingled with noise he himself made gasping his last breaths of air.

The irksome noises modulated to something more akin to snorts and snuffles as Joe awoke abruptly from his dream. Hot and sweating, and hardly daring to move, he looked up but instead of the swan towering over him he saw a near full moon high above the trees. The stiffness in his limbs told him that he was still in touch with his body and that he was probably not dead after all. However, he was not content in his mind , he was not yet completely free from his nightmare. And what about the noises? He could still hear them.

The Lincolnshire Tramp

Nothing more than a solitary glance towards the bed of the woodland revealed the simple explanation; the noises came from a family of badgers out foraging for food.

The revelation carried with it some mixed emotions for Joe. His primary reaction, motivated by anger, roused in him the need to jump up and chase the beasts away but, because he could not yet deliver himself from his nightmare, he had not the heart to do it. The badgers, he concluded, must have something to do with his wild dreams. Though not directly involved, were they there to bring home a poignant message? Was there a moral to the dreams?

Joe sat up and thought about the dream and his behaviour since becoming a tramp. He had been extremely nasty to a lot of people, and justly so, but had it achieved anything? The widow for instance – he had raped her sure enough but did it compensate for Marjorie's indiscretion? Did it satisfy him? What about all the other people and places he had abused – was he satisfied with that? Too many questions and not enough answers; that nightmare had shaken him all right.

On balance, he calculated his campaign of terror had brought him but little atonement for his losses and if, as it now seemed, he was to be haunted by his policy of reaping a full measure of retribution, then to continue with it would be pointless. He had done his utmost to cause misery to others but it had not given him any real satisfaction, it did not give him peace of mind.

Meanwhile, the badgers totally ignored Joe as he sat and worried over his deliberations, they were far too busy feeding and frolicking. Had he made a sudden movement then they would most certainly have gone to ground and returned to their set but as long as he remained reasonably still they would avail him of their company until sun up.

Watching the badgers in their natural habitat and still affected by his nightmares, Joe began to think about the swan. He had no right to kill that big bird, after all, he was only behaving as a good parent and protecting his young, he did not deserve to lose his life. That poor creature was not his enemy – fellow man alone had that distinction.

Although not immediately aware of it, Joe was being drawn closer to the creatures of the wild and in the years to come he would see more of them and develop a better understanding of their behaviour. The badgers, for instance, gave him an insight to their social structure. He may not have seen it straight away but it would come to him in time; for the present he was content to sit and observe their antics.

Long before the badgers deserted him, Joe drifted into an easier sleep and when he awoke they were all gone. The sun had replaced the moon and the woodland had donned its morning apparel; it was fresh and bright and alive with activity. Joe got up to stretch his legs for a while before settling down to breakfast. He ate the remains of a packet of biscuits and as he chewed the last biscuit he began to unfold the empty packet. The plain white card from which it was formed gave him an idea – it was an ideal base on which to sketch the badgers. With Molly's coloured pencils and his natural talent for drawing, Joe began to enjoy the idea. Sketching animals instead of hurting them would he his way of making amends for his cruelty to the swans.

Needless to say, he had to rely on memory when he started to sketch the badgers but time was on his side, he could observe them by night and touch up his drawings by day. With sufficient food and the badgers for company, laying low came as no hardship. For the first time in fifteen months Joe relaxed and almost enjoyed himself although he could not be completely off guard. After a week he returned to his restless self and wanted to be on the move again. A craving for alcohol and the lure of the open road became too much to bear, it was time to leave. He spent his last night in the wood with the badgers and at sunrise he set off to find the nearest road.

Later, by sunset, he was to be found tottering along the A373 towards Tiverton. He was blind drunk, vociferously foul and a menace to other road users. As usual, he had managed to lay his hands on a bottle of strong spirit and would not let go of it in case it finished him before he finished it; a race to nowhere for the result was of no real consequence – did it really matter if he keeled over before he emptied the bottle or after. In a sober state he might hare been more concerned about being run down by a car; many drivers were dazzled by the sinking sun and did not see him until the last moment.

Somehow he avoided death or serious injury and was to do so many times over during the next five years of tramping the roads. Whenever alcohol came into his possession he would drink to excess and when it did not he would befriend the animals and sketch them. His attitude towards people did not vary save for physical contact. He continued to curse them and insult them but he refrained from causing them actual harm. Furthermore, he refused to relinquish the chip on his shoulder, he had been ill-used in the past and would not allow himself to forget it.

The Lincolnshire Tramp

In general, he remained morose and embittered, and cared not for the joy of living. Rarely, if at all, did a twinkle appear in his eye or a smile cross his lips, or laughter fill his heart. Misery became a constant companion, always to hand if needed to sour his day-to-day existence. The future held nothing for him, so ambition fell by the wayside as he wandered from one place to another. Somewhere to rest at the end of each day and enough food and drink to nourish him were his sole priorities.

As the seasons slipped by so he lost touch with worldly affairs. He did not know – or care – what political, economic, social, or moral changes had been made. He became ignorant about the state of the nation and obscure about its welfare. He had his space and that was enough for him; never mind what was happening to the rest of the country.

In all, he spent almost five and a half years roaming the southern counties of England, a slow plod compared to his former pace. Prior to his arrival in Devon he averaged twenty miles par day but since then, because he had no particular aim in life, he reduced it to five. Indeed, for the first half of those years he never ventured beyond the boundaries of the three westernmost counties. The reason for this may have been found in his subconsciosness; probably the remorse he suffered for raping Townsend's mother, or killing the swan, caused him to seek a kind of mental comfort in the less populated areas. A theory he would never subscribe to although it could not be completely discarded.

However, memories do tend to fade a little with the passing of time; enough, at least, to give Joe renewed confidence in himself. He concluded his months of sojourn in Devon, Conwall and Dorset and made his way into Hampshire and the New Forest. It was not the enthusiastic arrival of a tourist seeking the natural pleasures of the area but that of a dishevelled tramp, unmotivated and disinterested.

He took for granted, much as he had done in the west country, the scenic landscapes, the historic buildings, the parklands, and the seascapes. He treated them all with equal contempt and saw in them no intrinsic value except for the odd moment when he was moved to sketch; usually after a bout of heavy drinlring.

From Hampshire he went to Surrey, Sussex and Kent but not until he had tired of each county in turn. An obstinancy within him came to dominance compelling him to leave no road unexplored lest he miss an opportunity to steal for his needs. Such diligence, not that it mattered, swallowed up time, weeks dissolved into months and months into years. And with the passing of those years, Joe aged considerably. He could easily have been mistaken for a man in his late sixties instead of one approaching his fifty second birthday. Not that he would celebrate the birthday when it came because he had long since erased all memory of anniversaries from his mind.

The fact remains, it was an older looking Joe who walked through the Kentish village of Pluckley. He pulled his greatcoat tightly about him to keep out a chill, autumn wind as he made his way through the main part of the village, he then descended a long gradient of a hill until he came to a cluster of cottages and the railway station.

There was something about the quiet little station that attracted his attention so he did not cross the humpback bridge which carried the road over the track, instead, he leaned on its brick wall and stared at the rails below. Presently a train rumbled through and came to a stop at a deserted platform, seven passengers alighted and the train moved on. Joe watched the passengers as they hurried out of the station and it occurred to him that none were checked for tickets. The station was unmanned.

If they get off the train without being challenged, he reasoned, then surely he could get on. After all the years of walking, a nice little ride on the tracks would do no harm. He made up his mind there and then, as soon as dusk closed in he would hop on the next train to stop at the station. In the meantime, he hoped to root out a bottle of strong drink from one of the wealthier households in the area.

Two hours later he sat in a comfortable carriage (the only passenger) and clutched a bottle of rum. The train moved forward and was soon swaying rhythmically as it rushed through the twilight, seemingly destined for a lengthy journey. That was what Joe thought as he settled back in the seat and contemplated the spirituous content of the bottle but barely had he taken a swig, or two, when he felt the train slowing down. Seconds later it coasted into the main line station at Ashford where, in railway jargon, it terminated. "All change! All change!" came an amplified voice. "All change here."

The lights in the carriage dimmed and went out. Joe cursed the railway for giving him short measure, an irony considering he was cheating them. He reluctantly stepped down from the train and, to his astonishment, he saw far too many people for his liking. The platforms were crowded with them, some in groups, some standing alone, some making enquiries, some drinking tee in the buffet, and some hurrying from one platform to another. There was also a

The Lincolnshire Tramp

small group, their journeys done, heading for the way out. They had to climb a staircase which rose up from the platform to join a concourse spanning the tracks, this would then lead them into the town.

At the top of the staircase there was a barrier manned by ticket collectors and nobody passed through it without the proof of a fare paid. This caused Joe some consternation, if he wanted to pass the barrier he would have to pay. Which, in effect, meant he would have to be polite and do the decent thing, and behave like a proper citizen. He could not agree to that, not after what he had been through.

Turning his back on the ticket collectors, he looked up and down the track to see if there was another way out. An expanse of tracks and endless high fences defiantly forbade egress. He was at a laos and could not think, or plan, his next move, he wanted to get away from the other passengers but did not know how best to achieve it. Perhaps the ride on the rails had not been such a good idea after all.

Ill at ease, he stepped back into the shadows and tried to merge into the iron structure of the staircase. A swig of rum, he decided, was needed to focus his mind so he raised his bottle to his lips, but before taking a drop he caught sight of an indicator board suspended from the roof over the platform. Drinking and reading at the same time, he learned that the next train in (on his side of the platform) was bound for Ramsgate and had several scheduled stops en route.

Problem solved, he thought. Catch that train and have a choice of two alternatives, either go all the way to Ramsgate or hop off at any unmanned station in between. If there was not a ticket inspector on the train then he could stay with it until it reached the Kent coast but if there was, then Joe could expect to be thrown off.

Joe was pleased with his plan although he would not allow a smile of satisfaction to express his feelings, however, he could not repress a rare moment of elation and was obliged to enjoy it until he regained the will to kill it off. When restored to his sullen self, he leaned against a steel stanchion and stared into the distance.

Bright flashes of light and frequent showers of sparks ushered in the coast bound express. It came out of the darkness and thundered into the station where it screeched and juddered to a halt. Doors flew open and the passengers inside changed places with the people on the platform, yet there was order in the general confusion and everyone quickly found an allotted space, including Joe. The carriage he scrambled into was long and of an open-plan design.

Down each side it had a row of seats (set in bays of four) and a central aisle, it was well lit and warm.

Joe had opted for a midmost postion in the carriage and sat alone in a four-seater bay. The bay opposite was vacant but others, fore and aft were fairly well occupied. There was the usual babble of conversation punctuated by loud laughter as the new intake of passengers settled down for the coming journey. Then, after a lengthy pause during which electric motors hummed and whined, the train jolted forward and gathered speed as it rushed through the suburbs of the town. Soon after, it tracked the darkened countryside and sped towards Canterbury.

The motion of the train and the warmth the carriage lured Joe into bouts of desultory sleep and during the moments of awareness he drank greedily from the bottle of rum. About thirty minutes into the journey, and a good half of the bottle's contents gone, he was brought to his senses by a desire to defecate. His first intention was to suppress it and relieve himself at a later time but it became a matter of some urgency and would not be held back. He considered looking for a lavatory on the train but the very idea of a proper facility seemed like an aberration to him, besides, he doubted if he could make it in the time anyway. Apart from anything else he was too tired and too drunk to make a move. Nature would have to take its course and that was that.

Out of control, the warm, putrid discharge seeped through his anus and spread unevenly over his buttocks and on the seat of his trousers. There followed the inevitable smell, pungent and vile and much worse than even he had expected. It began to pervade the air in the carriage and gradually spread to every corner. Eventually it stank the vehicle out.

When the smell reached the nostrils of the other passengers they reacted differently. To some the odour became intolerable and they abruptly left their seats to seek a more healthier part of the train, others made light of it but opened windows all the same or moved to the furthest parts of the carriage. The few who remained in their original seats did so because they could not see any point in moving when they intended getting off at the next stop. Whilst others, who tried to board the train, quickly changed their minds and moved on to another door in another compartment. In most cases, the passengers had not realized that there was a tramp in their midst and it certainly came as a shock to them when they saw Joe. He totally ignored the gasps of horror and the stares and drank defiantly from his bottle. It was warning enough and they kept their distance. Nobody attempted to approach him.

The Lincolnshire Tramp

By the time the train arrived at Ramsgate the carriage was deserted apart from Joe, and as the other carriages disgorged the few remaining passengers he settled back in his seat. By then he was extremely drunk and unwilling to move, indeed, it had crossed his mind to spend the night where he was. Unfortunately for him the railway executive had other ideas and wanted their train cleared of travelling public. A trainee driver was sent along the platform for just that purpose.

"Everybody out! All change! Everybody out," called a burly young man as he checked each carriage in turn. Drawing level with Joe and peering at him through the window he shouted, "Come on mate. Time to get out." To make sure his instructions were obeyed, the young man waited patiently for Joe to make a move.

Even though inebriated, Joe realized he would never be allowed to stay and made a determined effort to get to his feet. Clinging to the seat backs, he shuffled unsteadily alone the aisle until he came to a door opening onto the platform. His knees buckled as he stumbled through it but he managed to stay upright and proceed, not in the straightest of lines, towards the station exit; a large doorway in a victorian building.

"Ticket please," called a voice from within a little kiosk guarding the way out.

"Bollocks!" Retorted Joe as he lunged towards the exit.

The ticket collector emerged from the kiosk to bar the way. "You're not coming through here without a ticket," he insisted.

"Arseholes!" said Joe as he staggered back and away from the doorway. He had intended dashing through it but lack of co-ordination took him the wrong way. He continued to stagger backwards until he got a forward motion going again but, by then, he no longer faced the exit – he was heading for the other end of the platform.

"Hey!" called the ticket collector, "This is the only way out and you must have your fare."

"Let the old sod go," advised the train driver, standing not too far away, "He's not worth the bother at this time of night."

"You're probably right," agreed the ticket collector, "Besides, he was stinking the place out."

With that, the railway staff attended to other duties and completely forgot about Joe, they naturally assumed he would climb through a hole in the fence and run away. The fact that he remained on railway property and possibily become a liability did not occur to them. As for Joe, he had no idea where he was going as he rolled and swayed along the platform, he could do no more than follow it until it tapered and disappeared into the coarse aggregate of the track bed.

Stumbling and falling, he made haphazard progress along the track bed and did so in the belief that it would lead to a way out. He knew he was doing the wrong thing but somehow he was attracted to the lines, the more he tried to pull away the more he veered towards them. And whenever he fell, his head went perilously close the the rails – even the live rail. Mentally unaware of the danger he was in he always managed to get back on his feet and stagger on. On towards a viaduct.

Meanwhile, the empty train waiting in the station was scheduled to go into a siding where it should stay until called upon for the first journey out in the morning. Cleaners were busily giving the carriages a tidy up whilst the trainee driver sat at the controls and waited for a signal to move the train to the siding.

The signal came soon after the cleaners had finished and had taken away their buckets and brushes. The trainee glanced nervously towards the established driver as if to seek confirmation.

"Take it away then lad," encouraged the driver from the station platform, "Put it to bed."

The trainee rehearsed his movements before putting them into practise and after a hesitant start the train moved slowly forward. It gathered speed as it ran out onto the main line prior to reversing back into a siding. As it happened, the reversing procedure did not come into effect.

Perhaps the zealous young driver had taken the train too far and too fast along the main line for had it not been so then it would not have hit, at speed, the heavy object placed across the line (an act of vandalism) and would not have been derailed. Even more to the point, it would not have had the momentum to take it towards the wall of the viaduct.

Sound does not travel so well when coming from behind especially to the ears of a drunkard. So it was in Joe's case. He did not hear the train coming and only became aware of it when it struck him in the back and dragged him along. He might have gone under the wheels had his greatcoat not caught on a protruding bolt situated between the coupling and the buffer furthest from the point of impact. The engine of the train, when it leapt from the track, came at an angle to the viaduct wall, therefore, its leading corner busted through the masonry first and created a hole big enough for the whole train to pass through. Had Joe been an that corner he would have been crushed against the brickwork and killed instantly, but because he was nearer the other corner he was dragged unceremoniously through the hole and flung into the street below.

A strange sensation came over him as he plunged towards the ground. His head cleared suddenly and his whole life flashed before him, every detail was there and he saw it all so vividly. The fall may have taken a matter of seconds but the history of his life seemed to take a great deal longer. Was this then, a prelude to death? The question could not be overlooked.

In actual fact he passed out before he hit the ground and lost all mental record of the events taking place during the following hours. He never saw the railway carriage protruding from the viaduct high above his head, and he was never aware of the man with the bicycle who had stood and witnessed the incident. He knew nothing of the woman who had stopped her car to help him, or of the ambulance which took him to the hospital. It was to be part of his life that had no niche in his memory.

At that moment in time, he was the filthiest creature alive and of the lowest order, yet, in his broken and wounded state, he found sympathy.

Chapter 16

Virginia Harrison had taken a job in Ramsgate as a social worler. She dealt mainly with children and had been doing so for about eighteen months. Before that she was unemployable. Ramsgate welcomed her and she fell in love with the place, vowing to make it home for ever. She rented a small flat above a restaurant for now her needs were simple and not at all ambitious as they were when she was younger. A job, an income, a car and a home of her own suited her every requirement.

Being a social worker had its advantages especially when she could use the work to soak up the hours on some of her more melancholic days; she hated to have time hang heavily on her hands. It also gave her the opportunity, providing she was careful, to find comfort in other peoples' problems without becoming emotionally involved herself. Needless to say, she had to deal with children in distress but she had learned to distance herself from their miseries to keep her own sentiments intact.

On the other hand, with her hours so flexible, she could arrange her day to encompass extraneous visits; usually to other unfortunate souls. This is how she came to be calling at the Margate General Hospital on an October afternoon.

Upon reaching men's ward she paused to ask the duty nurse if an old tramp had been brought in the night before and if so, was he still there. The duty nurse knew exactly where Joe was. He had been the main topic of conversation from the moment he arrived. The nursing staff had a difficult time trying to clean him up, the doctors were amazed he survived the fall considering the exent of his injuries, and the surgeons tried to work miracles to mend his broken body. But in spite of all their industry, The Vagrant (as he was known to them because Joe refused to identify himself) showed no sign of gratitude, to the contrary, he cursed them for interfering with his person.

"You'll find him at the far end on the right," instructed the duty nurse, " But be careful, he's very abusive."

"Thanks for the warning," reciprocated Virginia, "I'll be on my guard. But before I go to see him can you tell me how badly he's hurt?"

"He's in a bad way," confided the duty nurse, "Got a lot of broken and fractured bones as well as cuts and bruises. He won't tell us

The Lincolnshire Tramp

what happened but the doctors think he was forced through a brick wall. Quite high up, apparently."

"Yes, I know," said Virginia pensively, "I was there soon after it happened. "

"I don't suppose he told you his name or where he's come from?"

"I'm afraid not. He was unconscious for most of the time." Virginia turned to enter the ward. "I think I'll go and see him now," she said, "See if there's anything I can do for him."

"Okay!" smiled the duty nurse, "See you later!"

Like an administering angel on a mercy mission, Virginia flitted through the men's ward, passing many occupied beds (with attendent visitors) on the way until she came to where Joe lay. For a while she stood and looked at him, not that there was much of him to see beyond the protective tent over his legs and the bandages to his torso, arms and head. Most of his face was visible, though not immediately recognisable, his eyes were closed, his beard had been shaved off, and his skin was ingrained with dirt. He looked old, weatherbeaten, and drawn.

Whilst Virginia watched him an uncanny feeling came over her. I've been here before, she thought. Last night when I found this tramp I had the same sensation. I feel that I should know him – but I can't do.

Aware of someone at the foot of his bed, Joe opened his eyes to see who it was but he did not see Virginia for herself and thought she was just another interloper come to meddle with his affairs. He wanted to shout at her and warn her off but in his weakened state his speech could not rise above normal pitch. "Who are you staring at, you gormless woman," he said sarcastically.

Virginia gasped. In that instant her troubled mind was eased. She may not have recognised his voice the night before but there was no mistaking it now. A verbal sentence complete with dialect convinced her of his identity. She moved to the side of the bed and looked into his eyes, "It is you, Joe – isn't it?"

For a moment Joe was at a loss for words. Who was this woman who pretended to know him and what was she doing here? Did she come as an interrogator for the hospital, or the police, or the social services, or what? Why was she trying to trip him up? Seeking the answers to his questions he looked into her face to see what it might reveal. Then, like a bolt from the blue, the truth hit him. "Virginia," he said slowly, "What are you doing here?"

She smiled and said, "Fancy seeing you again after all these years. Who'd have thought it." She drew up a chair and sat down. "If I'd known it was you lying in the road last night I'd have come here to the hospital with you. How are you feeling now? Is there anything I can get you? Anything you need? Is there anyone I should contact to let them know where you are? How have you been keeping all this time?"

Virginia was beside herself with excitement. It was good for her to see a friend from the past and Joe had been a good friend to her – she knew that now. In all honesty, she had never expected to see him again especially since she had left her home in Spalding and had vowed never to return. But here he was, in the flesh, and she had some catching up to do. There was so much to talk about she hardly knew where to start.

Conversely, Joe did not share her enthusiasm. He did not want to see anyone at all, let alone an associate from the past. There remained traces of bitterness and resentment in his heart and these could not be nullified, not even by the care given to him after his accident. If anything, the accident had made matters worse because he was in the hands of others and unable to fend for himself. He had no choice in the matter, he was dependent on them and he hated it.

Above all else, he wanted to be left alone. He did not care for company no matter from where it came, and was, therefore, in no mood to listen to Virginia's prattle. "I'll tell you that I need," he snapped, "I need peace and quiet. So why don't you take your backside out of here and deposit it a million miles away."

Virginia's mouth fell open as she stared in disbelief at Joe. She was all set for long conversation but – obviously – he did not want to know. Disappointed and deeply offended, she got up and put the chair back in its corner. "You were very rude to me last night when I tried to help you," she said, returning to Joe, "And you've been very rude today. I don't know why you have to be so nasty. I shall leave you now and I don't know if I'll ever come back." Haughtily, she marched out of the ward and out of the hospital. "Really! Of all the nerve" she said, over and over again.

Good riddance, thought Joe as he watched Virginia leave, I don't need to talk to her. But as soon as she had gone, and he had had time to mull over the interview, he sensed a feeling of emptiness. Perhaps his dismissal of her had been too hasty, he should have listened to her and maybe found out what had happened in their home town at the time her father died. He retained a great respect for old Harrison and was curious to know the circumstances of his death.

The Lincolnshire Tramp

"She's a social worker, you know." The statement came from the patient in the next bed and was directed at Joe. "Seen her in our street when the kids at the end were in trouble."

"Is that so," said Joe contemptuously.

"I thought she only dealt with kids," observed the patient, "Didn't know she did your sort as well,"

"What d'you mean – my sort?"

"Well – vagrants and tramps and suchlike. No offence intended.

"I don't want a bloody, social worker," groaned Joe, "I just want to get out of this place."

The patient drew a deep breath and shook his head, "Be some time before you leave this place, mate. From what I've been hearing it will be a couple of months, if not more. You've got some bad injuries there, I can tell you."

"Thanks for nothing," mumbled Joe as he sank deeper into his pillows. He became more aware of the pain racking his body, made worse, no doubt, by the mention of 'bad injuries'. Two months of this, he thought, I don't think I'll be able to take it.

For the rest of the day and well into the night, Joe tried to get Virginia out of his mind but no matter how often he forced his brain to pick out another subject it invariably returned to her. Her appearance bothered him most for she was not at all as he remembered her. In former days she was young and beautiful always well dressed and elegant, she had poise and charisma, and she wore delicate perfumes and careful make-up. Now, as he saw her, she appeared old and gaunt, plainly dressed and without a trace of make-up, and she smelt of stale cigarette smoke.

It also bothered him as to how and why she was in Ramsgate at that particular time. He even entertained the idea that she was part of some conspiracy, probably he was under surveillance by some statutory body or other. In any event, it was too much of a coincidence and it troubled him greatly.

Virginia, although angry with Joe, could not help being curious about him. Something about his demeanour suggested he had lived a life outside of the normal and it intrigued her. A week had passed since she stormed out of the hospital and at that time she had been in two minds whether to return or not but now she knew she was going back.

Simple logic told her that Joe had every right to be cross with her; did she not throw him out of her shop when she thought he was the cause of her father's death. And now, when he lay injured in a hospital bed, did he not have the same right? Why should he be expected to be anything but bad tempered so soon after a terrible accident? Her calling prevailed upon her to return to the hospital in case he needed her help and never mind the verbal brickbats he might throw at her.

Expecting the worst, she followed the other visitors into the men's ward and found Joe in his usual place. Nothing much had changed, he was still well bandaged and protected but she did think he looked a little healthier in the face. "Hello! Joe" she smiled, "How are you feeling today?"

" Not so bad," he said meekly." I didn't expect to see you again"

"Well – " sighed Virginia, finding the chair, "You know how it is. We go back a long way so I can't really ignore each other. The air has to be cleared."

Immediately Joe latched on to her unintentional cue and asserted, " I want to assure you that I did not steal any of your father's money, or the firm's money. I never embezzled a single penny".

"I know – I know," confessed Virginia ashamedly. "It was all Keith's fault, he stole the money and caused poor Daddy's death". She looked up into Joe's eyes and continued, "I was hard on you at the time and I am terribly sorry". She paused just long enough to take a handkerchief from the sleeve of her sweater and dab at her nose with it. "Later, when I found out the truth, I went to your house to apologise but there was nobody there, the place was deserted. I did try several times – honest!"

"Forget it," said Joe, "It's all in the past. It's gone now."

"That's my problem – I can't forget it. Things went terribly wrong then and it ruined my life. I should have taken your advice and disassociated my shop from the family business. I can see that now." She broke off to look wistfully into space and wished, for all the world, she could turn the clock back. After the pause she said, "I believed in Keith, you see. I thought he knew all about business because that's all he'd ever done. I had no idea he was so hopeless at it and he was being propped up by people like you and Daddy. Keith always sounded so convincing when he talked about commerce, now I know it was just a lot of hot air."

"Your brother was very selfish," interjected Joe, "He used what little skills he had to further his own ends."

"Did you know he gambled?" said Virginia sourly, "I knew nothing about it until they came to repossess my shop."

"The last time I saw Keith," Joe reflected, "We had a flaming row. The men were on strike and the works had closed down. That was the first time I heard about your father's death and I was never told the full story.

"Nobody knows the real truth," admitted Virginia, "Daddy collapsed in Keith's house and died of a heart attack in hospital later. I suspect Keith knows more but he wasn't saying".

Joe wanted to commiserate with Virginia for the demise of her father but a coldness within him excluded all such sentiment, instead, he resorted to more mundane matters.

"What happened to the firm?" he asked. "Did Keith keep it going?"

A pained expression crossed Virginia's face as she explained, "The men never went back to work and about a week after Daddy's funeral the entire contents of the workshops, stores and offices were sold at auction. A month later the site was sold – I understand there's a superstore there now. Keith said he had to do it because the firm had incurred too many debts."

"The idiot," barked Joe, "That firm had too many assets to go bankrupt. It could have easily ridden out the recession and be in production today." For a fleeting moment he was back behind his desk busily structuring the company for future success.

"And that's not all," continued Virginia with an air of confidentiality, "he moved his mistress into our house, a thin girl who wore too much lipstick. Her name was Millie Roberts – I don't know if you knew her at all, she was always around the town."

Joe shook his head. He did not recall a Millie Roberts.

"Anyway," resumed Virginia, "When he brought her there for the first time she was to keep me company because the house would be lonely without Daddy. His motive soon became clear and I could swear he spent more time there than he did at his real home. It was Shena and the children I felt sorry for. Without any real work on his hands he had time to waste and he behaved like a playboy, throwing money around as if it didn't matter. When I tackled him about it he said he'd won the money in a football pools syndicate with some of his friends. I can see now that it was the proceeds of the sales after the creditors had taken their cut. He lied to me and said they'd taken it all and there was nothing left for me. Foolishly, I believed him because I had no reason to challenge his decisions. I was doing well with my shop so I wasn't short of money and there was no animosity between us – not at that time." Once again she paused to stare into space and after a moment of reflection she added, "If only you'd been around then, Joe, you could have saved me with your good counselling."

Joe made no comment but he thought a great deal. He doubted if Virginia would have taken his advice, she might have found her brother to be a more powerful influence. Seemingly, she had not acted on his instructions when he did put himself out to help her. It would have been a waste of time.

Like a precipitant shroud, fatigue swept over Joe's body and rendered him too exhausted to listen to more of Virginia's ramblings. Such was his tiredness, it was as much as he could do to summon up enough energy to ask her to leave. Once again his feelings were in turmoil, he wanted to be rid of her for what she and her brother had done to him yet, for reasons beyond his comprehension, he wanted her to stay and be there should he awake from his next sleep. It was his intention to be rude to her but his words adopted an apologetic ring and he heard himself requesting, rather than ordering, her removal.

Slightly put out but condescending to understand his problem, Virginia took her leave. She had promised to wait another week before returning, by then (she hoped) he would have regained some of his strength. In the meantime she had plenty to occupy her mind.

Joe fell asleep almost before Virginia left the ward. It was the longest and deepest sleep he had had for many years; it might easily have been the turning point between life and death. However, he returned to the land of the living on the following morning and did so with restored vitality. And after breakfast he made an unusual request – he asked to be shaved. A small enough gesture at the time but it was the start of a better relationship between himself and the nursing fraternity. Reason had told him to be more tolerant of them since they and he were destined to spend considerable time together.

Getting back to gregariousness would not be an easy transition for Joe, he had spent too much time on his own and had come to accept solitude as the only way of life. But now he was a captive amongst so many busy people as is the way of a patient in hospital, he had to change. He was part of the community, whether he liked it or not, and as such he could not remain isolated. With this in mind he consented to a member of the staff to give him a daily shave, and tend to other personal matters. Beyond that, he kept himself to himself and as his treatment progressed so his protestations grew less.

On the day of her next visit, Virginia suffered a bout of depression. She had taken her prescription soon after breakfast but it seemed not to have had any effect by the time she arrived at the hospital. It was late in the afternoon but her melancholy continued to weigh

The Lincolnshire Tramp

heavily upon her. Nonetheless, she was determined to see Joe again and, this time, find out more about his recent activities. So far she had only told him of her own problems.

"You're looking well today, Joe," she said on greeting him. "I bet I look a right mess."

You do, thought Joe but declined to say as much. In fact he thought she looked a damned sight worse than she did the previous week, more haggard, more washed out. "Sit down," he invited, "And tell me about it."

"About what?"

"Whatever it is that troubles you."

She sat down "It's nothing really. I'm a bit low, that's all. It happens."

"As I remember," recollected Joe, "You never used to get down in the dumps, you were always above that sort of thing, always bright and perky. How come you've changed?"

"Alcohol," confessed Virginia. "I became an alcoholic."

"I can't believe that," said Joe, "You were always scornful of strong drink. Fruit juice was your tipple."

"Yes – with gin in it!"

"I didn't know that!" Joe was astonished.

You wouldn't have done," Virginia explained, "I didn't start adding the gin until long after Daddy's funeral. It was Keith's fault really."

"Why?"

"Because he drove me to it." Virginia became almost tearful. "He was such a pig – a selfish, rotten, arrogant pig. He swindled me out of everything. I lost everything I possessed because of him." Tears began to well up in her eyes.

A twinge of sympathy tugged at Joe's conscience. He wanted to comfort her but without the use of his arms and hands he could do nothing physical, also, he was at a loss for words. Thereupon, he assumed her little handkerchief would be employed to dry her moistened cheeks but it did not emerge from its hiding place in her sleeve. Instead, she clutched the straps of her handbag and recalled the most unpleasant of her memories.

"You wouldn't believe this," fretted Virginia, "But I caught Keith taking fifty pounds out of my shop till. It happened one afternoon when I was out sorting stock. I heard a noise in the shop and went to investigate. It was Keith and when I asked him what he was doing he just laughed and said he was taking some of what was owed to him. He said, because it was a family business he was entitled to half the profits."

"The bastard," exclaimed Joe.

Virginia nodded in agreement and then said, "We had one hell of a row, the first we ever had, and I saw him in his true colours – a shiftless lout with a greed for money, and he didn't care where it came from. I told him it was my shop and my business and all the money it generated belonged to me. I said he was to stay away from it and never come near it again. He got very angry and started to threaten me but I was determined to beat him at his own game. I ordered him to remove himself and his mistress from Daddy's house and, if he didn't, I would instigate legal proceedings against him. I wasn't sure what I could do at the time but I had to scare him off somehow."

"But surely," Joe intervened, "Your father left a will to cover all that."

"Keith said there wasn't a will and probate would take a long time. You know what I'm like about that sort of thing – I don't understand it. I was content to let Keith handle it – fool that I was." She paused for a moment and used the time to bite at the thumbnail on her right hand. "Anyway," she continued, "Keith stormed out of the shop and warned me to watch my step in future. I was so angry and frightened; I went out and bought a bottle of gin. It tasted horrible but I didn't care, I just wanted to drown my sorrows and forget everything. I got terribly drunk and was sick afterwards but worse than that – I got hooked on the stuff. I took it steady at first because I still had a business to run but when I lost that I really hit the bottle."

"So it was you who lost the business – nothing to do with Keith?" Joe surmised.

"It had everything to do with bloody Keith," Virginia raised her voice, "He sold the bloody shop from under me." Then her voice modulated as she explained. "I went to work as usual one morning and found three men waiting for me. They said they wanted to speak to me in confidence about my brother so I let them into my shop. Then, as I stood there and waited to be told what mischief Keith had been up to, they began to fold up my business. One of them changed the locks on the doors, another listed all the stock and the third measured up the place and listed the fittings and fixtures. And when I demanded to know what was going on they calmly told me they were official receivers and had come to seize all the assets, including the building. I was shown some documentation which seemed to verify their claim.

"The only person I could turn to was my Bank Manager but when I met him he shook his head and said he was very sorry; the matter was out of his hands. Then he explained that Keith had borrowed a large sum of money from another branch and had used my shop as collateral. Somehow the bank had discovered that Keith had used the money to gamble with and lost the lot. Naturally they wanted their pound of flesh – my shop. They certainly move fast when they smell trouble."

Joe shook his head in disgust. "What a dirty trick to play on your own sister," he said – then he added, "He was always trying the same tricks on your father but the old man was too astute to be taken in."

"Then I wish Daddy had confided in me and told me what Keith was like. I had no idea what was going on. If only somebody had warned me."

"Suffice it to say," said Joe with some severity, "I went out of my way to warn you all those years ago but I was thrown out of the shop and the door locked against me". He seized the opportunity to air that particular grudge.

With her eyes wide open and full of compassion, Virginia looked at him.

"Poor man," she sighed, "You were always so good to me in those days and I didn't have the decency to trust you. What a stupid woman I am. How can you ever forgive me."

"You were deeply distressed by the death of your Father so, understandably, your attitude would be irrational," said Joe benignly. In fact, he wanted to say, "It serves you right for not listening to me in the first place," but given his own despicable behaviour during the interim years, he was in no position to deride Virginia. Probably he could forgive her but who would, in all honesty, forgive him. It pained him to remember the wickedness he had perpetrated in pursuit of vengeance but he was not ready to face penance and wanted his mind to be free of the subject. "I hear that you are a social worker now" he enquired, "How did that come about?"

"Through drink, I suppose." There was sadness in her voice. "I drank too much and somebody helped me out. I wanted to repay my debt to society so I became one of its workers. I haven't been doing the job for any length of time because it took me too long to get over my illness."

"Alcoholism – you mean?"

"Yes, I got it really bad. Within days of losing my shop I had to get out of Daddy's house – that was also sold off. I moved into a rented room and started spending my meagre savings on drink; it was the only consolation I could find. I couldn't believe that Keith had lost in one year what it had taken Daddy a lifetime to achieve.

The Lincolnshire Tramp

It seemed so unfair; I was hurt and upset. I know I should have gone out and found myself another job there and then but I just couldn't face it – drinking was easier. Besides, if I had got back on my feet again how long do you think it would be before Keith came snooping. He'd be after every penny I earned. That lousy brother of mine ruined my life and I lived in fear of him. All I could do was to escape to my bolthole and blot him out with a bottle of gin.

You can guess what happened next – I became addicted. When I realised what had happened it was too late. I began to suffer from DT's and my body went to waste. My money ran out and I wasn't capable of earning anymore – I couldn't have held down a job, not in the state I was in. I was an absolute mess. Anyway, to cut a long story short, I collapsed in the street one day. I don't remember much about it but I was told I held up the traffic for almost an hour. Later, when I came round in hospital, I had a terrible craving for alcohol and I demanded to be given it. They refused, of course, and told me that one more drink would kill me – I was that close to death. What could I do? I mean, I was stuck in that bed, wired up to all sorts of machines and desperate for a drink. At the time, death was not an issue – getting through the night was more of a problem."

"You could have discharged yourself," said Joe wistfully. "That's what I'm going to do as soon as I can walk again."

"It's not as easy as that," scolded Virginia. "Mending a broken bone is one thing but trying to overcome the effects of alcoholism is another. Your mind is blown, your body is weak, you're afraid to walk through the next door and you think you are going to freak out all the time. You just lose all hope and don't want to go on living. It's really scary."

"You must have come through it," cut in Joe, "Because you're here to tell the tale."

"Oh! Yes," agreed Virginia, "I did get through it. I've been to hell and back."

"I know the feeling," muttered Joe.

Virginia ignored him and carried on with her reminiscence. "After a few days, I was transferred from the hospital to a nursing home to undergo a course of treatment. It was horrendous for the first month or so and I was suicidal for most of the time. I couldn't get it into my head that I was actually ill and until I accepted that simple fact I would never get well again. It took a long time but I did recover, with that and a lot of help from the AA I came back to being a real person. I haven't as much sipped an alcoholic drink since then – isn't it marvellous?"

The Lincolnshire Tramp

Joe licked his lips at the thought of a strong drink and said, "I've drunk a lot in the past years but it hasn't affected me like that. Mind you, I could do with a good whisky now."

"I could help you there," promised Virginia.

"What! Smuggle a bottle in? Though light hearted, Joe had expectations.

"No – silly!" Virginia smiled. "Help you with your craving for alcohol is what I meant. I could take you along to the AA and get you sorted out." She became aware, at that moment, of a great weight lifting from her shoulder – her melancholy had receded. She felt refreshed and revitalised. Talking to Joe had done her a power of good.

"I don't want to be sorted out," protested Joe, " I like to drink."

"On your head be it," she construed, "But don't say I didn't warn you."

She leant forward to brush his hair out of his eyes and then said, "I've told you all about me, now I want to know what you've been up to?"

Joe paled and alarm bells rang in his head. How could he tell her the truth about himself? It would mean confessing to, arson and robbery in Essex, sexual abuse in Suffolk, house breaking and sexual harassment in Norfolk, indecent exposure and burglary in Northants, attempted murder in Bedford, killing a swan and raping a woman in Somerset and a string of minor offences. She might not take kindly to such confessions and deem it her duty to report the incidents to the police. Besides, Joe was anxious to draw a thick membrane over the episodes and hide them in a corner of his mind; they were beginning to haunt him.

"I'm feeling rather tired just now," he proffered, "perhaps I could you about me at some other time. After I've rested." It was a hasty, yet substantial excuse designed to foil her curiosity. In her absence, presuming she left him alone, he could dream up a convincing answer to her question.

Virginia exuded sympathy. "I understand," she said, " I know what it's like to be confined to bed. You rest now and I'll come back again – probably next week." She stood up and prepared to leave. "Before I go – is there anything I can get you?"

"No – nothing!"

"Bye then, see you next week!"

Joe nodded rather than voice a parting salutation. He was sorry for bringing the visit to an end but he feared she would pry too deeply into his recent past. All the same, he had enjoyed talking to her and listening to the account of her life; she too had suffered. He could now make allowances for her and accept her for what she was. What is more, he looked forward to her visits.

When Virginia, on that fateful night in October, tried to render aid to an unconscious tramp, she had no idea how much it was to change her life. She thought she had sorted herself out after the traumatic events that had taken her to death's door. Her future, as she saw it, offered nothing out of the ordinary, nor did she want there to be. Her plan was simple, twenty years service in the local community, retirement with a pension, a bungalow with a garden, and a cat. Undoubtedly, she would meet many people during the course of her work but an emotional attachment to any particular being was never envisaged. She certainly did not expect a ghost from the past to return and progressively dominate her very existence.

From the outset, both she and Joe had not the slightest intention of renewing their former friendship. They were both very independent people who abhorred the thought of a meaningful relationship with another person. However, coming together was inevitable and no matter how hard they fought against it they could not ward off their destiny. It was not an instantaneous bond but one that gradually developed as an underlying theme to their subsequent conversations; a bond too strong to break when they eventually became aware of it.

Up until late December, Virginia's visits to the hospital became more regular, and as Joe's bones began to mend she took on some of the work of the Physiotherapist. In the main, Joe' superficial wounds had healed and he had regained the use of his hands and arms but his pelvis and legs had been greatly weakened and needed lengthy convalescence to rebuild them. Nevertheless, everyone was delighted with his progress and many claimed it as a miracle.

"I shall never know how he survived that terrible fall," was the common opinion at the time.

Although his body responded well to treatment, Joe could not say the same for his conscience (not that anybody found it necessary to apply healing to his mental disorders) so that whenever he cast his mind back to the darkest of his days, he cringed with shame. There was no use denying it, he had sunk to the lowest levels of depravity and deserved only to be banished to the sewers where he should be no more than subservient to the vermin. On all counts, he was not worthy of the care and attention lavished upon him by Virginia and the staff of the hospital. After all, she (and they) were never told about his wicked deeds; he kept his secretes to himself because he lacked the courage to tell and he suffered for it.

With Christmas just around the corner, Virginia had an idea. She thought it would be nice if she and Joe could spend the holiday at her flat. She had a spare room and a suitable bed and a willingness to attend to his needs.

Although apprehensive, Joe did not rule out the idea and offered to consider it, but the hospital authority welcomed the plan and pushed hard to achieve it. Because they could not discharge him back into the wild they were duty bound to find him a suitable place to start his convalescence, after that he could become the responsibility of the Social Services and it would be up to them to find him a more permanent place of residence.

With the odds stacked against him, Joe reluctantly accepted the inevitable. It was arranged to convey him to the flat on Christmas Eve with the proviso that he would be carried, by ambulancemen, up the stairs to the level of the first floor rooms. Clutching his meagre possessions and escorted by Virginia, he was wheeled in a chair to an ambulance and driven the few miles to Ramsgate.

Chapter 17

Joe had his qualm about living with another person. Although he knew Virginia reasonably well, he had misgivings about their compatibility. True, their relationship proved amicable on an hour to hour basis but how would it stand up over a period of several days? Several days of confinement to be precise because he was well aware of his limited mobility; he could not walk away if he was dissatisfied. Then again, would sharing a flat with Virginia be too much like living at home with Marjorie? If it proved to be the case then he would certainly have to leave, a means would have to be found if he was to be haunted by memories of his marriage.

As for herself, Virginia was looking forward to the arrangement, it excited her but she could not say why. Maybe it was an ego trip, or just another adventure, a new lease of life – perhaps, or was it for some deep-seated reason beyond her powers of deduction. No matter, she could not waste the time to figure it out; she had too much to do.

Entertaining a man in her home was a new departure for her and she was desperately anxious to do all the right things. Hitherto, she had known only two men in a domestic way, her father and her brother and she had grown up with them. Now there were new roles to play and many moves to learn.

It had been decided, between the two of them, to keep Christmas as a low-key affair. The mass and its subsequent revelry had lost a lot of its magic and meaning for both Joe and Virginia. They agreed not to exchange presents – or sentiments – and take each day as it came. Relaxation, conversation and companionship became a matter of course.

On Christmas Day, Virginia cooked an excellent lunch with trimmings and offered to slip out and get Joe a bottle of his preferred drink to have with his meal. All too aware of his own failings, Joe declined the offer. One drink from such a bottle would lead to another and before long the bottle would be drained. Beyond doubt, he would end up blind drunk and ruin everything. It vexed him to turn his back on alcohol but he knew it was the best thing he could do, especially in consideration of Virginia's problem.

With a smug little smile on her face, Virginia welcomed Joe's decision. She secretly hoped he would refrain from drinking, at least for the time being and give her a chance to know him as his sober self. "Can you tell me something?" she asked as soon as luncheon was out of the way, "How come a clever man like you ended up as a tramp?"

Joe gave the question a moment's thought before he said, "It's a long story really but, to put it in a nutshell, I gave up on life. I tried to please everyone yet pleased no one. Everyone kicked me in the teeth so I just walked out."

"Including me," muttered Virginia, lighting up a cigarette. "But – what I don't understand is," she paused to wipe a tiny strand of tobacco from her mouth, "What did you do with your wife? Did she die, or what?"

"As far as I know she's very much alive," sighed Joe, "And I don't think she ever knew I'd taken to the road. If she did I don't suppose she'd care."

"You just walked out on her – just like that. I mean, I can understand you being cross with people like me and Keith, but your own wife – how could you?"

"It wasn't that difficult," recounted Joe irately, "I'd been away trying to save the firm and everybody's job and when I returned home I found her in bed with another man. That day, I was made to feel the most useless person in the world. What would you have done?"

"I don't know," confessed Virginia thoughtfully, "I might forgive and forget or I might do as you did and walk out. I've never been married so I don't know how I would react. I know I would be very hurt."

"Best not to get married if you have sensitive feelings," observed Joe. "I shall not get involved again, I know that."

"What will you do when you're well again?"

"Back on the open road, I suppose."

"You liked it then?"

"I was free to do as I pleased."

"So you'd go back to being a tramp rather than get married for a second time?"

"Why should I want to get married for a second time?"

"I don't why I said that." Virginia blushed vehemently. "How silly of me." She moved towards the window and looked out, "It must be very cold out there. And it's getting darker."

Joe made no comment, his mind was elsewhere. He wondered where he would have spent Christmas if it had not been for the accident.

The Lincolnshire Tramp

Throughout the remainder of the holiday, Virginia avoided further mention of Joe's marital status although she thought about it quite often. Instead, she contented herself with his general well being and was delighted with the progress he made. In that short space of time she could see a marked difference in him, he looked healthier, he gained weight and he was beginning to find the full use of his legs.

All too soon, the day came for Joe to be handed back to the hospital and the care of the Social Services. However, Virginia had plans of her own. She did not make the necessary arrangements for transportation and went alone to meet the authority. Acutely aware of the shortage of accommodation for the homeless, more so for the injured homeless, she argued for, and was granted the release of Joe into her care for a term of six months. Of course, certain formalities had to be attended to and she must expect visits from other social workers.

Later in the day when a jubilant Virginia returned to her flat, Joe was told about the new arrangement. He chose to be philosophical about it and agreed to comply with her wishes in as much as his convalescence was concerned. After that (he emphasised) he reserved the right to leave and go his own way. His rider was not part of Virginia's plan but she accepted it for the time being, knowing full well that she would change it at some later date. Until then, she vowed to pander to his needs and win him back into normal civilisation.

From time to time during the next few weeks, Joe suffered recurring nightmares – stemming from his experiences with the widow and the swan – and put it down to sleeping in a proper bed. He began to nurse a desire to sleep out of doors once again but was reluctant to leave the comparative luxury of the flat.

For a while he was torn between the different life styles until finally, when he could not make up his mind, he mentioned it to Virginia. One evening, soon after she had returned home from her work, he explained, " I don't know why it is, but I seem to have trouble sleeping in a bed. I feel that I should be sleeping in the open."

"I see," said Virginia unemphatically, giving lie to the turbulance in her mind for she thought he was about to announce his departure and move out of her life. "There must be a simple explanation," she urged searching for a solution. "I know I'm away most days and have to leave you on your own, that must be pretty boring for you, especially as you're virtually a prisoner here. I think a change of air is what you really need. Perhaps you should get out of the flat for at least an hour every day, go for a walk, and get some exercise. Do you think your legs are up to it now?"

"I'm sure my old legs are up to it," confirmed Joe, tapping his thighs. "With a good stick I know I could manage a daily walk."

"You must take it easy," warned Virginia, "I don't want you overdoing it on the first day." She was happier in her mind now, he was not thinking of wandering too far away. "First thing in the morning, I'll go and get you a stick," she promised.

Joe had always believed he would walk forever, considering the time he had spent tramping the roads, but his first outing (alone and to some distance) proved his belief unsound. His legs were nowhere near strong enough to support him for any length of time and he realised that much effort would be required to build up the muscles again. He also realised that he could not discard the bed that Virginia had provided, he would have to sleep on it – nightmares or not.

By mid-February, Joe was due at the hospital for a check up and an assessment. Virginia accompanied him and seemed to spend the entire afternoon smiling as Joe was complimented, time and time again, for the good progress he had made; to everyone's credit, he had done very well. However, care was still needed if he wanted to gain full use of his legs.

Before leaving the hospital, Joe was handed the remainder of his personal effects (items taken from him and put into safe keeping whilst he was confined to the wards) two bulky envelopes marked "Vagrant". The larger contained his collection of sketches and the smaller, his money; money he had stolen or found during his years of vagrancy.

He was pleased to have his sketches back, he had almost forgotten them but he felt uneasy about the money; it was suddenly repulsive. "Take it," he said thrusting the envelope into Virginia's hand. "It'll help to pay for my keep."

"There's no need," objected Virginia, "I'll gladly take care of you for nothing." She wanted to hand the money back and then thought it wiser not to go against Joe's wishes. "I'll look after it for you," she decided and tucked the envelope in her bag. "About the sketches," she continued. "Do you know I nearly stole them from you on the night of the accident. I came across them in your pocket and took a liking to them."

"They're nothing really." Confessed Joe, "But they did help me through some bad times. I might let you have them if I think they are worth saving."

"I shall have them," laughed Virginia as she guided Joe towards her car, "You can be sure of that." For a moment she was her old self again. She had slipped back to her former days and she bubbled with exuberance and youthfulness returned to her voice. Being with Joe was like a tonic and as she drove him back to her flat she glowed with happiness.

On the way she found herself planning her future with Joe. Wouldn't it be wonderful to have him as a more permanent companion, she thought. Her mind raced on as she examined the possibility of making him more dependent upon her. She had to find a way to make him stay with her. It was not going to be easy because he was such an independent man and had ideas of his own. As yet, she still did not realise why she needed to go to such extraordinary lengths to bring him closer to her. All she could accept was an overwhelming desire to hang on to him at all costs. If it meant resorting to trickery then so be it.

That evening, when she had prepared dinner, a new scheme evolved in her head. It needed a certain amount of tact and courage that she hoped to gain when they watched television together. Eventually, her plan came into being when at ten p.m. she ran a hot bath for Joe. Only then did she have the daring to suggest, "After your bath, Joe, I want you to do something for me – okay?"

"But of course. Just name it."

"I don't want you to go into your room tonight. I want you to come into mine and into my bed. Will you be a darling and do that for me?"

After some hesitation, brought about by a loss of words rather than a lack of desire, Joe gave one of his rare smiles and nodded in consent. He gently gripped Virginia's arm before making his way to the bathroom.

Virginia breathed a deep sigh of relief and then skipped into her bedroom to prepare herself. She was pleased to have caught Joe in such an amiable mood; surely now he must find pleasure in her bed and make meaningful love to her. The intercourse they would enjoy would establish a bond between them and carry their relationship to a higher plane.

With her heart pounding like a bass drum, she went to her wardrobe and selected the prettiest and most daring of her nightdresses. She laid the garment on the bed and then stared at it to envisage the sexual satisfaction it would evoke. It had been a long time since a man had sought the delights of her body, which is not to say she was entirely without experience. In the past, her lovers came from wealthier ranks; one night stands after the Hunt Ball or brief affairs at the tennis club. Such were mere flings and never taken seriously. Sex was par for the course amongst the bright young things, nobody attached any real importance to it. A successful career was the main attraction.

As she took he day clothes off and sprayed her naked body with perfume, she began to think about the meaning of love. Was she really in love with Joe or was it something to do with being left on the shelf? Why was it so important to hang on to this common tramp? He was a man without prospects and a good twenty years older than herself. He was not a particularly handsome man or a healthy one and he did not readily display a sense of humour. The more she thought about it the less important his attributes became. The overriding factor was the extent to which she was drawn to him and wanted him for herself. What about him? Would he ever come to love her?

Oh dear! Was it sex she wanted or love? Or was she afraid this would be her last chance of either? Did she really need to have someone else cluttering up her life? With so many questions bombarding her brain it was little wonder she trembled when she donned the nightdress and slipped into bed.

If Virginia suffered anxieties then Joe fared no better. He lay back in the hot bath and tried to fathom things out. Her request had caught him off guard and he was not sure what to make of it. It all seemed so unreal. It disorientated him; he could not be sure if he was the same person anymore. Reason would suggest he had undergone a change of image and had done so without conscious effort on his part. Fate must be manipulating his life now. How else could the transition from obnoxious tramp to prospective lover be explained? In the same light, he no longer saw himself as a lover either.

He had never been invited into a female's bed before nor had he ever been propositioned and it unnerved him. He began to suspect an ulterior motive but could not see what it might be. Perplexed and apprehensive he eased himself out of the bath and towelled himself down.

Soon after when he had cleared the mirror of condensation prior to shaving, he was alarmed by his own reflection. It suddenly came home to him that he was looking at an old man. "Christ!" he muttered. "Whatever can she see in me? I've aged so much." Then, as he lathered his chin, he remembered Virginia also looked old for her years, more like a maiden aunt than a seductive young siren. If he was going to make love to her then he would have to look beyond the barrier of time and see her for the youthful beauty she was. It was an unkind thought on his behalf and he need not have entertained it because he was more than confident of his own sexual prowess.

It took only a matter of minutes for him to complete his shave and then put the bathroom in order before making his way into Virginia's bedroom. He entered her room and saw her in the light of a small, bedside lamp, its mellow glow softening the hard lines in her face. He particularly noticed the pretty nightdress, which gave the illusion of sensuality to a neglected body. He sensed a heady atmosphere with its symptomatic invitation to delicious sex and he smelled a delicate perfume designed to rouse the most reluctant of lovers. In all, the scene was set for a most pleasurable copulation.

Virginia smiled and opened the bed clothes to welcome him to her side. She was warm and affectionate, lustful and passionate, breathless and eager and above all, most anxious to please her man. Her body quivered with anticipation and she was as ready as she ever could be for a stiffened phallus. "Come to me, darling," she sighed, "Come and make love to me."

She had, in effect, worked herself up into a state of wild abandonment, an unusually rare occurrence for her as she craved the union which she hoped would bring Joe closer to her. There was no escape from the desire within her breast, she wanted him for herself and now she was sure of it.

The main function of a female on heat is to arouse the mating instinct in her partner, none more so than in Virginia's case. Unfortunately, despite all sexual enticements, Joe could not rise to her expectancy. To his horror, he discovered impotency.

In a desperate effort to bring some rigidity into his limp and pallid penis he recoursed to his unpractised knowledge of foreplay. He kissed her body from her neck to her toes and clumsily fondled her breasts and vagina. He encouraged her to play with him, even to the point of taking his penis between her lips. But, to his obvious disappointment, their combined efforts did not produce the desired erection. By not being able to enter her he denied them both the

The Lincolnshire Tramp

pleasure of intercourse. Dejectedly, he rolled away and complained bitterly about being a failure as a man.

Virginia touched him gently and kissed his cheek. "Don't worry," she whispered, "It's not the end of the world. We can try again tomorrow."

"I don't think so," Joe said solemnly, "This impotency thing looks to be permanent." He started to leave. "I think I'd better go back to my bed."

"You can sleep here tonight," urged Virginia, preventing his departure, "And if I were you, I wouldn't worry about being temporarily impotent. It's probably caused by that terrible accident you had. You'll get over it."

Joe thanked her for her kindness but as he settled down to sleep he knew his problem was not a physical one – it was a psychological one. He had raped the widow and he was to be punished for it. For as long as this spectre haunted him he would never be able to make love to Virginia; the thought depressed him. A sexual relationship with her would be more than ample compensation for the loss of Marjorie.

Unaware of Joe's thoughts, Virginia cuddled up to him and dreamt of happier times ahead. Who knows – they might marry and raise a family? Foolish dreams, no doubt, but they made her feel good.

From then on Joe always slept with Virginia although he remained permanently impotent. They came to accept that sexual intercourse would never be part of their life together but would not allow it to impede their friendship. For most of the time Joe was quite content to stay with Virginia in her flat but too much inactivity unsettled him and he fell victim to bouts of restlessness. When such incidents occurred, Virginia responded swiftly. She was always keen to find something to occupy his mind in order to wean him from his wanderlust.

That is why she found him some part time work in the restaurant beneath the flat. He was hired to help with the washing up but when the more permanent staff discovered that he was a rehabilitative tramp they mistrusted him and believed he was out to rob them of their modest possessions. Essays were made to reassure the staff that Joe posed no threat to them but the uneasy atmosphere prevailed and Joe was forced to give up the job. In fairness to himself, he made a concerted effort to stay with the work and not lose heart at the first set back. Proving his worth suddenly became a matter of principle.

Virginia was sympathetic and understood his reasons for leaving the job, but she remained undeterred and encouraged him to consider self employment, that way he would be in control of his own destiny yet remain under her spell.

"Nice idea," admitted Joe, "But what work d'you suppose I should do?"

"You should try accountancy – you're good at that."

"No – I don't think I could do that. It would bring back too many bitter memories. It would have to be something else."

"Handyman then! Can you do odd jobs around the house and garden?"

"I liked to do a bit of gardening but otherwise I'm useless with my hands."

Oh! I wouldn't agree. Look at those sketches you did – you need clever hands to do something like that."

That's different," said Joe with a bashful smile. "You can do anything you like when it's your hobby."

"And you could also do it for money," interjected Virginia. "I'm sure you could sell all the pictures you painted." The idea appealed to her more than it did to Joe and she was quite carried away with it.

"Hold on a minute," urged Joe, "I'm not sure that I can paint a picture let alone sell it. Just because I've made a few sketches it doesn't mean to say I can paint. I'm not an artist."

"How do you know until you try," said Virginia firmly. "You have some money to come from the restaurant so I suggest you go out and buy some paint and brushes and something to paint on and make a start."

Joe began to take to the idea and in his mind he weighed up the feasibility of the project. "I'd need somewhere to work," he said, "It could be a messy business."

"No such problem," smiled Virginia. "Now that your bedroom has become vacant there's nothing to stop is turning it into a studio. Let's have fun, let's do it now."

Before Joe could utter another word, be it in protest or be it of approval, he was ushered into the spare room and instructed to dismantle the bed. Virginia donned a headscarf and an overall coat and set about rearranging the rest of the furniture. Two hours later, the room was officially designated, by a laughing Virginia, as a place of work and not a place of rest. "Resident artist." She announced, "Mr Joseph Glasson."

The Lincolnshire Tramp

Joe looked at her and smiled, he was pleased to see the "old" Virginia coming back into her own. He hoped he could do justice to the faith she had in him and produce the pictures she wanted. To show his commitment and to fire up his own inspiration, he put his sketches on display so that they could go through them together and judge them for their merit.

Days later when the money for his work at the restaurant came through, Joe took Virginia shopping. They made an excursion to Canterbury and had a wonderfully exhilarating time buying up an abundance of artists' materials. They purchased a box of watercolours, a box of oils, a box of acrylics and boxes of coloured pencils and crayons. They also bought paper, card and canvasses as well as a selection of brushes. The incessant conversation between them conjured up all kinds of pictorial images that might, one day, adorn the walls in many a house.

The ecstasy was in the purchase of materials and not in the practical application of them, as Joe soon realised when he sat down to try and sort them out. He may have been gifted in the ability to draw but that gifted ability did not extend to the actual techniques required to work the various mediums. In fact, he did not get on at all well with the oil paints and only marginally better with the acrylics. He had hoped to do better with the watercolours but the results were disappointing.

In time, with encouragement from Virginia, he went along to the local library and spent many hours reading all he could find on the subject of art and its construction. Painting pictures was not going to be as easy as he thought, he would have to develop some skills before he completed a single work. Nonetheless, he learned sufficient from the books to strengthen his resolve and set about his task with renewed vigour.

A month slipped by and still he had not produced a worthwhile picture. Virginia detected a slight despondency in his manner and thought she saw that telltale look in his eye. Deeply concerned she suggested he take a short break from his work and accompany her on a visit to a foster home where she had four small charges. Joe agreed to go with her although he confessed to not having had a lot of contact with small children, he was not sure how they would respond to him.

By car, it took about twenty minutes to get to the foster home and on the way Joe was told about the plight of the family in care. "Three boys and a girl," explained Virginia. "Their father is in prison for committing armed robbery and their mother is receiving psychiatric treatment. Poor thing – completely lost her marbles."

"Do you get many cases like this?" As Joe asked the question he realised how little he knew about Virginia's work.

"No –," replied Virginia, "This is the only one I've had. They're good kids really, it's a pity that life has given them such a raw deal. At the moment we're having trouble with the eldest, a boy of eight who habitually wets his bed. I think he feels the loss of his parents more than the others."

It was raining when the car came to a halt outside the foster home. "Is this the place?" asked Joe viewing a detached, double bayed house of the nineteen thirties style.

"It is and we were lucky to find a home as big as this. We like to keep the children of a family together whenever possible." Virginia got out of the car and raised her umbrella. "I expect they'll be inside today," she said, "Hardly the weather for playing out of doors. Are you coming?"

Joe was soon at her side, taking charge of the umbrella he escorted her to the front door. After a short wait a large but pleasant woman opened the door and welcomed them in. They were then guided into the spacious living room where they met the children who were seated at a polished table. Obviously prepared for a visit from their welfare worker, the children were clean, neat and tidy; although their clothing had seen a lot of use.

From the moment Joe stepped into the room he became a focal point for the children. They sat absolutely still whilst their eyes followed his every move. The children were unsure of him and wary of his presence, already in their young lives they were deeply suspicious of strangers. Joe looked into their eyes and saw the misery and the fear that kept the youngsters permanently on guard. He swallowed hard as he remembered his own unpleasantness towards children in recent years. He had been brutally unkind to them and had denied them the entitlement of any emotions.

With something akin to her former panache, Virginia introduced Joe to the children and asked would they mind looking after him whilst she went out of the room to talk to the foster mother. For the shortest of moments the children's faces shone with pleasure as they agreed to her bidding but in their hearts they nursed a certain foreboding. However Virginia was not aware of this as she settled Joe in a comfortable armchair and promised not to leave him at the mercy of the children for too long. "Be good," she called as she left the room.

In the silence that followed Joe began to feel uncomfortable under the relentless staring from the children, even so, he tried to think of something to say that would break the ice but not alarm them. He was not at all skilful in this area – he would admit to that. In fact, it could be said that he was out of his depth when it came to conversing with such young people.

He need not have concerned himself for the only girl in the group could contain her curiosity no longer (she was the second born into the family and now in her seventh year). She had noticed the care with which Joe had been settled in the armchair and knew that something was amiss. "Have you hurt your leg, Mister?" She asked bluntly.

"He's not Mister," whispered her younger brother, "He's Joe!"

"I know," snapped the girl, "Now be quiet."

In a reassuring manner, Joe smiled at the children and said. "I got my legs broken in an accident many months ago. They're almost mended now."

"What sort of accident?" asked the eldest boy.

"I was knocked down by a train," Joe replied then he laughed and added, "I was so angry I got up and pushed it off its tracks." His little joke worked and the children relaxed; they laughed together and the tension crept out of their bodies.

"Do you know any other funny stories, Mister Joe?" The question came from the girl.

"What sort of funny stories?" It was not an answer Joe was looking for but an actual story to tell. His question was merely to stall the girl whilst he racked his brain for a yarn.

"A story about animals," requested the eldest boy; a subject dear to his heart.

The simple request was enough to spark an idea in Joe's mind; he knew a lot of stories about animals and could easily select some of them to tell the children. "I know a story about baby badgers," he said, "Would you like to hear it?" A rapturous chorus came from the children as they shouted, "Yes". Then they settled down to listen.

Joe cast his mind back to that early morning in the woodlands of Somerset when the foraging badgers broke up his nightmares. He picked out an incident when the youngsters of the sett were particularly playful and ambushed an old uncle. With some minor embellishments, Joe related a fascinating tale.

Very soon, he had the undivided attention of the children as they now sat on the floor in front of him and hung on to his every word.

The Lincolnshire Tramp

The story about the badgers was followed by another about ducks and another about fallow deer and so on. By the time Virginia returned he was well into his sixth story.

Mildly surprised by the congenial scene – which she almost interrupted, Virginia selected a vacant chair and sat quietly down. She listened in awe to Joe's story telling and was pleased to see him getting on so well with the children. "I don't know," she declared as soon as the story telling was over, "When I left this room you could have cut the atmosphere with a knife and now, when I come back, it's the cosiest place in the world. What happened?"

She did not really expect an answer but the children gave her one all the same as each had a favourite story to recall and when she told them that it was time to take Joe home they begged her to bring him back again; the sooner the better.

"You had them eating out of your hand," she observed as she started the car for the homeward journey, "I didn't know you had it in you."

"I didn't know either," confessed Joe. "Something must have clicked between me and those kids to set it all going. When we get home I'm going to do something for them. I've made up my mind to paint a picture for each one and link it to their chosen story. See – I've made a list of their names and the story they liked." He held up a list to show Virginia. "I'm glad you brought me here today, it may give me the inspiration I need." He could not have been more impatient to get back to the flat and make a start.

In the days that followed, magic flowed through Joe's fingers. He could not put a solitary line in the wrong place or mix a disagreeable colour. He worked on white card and used gouache as opposed to pure watercolour to create his effects. Each of the four pictures illustrated a group of small animals acting out a particular story and beneath each picture – with the neatness of an accountant – the story was printed.

To tease Virginia, Joe kept the pictures from her until they were all complete, then he arranged a special unveiling ceremony for her benefit. He knew he had done well.

"Joe," she enthused, "They are absolutely brilliant. They're all so good that I don't know which one I like best. You are a clever old thing.

"In the morning," Joe said proudly, "I shall go out and buy frames for them and then we can go and present them to the children."

The Lincolnshire Tramp

Virginia was not listening; she was too engrossed with the pictures. "Do you know," she purred, "I think you've found you metier. I think you could do a complete book on the subject. A book for children – such books are always in demand. It could be the making of you."

"Steady on," spluttered Joe, "That's a bit ambitious for me."

"Not at all," insisted Virginia. "You never know what you can do until you try. Why not give it a go?"

After some erratic thought, Joe declared, "No – it's not possible. I couldn't do it. Where would I begin?"

Virginia lost her patience with him. "Don't talk silly," she said, "You have everything you need. You have paint, you have paper. You know a lot about wild animals and you have sketches to work from and you know enough about life to compose a simple story. For instance – why not write about an old tramp that helps animals? There's an idea!"

A pained expression crossed Joe's face but he could not find it in his heart to reprimand her for drawing his attention to his recent past. Instead he graciously made an allowance for her slip of the tongue and put the issue to the back of his mind. However, he could not entirely rule out her suggestion; there was much sense in what she had said and an idea did lodge in his head.

"Not a tramp," he insisted, "But a little man no more than three feet tall. He could live in a secret cave near Cheddar and, as you say, help the animals."

"You see," beamed Virginia, "You can do it."

Even as she spoke, Joe had a vision of the little man. He would be dressed in an old tweed suit, gardening shoes, cravat and fishing hat – the very clothes that Virginia's father had worn at the last Christmas party they had enjoyed together. In his mind, Joe could see Alfred clearly (even after the passing of so many years) which made him an ideal model. Naturally he would have to clear it with Virginia because she, at some stage, was bound o recognise her father and might be upset by it. He told her there and then.

"It's a wonderful idea, Joe," she said excitedly, "Daddy would have loved it – I know – and I will not be the slightest bit upset by it. I'd take it as a compliment."

In due course, the children were presented with their pictures and Joe made a start on his illustrated book. He was to visit the children regularly for many months and use them as a sounding board for his narrative. He came to accept them as shrewd judges of his work and soon discarded any part that met with their disapproval. Thus the book progressed.

Chapter 18

The summer months were most agreeable and Joe could not have been happier. His relationship with Virginia blossomed into a unique friendship, they were devoted to each other and he had regained his job at the restaurant. He could earn a modest income from washing up dirty dishes for five hours a day, then have three to four hours to work on his illustrated book and still have time for Virginia.

Indeed, they spent a great deal of time walking the Ramsgate Sands or strolling along the tiny harbour or wandering in the parks. They ventured further along the coast to Broadstairs and Margate and inland to Canterbury. They even found time to visit the summer shows at The Granville, The Lido, The Winter Gardens, The Marlowe and other smaller theatres.

For the two of them life became heaven. The miseries of their individual pasts were but a distant blur in their memories but if ever their thoughts were drawn to those infelicitous days then Virginia would easily dismiss hers on the grounds that she justly deserved her new found happiness. Joe, on the other hand, could not make the same claim. He had caused as well as suffered misery; there was no excuse for him. Now he was on top of the world but he knew he had no right to be.

By the end of September, he put the final touches to his illustrated book. Virginia had not seen the work in its entirety because he had – again, to tease her, - deliberately held back the greater part of it. But now he planned to unveil his masterpiece over a candlelight dinner and surprise her.

The flat was almost in darkness when Virginia returned from her working day. She was puzzled and thought that something might be amiss but then she saw the table set for two and candles burning brightly in brass holders; she guessed something good was about to happen. "This looks interesting," she purred, "Is it a special treat for me?"

"Especially for you," confirmed Joe, taking her outdoor coat and putting it on a hanger in a closet. "Now – if you'd like to make yourself comfortable I'11 pop down to the restaurant and pick up a meal." He kissed her but before leaving the flat he added, " And after we've eaten I have something I'd like to show you."

"It sounds very intriguing – I can hardly wait."

The Lincolnshire Tramp

Joe laughed and made his exit. When he was gone, Virginia sat herself down and glanced around the room, she hoped to espy the mysterious object of which the dinner was so obviously in honour. That is not to say she did not have a clue as to what the object might be – far from it – because she did have a fairly shrewd idea.

Since their gastronomic tastes rarely extended beyond wholesome English cooking, the meal (when it came) was not a lavish affair. Nonetheless the food was excellent and ample for their needs; it also served to set up a very enjoyable evening.

During the genial conversation over dinner, Virginia relinquished her emotions to an inner warmth. She was blissfully happy and desired nothing more from life. She now had something to cling to – something to believe in. Through her eyes, her heart looked lovingly at Joe and she marvelled at the changes she had seen in him. In the first place she had known him as an efficient accountant and then, years later, as a foul-mouthed tramp. She had nursed him when he was vulnerable and she adored him for what he had become. It was of no use, she could not hide the truth from herself any longer, she was in love with him and the feeling was fantastic.

Look at him, she thought, he hasn't the faintest idea of what I'm thinking about. He's too busy eating and talking about his future plans to know that I can't live without him. Oh God! Please let us always be together.

Joe looked at her and smiled. "That was tasty," he said viewing the empty plates and dishes, "Now I'll make the coffee. Have you had enough to eat?"

"Yes – thank you. It was delicious," Virginia got up from her seat to clear the table whilst Joe prepared the hot drink. "What was it you wanted to show me?" she asked.

"After coffee", teased Joe.

"Not fair," scowled Virginia in return, "I want to see it now."

"When you've finished your coffee," insisted Joe but he, like her, was getting impatient for the big moment and could hold out not another second. Like an excited schoolboy, he grinned sheepishly, excused himself, and hurried into his room. He returned within a minute carrying a large, cardboard box tied with coloured ribbon.

"Would my lady do the honours?" he begged as he placed the box on the table in front of Virginia.

"Gladly sire," cooed Virginia, sitting back to admire the box and contemplate its contents. With delicate precision, she untied the ribbon and opened up the box. "I thought so," she murmured in breathless anticipation, "It's your book. It's finished, isn't it?" She carefully lifted out the work and began to appraise it.

"I can't say if it's any good or not," observed Joe in all modesty. "I'm not able to adjudge it."

"But – you are pleased with it?" Virginia posed the question as she studied the colourful pages.

"I enjoyed doing it – let's put it that way."

"I can tell you in all sincerity, Joe, it's absolutely brilliant. It's the best thing I've ever seen. There's so much fun in it, the children will love it." Virginia smiled broadly when she reached the last page but for her it was not the end because she simply had to return to the beginning and start all over again. "Brilliant – absolutely brilliant," she repeated.

"You're easily pleased," laughed Joe, "But what about my discerning public. Will they be so enthusiastic, I wonder?"

"You haven't got a discerning public," Virginia retorted lightheartedly, "But I think you will have when this comes out." Then, in all seriousness, she said," What's the next move? How do we get it printed?"

"And marketed," responded Joe. "Do you know I hadn't thought about any of that; it never entered my mind. I suppose I was just too busy with the story to worry about production. I'll have to start making some enquiries."

"There's a place that does printing in Margate," confirmed Virginia, "I don't know if they'll be able to help you."

"Could give it a try," Joe replied, "What can I lose?" He picked up the local telephone directory and began to search for the name and address of the printer. Meanwhile Virginia browsed through the illustrated book yet again.

The following morning Virginia drove Joe into Margate and left him outside the printer's office. She went off to attend to a charge in the town and promised to be back within the hour. Joe, having telephoned for an appointment with a Mr Reid entered the office and waited for his interview. He had with him the box containing his work and he had high hopes of a very successful meeting.

"A nice piece of work and I can see it has a lot of commercial potential," declared Mr Reid ten minutes later. He had studied Joe's book with great interest. "But you realise, of course, we are printers not publishers. We can certainly print the book for you – and print it to a first class standard – but the rest will be up to you or somebody acting as an agent for you. In other words, you'll have to find your own markets."

"I thought it would be something like that." Affirmed Joe.

"Now let's see," said Mr Reid, glancing over the illustrations, "This will require a multi colour printing process which means many coloured plates will have to be made for each drawing. I know a company that can do this for you but it doesn't come cheap." He looked up to see the reaction on Joe's face.

Joe's expression gave nothing away as he asked, "And then what happens?"

"We do a print run according to the number of books you require. For a book like this, as a commercial enterprise, you'd need something in the region of fifty thousand copies for a modest profit. After the printing, the whole lot is sent to the book binders to make up the finished article."

"It sounds very expensive," said Joe thoughtfully, "What sort of money is involved and what terms can you arrange?"

After a long pause and a good deal of consideration, Mr Reid sighed and said, "I think we are looking at a figure of thirty thousand pounds – half up front before we start the job and the remainder when the last book is bound."

"I'm afraid we shall insist on being paid in full before we release the first batch of books. It's the way business is these days."

Joe was visibly shocked by the terms and the amount of money involved. It was not the way his old firm had conducted their business in the past; things must have changed dramatically during those days. "It's a hell of a lot of money to lay out," he said, "Money I don't have."

"Forgive me for saying so," said Mr Reid, "but that is exactly why we impose such strict terms. My advice to you is two-fold, firstly go out and find your market; children's books are usually a winner so you shouldn't have too much of a problem there. Do get orders confirmed in writing. Secondly use someone else's money. If you manage to sell the entire first printing you'll have enough money to pay a hefty interest on a bank loan and still keep a profit."

By now, Joe had done some mental arithmetic and could not fault Mr Reid's argument. All things being equal, a profit was there.

"Of course," continued Mr Reid, "as far as you're concerned the icing on the cake comes with the second printing. With the initial costs out of the way the second print run might well be forty percent less."

"A nice idea," said Joe. "But not one I could consider until I've shifted the first fifty thousand. That sounds like an awful lot of books to me."

"Start talking to the big chain stores and that figure will soon shrink."

The Lincolnshire Tramp

"You're probably right," admitted Joe as he prepared to terminate the meeting. "I think I'd better get back home and start doing some serious thinking."

"In the meantime," assured Mr Reid, showing Joe to the door, "I'll get somebody to draw up a complete estimate. It may work out cheaper than the one I've given you off the cuff. I've got your name and address, haven't I?"

The two men shook hands and Joe made his way out into the street to wait the return of Virginia. Whilst he waited, he mulled over the issues raised during the conversation with Mr Reid; the meeting had not gone as well as Joe might have expected. In fact, the more he thought about it the more he became downhearted. Where in the world would he find that amount of money to start a project? Neither he nor Virginia had such funds available and he could hardly borrow from a bank when he was (in their eyes) *persona non grata*. Virginia could not help out either, being an undischarged bankrupt she had less than a remote chance of borrowing a large sum of money. In every respect, the chances of getting the book published were ebbing away.

The very thought of hawking this idea around the book retailers in order to drum up a market filled him with horror. He had tried that before when he was selling joinery and look where it got him! "No! no! no!" he said to an impudent seagull who thought a bag of household rubbish contained more food than the sea, "I am most definitely not in favour of another sales campaign. I'd rather throw my drawings in the fire than go through that experience again." Downcast and forlorn, he leaned against a brick wall and stared at the rubbish on the pavement.

"Hi there!" called Virginia as she brought her car to a standstill beside him. "You look as though you've lost a pound and found a penny. The meeting not go well?"

"As meetings go it wasn't too bad," explained Joe, "But the future of the book isn't too rosy."

"I'll tell you what," offered Virginia, glancing at the street ahead, "I'll park over there and you can put your box in the back, then I'll treat you to lunch and you can tell me all about it – okay?"

Joe nodded, picked up his box and walked carefully, across the street to a parking bay. Virginia followed and as soon as the car was settled they locked the precious book in the boot and went off in search of a coffee house.

Lunch was a very light affair, toasted teacakes and plenty of coffee. Joe related the events of the morning and Virginia listened attentively. "It's not the end of the world." She declared, having noticed a hint of bitterness in his voice, "there must be another way. After all, not all authors are rich when they start to write."

"Or draw " corrected Joe.

"Exactly." continued Virginia, "That's why I think a visit to the library might be a good idea. They must have some information about it."

"Why do I always feel better when I listen to your simple logic?" Beamed Joe.

"That's my boy," coaxed Virginia, reaching across the table to give him a friendly pat on the shoulder. "We'll find a way to get the book published, don't worry." With that she stubbed out a cigarette and gathered up her bits and pieces. "Drink up," she said, "And let's go find a library."

Joe smiled and looked at her affectionately. She was her younger self all over again – bubbling with enthusiasm – and he adored her for it. She could lead him anywhere and he would gladly follow. Thusly, they entered the town's library and Virginia made the appropriate enquiries. A demure, young woman directed them not only to the reference section but also to the exact shelf whereupon lay a directory of book publishers.

There followed an informative half hour as names and addresses sprang from the pages and a new world opened up before them. With so much information available, care had to be taken to select the likeliest of publishers; a short list of six was compiled. The prospect of getting his book printed without disbursement to himself appealed to Joe and he was keen to get back to the flat and draft the introductory letters.

Later, in the evening of that same day, he sealed down the flaps of two separate envelopes and checked them. He thought it best to sound out the publishers two at a time and await their responses before proceeding further. He had hoped to slip out of the flat and pop his letters into a nearly pillar box but the absence of postage stamps prevented him from doing so. "Never mind," he sighed, "I'll post them in the morning."

"It's time for bed, anyway," yawned Virginia. "Got a busy day tomorrow."

With a feeling of wellbeing, Joe went happily to bed. He fell asleep instantly and slept well for a few hours but, at sometime during the night, his subliminal self turned his emotions upside down and fears crept back into his mind; fears to fuel nightmares. In the early hours of the morning he drifted back into consciousness through a series of deeply disturbing dreams, the evil he had perpetrated in the past had come back to haunt him. It was all there, the swan, the widow, the young mother, and the others. They were mixed up in never ending plots to destroy him. Stricken with terror, he opened his eyes and tried to see in the darkness of the bedroom. He perspired and panicked and wanted to run away.

Accordingly the constant ticking of an alarm clock brought him back to his senses. When he realised he had been victim, to nightmares he calmed down and tried to reason with himself. Why, he wondered, should I start to have these dreams again? I've been so long without them.

He could not – or dare not – go back to sleep. He was convinced he had a problem and it, above all else, must be put right before he risked closing an eye. After more concentrated thought he began to see the events in his dreams, in a peculiar way, parodied the stories in his illustrated book. If this proved to be the case, and he felt sure it was, then he must accept it as a bad omen. His reading of the signs suggested that he should not profit from his work.

On the other hand, he could not see the sense in scrapping a work that had come so easily to him, a work that was manifestly meant to be. Clearly, the fault lay not with the book and its content but with the money it could attract, money he should never be entitled to. Seemingly, the nightmare had distorted the book's origin.

Further to the point, if the book did bring in a certain wealth then he saw only a negative side to such wealth, heavy taxation, a proper identity, public exposure and a loss of privacy. It was too high a price to pay and he would not entertain it. To become embroiled in any form of commercialism nauseated him, he knew that now. He had discovered an intrinsic value in the simple life and provided his needs were catered for he wished for no more. Washing up dirty crockery in the restaurant and selling the occasional picture satisfied his pecuniary needs. Other than that, he enjoyed his leisure time with Virginia.

He continued his cogitation until six a.m. When he got up to brew tea. Even so, his views had not altered. The book had to be published yet he must not accept payment of any kind for it. How it should be done remained a problem.

Some minutes later, a flash of distant memory came to him as he poured boiling water into a teapot. Whether it was steam, or the smell of scalded tea leaves, or the pot itself, was not at issue because any one of them could have triggered off the memory; the fact remains that Joe recalled the charities dispensing hot drinks when he was in need. Surely, any one of them would welcome the donation of his work to boost their funds. Elated by the idea, he quickly assembled, teacups, milk jug, sugar bowl, teaspoons and teapot and placed them on a tray. They rattled noisily as he carried them into the bedroom where he intended to tell Virginia about his latest plans.

His arrival awakened her and she opened her eyes and smiled. "Tea – how nice." She purred. Whilst Joe poured the tea she sat herself up and rested back against the pillow. "You're up early," she said glancing at the clock, "Couldn't you sleep?"

"I've been awake half the night," explained Joe, "Been thinking about my book." He handed her a cup of tea. "I want it published but I'm unhappy about taking money for it so I've decided to donate it to charity. I hope you don't mind?"

She was shocked by his decision but would not challenge it for fear of breaking the fragile thread that held their relationship together; a misguided assumption on her behalf. "Of course I don't mind," she affirmed, "I'm happy to go along with whatever you want to do."

"I'm glad you said that. It really is important to me to do it this way."

Virginia was also glad, she was assured of the strengthening of the bond between them. "Have you thought of a particular charity?" She asked.

"Not yet," said Joe squeezing her hand, "I'd like you to pick one. Any one you like."

"Oh Gosh!" Squealed Virginia. "There's so many to choose from. I don't know which one to have." She gave the matter some frantic thought as she drank her tea. "I think it will be one that helps children," she ventured, "So I think I'll choose – Save the Children Fund. Will that do?"

"Excellent choice," declared Joe kissing her on her forehead, "Save the Children it shall be." Much relieved and at ease with the world, he sat on the floor to drink tea and contemplate his new venture.

In the weeks that followed, he made contact with the chosen charity and after the exchange of many letters they agreed to accept his work and put his proposals to a selected committee. He was happy to sign over all rights to the work providing it was published and the proceeds went into the charity's coffers. He was warned that it would be a new departure for the organisers and may take time to get it off the ground but it was a risk worth taking.

The Lincolnshire Tramp

With his illustrated book now out of his hands, Joe encountered emptiness in his life. However, the encounter was short lived; for he soon filled the void with a series of drawings which he was able to sell locally, usually at the restaurant where he did the washing up.

Virginia brought him some wood working tools for Christmas so that he could make up his own picture frames. He was pleased with the tools and the frames he made; it was good to have a new dimension to his skills. His present to her was not half so exciting; a gold chain with a pearl pendant. There again, it was the first Christmas present he had given anyone for seven years. Virginia was delighted with it and confessed to it being the only piece of jewellery she had ever received as a present; her father always gave her perfume for Christmas and her brother, if ever he made the effort, handkerchiefs.

The months rolled by and at the end of May in the following year a little package awaited Joe. It had just been possible to pass it through the letter box cut into the main door of the flat and it had fallen to the floor. Joe almost stepped on it when he returned from his work but avoided it with a swift side movement. Compulsively he picked it up and muttered, "What have we got here?" But before he had completely removed the wrapping he knew what it was. "Well I'm damned," he said, I'd forgotten about this. He held out a brightly coloured, yet smallish book designed for children – his book.

He carried the book into the sitting room and sat down to study it and the accompanying letter. The letter apologised for the delay and not having made contact with him during the preparation of the book but it did hope he would be pleased with the end product. Joe grunted and put the letter to one side so that he could examine the book and its thirty six pages. He was pleased with it and could not fault any part of it, all of his original work was there and, as was his request, it did not display his full name. It simply attributed the story and the artwork to "Joe".

"It's a lovely little book, Joe," exclaimed Virginia when he presented it to her that evening. "It's beautifully done. You must be very proud of it."

It does give me a lot of satisfaction," Joe claimed with modesty. "But the real praise should go to the people who produced it. I only hope it was worthwhile and they make money out of it."

"It's a pity you can't be recognised for your part in it," sighed Virginia, "But I know that's the way you want it and I respect that."

"One day – perhaps," said Joe as if to mollify her.

Virginia smiled and caressed the little book. "You don't have to – you know." She said softly, "All I need is here."

"If it goes really well," propounded Joe, "I think I'll do another one. I shall enjoy that." An embryonic plot found a place for itself in the forefront of his mind. "In fact, I could do several more." He boasted.

To Virginia, this was like music to her ears; his ambitions promised to keep him close to his new home. "I'm sure it will do well." She urged, "And you'll do many more."

As it happened, Joe did not make a start on his second illustrated book until mid-August. His excuse for the delay was threefold; he had a backlog of orders to fulfil for his framed pictures, it was the height of the summer season for the restaurant and he was obliged to put in extra hours and he needed a report from the charity to confirm the movement of his first book.

The good news came on Thursday morning. Virginia was at home suffering from what she called a *summer cold* when the postman came to the door. She did not answer the door but waited for the clutch of letters to drop through the letter box. As she expected, most of the mail was addressed to herself but there was just the one letter for Joe; the discernible markings on the envelope identified the sender as the chosen charity. Virginia did not open the letter, that was for Joe to do, but she did have a feeling about it.

When Joe returned from his stint in the restaurant, he complained of tiredness. He had been particularly busy lunch time and he had been given extra work to do. However, he soon bucked up when he read his letter. Then he infuriated Virginia by saying, "Do you know – I haven't seen a single copy of my book for sale around here. Never seen it in any of the shops."

"That's isn't what your letter is about," snapped Virginia. "So don't be a pain and tell me what it really says."

"You want me to tell you if they've sold any of the books, don't you?" Joe chuckled.

"You know I do."

"Okay. They've sold some – about fifty."

"Only fifty books!" Virginia was dismayed. "That's not many."

Joe chuckled again. "Fifty Thousand," he declared, "The entire first printing. Here – see for yourself," He passed the letter over to Virginia. "They're planning a reprint."

Virginia took the letter but before she could read it she suffered a coughing fit and had to sit down for a short rest. She duly returned to the letter when the fit had abated and she had taken drinking water administered by Joe. "It really is good news," she said, "they've done wonderfully well with it. You must be thrilled." The look of admiration in her eyes outshone the discomfort of her viral infection. "Will you start your new book now?" She asked.

"I suppose I could." Joe said thoughtfully. "After all – I do have the rest of the day free and I have no other urgent commitment. But there is a condition."

"Oh! And what is that?"

"I want you to go to bed and have a long rest. You're far from well and I'm sure it will do you the world of good."

"Don't be silly. I can't go to bed at this time of day, it's only four o'clock. Besides, I've got too much to do."

"There's nothing that can't be left for another day," insisted Joe as he helped her to her feet. "Your health is more important than odd jobs around the home."

Virginia knew he was right, she did not feel up to doing anything strenuous and would be better off if she relaxed in bed. "I will go and lay down for an hour or so."

"Until morning at the very least," commanded Joe. He ushered her into the bedroom and helped her get into bed. "Just call out if you want anything," he said, "I'll be working in the next room."

The bed was cool and comforting and it lured Virginia in a light but lengthy sleep. Meanwhile, Joe settled down in his own room and mapped out a sketch of his new illustrated book. He also kept an eye on Virginia, often visiting the bedroom to check on her progress.

About four hours later, she came out of her sleep and called for tissues. Her nose was running and she started to sneeze. "I think this cold has really come out now," she spluttered as Joe took in a box of tissues. "Never had one as bad as this before."

"It's bound to get you down," said Joe sympathetically, then he asked. "Can I get you a light snack or something?"

"I know I should eat to starve a cold," said Virginia, "But I'm not at all hungry. Perhaps I could manage some soup and a slice of toast; there's a tin of oxtail in the cupboard."

"I'll see to it." confirmed Joe, "And when I have done that I'll pop out to see if I can find a shop open. You'll need some more aspirin and probably some other medicines."

True to his word, Joe prepared the snack and then set off to scour the streets of Ramsgate to find the required pills and linctus. When he returned, some forty minutes later, he found Virginia in a sound slumber. She had taken her meal and obviously dozed off again. Not wishing to disturb her, he quietly left the bedroom and went into the kitchen where he placed his purchases on the kitchen table. They would be readily to hand if needed in an emergency.

He thought about returning to his illustrating but decided to clean up the flat instead, after that, he flopped into his favourite armchair and watched television until midnight. It was when he toyed with the idea of spending the night in the armchair so as not to be a nuisance to Virginia, that he heard a slight commotion coming from the bedroom. Instantly, he went to investigate and found her in a state of mild delirium. She was extremely hot and had a high body temperature.

Joe calmed her down before persuading her to take some aspirin in water. Then he made her as comfortable as possible and coaxed her back to sleep. He stayed with her in the bedroom for the rest of the night, sometimes he slept on top of the bed and sometimes on the floor, but always ready to attend to her needs.

In the bright light of the morning he got up and placed his hand on her forehead. He was sure that her temperature had dropped to near normal but he was unhappy about the sound of her breathing. A few seconds later, when she awoke and tried to speak to him, he knew she had a respiratory problem.

"I'm afraid it's the doctor for you my girl," he said, gently squeezing her hand. "Then we'll get you sorted out." He knew she had a Practice listed in her address book and it would be a matter of hours before the doctor could attend to her. Nevertheless he had to telephone the surgery as soon as it opened and make an appointment.

In the meantime, he did what he could for Virginia. He gave her some breakfast, washed her, put her into a clean nightdress and tried to comb her hair. He was not well practised in many of these pursuits but he did his commendable best. This, despite her weakened condition, was greatly to Virginia's amusement for she likened him to a Mother Hen.

The doctor when he arrived was a young man in his late twenties. Although extremely proficient he lacked the experience of a longer serving member of the profession. This minor handicap served only to delay the diagnosis of Virginia's disorder but once it was established in his mind he swiftly acted upon it. He asked for the telephone and made a call to the hospital in Margate then, having found a bed, he contacted the local ambulance service.

The Lincolnshire Tramp

By noon, Virginia was in hospital to undergo a series of tests and treatment for a viral infection. The young doctor has deemed the virus to be too unstable to treat at home and fearing complications had committed his patient to the institution where the proper facilities were available. In short, he needed a second opinion to confirm his diagnosis.

Through some parochial directive from the Local Health Authority, Joe was not permitted to travel in the ambulance with Virginia. He was advised to make his own way to the hospital. Virginia was unhappy with the ruling but was far too weak to protest. However, she did insist on Joe taking the car keys out of her handbag and keeping them to drive himself to the hospital and back. Reluctantly he agreed although he was in some doubt about his ability to handle a car after so many years.

As soon as the ambulance moved off, Joe secured the flat and went down to the street to find Virginia's car. It's funny how the tables have turned, he thought, not so long ago she packed me off to hospital in an ambulance. I say it was not so long ago but it must be...let me see...over twenty one months ago. Good God! How time flies.

Gingerly he climbed into the driving seat of the car and adjusted himself to a suitable driving position. His legs had healed considerably well, he had no qualms about that, but were they ready to respond to controlling the movement of the car. He did not start the engine for a full five minutes, he needed that time to become psychologically prepared to drive.

The car jerked forward and so began an erratic peregrination to Margate. Joe was not happy to be behind the wheel of a car again, he suffered from a loss of confidence and he was disturbed by too many unpleasant memories. He would rather be a passenger.

Chapter 19

On her second day in hospital, Virginia perked up. She was on a course of antibiotics and her body was responding well to it. When Joe arrived for his daily visit she was sitting up in bed and when she saw him she smiled.

"This takes some believing," he said, stepping back to admire her. "You really do look good today. Quite a change from yesterday when you looked as though you were at death's door. It's wonderful to see you smiling again."

"I feel wonderful," agreed Virginia, "And so much better. But isn't it just awful. I'm gasping for a cigarette because I feel so good and they tell me I must never smoke again. What a liberty!"

"Better do as they say," warned Joe, "We don't want you staying in here a day longer than you have to. They do know what they are talking about."

"All the same –" pleaded Virginia, "To give up me gaspers!"

"As it happens," said Joe, unpacking a carrier bag, "I forgot to get cigarettes. I bought you some fruit and some chocolate, some magazines, a clean nightdress, a bottle of squash, " he introduced each item before placing it on the bedside locker. "Some 'Get Well' cards from various acquaintances and some toothpaste. Everything you asked for."

"Except the cigarettes."

"You're not to have them – so it doesn't matter."

"Then I shall eat chocolate and get fat," Virginia giggled.

Joe sat on the bed and held her hands. "Get as fat as you like," he said, "But get well first."

She looked into his eyes and saw the sincerity in his words. It was nice to know that he cared about her; it made her feel wanted. She desired to tell him how much she loved him but thought it more prudent to ask about his latest endeavour. "Have you been able to work on your book?" she asked.

"As a matter of fact," Joe replied, "It's coming along nicely. I couldn't put my brushes down last night. Mind you, I couldn't get to sleep either – I think that's because you were not there. I don't know if that was a good thing or not, but I did finish three of the pictures."

"Charming!" teased Virginia, "Nice to know you get on so much better without me."

Joe responded instantly. He pulled back the bedclothes and exposed her feet. "That is most unkind," he said authoritatively, "And you shall be punished for it." He knew she could not stand having her feet tickled so he deliberately ran his finger up and down her soles.

Virginia howled with laughter and tried to bury her feet in the firm mattress of her bed. "You beast," she squealed, "I'm an invalid and should be treated with care."

Unmoved by her plea, Joe did not let go until he had exacted a full meter of punishment. By then, he and Virginia had become the centre of attraction for everyone in the ward, patient and visitor alike. Virginia's laughter was so infectious it caused an epidemic of smiles and giggles within the group.

Such was the elation in the ward on that Sunday afternoon that it came as a real shock when Virginia suffered a relapse during the early hours of the following day. A watchful night nurse had seen the change and had mobilised an emergency procedure. For nearly two hours, Virginia was in a critical state and then, thanks to the medical staff, she started again on the path to recovery.

The incident, when he heard about it on his next visit, stunned Joe. It was the last thing he wanted to hear. Virginia was not in her usual place but in a room of her own; she was attached to a monitor and was sedated. Unable to understand the situation, Joe had approached the Sister-in-Charge and had asked for an explanation. He was told that Virginia had undergone a minor operation to remove fluid from her lungs but that was only a stop gap because she really needed major surgery – a heart and lung transplant.

"That's a blow," said Joe, trying to take in the information. "Has Virginia been told about it?"

"I told her just before I gave her the sedative," replied the Sister, "She took it calmly."

"So what happens next?"

"We make her as comfortable as possible and simply wait for a donor. She can wait at home if she wishes."

"I think she'll do that," said Joe deep in thought, then he asked "This is all so sudden, what brought it on?"

"Surely you know," retorted the Sister, "Too much smoking." Then, with sympathy, she added. "Her lungs are so bad they cannot offer immunity to a virus attack, her only chance is a transplant".

"And her heart?"

"That too."

Clearly shaken by the news, Joe turned to go. "Will it be all right if I sit with her for a while?"

The Lincolnshire Tramp

"Stay for as long as you like," encouraged the Sister. "And when she wakes up try to convince her to give up smoking, one more cigarette might be one too many."

"I understand," nodded Joe, "and thank you for your help." He made his way back to Virginia in the lonely room and sat himself down on a convenient chair. And as he watched her the gravity of her illness came through to him, such a change from the previous day when she had been so ebullient.

He sat in the chair for a good three hours and spent most of that time thinking about his life with Virginia. In some ways it was so unnatural because they could be considered as incompatible yet in other ways it seemed so right to be together, they belonged to each other.

Virginia stirred and opened her eyes. "Hello," she said weakly, "I'm glad you're here."

Tenderly, he stood up and kissed her and when he sat down again he said, "It sounds as though you've had a rough night. Do you feel any better now?"

"I've no pain or anything like that. Just very tired – that's all."

"The nurse told me about the transplants you need. I really do feel sorry for you."

"I know – isn't it a bind." She displayed a faint smile and tried to make light of her predicament. "Don't look so worried," she continued, "As soon as I get me spare parts I'll be back to my old self again. There's a treat in store for you – I don't think!"

"I don't care what it takes," said Joe passionately, "But I want things to be as they were. I've grown to enjoy the life we have together and I want it to go on like that. I know it is cruel and selfish but I hope a donor is soon found and you are made well again."

"So I do mean something to you?"

"Oh! Stop teasing. This is serious."

Virginia would have laughed had not her little bit of fun exhausted her; even a moderate conversation was fatiguing. She lay back in the Health Authority's pillows and looked wistfully into space. "They tell me I can go home and wait for a donor but I can't see how I can do that without getting some extra energy from somewhere."

"You'll get it – don't fret. They're good at that in here – building people up to face the future. I'm sure you'll be home in a couple of days."

An appreciative glance darted from Virginia's eyes before she closed them in an instant, she went to sleep again.

The Lincolnshire Tramp

Joe waited for a few minutes just to be sure she was sleeping comfortably before he silently left the room. On his way back to their flat in Ramsgate he came to a definite decision; he would not surrender his rights to his new book to charity. It would serve his interests better if he kept the royalties for his personal needs. In fact, it was Virginia's needs he had in mind rather than his own, he had no illusion about the cost of her treatment and the subsequent convalescence; he had to have the money.

By the time he parked the car and entered the flat, his mind was firmly made up. He went directly to his room and settled down for a long night of drawing and colouring. He ruled out all thought of rest until he had completed, to his entire satisfaction, four more paintings, only then did he relax and sleep.

Whether he had completed his allotted span or whether it was the postman who woke him up, Joe could not say for certain. All he could be sure about was the ominous envelope hanging precariously from the flap of the letterbox. Catching hold of it before it fell to the floor, he studied it for many long moments and did so with ever increasing suspicion. It was certainly addressed to him, even though his surname was spelt incorrectly and it seemed to demand instant attention.

"How in hell," he growled, "Have the tax people tracked me down after all these years? How did they know I was here?" He tore open the envelope and feverishly extracted the letter. "Somebody must be spying on me."

The content of the letter was brief and to the point. It politely summoned him to call at the local Inland Revenue Office and explain his means of income. Until recently they had no record of him on their lists but they did have certain information confirming his existence in the area and working as an artist. Failure to comply would result in an estimation of his income which would then be liable to taxation under Schedule E of the tax code and any assessment due to the Treasury would be recovered.

"The bastards." roared Joe, "How dare they write letters like this. What information have they got and where did they get it?" In a search for the answers, he re-read the letter over and over again. They couldn't have got it from the organisers of the charity because that doesn't make sense. There's no mention of a book, only a hint at pictures. It must be those damned pictures I sold. How can they tax me on a few measly pictures?"

In a fit of temper he began to tear up the letter but then common sense prevailed and he stopped himself. If he did not sort the matter out there and then it would re-surface at a later date, probably at a time when it would most inconvenient Virginia. He could not allow that. "Once a Tax Inspector smells blood," he muttered, "They never let go until they've taken a good measure. And you can't ignore them because they simply do not go away – the bloody parasites."

He collected the fragments of the letter and pieced them together on the dining room table. "I suppose I'd better find out who sent this damned things and go and have it out with 'em. I could do without this sort of hassle right now."

Within an hour, he had made an arrangement to meet the Inspector on the following morning. He had timed his appointment to avoid clashing with his work at the restaurant and his visit to the hospital.

Although disturbed by the letter, Joe refused to be intimidated by it and put it to the back of his mind until the appointed hour. In the meantime he had enough to keep himself fully occupied so much so that he completely forgot about it when he went to see Virginia. She was looking a lot better and ascending another peak.

"If you continue to make progress like this, " he encouraged. "You'll be home in no time at all."

"Funny how it goes," observed Virginia, "Yesterday I didn't have the energy to move but today I feel like dancing. I suspect it's the drugs I'm on."

Joe smiled. "It's incredible," he said "You always manage to spring back after a bad turn. It must be a good sign for the future."

"Talking of which," intervened Virginia, "I've had some thoughts about that. You know how it is – when you're in here you have plenty of time to think, specially about the future." She paused to sip a drink. "I've done a lot of thinking and I've decided how nice it would be to have a little shop again. Not fashions or anything like that – that's too hectic. It would be something quieter, like a little studio to sell pictures, your pictures."

Both flattered and flustered, Joe almost tumbled over his own words, "But but, but," he stammered, "I couldn't paint enough pictures to stock a gallery, besides, I'm not that good."

"You are good," Virginia insisted, "And what is more – you are developing a style. That's what it is all about – style. Believe me." She rested for a moment to regain her breath and give Joe a chance to respond. But when he did not, for he was deep in thought, she continued. "It's a pity you gave away all the rights to your first book because we could have had lots of prints made of the first set of pictures and sold them."

Enlightened by her comments, Joe could see how a small gallery might work, it also reminded him of a decision he had come to on the previous day. "Don't forget the pictures for the second book," he said, "We can have all the prints we want from them. I know I haven't mentioned it before, but I have decided to keep the second book for our needs. I've a feeling we shall want a lot of money in the weeks to come. I just hope I can get it published."

Caught off guard by his decision, Virginia did not know what she could say. Her instincts told her that he was right to think of himself but her sympathies lay with the charity. "What about the children?" She heard herself say, "Won't they need the money?"

"I think they'll be all right," said Joe reassuringly, "They're sure to reprint the first book and that'll keep them busy for a while. I can do another for them later on."

"Yes". Agreed Virginia pensively, "That would be okay." Then on a brighter note, she adjured, "So I can have my little shop – can I?"

"Of course you can." Enthused Joe, "And we can open it up in time for Christmas. How about that?"

His approval heartened her and the strength she gained from it enabled her to stay alert until well into the evening. By the time Joe kissed her a good night and took his leave, dusk had descended over the hospital.

At precisely nine-thirty on the following morning, Joe entered a Tax Inspector's office. He offered a pleasant salutation to the poker-faced man sitting behind a desk and received a derogatory grunt in reply.

"Sit down." Commanded the man, pointing to a worn and battered chair. "I understand we have your surname incorrectly written in our file. We must put that right for a start." He opened up a slim folder and compared its contents with a slip of paper previously handed to him by a clerk. "Joseph Albert Glasson – is that you?"

"Yes," confirmed Joe, taking an instant dislike to the Inspector.
"And how long have you been at your present address?"
"About a year and a half," Joe replied; unintentionally inaccurate.
"And where were you before that?"
"Nowhere."
"What d'you mean – nowhere?" The Tax Inspector cast a quizzical glance towards Joe.

"I walked the roads for six years," Joe explained angrily. "I was a tramp."

"I see", said the Inspector in doubtful tone. "So where were you before you became a tramp?"

"Spalding – Lincolnshire."

"No doubt they have a record of you there."

The Inspector's comment irritated Joe. "Look here," he snapped, "I've always paid my tax demands. I owe the Inland Revenue nothing."

"Is it true to say you haven't paid any income tax for the last seven and a half years?"

"Yes – but that's because I haven't earned any money."

"So you say!" The Inspector broke off to glance through his notes then he admitted, "Very well, as we appear to have no address confirming your whereabouts prior to the address you have given us, we shall assume you were a vagrant. That leaves us with eighteen months, on your own admission, you have lived in this district. Presumably you have had money to pay for accommodation and living expenses. Where did that come from?"

With an ever-increasing feeling that he was banging his head against a brick wall, Joe sighed deeply and tried to reason with the Inspector. "The sort of money you are talking about would certainly put me in a tax bracket but I can honestly tell you I've never handled such sums. The reason for me being in this area is because of an accident. I was knocked down and had my pelvis and legs broken. Luckily I was found by an old friend who took me into her home after my spell in hospital. I've lived with her ever since and it doesn't cost me a lot of money. She's been very good to me."

"Hmmm!" mumbled the Tax Inspector, "I shall need to look into that." He remained silent for the best part of a minute whilst he jotted down some notes. As he watched him, Joe realised how flimsy the Inspector's case was; so far he had not produced a scrap of evidence to support his allegations. "So," continued the Inspector, "You have earned some money. Tell me about that."

Joe was glad he had kept his head and not lost his temper for now he could anticipate the Inspector's questions and readily find the answers. "Since I have been on my feet again," he offered, "I have been able to do some casual work and I have painted and sold a few pictures. But that was in recent months and you know damned well you can't tax me on that until April of next year."

"Since you are so familiar with the system." Quipped the tax Inspector, "I need hardly remind you of the penalties for making a false declaration." He reached down to open a drawer. "I'm glad you mentioned the pictures." He said, "Because I have one here." He produced his exhibit.

To Joe's astonishment it was one of the paintings he had sold earlier in the year, he certainly did not expect to see it in a Tax Inspector's hands. "Don't tell me you went out to deliberately buy a picture to catch me out," he said.

"I can assure you we do not stoop to those levels in this office," insisted the Inspector. "This picture was bought by a relative of mine because she liked it. What interests me about it is the actual transaction. You did sell this picture for twenty pounds, did you not?"

"Yes."

"And how many of these did you sell before April the 4th this year?"

"Hardly any."

"What does that mean? Ten, twenty, thirty, a hundred? Just how many?"

"About fifteen, but as I said – mostly this year."

The Inspector examined the picture with great interest. "This one appears to be very well done." He said, "So much so that it suggests a well practised hand. Could it be that you have painted more pictures than you admit – I wonder?"

Joe knew the Inspector was bluffing; the picture was of poor quality and not done at all well. It was just a taxman's trick to catch him out, to make him confess to selling many more pictures. The obvious intention to extract a confession by flattery was not going to work. "About fifteen, I told you," snapped Joe, "And about fifteen it is. I defy you to prove more."

"What about your savings? The Inspector tried a different ploy. "How much money have you got in the Bank, or your Building Society, or the Post Office?"

With a look of incredulity, Joe glared at the inspector. "How can I save money if I've never had any to save. How many more times must I tell you this?"

"Very well," concluded the Inspector, "This interview is now at an end. I shall have to look further into your claims but in the meantime I want you to go home and prepare a statement of your financial affairs for the past seven and a half years. I shall be contacting you again in the near future. Good day!"

Greatly put out but with no desire to stay and argue his case, Joe walked briskly from the Inspector's office. Memories from the past stirred within his breast as he recollected the rows he had had over money in his former office. False claims had blighted his life then and now he feared it would happen again. He resented the Tax Inspector, partly for his unsympathetic attitude and partly for bringing some distant fiscal grievances back into focus. At that moment in time, Joe could have easily run away again just to get away from the petty bureaucracy. Instead, he returned to the flat to prepare himself for his stint in the restaurant.

Yet another letter awaited him on his return; it was from his chosen charity and it lavished praise on him to disguise its real intent – begging. It told of the rapturous reception his book had received all over the world and how the children had taken it to their hearts; it praised him for his deep understanding of the young and his ability to communicate with them; it expressed its delight at the sell out of the first print and the demand for the reprint and finally, it explained how much children were looking forward to his second book.

On first reading, Joe found the letter to his liking and drew much pleasure from it, but on second reading he realised its true implication. A huge demand for his second book appeared to be on the cards and the charity was depending on the cash it would generate.

Suddenly a host of perplexities flooded into his head. If, as he proposed, he kept the income from his second book for his and Virginia's needs then the children would lose out. But, vice versa, he and Virginia could be the losers if the charity was to gain. From another point of view, the Tax Inspector could come down on him like a ton of bricks if he discovered him reaping a fortune from the work. There again, if he gave the book to charity it would not necessarily rid him of the Tax Man.

"Sod it," shouted Joe, "All this nonsense is making my head spin. Best if I go and do some washing up and forget about the bloody Tax Man, the bloody book, and the bloody charity."

Clearly the meeting with the Tax Inspector had put Joe on edge and that, together with his other worries, affected his reformed disposition; he was beginning to lose his temper again. However, a spell of washing up and a pleasant few hours with Virginia restored some lost ground and as long as the meeting and the letter were not foremost in his mind he functioned calmly.

For four more days, he was not to have his temperament disturbed again even though Virginia's condition had its ups and downs; he had learned to accept that. But on the fourth afternoon, when he hurried into the hospital to show her the final draft of his book, he was told that she had been transferred to another hospital. The revelat irritated him.

"Why didn't anyone telephone me about this?" He barked at a Staff Nurse who was seated at a desk. "I left strict instructions and a telephone number!"

"We did try and phone you," explained the Staff Nurse, "But nobody answered. Virginia thought you might be at work."

"But why was nothing said about this yesterday – when I was here?"

"I'm afraid Virginia had another bad night – this time it was her heart." The compassion shown by the Staff Nurse rose above the anger displayed by Joe. "She needed more specialised treatment than we can provide here. Luckily there was a cardiothoracic bed available at Harefield Hospital and she's been rushed over there."

"I've heard of that place," said Joe with less aggression in his voice, "but I don't know where it is."

"It's in Middlesex," advised the Staff Nurse, "Just north of Uxbridge. Take you three or four hours if you're going by car."

Joe thanked the Staff Nurse for her help but before contemplating the journey he had to know more about Virginia's state of health. "How was she when they took her?" he asked, "Was she in a very bad way?"

The Staff Nurse gave him a reassuring smile and said, "She was very comfortable when she left here and she would have been well looked after on the journey. Don't look so worried, she'll pull through okay. She's probably tucked up in bed right now and having a little sleep. I'm sure she'll be her cheerful self when you get there".

"Yes! Right! Thank you!" Joe was not capable of stringing words together as he excused himself from the ward and dashed out of the hospital. There was so much to think about yet he could do nothing constructive until he had come to terms with the latest news. Obviously he had to return to the flat, pack an overnight bag, gather up all the money he could find and consult a road map. Then, with the flat made safe and securely locked, he could start the journey.

At a quarter past three on that Friday afternoon, he set off to cover the distance between Ramsgate and Harefield, some one hundred and twenty road miles with diversions. Four and a half hours later he arrived at the hospital, agitated and tired.

It had not been the most enjoyable of journeys for many reasons. His time away from distance driving affected his reactions, he felt claustrophobic in the rush hour traffic, he was unnerved on the motorways and he lost his way on several occasions. The anxiety he felt for Virginia was not helped by the frustrations he endured on the road. For a man who was not in a patient mood, the journey seem to take forever.

Fearing the worst, he entered the hospital and began his search for Virginia. Within minutes he was guided to her bed in a specialised unit and when he saw her the misery of his journey fell away. "Hello," he said softly, "I'm sorry it has taken me so long but at last I'm here."

Virginia, looking so fragile and helpless against a stack of gleaming white pillow, smiled back. "Thank you for coming," she said, "You're just the tonic I need." She reached out and beckoned him to kiss her.

After the gentle, but no less passionate, kiss she held onto him and confessed, "I'm not afraid now you're with me."

Joe's next question had to be suppressed because he had the answer before he could ask for it. Virginia would have claimed to be feeling fine but he could see she was far from well. Her latest relapse had taken its toll and it had frightened her. Instead, he stroked her hair and declared, "I've got lots of good things to tell you so cheer up and put on a happy face".

Virginia smiled.

"That's good enough, " he joked. "Now where shall I begin?" Ah! Yes! The latest book. I'm proud to announce that it is all finished. I shall show it to you in a little while, but first I must tell you about the letter I had."

His enthusiasm about his latest book put fresh life into Virginia and her eyes took on a sparkle as she begged, "I must see your new book first – please."

"I shall show you later," insisted Joe, "Otherwise I shall forget all the things I want to tell you." He tweaked her nose. "Now about this letter. It was from Save the Children and it was full of praise for the first book, apparently the children love it. It seems the reprint is almost sold out and it hasn't come off the press yet. That's good, isn't it?" He deliberately held back that part of the letter which, all but, demanded the second book.

"I'd like to see that." Admitted Virginia.

"Sorry, darling, in my rush I forgot to bring it. I also forgot to bring some details I picked up at an estate agents."

"What sort of details?"

"Shop premises," said Joe. "It seems there's a glut of empty shops in the town but the rents are a bit hefty. However, I'm sure we'll be

The Lincolnshire Tramp

able to come to some arrangement with the owner if we find one we like."

"You are a chump," sighed Virginia, "I would love to have seen them as well."

"I know," agreed Joe, "I'll get them for you at the first opportunity – promise."

"You'd better," threatened Virginia. "I'm looking forward to my little shop."

"I've also had a meeting with the Tax Inspector," continued Joe. "I think it might be best if I get my tax affairs sorted out before we start a new business." Not only did he try to make light of the acrimonious meeting with the Tax Inspector but he avowed to resign himself to the demands made upon him, if only for Virginia's sake.

"How boring," gasped Virginia, "But I suppose that sort of thing has to be done. Now can I see your new work?"

Joe had thought of leaving his work at the flat, or even in the car, but at the back of his mind he was obliged to keep Virginia in countenance; the work would come in useful as a device to keep her spirits up. In the event, the work had stayed by his side and was ready to hand if required.

"I hope you won't be disappointed with it," he said, withdrawing a package from a carrier bag. "You see – I didn't have time to get it vetted by that little family we used to visit." He unwrapped the package and offered its contents to Virginia.

"I'm sure it will be perfect," purred Virginia as she sought out the first of the brightly coloured pages. "I know you too well. Your work is always so meticulous."

Joe would have apologised further for the poor quality of his painting but, instead, he sat back in the chair and could only smile as she examined each page in turn. He could not even comment when she squealed with delight as and when the images pleased her.

Virginia had just scrutinised the last page and was about to lavish praise on Joe on the excellence of the work when a Staff Nurse hurried into the unit.

"Good news," she called, "A donor is on its way here and we must get you ready for some tests." She picked up the clipboard from the foot of the bed and examined the charts. "When did you last eat?"

"I've had nothing since I left Ramsgate, explained Virginia. "I haven't felt like eating." She smiled at Joe as he gathered up his illustrations and packed them away.

"That's okay," said the Staff Nurse, putting a thermometer into Virginia's mouth, "Now your pulse," she added as she checked her watch.

"Does that mean I'll have the operation soon?" asked Virginia as soon as she was free to speak again.

"Probably tonight," asserted the Staff Nurse, "providing the tests prove compatible." She replaced the thermometer in its receptacle on the wall before marking the chart. "We'll be getting you ready for the theatre in the next few minutes. All right luv!" She tapped Virginia on the shoulder and winked at Joe before she left the unit.

"This could be it", said Joe, taking Virginia's hands in his. "This could be the chance we've been waiting for." His excitement barely getting the better of his emotions.

Looking into his eyes, Virginia begged, "Wish me luck, my darling, I feel so nervous".

"All the luck in the world," smiled Joe, "And more."

"What will you do? Will you wait for me? Will you be here when I come round? You won't go away – will you?"

"Hold on a minute," said Joe, trying to calm her down, "I'm not going anywhere. I shall be here waiting for you. Now just relax and let these hospital people take you over for a little while."

"I'm being silly – that's all. I know everything will be alright and you will be waiting for me."

Glancing through the doorway of the unit and into the corridor, Joe could see the Staff Nurse in conversation with the doctor. Virginia was the apparent subject. Any minute now, thought Joe, they'll be in here to start the proceedings. He returned his attention to Virginia and took her in his arms. "I'm going to have to leave you now," he whispered, "So be brave and I'll see you in a little while." He kissed her and made his way out of the unit.

Before he could pass the Staff Nurse in the corridor, she caught hold of him, "Come back in a couple of hours," she suggested, "Virginia won't have had her operation by then and she might need a little comforting whilst she waits."

"Yes! Thank you! I shall do that." Joe was grateful for the information because he now knew how long he had to find himself a meal without risking too much time away from Virginia. It had been nearly eight hours since he had last eaten.

Two hours of anxious waiting can seem like an eternity even though there are things to be done. And when Joe tried to fill that gap, he found himself responding automatically to his personal needs, of which none was demanding enough to divert his mind from constant worry. But as time has a habit of passing, the two hours slipped by and he could make his way back to the unit.

Yet again he was stopped in the corridor, this time by the doctor he had seen earlier with the Staff Nurse. "A quiet word if I may," said the doctor, taking Joe to one side. "I'm afraid I have some unpleasant news for you. Virginia will not be the recipient of the recently donated heart and lungs after all. Regrettably, her other organs are failing rapidly and she is in no fit state to undergo major surgery. I am very sorry."

Joe, in a state of sudden shock, could only murmur, "The viral infection I suppose?"

"Yes," nodded the doctor.

"It must be a wicked bloody virus to do that to a person," said Joe bitterly. "Is there no chance of a cure?"

"You're right. It is a particularly vigorous strain. There's little chance of defeating it in a person in poor health."

"You mean – Virginia might not get over it?"

"She is quite calm now," explained the doctor. "But I kept nothing from her. I had to tell her the truth. She only has a matter of days to live. We shall do all we can to make her comfortable. It would help if you could give her all the time you can."

Ashen faced and close to tears, Joe thanked the doctor and walked on to present himself at Virginia's bedside.

"Just like at school," croaked Virginia when she saw Joe standing beside her, "Failed all me tests." She looked up and saw the dazed expression on his face. "You know – don't you?" she whispered. "The doctor has told you." She all but flung herself into his arms and started to sob.

For countless, long minutes, Joe leaned over the bed and cradled her heaving body. He desperately searched for soothing words to comfort her but his inept mind failed him so he remained silent, besides, he knew he would break down himself if he tried to speak.

Fatigue alone brought an end to Virginia's tears. Too tired to cry any more, she lay back in Joe's arms and tried to be positive about the future. Despite her heartache, brought about by the prospect of an unfulfilled life, she made an effort to come to terms with her illness and accept her pending death. "It hasn't been all bad," she said softly, "The last year or so I have had with you has been the happiest part of my life."

"And mine," concurred Joe. "That's why I can't lose you now."

"Nice of you to say that but we both know my time is nearly up."

"There's always tomorrow, darling. You might make a recovery. Miracles can happen."

The Lincolnshire Tramp

"You're a wonderful man and I love you dearly but your good heart cannot save me now. My body feels old and worn out and I haven't the strength to restore it. In fact, whilst I still have the energy I must ask you to do me some favours and I want your promise."

"You know I will do anything in this world for you; my word is my promise."

"Bless you. I know how reliable you are." She paused for a few moments as if to recharge her batteries before issuing her final instructions. "When I die." She charged, "I want to be cremated and have my ashes buried in my father's grave – the authorities in Spalding will tell you where to find it – and I want my little book with me when I go. I haven't made a will because there's no point. I have so little to leave. You shall have whatever there is, Joe."

"What about distant relatives?" Joe put the question out of courtesy rather than immediate concern, he was not yet convinced of her imminent demise.

"There are none worth worrying about," said Virginia slowly, "You need not bother about them. When the time comes, my handbag will contain all the information you'll want."

"Everything will be just as you say, darling," said Joe, aware of the tension in her body, "So put your mind at ease and relax."

"Yes – I need to rest now. But first, can I have my little book?"

Joe made sure she was comfortable before he looked through her effects to find the book, his first book.

"I just love this book," sighed Virginia, "It reminds me of so much. The day I found you in the road and discovered your sketches, the success it has made, and – best of all – it reminds me of Daddy. In your drawings I can see him talking to the animals."

As a transient measure, Joe put his hand on hers to prevent her opening the book. "I love you more than I could love anything on this earth," he said passionately, "And I've wanted to tell you so for a long time."

Virginia looked into eyes and perhaps saw too much. On the point of tears, she begged him to kiss her and after she whispered, "I love you to and I want to thank you for everything you've given me. It's a strange thing to say right now, but you've made my life complete."

Once again, for fear of breaking down, Joe remained silent. To ward off the emotion, he removed his hand from hers and opened the book for her. Then he sat down in the armchair, placed adjacent to the bed and watched her as she slowly turned each page to find a place for herself in every scene.

When done, Virginia looked up to smile at Joe before she closed the book and clutched it to her bosom. "Good night," she whispered as she drifted into a restful sleep.

Joe leaned forward and kissed her. "Sleep well, darling," he said softly. "See you in the morning." He got up to turn the lights out and then returned to the armchair for a night of vigil. An hour later a nurse entered the unit to check on Virginia's condition and when satisfied that all was well she went off to find a blanket for Joe. "You'll need this if you're staying the night." She said in a hushed voice.

Although not intending to sleep, Joe appreciated the offer of the blanket and, in time, made use of it. He had planned to stay awake all night just in case Virginia needed him but he could resist the serenity of the room and succumbed to sleep.

It seemed his slumber had lasted only a matter of seconds when it was disturbed by an ear splitting clap of thunder. In reality, he had been asleep for three hours prior to a storm breaking out over Harefield. A howling wind lashed torrential rain against the windows as flashes of lightening illuminated the overcast sky and the intermittent thunder reached crescendo.

Sitting up abruptly, Joe cast an anxious glance towards Virginia in case the storm had disturbed her but she appeared to be sleeping peacefully and in no way distressed. With his mind at ease, he settled back in the chair to await the abatement of the storm but sleep returned to his tired eyes long before then.

It was daybreak when he awoke again, and he did so to an altogether different situation. As soon as he saw the empty bed beside him he knew the worst had happened. The gentle hand on his shoulder – a nurse offering him a cup of tea – confirmed his suspicions. He looked inquisitively up at the nurse.

"I'm afraid so," she said compassionately, "Virginia passed away in the early hours of this morning. You were asleep when we took her out. We didn't want to wake you."

Chapter 20

Throughout the days immediately after Virginia's death, Joe behaved like a programmed zombie. He attended to various matters with the indifference of an automaton and took each day as it came. It was as if he had lost his way for without Virginia his life was bereft of purpose and the future no longer existed. His inspiration expired on the day she expired and now there was nothing ahead of him but a vast, meaningless void. Into the mists of intense sorrow went his hopes, his aspirations, his plans and his newly found salvation. He simply existed because he was there and for no other reason.

As he had no compelling desire to return to the lonely, empty flat in Ramsgate, he took up temporary accommodation in Harefield; this was to last until he had completed Virginia's cremation. In the meantime, he had to collect the last of her possessions from the hospital and dispose of them as he thought best. Her handbag, however, had to be carefully examined; a task he had no appetite for. With reluctance, he opened the handbag and tipped out its contents. Virginia, intuitive as ever, had made all the necessary preparations for her demise, even to the point of some last minute instruction for Joe.

Her main concern was with the insurance covering the cost of her funeral expenses. With all the information to hand, Joe's task was simple. He had to link a funeral director to the insurance company, providing he had the death certificate. And after that, when her ashes were safely buried with her father, he was to contact a solicitor in Ramsgate and claim the remainder of her estate. Finally, she hoped he would live on and become very successful, and, perhaps, think of her from time to time. She promised to love him in death as she had done throughout the last months of her life.

Seven days later, Joe sat alone in what he could only see as "some distant crematorium" and watched the pallbearers reverently deliver Virginia's coffin to the altar before the covert furnace. The pallbearers then joined Joe for a short service given by a local priest. In a moment of prayer, the coffin moved forward to be engulfed by an ornately curtained aperture and Joe shed a tear. Such a final and decisive act brought the truth home to him, with the disappearing coffin – Virginia had gone forever. She must be so lonely, he thought, with just me, the priest and the pallbearers to mourn her passing.

The Lincolnshire Tramp

Having paid his last silent tribute to Virginia, Joe walked quietly away from the crematorium. He needed to walk in order to channel his thoughts and bring them to a common conclusion. Somehow he must force his mind to concentrate on the next phase of his life, he had to plan ahead whether he wanted to or not. But no matter how he compiled his options, nothing wanted to fall into place. There was no obvious direction to take, After two hours of walking, the only conclusion he came to was to leave his decision until after his trip to Spalding.

As soon as possible on the following day, he collected Virginia's ashes from the crematorium and placed them carefully in the car. Without further delay he set off to find the A1 (motorway and trunk road) to Peterborough and the subsequent road to Spalding.

In his case, going home did not exactly fire him up with the ecstasy normally associated with a return to one's roots. With past adversities so deeply ingrained in his memory he had developed a loathing for the place and had covenanted himself never to go within a mile of it again. However, Virginia's dying request must be honoured and he had to go back.

On the long journey north, his relationship with Virginia played heavily on his mind, so much so that he began to blame himself for the tragic events that came to blight her life. If he had not been so selfish and stayed in Spalding instead of running away, then he would have seen what Keith was doing to her. She would not have suffered at the hand of her brother if he had been around to protect her. He would have run Keith into the ground and have no qualms about it, more so, since Alfred could no longer be offended.

Indeed, he and Virginia might have come together all the sooner, albeit under different circumstances and she would have had a better chance to fulfil her life. If only he could have seen it that way at the time then he, as well as Virginia, need never have wasted so many precious years.

Whenever the name of Keith Harrison entered Joe's head it invariably induced anger. "That bastard." He roared above the noise of the traffic. "He should be punished for the harm he's done. I just hope I don't run into him in Spalding because I won't be held responsible for my actions." There was no definite manner in which he would deal with Keith should he meet up with him but no doubt a means would present itself on the spur of the moment.

In order to rid his mind of anger, Joe pulled into a roadside restaurant and ordered a lunch. And whilst he waited for his lunch to be served he began to think about the anger he had just felt.

Could it be that his old emotions were taking him over again? Was history about to repeat itself? Was he going to turn his back on society once more? No...No...No... He would have none of it, especially now that he had success within his grasp. He owed Virginia that at the very least.

A good rest, a good lunch and a more agreeable line of thought set him up for the remainder of the journey to Spalding. He arrived late in the afternoon but he did have time to locate Alfred's grave and make arrangements to have it opened on the following morning. He had to pay for the attendance of a grave digger but he would not argue against that since he wanted to place Virginia's ashes as close as possible to her father's coffin. To sprinkle them haphazardly at ground level was out of the question.

Joe wondered what he might do in the meantime, he had the evening and part of the morning to kill. He did consider a sight seeing tour of his old haunts but quickly discounted the idea lest he disturb too many ghosts; images from the past were bound to be ugly and he was in no mood to face them.

In the end, he settled for a quiet evening in a motel some miles east of Spalding. He wanted to mull over his memories of Virginia whilst they were still fresh in his mind. Later, as he prepared for bed, he cursed his luck when a stirring in his groin proved to be the return of his virility. Fate had played another trick on him, at least that is the way he saw it, for when he wanted to have a sexual relationship with Virginia he was rendered impotent but now, with his blossoming erection, he could only think of what might have been. If only he could have her back for a short while, just long enough to satisfy both their carnal desires. Just long enough to consummate their love for one another. He fell asleep, his lust unfulfilled.

There was a definite chill in the air on the following morning and it caught Joe's attention as he waited patiently beside Alfred's grave. Was it, he speculated, a condition of the weather or was it a phenomenon peculiar to all burial sites. He was about to expand his theories when he noticed the stunted figure of a grave digger coming towards him.

"Ooh! It's all go this morning." Remarked the grave digger, by way of introduction. "I've just this minute finished digging a grave for today's burial." He paused to catch his breath and then, having glanced at Joe and at Alfred's grave, he said, "This the grave you want opening up?"

"This is the one," confirmed Joe.

The Lincolnshire Tramp

"Ah! This is Mr Harrison's grave. He was a nice old boy, you know." The grave digger prodded the neglected plot. "You would have thought the family would 'ave put a proper 'eadstone on 'im, wouldn't you?" He thrust his spade into the soft earth.

"I'm not surprised." Asserted Joe.

"I knew all the family," continued the grave digger as he set to work. "His wife is buried here as well. Did you know that? Of course she died a long time before 'im when the children were small."

"So I understand," said Joe, "But I didn't know she was buried here."

"Oh yes, it's a family plot. It's for all of them."

"I have Virginia's ashes here with me now. I expect you remember her?"

The grave digger stopped work that instant and looked up in astonishment. "Oh no! Not little Virginia. Don't tell me she's gone as well. This is tragic."

"She was in such poor health at the end," said Joe solemnly, "Her passing may have come as a relief."

"That is sad." The grave digger shook his head. "She was such a lovely girl." He resumed his task in silence but after a minute, or so, he observed, "Pity it wasn't her brother. Now he is a nasty piece of work. If anyone deserved to come to a sticky end it should 'ave been 'im."

"I couldn't agree more," Joe concurred, "I've never met such a selfish and greedy person. I suppose he still lives in Spalding, does he?"

"Not anymore," emphasised the grave digger, "Been gone some years now. Seems he got into a lot of trouble with the trades people and had to move out of town. Don't know what he's doin' now since 'is firm folded up."

"He was no businessman either." Joe remarked sourly.

"Don't know about that," said the grave digger knowingly, "But I do know the firm went bust because the accountant ran off with all the money. There wasn't as much as a penny in the bank after he'd gone. That's what really killed off the old man –'e had so much faith in that accountant 'e just couldn't believe what he'd done."

"Is that so?" Joe asked, trying to gauge the depth of the rumour.

"It's common knowledge," returned the grave digger, Everyone knows it."

Joe wanted to explain the truth but telling it to a humble grave digger would not carry a lot of weight. If it was to be made known then it would have to come out at a higher level, a court of law perhaps where it would be more effective. There again, as Keith had remarked all those years ago, mud sticks and even though, after all that time, the mud may have dried and blown away the stain will remain. It was not worth the effort.

There was nothing more to be said until the grave digger had completed his dig and asked if the hole was deep enough. Joe was satisfied that it was and reverently placed the little urn of ashes into it. With bowed head, he stood back and rendered his last, silent farewell. The grave digger stood beside him.

No longer able to control his emotions, Joe rewarded the grave digger with a generous gratuity and left him to restore the grave to its formal condition. Virginia was now with her father, indeed, back with her parents who had given her life.

As Joe made his way out of the graveyard he met a funeral party coming in. Out of politeness he stood aside to allow the cortege to pass. The mourners, their eyes downcast, paid little, or no, attention to him as he watched them approach and solemnly trudge by.

Joe did not expect to recognise any of the mourners, therefore, it came as all the more of a shock when he saw Vernon Townsend walking immediately behind the coffin. The sight of his former colleague threw Joe into a moment of mental turmoil, so much so that he failed to recognise any other member of the party. This proved something of a hindrance when he tried to discern the occupant of the coffin. Since Townsend appeared to be the chief mourner then the deceased must be of his immediate family. It could be his wife in the coffin, or one of his children. Maybe it was his brother or his sister, or —which was much more likely – his mother.

The last motion hit Joe like a bolt out of the blue. Was it really Townsend's mother – the woman he had raped – being interred on the same day he had buried Virginia's ashes? How cruel to be reminded of such a distasteful crime on this day of all days. Why does the hand of fate constantly deal these merciless blows? Why must he suffer the memories of his shameful past?

Shaking his head in disbelief and wishing he had never abused the woman, Joe turned away and followed a path which was to lead him out of the graveyard. It was easy to turn his back on the cortege but it was not so easy to do the same with his thoughts. He was to be plagued by them for many a long hour as he journeyed south on his return to the flat in Ramsgate.

Time and again, his mind dwelt on the words of the grave digger who had, somewhat unwittingly, accused him of stealing Harrison's money. With so many people believing this to be true, how could he hold his head high in Spalding again? Moreover, what right had he to hold his head high anywhere? After all is said and done, Joseph Albert Glasson was not a saint. He was just as guilty as Keith Harrison when it came to transgressions against others. Just because time had intervened it did not mean his sins were forgiven. They would always be on record somewhere, if only in his own mind.

As he drove on, Joe recounted every detail of every crime he had committed, then he searched for a good enough reason to justify his actions at the time. In those days, he thought he had reason enough but now, in the cold light of day and many years later, he was not so sure. His deeds seemed to merit shame rather than justification.

The gloom of the late afternoon matched Joe's melancholy and as it grew darker so did his mood. By the time he arrived at the flat in Ramsgate his future had all but been decided. He was so low in self-esteem that he saw only the one course of action – to take to the roads again. In all honesty, he could not consider himself worthy of a successful career, besides, there were too many skeletons in his cupboard and they would surely come out at the most inappropriate moments. He was sorry to go against Virginia's wishes but, deep down in his heart, he knew he would never achieve the kind of success she had in mind for him.

Resigned to his inevitable fortunes, Joe stepped into the flat and fumbled for a light switch. Even before the light came on, he sensed Virginia's presence, she seemed to be everywhere. After all, it was more than just a flat to her, it was her home. She had created this new world for herself out of the debris of her tortured and wasted years, and had done so with fortitude and courage. It was her special place, designed to suit her needs and never tainted by outside influences. Joe, like everything else, was introduced into the home for a rightful and proper purpose and he, like the rest of it, was never considered as obtrusive or out of place.

Virginia had been proud and happy with her little home but sadly, as Joe now perceived, it reflected too much of the last years of her life and it upset him. He went into the kitchen to make himself some tea and she was there, in every pot and pan, in every cupboard and in every appliance. He could not touch a thing without recalling some small anecdote or incident connected with it. All influenced by Virginia.

It was the same when he tried to relax in the lounge. And in the bedroom, it seemed worse than ever. Virginia reigned supreme within the confines of the flat and she could easily weave her way into his susceptible mind. In time, it caused him great anguish for he began to pine for her.

He did eventually settle down for the night but he lay fully clothed on top of the bed. He could not bring himself to undress and get between the sheets, it would not be right to sleep in the bed without Virginia. Indeed, it did not seem right for him to stay in the flat for the same reason; it would be impossible to live without her. Such reasoning could only add weight to his earlier decision – he would take to the roads at the first available opportunity.

With the morning came a batch of post, the first delivery since his departure to Harefield. There was some junk mail addressed to Virginia and three letters addressed to himself. Without thinking, he ripped open the envelope of the first letter and withdrew its content. It was a demand from the Department of Health and Social Security and it claimed his contributions for the past seven years.

"Pay up or else," sneered Joe as he screwed up the offending letter and threw it to the floor. "What next I wonder?" He examined the second envelope with a little more care and as soon as he realised it contained yet another demand, this one from the Inland Revenue, he threw that to the floor. The third envelope did not hide any secrets either, at least that is what he thought, it was from Save the Children Fund and he assumed it begged for his second book. "Don't panic," he declared, casting the envelope away, "You will get the book."

Had Joe been over-inquisitive he might have read the letter and changed his whole outlook on life. It was an invitation to lunch with the patron of the Fund; the Princess Royal had taken a great interest in his book and had expressed a desire to meet him. He was also to be presented with an award for his work for charity.

No right minded person would have turned down such an invitation, least of all Joe, especially when it would have fitted in with Virginia's wishes. And had Joe attended the luncheon, he would have been drawn deeper into the circles of the charity which, in the fullness of time, would have made an honest citizen out of him. Never again would he have walked the highways and byways as a tramp.

But, such being the instincts governing behaviour, Joe had wrongly determined the content of the letter and had disregarded it on that basis.

The letters from the government departments were to the forefront of his mind and they had obviously influenced his decision. Kicking the envelopes to one side, he returned to the lounge and promptly parcelled up his second illustrated book. After breakfast, he took the parcel to the post office and sent it on its way.

The Lincolnshire Tramp

He had other business in the town that morning, namely, a visit to a local solicitor's office to discuss Virginia's estate. It proved to be yet another acrimonious meeting. The solicitor wanted to drag the proceedings out over a period of weeks whereas Joe wanted them wrapped up there and then.

"I can't see the problem," snapped Joe, rather heatedly, "Miss Harrison has left everything, such as it is, to me. And I, in turn, want to pass it on to charity. Why can't you do that?"

"Because probate doesn't work that way," insisted the solicitor. "Before I can prove her will I must search for other members of her family. They may have a valid claim to her possessions."

That means Keith, thought Joe, and I'll be damned if I let that bastard take any more from Virginia. There and then, he made his mind up about certain matters and instructed the solicitor to deal with the rest; if he was smart enough he could sell Virginia's car and jewellery before the solicitor became aware of their existence.

Without further protest, Joe handed over a key to the flat and some of Virginia's papers – bank statements and the like. If the solicitor was going to be awkward about it then he might as well earn his money and sort the problems out for himself. Chances were, the solicitor would find enough money to cover his fees but little, if any, for anyone else. As for Joe, he planned to be well out of the way in case there were any recriminations.

By four in the afternoon, Joe locked up the flat for the last time. He had been coming and going for most of the day but now it was time to be moving on. With him he had warm clothing, a stout pair of boots, photographs of Virginia, some food and just over three thousand pounds in cash. The money, being the proceeds from the sale of the car and other effects, was pledged to charity and would be – apart from a few pounds to buy a couple of bottles of whisky – handed over at some time the next day.

Leaving the Thanet towns behind him and taking the coastal road to Herne Bay and Whitstable, Joe felt easier in his mind. He was back in the gutters where he thought he belonged and, somehow, it made life more tolerable. Self pity may be a human condition frowned upon by others but to Joe it was the only tangible means of consolation; there was, of course, the whisky but that did no more than blur the mind – not ease it.

He counted himself as a lost and broken man who, for the second time in his life, was cheated of real happiness. How could he cope with the restraints of modern living when he was always being denied supportive and loyal companionship? How could he be expected to function as a normal human being when he was destined always to disappointment? To journey through life as a tramp was his safest bet, that way he had nothing to lose.

Soon after midnight, he strolled along the gently sloping beaches of Seasalter. The moon, in its first quarter, gave sufficient light for him to pick his way through the soft sand spreading between the endless breakwaters. To his left was the higher embankment of the coastline and to his right, the restless sea. The lapping waves at the water's edge gave tranquillity to the scene for it was an unusually still and mild night considering it was the first of October.

There could have been no better place for Joe to start his second term as a vagrant. Spoilt for choice, he flopped down in the soft sand as and when it suited him and, as if to mark the event, he took his first swig of whisky for more than two years. At first, the draught bit into his throat, but the after taste was pleasant and rewarding. Joe was back where he belonged.

The night passed without incident and in the morning he awoke to the commotion of scavenging seagulls. Without malice he cursed them and then laughed when they totally ignored him. He watched them for a while and then, mindful of some urgent business that day, he got up and shook the sand from his clothing. Collecting up his paltry belongings, he found a way off of the beach and went in search of the road to Faversham. He knew there was a charity shop there run by Save the Children Fund.

Slightly before noon, he found the shop and was fortunate enough to meet the area manager, an energetic young woman making her regular call.. She continued to price up a batch of second hand garments whilst listening to Joe's bequest.

"I want to donate a large sum of money to the charity." He said.

"That would be nice," replied the area manager. "How much is it?"

"Three Thousand Pounds."

"Wow! That is a hefty sum." The young woman, not believing her ears, looked up for confirmation and when she saw it in Joe's eyes she added, "If it's a cheque you could send it to head office. I can give you the address."

"It's cash," Joe said emphatically, "And I'm afraid I must insist on you banking it today under my supervision."

The authority in his voice pre-determined the area manager's reaction. "But of course," she said, "I'll get the paying in book." She flustered around in an over-sized shoulder bag to find a pen and a collection of bank books. Meanwhile, Joe unloaded the money from his pockets and counted the notes out into one hundred pound piles.

"There is a condition," he announced as he counted, "This donation must be shown in the annual report as a bequeathal from Miss Virginia Harrison of Ramsgate in Kent. Do you understand that?"

"Yes. I understand. It is very kind of her." The young woman paused for a moment of thought. "Perhaps," she concluded, "You'd better write it down so I won't forget to pass it on." She pushed a pen and a note pad towards Joe.

Eventually, the money was checked, counted and recorded before being stuffed into a plastic bag and taken to the bank. Joe accompanied the area manager to the local branch and as soon as the money was safely over the counter he took his leave of her.

The young woman was in a state of bemused bewilderment when she returned to the shop. She had never before handled such a large cash donation and it quite took the wind out of her sails.

As for Joe, he was very pleased with himself. He considered it to be a job well done because it established a place for Virginia in the history of the Fund. He could be sure that she would get a well-deserved mention for her care for others.

On the road from Faversham to Sittingbourne, he thought a great deal about Virginia and hoped she would understand his reasons for not complying with all of her wishes. And when he thought about their time together it came as a strange episode in his life, completely unexpected and more akin to another existence. Like a huge dream played out in a different world with different characters and different ideals.

Likewise, life before Virginia had an air of immateriality about it and he began to wonder if he really had lived those dreadful days as a tramp, a mean and despicable tramp. Of course he had, how else would he know the names of Bumble Drage and the Obday Brothers, Lizzie Tish and Mad Molly. These had been real people and he had met them. There had been no dream.

The more he thought about his fellow vagrants the more he realised how hostile he had been towards them. In future, should he meet up with them again, he would make amends for his insults and try to be friendlier. After all, they were all creatures of the same ilk and should be able to tolerate each other.

Many topics flooded his mind as he threaded his way along the busy A2 but that was not necessarily a bad thing since he did not have to act upon any of it. That is what vagrancy is all about – thinking a lot but doing very little.

However, Joe did have to come to terms with one small problem – his legs. Although healed well after his accident they were not so strong as they used to be and needed frequent resting. He was not aware of it at first but it soon became apparent when the days grew colder and damper. On the other hand, why should he worry about it, he was not going anywhere in particular nor was he in a hurry to get there. He had all the time in the world to rest so why not take advantage of it.

After a night spent in a playing field west of Sittingbourne, he journeyed on to Gillingham, Chatham and Rochester and then south to Maidstone. During this time, dark clouds laden with showers rolled across the autumn sky and all too often discharged a deluge of drenching rain. For the most part, Joe was able to find shelter but there were times when he got caught out in the open and suffered a soaking.

For about fourteen days, on and off, the showery weather persisted and many parts of Kent and Sussex became waterlogged. At the time, it was of little importance to the inhabitants of the two counties but some days later, in the early hours of Friday the sixteenth of October, it had a significant effect on the events of the day.

Before then, on the afternoon of the fourteenth, Joe entered Knole Park (a manor house and parkland on the southern outskirts of Sevenoaks) to seek a place of rest. His arrival was not planned, for had it been then he would have passed through the town some ten days earlier. He had simply wandered out from Maidstone and scoured the Kentish Weald before picking his way to Sevenoaks by way of Tonbridge and Tunbridge Wells.

His impression of Knole Park was always favourable. It appeared to be a vast parkland dotted with trees. It had gently sloping hills and valleys as well as many densely wooded areas. It also had herds of fallow and Japanese deer which roamed freely in the thousand acre estate. Joe had seen them two years previously and had drawn them often in his books.

During the day, the park was visited by the general public (much more so in the summer months, of course) but this did not deter Joe from hanging around for a day or two. He could easily blend into the background if he felt troubled by other visitors, there were plenty of places to hide. All too quickly, he had slipped back into

The Lincolnshire Tramp

his old habits of vagrancy and could not be accepted as anything other than a tramp. He could not mix with the public now.

For the rest of that day (the 14th) and for the whole of the following day, he did not leave the park. He was enchanted by the place for it seemed to invite him to stay, it offered him shelter and protection and it offered him its animals to befriend. Indeed, he was fascinated by the deer and spent as much time as he could with them. Virginia would have loved them, he thought. Such a pity she could not be there to see them.

On the night of the fifteenth, Joe settled down to sleep. For the first time in nearly a month he felt at peace with his world. It was a rare moment for he could put his troubles behind him and allow himself a degree of contentment. He relaxed on his leafy bed and lulled himself into slumber with warm and pleasant thoughts.

He slept peacefully until about four in the morning when he awoke with a start. Everywhere was still and quiet and there was not a sound to be heard. He listened out for the deer and other creatures of the night but heard nothing. Then, as he sat up, a shiver ran down his spine, he became aware of an eeriness descending over the parkland.

Peering into the gloom, he got to his feet and went in search of the animals but they were nowhere to be seen. They had all vanished. He was totally and utterly alone.

Presently, his attention was drawn to a slight rustle above his head. He looked up and hoped to see a bird or a small mammal in an overhanging bough but it was too dark to see anything properly. And when the leaves rustled again, he knew it was the work of a freshening breeze.

Puzzled by the phenomenon, he stepped out into the open where he expected to first traces of dawn to shed some light on the mystery. He had gone nor more than twenty paces when he stopped dead in his tracks to listen to the strangest of sounds. It was not exactly a rumbling noise or a swishing sound, nor was it a howling sound or a crashing sound. It was, if it could be described as such, a combination of all four. Furthermore, it was, as yet, some way off and seemed to spread along a lengthy southwestern horizon.

As he stood and listened to the sound so the breeze around him changed to a more forceful wind. Then the penny dropped, he was listening to an approaching hurricane. Obviously, the animals had come to the same conclusion, only much sooner, and had gone to ground. He did not quite know what he should do but he was easier in his mind now that he knew what was happening.

The Lincolnshire Tramp

The hurricane was the worst natural disaster to hit Southern England this century. It was widespread and powerful and caused tremendous damage to plant life and property. Its constantly strong winds, gusting to over seventy miles an hour lasted for several hours and left parts of Sussex and Kent looking more like battlefields.

Apart from ripping out house tops and sending chimney stacks crashing to the ground, from upturning caravans and rolling high sides vehicles, from disrupting endless miles of power cable and telephone lines, the wind storm did its greatest damage to trees. Thousand of trees were lost, the majority being uprooted by the wind but others were to suffer total destruction by a falling neighbour. Some of Britain's biggest trees, of a hundred or more years standing, simply keeled over like submissive giants. In every direction, fallen trees barred the way.

With hindsight, it was established that the problem was compounded by the heavy foliage still on the trees at that time of year and the earth at the roots being loosened by too much rain. The hurricane had struck at precisely the wrong time, a month later and many of the trees would have resisted its force.

Miraculously, there was very little loss in human life during the storm, the population was still abed at the time and, therefore, in the relative safety of their homes. But some unfortunate souls did perish in those early hours, Joe being amongst them.

At the height of the storm, Joe was struggling against the wind in an effort to reach the protective walls of the manor house. He had still some way to go and found it difficult to cover the open ground especially when he was being bowled over by the swirling, gusting winds. With his legs weakening by the step, he entered a grassy avenue bordered on both sides by hefty beech trees.

The long columns of majestic beech, their trunks measuring sixteen feet at the girth, stood like pillars of a great Greek Temple. Such bulky plants should hold firm against the worst excesses of the weather, at least that is what Joe thought as he leaned against one huge trunk. He had stopped to catch his breath and seek a moment's respite from the wind. All around him, trees of every description crashed to the ground as if felled by an army of mad axemen.

The howling, roaring wind with the groaning, splintering trees put fear into Joe's heart. And when he felt his tree (the one he leaned against) tremble and shake, he began to panic. Instinct told him the tree would not stand a moment longer and he should get away from it as soon as possible. He started to run, to the best of his ability, towards the stone walls surrounding Knole House.

Without warning, the columns of beech trees started to tumble. One after another they hit the ground with resounding thumps and the whole park seemed to vibrate with their falling. In the midst of it all Joe's legs buckled and he stumbled into the path of a falling tree. The massive trunk completely smothered his fragile body and in an instant he was gone. Gone as though wiped from the face of the earth.

If his soul were ever to rise from his broken and crushed body then it would have soared to the realms of blissful tranquillity. No more the feelings of remorse, grief and guilt. No more would his troubled mind worry about the past, the present or the future. His lifespan was done and with it the misery and the hardships he had endured.

How different it might have been if he had not interfered with the march of time. He did not have to be a hero and try to save the Joinery Firm; he should have gone down with it. Like many of his fellows he would have survived and gone on to a more fulfilling life – or did destiny really play a hand?